Hidden Between The Lines

Hidden Between The Lines

Sally Laughlin

Published 2021 by Next Chapter
Cover art by http://www.thecovercollection.com/
Back cover texture by David M. Schrader, used under license from Shutterstock.com
Large Print Edition

Chapter 1

Terror built in her as she ran. Her breath came in rapid gasps. The rain and mud were weighing down the hem of her dress making it difficult for her to run. Someone was chasing her. She glanced behind her. A dark, shadowy form of a man lunged for her.

Rachel's eyes flew open. Her heart was pounding, and she felt out of breath. Relief washed over her when she realized she was still in her own bedroom. She rolled over on her side and looked toward the windows.

The dusty rays of dawn crept through her window greedily stealing toward the dark hidden places in her room. Familiar shapes and spaces covered by the black shadow of the night soon began their daily transformation.

Excitement built in her as she flipped the quilt off and jumped out of bed. The nightmare was quickly forgotten as she thought of meeting Lieutenant Phillip Prescott again in town today. Phillip always told her he thought of her as his Lady Fair, and he was her brave Knight. And, how he thought she was the fairest maiden he had ever seen, with her golden hair and big, blue eyes. She had only known him three months, but knew he was the man she would love forever.

Rachel dressed and hurried down the stairs to have her morning meal and wait for Edith to pick her up for the ride into town.

She was surprised to see her father already sitting at the morning table having his meal. "Good morning, Father," she said respectfully. "I am surprised to see you rise so early. I usually eat alone in the morning."

"I wanted to talk to you about some good news," he said smiling at her. "But it was late when I got home last night, and you were already asleep."

"Oh?" Rachel was confused. Her father almost never talked to her, and never as nicely as he did now.

"You have grown into a beautiful young woman." He reached over and patted her hand, smiling broadly at her, "And it has not gone unnoticed."

"Thank you, Father. But I don't understand," she replied.

"In two weeks, Lord Symington is planning a lavish party that will be thrown in your honor on his vast estate." His face was aglow with his news. "He will announce your engagement to him."

Rachel gasped in horror. "Surely, you jest, Father."

"No, I do not jest about such things," he said briskly. "You shall be married in two months' time."

"Father, you cannot be serious. Father, he is so old, and ..."

Lord Ramsford cut off her sentence. "You are eighteen." He glared at her, "At your age; I am lucky any man would want you, let alone a very rich man," he snapped.

Rachel pushed away from the table and stood up facing him. "I will not marry him, Father. I will not. He is old and bent." She wrinkled her nose in distaste. "He has foul breath and rotting black teeth. Even his lips are blackened. You cannot ask this of me."

"You will do as you are told. He has given a very generous bride price for you. All of my debts and those of your brother, Harold, will be paid with money to spare."

"Father, I know you have heard of the terrible things this man has done. I would be his fourth wife. Can you want this for me?"

His lips curled in anger, "You will do as you are told, and that is the end of it."

Now Rachel's anger mounted. "How can you say such a thing? His first wife died in childbirth along with the child. This hideous man said it was of no consequence because the child was a girl. His second wife ran off with one of his henchmen." Her voice pleaded with him to listen. "They say he had them found and murdered. And what of his last wife? They found her body at the bottom of one of his towers. No one knows if she jumped or was pushed."

"Enough," he snapped. "Yes, I have heard all of those rumors, and that is just what they are - rumors. No one can prove any of it. I believe the townspeople made up all of those things because they are jealous of his wealth and power."

Rachel turned and headed for the door followed closely by her father. He grabbed her arm whirling her around. His lips curled back, his teeth bared, and anger poured from his eyes as he snarled. "You shall marry whomever I say. You have no choice in the matter."

"No, I will not marry him." She yelled.

Rachel yanked her arm free just as his hand came up and slapped her hard across the face knocking her to the floor.

"You will do as I say you ungrateful child. Your brother and I will be able to live comfortably the rest of our lives. You would be so selfish as to deny us this?" He stood over her shaking his fist and screaming at her. "I will not speak of this again. I have accepted his generous offer, and you will be married in two months' time. The banns will be posted this week."

"No, no," she sobbed uncontrollably.

Lord Ramsford raised his hand to strike her again, but stopped. "You had better not try to undo what has been done," he snapped. He walked away leaving her to cry on the floor.

Rachel had no idea how long she lay there crying when she heard her cousin, Edith, bursting through the door.

"Oh, my dear, Rachel," she scooped Rachel up into her arms rocking her gently. "I heard you crying. What has happened?" She pulled away from Rachel and spoke to her in a soothing, gentle tone. "Now stop crying and tell me what has happened."

When Rachel had finished, Edith's small, gray eyes narrowed. "You shall not marry that foul old man. I believe all the evil things they say about him." She released Rachel from her embrace and stood up holding her hands out for Rachel to grab. "You are too small and lovely a thing to marry such a hideous creature." She threw back her head and laughed. "That horrid man would not want me as his wife. I am quite a bit taller and heavier than him, and if he gave me any trouble I would just sit on him."

Rachel laughed in spite of the situation and grabbed Edith's hands as she was pulled to her feet. "But what can I do?"

"We'll go to my father's house and think of something." She leaned in and whispered in

Rachel's ear. "We are meeting your lieutenant today, maybe he can think of something."

Later that afternoon they met up with Phillip, who paced back and forth in anger.

"Married?" The tall, handsome lieutenant shouted. "No!" He said firmly. "No man shall have you but me."

"But he is very rich and powerful," Rachel dabbed a handkerchief to her wet eyes.

"My father is very rich and powerful, too. He is a very influential barrister in London. I will appeal to him for help."

"How can he help us? Do what?" Rachel sniffled.

"I may be his second eldest son, but I am his favorite son. He will do whatever I ask."

"What will you ask?" Edith inquired as confused as Rachel.

"He can get us a license to marry," Phillip moved quickly to his horse tied to the branch of a tree. "Let my father work this out," he stopped and walked back to Rachel. "He will have to get permission for me to wed, and a special license. He will know what has to be done." He grabbed

Rachel into his arms and kissed her hard on the mouth. "No man shall have you but me, my fairest of maidens."

"Married?" Rachel was still whirling from his words.

"Of course," he kissed her again quickly.

"But I …" Rachel stammered.

"I know that a regiment has just left for Nova Scotia. I could possibly join them as an attaché or something. It would mean a couple of years there. Let me have my father deal with this. Now, I must get to London and have him procure our future. I will get word to you through Edith with the plans." He nodded respectfully to the two stunned women and rode off.

"Well, that was a very quick solution to your problem. He didn't even ask if you would marry him, although I am sure he already knew the answer to that." Edith placed an arm around Rachel's waist. "Not a very proper proposal, but a very good idea."

"I hope his father thinks so as well," Rachel grimaced.

"He will love you as father, and I do," Edith untied the reins to their buggy from the low-hanging tree branch.

"Whatever shall I do without you Edith? You are more like a sister to me than a cousin. I do love you dearly." Her head dropped as tears rolled down her face.

"You are only going to be gone for a couple of years to Nova Scotia, and by that time that hideous old Lord Symington will have either forgotten about you or be dead." Edith motioned for Rachel to get into the buggy, and spoke to her in a very comforting voice. "All will turn out well. You will see."

Rachel dabbed at her eyes again and climbed into the buggy. "I look at the portrait of my mother, and wish with all my heart she had lived. She would never have let father try to marry me off to the likes of Lord Symington."

"They say she was quite a beauty," Edith looked over at Rachel, "just like her daughter."

"Why is it that your mother died in birthing you and your father still loves you dearly? And my father, well, they are so different?"

"I do not know, Rachel. One cannot figure out what makes people be who they are, well, at least not me."

"Nor I," Rachel sighed. "In one of father's drunken fits, he told me that I was a terrible exchange for losing his wife."

"Oh, my dearest, that is a horrible thing for him to say," Edith shook her head. "That angers me greatly."

She looked over at Edith and shrugged. "I have to accept that which is." Tears began to form in Rachel's eyes. "I am really going to leave you. What shall I do without you?"

"You will live happily with Phillip and return to me in a couple of years; that is what you shall do." Edith straightened her shoulders. "Now, let us not think of this right now, or I truly shall burst into tears." She quickly changed the subject. "I think you better start bringing over what you want to take with you. We will start storing your things in a trunk I have in my room."

"Yes," Rachel laughed. "I have dresses and pelisses that I wouldn't have had if it weren't for you. It took me a while to figure out that when you were making an outfit for yourself, you always ordered extra material, so I would also have an outfit."

"I did no such thing," Edith said. "I am just very bad at figuring out how much material I would need."

"I shall miss you more than you will ever know," Rachel started to cry again.

"Now, stop that." Edith tried to keep from crying, but it was to no avail as the tears began to slide down her face.

A week passed since Rachel, Edith and Phillip had solidified their plan of escape.

Rachel moved restlessly on the bed. She had hardly slept all night and when she did her reoccurring nightmare of a dark shadow chasing her would appear. She pushed it aside as she always did, especially today. The excitement and anticipation of her elopement were almost too much for her to bear. "Today is the happiest day of my life. Nothing matters now except our being together." She said softly as she stretched her body and smiled.

She pulled back the feather quilt from her bed and raced to the window. Her bare feet flew across the room barely touching the cold wooden floors. She plopped down on the window seat, and shivered. She was not sure if it was from the excitement or the cool morning air as she pulled the neatly folded crocheted blanket up around her.

This would be the last time she would ever sit in this window and stare out at the beautiful landscape that circled her father's manor. However, it held little importance to her because there were no fond memories attached to it. All Rachel could think about was escaping from here for good.

She sighed happily. She was going to be with the one she loved for the rest of her life. They were going to live happily ever after, of that she was certain.

However, for now, everything had to be a secret. Her life … and his depended upon it. She pulled her knees up tightly against her chest. Her head fell back gently to rest on the window frame.

"This has been the longest night of my life." Rachel said thinking of Phillip. "Did you sleep fitfully, my dearest? Are you just as excited and nervous, my love? Once we're married and on the ship, we will be free to love each other forever."

Today, she would cheat the foul Lord Symington of the pleasure of her company. "Today," she sighed aloud. "My love - my life - forever." She grinned and brought her chin down upon her knees. "Phillip," she whispered softly, lovingly, and hugged her knees even tighter to her chest.

A mourning dove flew past her window. She reached up and opened the window letting the cool morning air stream in.

A small breeze tugged at her hair as it fell in complete disarray around her face. Her eyes followed the flight of the dove until it disappeared around the side of the manor. She got to her knees and pushed the window open further. Rachel breathed in deeply. This would be the last morning of English air that she would breathe for a long time.

Suddenly, Rachel realized that she had better stop thinking about such things and start getting ready. She reached over and shut the window, snapping the closure tightly. She went to her wardrobe and carefully dressed.

She had to leave some dresses behind so that no one would know she had left for good. Although she knew her father did not know what was in her wardrobe, because if it were not for Edith, she would probably only have one or two dresses. Her father felt a dress should be able to last for years if properly cared for.

Rachel crept quietly down to the breakfast table, and was startled to see her father at breakfast so early in the morning - again. Her stomach began to churn, because the last time that happened, he had unpleasant news for her.

"I have good news for you about picking your trousseau," he reached into his waistcoat and pulled out a wad of money. He peeled off a few bills placing them firmly on the table and quickly pocketed the rest. "Lord Symington sent over some money for you to choose your bridal clothes. That is all you need for now. He wants it bought before the wedding, of course."

"Thank you, Father." Rachel picked up the money and carefully put it in the pocket of her dress. She knew they would need all the money they could get, because she was sure, a Lieutenant's pay was not very much. Even though his father was very rich, Phillip's older brother would inherit everything. But she didn't care about that: They had their love to get them through everything.

"Good morning everyone," Harold's voice was cheerful and hearty. He inherited her father's good looks, with his blonde hair and blue eyes. Both were very thin and tall. They could have passed for brothers if it were not for her father's thinning, gray hair. "This is a glorious morning. Aren't you excited about becoming a bride?" His face beamed at her, "a very rich bride, I might add."

"It appears you and Father will also benefit from my marriage," she said trying to hide the disgust creeping into her voice.

"That's enough insolence from you," her father growled. "You can thank your lucky stars; I am marrying you to someone who can give you everything you will ever want."

"You are an ungrateful chit. Most women would be happy to be married to someone who is so well off," snapped her brother.

"Do not ruin this opportunity of marriage," her father leaned toward her menacingly, "or you will regret the day you were born." He returned to his boiled egg and reached for a toasted piece of bread. "On a more pleasant note," his voice returned to a non-threatening tone. "Lord Symington has announced that he will be coming to the manor for lunch."

"Oh, when?" She wanted to laugh out loud, because she knew she would be gone.

"Today," he said. "I want you dressed in your finest afternoon gown. I do not want him to think I have not been giving you fine things, or that we are paupers." He shoved a piece of toast in his mouth and began working on the hard-boiled egg.

Rachel let out a gasp. "Lunch today?"

"What is the matter with you now?" He asked, annoyed with her outburst.

"It is just that Edith, and I have plans to go into town at noon." Her mind was racing. What could she do? All of her good clothes were at Brekmore Manor. What about Phillip? But more importantly, how could she get away without causing suspicion?

"Is that all?" Harold picked at his food with his fork. "You can go another day."

"I will have to go and tell her that I cannot make it," she said trying not to sound too nervous.

"That is what we have servants for." Harold threw his fork on his plate and pushed himself away from the table. "I really am not that hungry. I must get myself ready to ride over to see Lady McLean this morning, but I will be back by noon to visit with Lord Symington, my future brother-in-law." He smiled broadly as he stood up causing his chair to scrape against the wooden floor.

"Go and write a letter to your cousin and inform her you have to postpone your shopping trip until tomorrow and have one of the servants deliver it." Her father got up, threw his napkin on the top of his plate, and left the table without any pleasantries.

All she could do was sit there and stare at the plate in front of her. Of all days, that foul man was coming today. Had he somehow learned of what their plans were? Maybe one of his servants spotted her in town with Phillip. They tried to be discreet and act as just friends in public; although a couple of times when they were alone they would steal a quick kiss.

Now, she had to figure out what to do. She had not seen Lord Symington for over a week and today of all days he was coming to visit. She feared it was just too coincidental to be happening.

Trembling she got up from the table and walked into the foyer. The large grandfather clock stood like a soldier guarding its post. The tick-tock of the pendulum beat a steady rhythm that seemed to say, "too-late, too-late."

It was just a little after seven in the morning. It was only five hours to freedom, and now to have it snatched away so cruelly. She raced up to her room and threw herself onto the bed. Tears ran down her face falling softly onto her quilt. She rolled over on her back and lay quiet trying to figure out what to do.

Rachel was unsure of how long she rested there. Her mind was numb and her heart full of pain. "I will not give up," she kept saying to herself. "I will not give up." Then slowly, a plan began to form in her mind. She jumped up and ran to her wardrobe flinging the doors wide open.

After carefully studying the remaining clothes, she selected a frock that was halfway decent and pulled it out. Rachel found a thread and pulled it hard; it came out leaving a gaping hole. Not wanting to take any chances, she pulled and tugged until a large rip appeared on the front of the frock. She took a deep breath and prayed that her father would not have stopped his morning ritual of drinking too much sherry.

As she had thought, he was in the library sipping a large glass of sherry by the unlit fireplace.

"Father," she said in her most apologetic voice. "I do want to please Lord Symington. You are right." Rachel hoped her tone sounded sincere. "I have been very thoughtless and selfish. I want him to see that I am worthy of his attention"

"Yes, yes," he said with an irritable wave of his hand.

She walked in front of him and the cold, barren fireplace. She waved the ripped dress in front of him. "My frock is badly torn. I will need a seamstress to fix it. It should not take long, and I will be back in plenty of time before Lord Symington gets here."

"I do not feel that is necessary," he said gruffly. "Just pick another dress."

"But you know I do not have many dresses." She held up the dress waving it in front of him again, "And this is the one that Lord Symington liked the best." She lied effortlessly.

"I see," he glanced over at the torn garment and nodded. "See to it that you are back before Lord Symington gets here. Have the coachman take you to town."

Harold appeared in the library door. "I'm afraid he has gone into town to pick up supplies for this afternoon's luncheon. Well, I'm off to Lady McLean's."

"Wait," Lord Ramsford called out to Harold. "You will escort your sister to town. She cannot go unescorted."

"I have an appointment, father. I am late as it is. I don't have the time to take her into town." Harold whined and pouted, which usually worked on his father.

"You won't have to take me into town, just to Edith's. She will go with me into town." Rachel's heart was beating so fast she was afraid she was going to faint.

"Cousin Edith's manor is in the opposite direction I am headed." He looked at his father's face and knew he could not win on this. His shoulders heaved as he said, "Well, it is a lot closer than taking you to town." He motioned for Rachel to follow him. "You see how I am sacrificing for you." He chided her.

"Rachel!" Her father's voice darkened with warning. "I want you back here before Lord Symington arrives." Lord Ramsford turned his back and stared into the unlit fireplace.

"Oh, yes!" She exclaimed with excitement in her voice. Rachel realized the enthusiasm was a little too much. Her father raised his head and turned looking at her.

"And I will use the money you gave me for my trousseau to pay for the seamstress."

The mention of money seemed to take his mind off her over-exuberance, and he nodded toward her. His hand came up, and he motioned for her to leave. "Do not be late, or you will meet with my wrath, as well as Lord Symington's."

"I must get my bonnet and shawl from my room. I will be right down." It was now or never. Quickly, she climbed the steps to her room. She threw open the door and looked for the last time at her sparsely furnished room.

The large, cold room, held a few pieces of furniture. An old bed, a chair, a small table, and a wardrobe to house her dresses sat clustered close together making the rest of the room look barren. A large, worn quilt and an old, crocheted Afghan were the only other things in her room.

Rachel picked out a shawl and bonnet when she heard a horse neighing outside her bedroom window. She looked to see the groomsmen bringing a saddled horse for her, and Harold fidgeting impatiently, as he waited for her to come down.

A deep, nervous sigh escaped her lips. She picked up the ripped frock, opened her bedroom door, and raced down the stairs to freedom. Her heart and mind were reeling; she was free at last.

But just as she grabbed the front door handle and opened the front door, she heard her father call out her name. Her heart was beating so loudly she could barely hear him as he called again from the library.

"Rachel!" He yelled.

Holding her breath, she walked toward him and stood at the library door. "Yes, Father?" Her voice trembled slightly.

"With the extra money that I gave you, pick up some fine sherry for lunch today. We seem to be low on it, and I want to make sure Lord

Symington has the very best sherry." He gave her his usual wave of the hand to dismiss her.

"Yes, Father." She could hardly contain a laugh from relief. "Oh, yes. We certainly must think of Lord Symington." Rachel gave a quick curtsey and hurried to the opened front door. She wanted to fly down the front steps of the manor to her horse, but instead walked calmly, with great effort, toward it.

Fifteen minutes later, they arrived at Edith's small manor. Harold raised his hand and motioned for a footman to help her down from her horse.

"You have made me late for my appointment with Lady McLean. But soon," he sighed deeply, "I will have no need of the widow McLean, and her money." He almost spat out the word 'McLean'. "Until then, I must appease her. She is such a plain, boring, simpleton. Unfortunately, I cannot afford to dismiss her attentions until you are married, and I have the money safely in my hands. After all, Lord Symington is a very old man, and he may die before you marry him. Oh, well, I must be off." He gave a slight nod to Rachel.

Rachel waited until Harold's horse was turned, and his back to her, and then flew up the steps of the manor. She burst through the door and raced into the foyer startling Edith, who was coming down the staircase. Edith's eyes grew wide, "What is wrong?" She ushered Rachel into a small parlor off the foyer and closed the two doors.

"What has happened? What is this?" She asked looking at the dress in Rachel's hand. "Wait." She walked to the door and opened it as she looked into the foyer. She quietly pulled the doors closed again. "We're alone, but speak softly."

It took every bit of restraint for Rachel to explain what had happened in a quiet, soft tone.

After Rachel had finished, Edith sat for a moment in thought. She leaned her face close to Rachel's and said, "It is just after nine o'clock." She patted Rachel's hand. "We still have time to make our plans work." Edith stood up, opened the doors, and called out. "Millie, come to the parlor at once."

A young girl, wearing a white cap that kept her dirty brown hair from falling about her pudgy face came into the room. Her small, brown eyes went from her mistress to Rachel and back again.

Edith seemed unnerved at the young girl who seemed to be too interested in Rachel's disheveled appearance. "Have Albert ready my carriage," she paused for a moment. "No, have him ready the buggy so that he can take us into town quickly." She took the torn dress from Rachel and held it up so that Millie could see it. "We have to get this frock fixed immediately so you look fit when Lord Symington calls." She turned to Millie, "Hurry now."

"Yes milady," Millie curtseyed and left the room.

"I do not trust that one," Edith said softly. She placed Rachel's ripped dress next to her on the sofa and continued "She is one of the servants whom Lord Symington sent over just recently. He told father she was very poor and needed work. Lord Symington said he had too many servants. You know father and his kind heart. He agreed to have her work here for a while until he could find her another position."

After a short period, they heard the rumbling sound of the buggy pulling up to the front doors.

Millie appeared in the doorway so quietly it startled them. "Your buggy is 'ere, milady. Would you be needin' my 'elp?" Her eyes narrowed into small slits.

"No," Edith replied in a firm, authoritative voice. "We can manage things quite well. I want you to help Mrs. Dawson in the kitchen." Quickly, she motioned for Millie to go. "Leave and shut the door behind you."

"Yes, milady." Millie curtsied again, lingering a bit longer before she left the room. Slowly, she closed the parlor doors. It was a moment before they heard the floor creak as Millie walked down the hallway to the kitchen.

"Quickly, we must leave now." Edith grabbed Rachel's arm, and the two raced out the door to the awaiting buggy. Before getting in, Edith walked toward the back of the buggy.

"'Tis all there, milady."

Edith looked up into the smiling face of the coachman, Albert. She nodded and smiled back. Albert had covered Rachel's trunk in the back of the buggy so no one could tell what was there. "To town, Albert, we have to get back here as quickly as possible." She yelled loudly so that anyone, especially Millie, who she knew would be listening, could hear her.

When Edith was confident that no one could see them from the manor, she ordered Albert to veer off the road to town and take a road less traveled in another direction. She knew he was loyal and would not question any orders given to him.

Once they were on the road, they kept a watchful lookout for any other carriages that might be traveling near them.

"I see another carriage coming our way," Albert peered back at Edith and Rachel.

"What? Oh, this cannot be. We cannot be seen. It may be one of Lord Symington's men." Edit said excitedly. "Is there another road we can take to avoid it?"

"Yes," Albert said. He jerked the reins, turning the buggy. He headed across a field of wildflowers at a fast clip. "I can cut 'cross here to get to another road. There be a little hill coming up. Hold on." He yelled back to them.

The ride through the wildflowers was a bumpy ride, causing the two women to hold onto the side of the buggy until it finally stopped on a small dirt road. Albert turned and smiled at the two disheveled women. He headed the horses down the dirt road walking them at a normal pace.

"No one uses this road much," Albert smiled back at his two passengers.

"Thank you," Edith said regaining her composure.

"Edith," Rachel looked over at her cousin sitting quietly next to her. "I am afraid when they find out what happened that you may get into trouble."

"Nonsense," she squeezed Rachel's hand. "I am to be married to a wonderful man. Our banns will be posted in a couple of days. I will be more than safe with him."

"He is a kind and generous man. And, I know he loves you very much."

"Yes, I know." Edith leaned forward to gaze into Rachel's face. "He is quite a bit older than me. I believe he said he was twenty-seven."

"Older?" Rachel threw her head back and laughed. "I was supposed to marry a man in his seventies."

"You cannot call Lord Symington a man. He is more like a toad."

The both laughed heartily at the comment, when Rachel grabbed at her throat and gasped.

"What?" Edith gripped Rachel's arm.

"I left my torn garment at the manor." She cried out.

"I thought you had grabbed it. But I had put it on the divan next to me." Edith moaned into her hand. "It is my fault."

"It is not your fault. 'Tis mine." Her blue eyes widened in terror.

"Millie will have found it by now and will be on her way to alert Lord Symington." Edith ordered Albert to stop.

"What are we going to do?" Rachel's eyes began to brim with tears.

"Well, first things first, we must protect Albert." She looked over and smiled at the man who had been with her family for over twenty years.

"Don'tcha worry bout me none, milady," he nodded to her. "I'll be taken ya to wherever ya needs to be." Albert's brown eyes narrowed with determination.

"Albert, I cannot risk having the anger of Lord Symington fall upon you," she patted the older man on his shoulder. "How far is it for you to walk back to Brekmore Manor? Would it be too much of a walk for you?"

"I am a fit man in my forties, and the walk would be doing me good, milady." He said, as his shoulder length, black hair whipped about in the wind.

"All right," she nodded. "Just say that we ordered you to stop and pick some berries for us, and when you got out, we grabbed the reins and left you there."

"I'll find where we went off the road. I'll take me some branches and cover the wheel tracks of the carriage where we turned off onto that field." He looked up sheepishly, and smiled at the quizzical looks from the two women. "I knew a sea captain who told me that the Indians across the Atlantic cover their tracks that way. Clever lot they are."

Albert jumped down from the carriage and after helping the two women onto the driver's bench he handed Edith the reins. "You be careful." He pointed down the road. "Keep going that way and you'll come to a main road." He walked away from the carriage and headed up the steep hill.

"Be careful, Albert," they yelled after him. He didn't turn around, but raised his arm and waved.

"Will he be alright, do you think?" Rachel's voice filled with concern.

"He will be fine. He is a very clever and brave man." Edith snapped the reins, and the horses began to move. "Now we must hurry to the rendezvous point and hope that your intended will be there waiting."

"Waiting?" Rachel cocked her head in question. "Isn't it too early for him to be there?"

"He said he would be there waiting for you hours before you could get there," she shrugged. "Let's hope that is true."

They had been riding for quite a while when Rachel suddenly grabbed Edith's hands. "Slow down!" Rachel yelled and pointed toward the horizon off to their right. "Look at the dust being kicked up over there. Someone has noticed us. It is a covered carriage. Oh, no! It looks just like Lord Symington's carriage."

"You are right," Edith slowed the horse down to a canter. "Look, they are headed our way."

"This cannot be good."

"I am going to get off the road." Edith turned the horses and headed toward a dense copse of trees.

"Yes, good idea! They will not see us in there." Rachel turned and looked back at the speeding carriage. "Maybe we should go a little faster. I would stay on the grasses so that there will be less dust."

"I was thinking the same thing."

The carriage chasing them seemed to have picked up speed and continued at a fast pace toward them. Edith had to slow the horses at the entrance into the woods because of the low-hanging branches, and the ground covered with fallen debris.

Cautiously, they entered the woods as the branches grabbed at their bonnets and tugged at their clothing. They stopped at a clearing in the woods that was wide enough to turn their carriage around, and waited.

But the approaching carriage seemed to be getting louder and coming right at them. Rachel looked around for an escape route, but there was too much fallen debris to dare go any further into the woods. The two cousins looked at each other for a moment and then threw their arms around each other. The coach was now coming through the forest and would be upon them in minutes.

"Rachel!" A familiar voice yelled out to her. "It's me!"

"Phillip?" Rachel whirled around. "It's Phillip," she said with relief.

"Oh, thank goodness," Edith sighed as she pulled away from Rachel.

"We saw your carriage at the top of the hill and followed you here," he leapt off the coach and ran toward her. He extended his arms and Rachel quickly fell into them.

"How on earth did you spot us from so far away?" Edith asked.

He produced an army telescope. "My friend here is a navigator and always carries this and a sextant in his case."

"But how did you know we were on our way." Rachel held him tightly.

"Yes, we are much earlier than we had planned," Edith said holding the reins to the skittish horses tightly in her hands.

"I hired a coach, but didn't want anyone driving it unless it was someone I could totally trust." He turned toward the man exiting the carriage. "This is Sir Horace Black. Let me introduce Lady Brekmore and my future wife, Lady Ramsford." They all nodded cordially toward each other. Phillip continued, "Horace got the coach earlier than we had planned so we stopped at a small inn to get some refreshments. Looking back at it now we were lucky that it was full with travelers."

"Why is that?" Edith asked.

"Three men came in a short while after we had been there. I caught a glimpse of an elderly man looking everyone over that was in the inn. We were facing the warmth from the hearth, and they sat directly behind us. After a short while, a servant girl raced into the inn. The girl was so winded she barely got her words out."

"Millie," Edith gasped.

Phillip continued. "There was a slapping noise. I can only guess that one of the three males struck her. Between her sobs, she told them that his future wife had lied about where she was going, and she suspected that she had run away. A man asked her if she knew where they went, and she said no. There was another slapping sound, and the girl ran out of the tavern crying."

"I will have her dismissed the moment I get back to the Manor," Edith gripped the reins even tighter. "I must hurry so that I can stall them as long as I can. Get her trunk from the back and put it on your carriage. You must leave now and hurry."

Horace helped Phillip carry the trunk to the back of their carriage and secure it. He quickly threw open the door to the carriage and helped Rachel climb in.

Phillip walked to Edith and gave her a slip of paper. "He is a family friend who will be sure to relay your letters to each other in the strictest of confidence. I have written his name and address for you. I might add I have paid him quite well to do so." He walked to the carriage and climbed in next to Rachel.

"Edith," Rachel called out to her from the carriage window. "I shall write to you and let you know how well things are going. Do not worry about me. I will be fine. But I am so worried about you and what may happen to you if Lord Symington finds out you helped me."

"Please, Rachel, do not waste your time worrying about me. I will be fine as well. It is you I will worry about."

Rachel sat inside the carriage trying to fight back the tears at leaving her Edith. She pulled away from the window for a moment to regain her composure and then for the last time stuck her head out the window and shouted. "I love you, Edith. I will miss you terribly."

"And I you." Edith's voice broke into little sobs. "Now, let's get going." She grabbed the reins and headed toward the forest opening.

"Be careful." Rachel yelled after her.

Edith could not reply because she was choking back the tears.

"We must hurry," Phillip said. "He might have put things together and may be out looking for us by now. This is some adventure, is it not?" His voice filled with excitement. "I am whisking away my Lady Fair to safety. Protecting her from the evil clutches of that vile old man."

Rachel cried softly into his coat. "Now, now," he patted her shoulder. "Stop crying, soldier's wives don't cry. You will see her again. We are only going away for a couple of years, not forever. And, with any luck, that rank old man will have died off. To think he thought he could have you. It is just too ridiculous to think about." He shook his head and laughed.

"Phillip, we have to hurry." Horace leaned down from the driver's seat. "You have the special marriage license your father obtained, right?"

"Yes, let's get moving." Phillip reached down and gently squeezed Rachel's hand.

"Hold on, this is going to be a very bumpy ride." Horace snapped the reins, and the horses burst into the clearing and down the road to the chapel.

It was an hour before they pulled up to the quaint little village, and less than fifteen minutes before they left the Vicar's cottage as man and wife.

Rachel rested her head on her new husband's chest as their carriage sped toward the wharf where their ship lay harbored. She placed her hand over his heart and closed her eyes. Rachel felt his arm tighten around her shoulders. She smiled and snuggled deeper into the safety of her husband's arms. They were safe. Nothing could hurt them now. Nothing.

Chapter 2

Edith cleared the patch of cover in the forest and raced the carriage to the main road. After she was sure that Rachel was totally out of sight, she pulled the reins in and slowed the horses down to an easy gait.

"If I get back too soon they might be able to figure out which way they went," she spoke to the horses, as if they understood what she was saying. "I think we should pick some berries on the way. It will give me time to think of something to tell them. Do you think that's a good idea?"

As if on cue, one of the horses neighed, causing Edith to smile, "Me, too." She pulled the team onto a grassy knoll where the strawberries were hanging in vivid clusters.

Edith climbed down from the buggy and tethered the two horses to a slender tree. She fumbled around the back of the buggy to find some place to put the berries. Finding an old bonnet that had been smashed by Rachel's trunk, she shook the dust off of it, and walked leisurely toward the bright, red fruit.

Edith purposely took a very long time to fill the bonnet, inspecting each berry individually. Finally, she stood, stretching her aching back, and looked up. "Oh, Mr. Sun, you are sitting high in the sky. I am quite hungry, so it must be near afternoon tea." She straightened her back twisting her body left and right to try to ease out the discomfort. "I do not think my back could take picking another berry."

Edith untied the horses from the tree and climbed into the buggy when she heard the pounding sound of horses off in the distance. She placed the bonnet on the seat next to her and took the reins in hand. The thundering noise was closer now. She hoped it wasn't someone intent on finding Rachel. Unhurriedly, she turned the horses toward the sound. It was coming from the direction of Brekmore Manor.

Over a slight hill crest, a large carriage pulled by four horses raced toward her. She recognized the men riding ahead of the carriage as two of Lord Symington's henchmen. Edith's heart began to race. "I hope my story will be believable. Believable enough for Rachel and Phillip to sail out of port," she sighed softly.

The carriage and riders pulled up alongside of her. Lord Symington burst opened the carriage door. "Where is she?" He screamed.

"Why, I thought she was with you?"

"What do you mean?" His blackened mouth twisted into a sneer. The blanket over his lap slid down as his hands clutched the side of the carriage door.

"I am sorry," her eyes blinked a couple of times in mock innocence. "I thought I made myself clear." She smiled insincerely, "I said, I thought she was with you."

"I heard what you said, you chit." He spat out his words. "How could you think she was with me when I am here?"

"First, do not dare to call me a chit again." Edith looked at the withering, old man straight in the eyes. "You may threaten and scare others, but not me." She leaned forward peering over at the scrawny little man.

"Second," Edith hoped she could keep her loathing of this foul man out of her voice. She continued, "Lady Ramsford waved at someone in a carriage, much like yours, and said she was leaving. I could only assume it was you in the carriage as I did not see a face. Nor did I think you would want me to intrude upon your time with Lady Ramsford."

"Which way did they go?" He growled more than spoke.

"Well, let me see," she raised a finger to her chin and began to tap it slowly, as if in deep thought.

"Well?" the veins in his neck began to protrude through his winkles.

"Well," she replied. "I do not know. The carriage did not move."

"What nonsense is this?" He screamed.

"What I mean is," her voice was short and discourteous. "I left before you did … I mean … I left before the other carriage moved. Therefore, I would have absolutely no way of knowing which way they traveled. After all, I thought she was with her intended; it was none of my business. I even stopped to pick strawberries because I felt it was of no importance."

"You think you are clever, my dear," his mouth twisted and spewed out spittle as he yelled. "Do not think to trifle with me. You are no match in wits. I would be very careful."

"I have had enough of your threats and unpleasantness. Good day." Her gray eyes narrowed and her back straightened as she snapped the reins causing the horses to move forward.

The two men on horseback quickly pulled in front of her to block her passage. Edith pulled out the whip she never used on the horses, but she would have no problem using it on these men.

"Let her go," Lord Symington ordered. He slammed the carriage door shut and pulled the blanket back around his legs. His two henchmen made room for her to pass.

Edith held the whip firmly in her hand, just in case one of them tried something. She wanted to race as fast as possible back to Brekmore Manor, but instead she made the horses move at a slow gait. The last thing she wanted to do was to have Lord Symington think that he had frightened her, although he truly had. Her false bravado held out until she spotted the sanctuary of her home. She fell back onto the buggy seat and sighed deeply.

It was a great relief when she spotted her father waiting for her by the front door. He waved frantically, his face filled with concern. He walked down the steps and waited for the buggy to stop next to him. He reached up and helped Edith from the buggy. "My dear! My dear. You are safe." He circled his arms around her and held her tightly. "Albert told me what happened. My dear, what have you done?" He motioned for one of the servants to take care of the buggy and horses.

She was about to speak when she spotted Millie standing directly behind her father.

"We must talk," she grabbed his elbow and led him into the house.

Millie shut the front doors and began to follow them.

"Millie," Edith stopped in the foyer and turned toward the young informer. "Have Mrs. Dawson prepare me some tea and bring it to the parlor."

"I thought milady would want me to stay near in case you needed me after your tiring trip."

"I have no need of you," she continued into the parlor on her father's elbow. "Just do as I asked."

"You seemed very impatient with the poor young girl. It is so unlike you to treat servants in that manner." Her father escorted Edith to a nearby chair and waited until she had seated herself before he sat down on the chair next to her. "She was very concerned about you and Rachel."

"How is that?"

"She asked many times if anyone knew where you were, as she feared for your safety."

"Father," Edith lowered her voice and leaned toward him. "I must tell you ... " A squeaky floorboard by the parlor door alerted Edith that someone was just outside the door. "Millie?"

Millie walked across the room carrying a large tray with Edith's tea. The tray looked hurriedly put together with unfolded napkins, a sugar lid not seated properly, and cream spilt onto the tray. "I am sorry, milady. Mrs. Dawson had the tea already prepared. I hurried this to you as fast as I could."

"That was very thoughtful of you," Edith's father smiled warmly at the nervous young girl.

"Yes, indeed." Edith gave a half-smile and added. "Seeing that you are being so thoughtful," the servant girl missed the sarcasm in her remark. "I want you to go to the carriage house and bring back my bonnet filled with strawberries, and take them to Mrs. Dawson. She will know what to do with all the berries."

"But … I," Millie started to protest, thought better of it, gave a short curtsey and left the room.

"Oh, Millie," Edith called out.

She turned and replied. "Yes, milady."

"Shut the door behind you."

"Yes, milady." She left the room quietly shutting the door behind her.

Edith waited until Millie's footsteps became faint sounds. "Father, you must release that servant immediately."

He reached over and patted her hand. "Whatever for my dear?"

"She watches us and reports back to Lord Symington everything we do and say."

"But why would she do that." Lord Brekmore leaned back into his chair.

"Because Lord Symington wanted to know every move that Rachel made." She picked up the teapot and made a cup of tea, offering it to her father. "He knows Rachel spends most of her time with us here."

He declined the offering of tea with an upraised hand. "I would like to know just what happened with Rachel and you."

"Rachel is hopefully on her way to Nova Scotia with her new husband."

He gasped and looked at his daughter with widened eyes. "What?"

"Yes, I helped her join up with him this morning."

"Albert said that you two took the buggy and a trunk of Rachel's belongings. He thought that she was going to stay with someone so that she did not have to marry Lord Symington. He sent everyone in the opposite direction looking for you two."

"Oh, my! He will be in grave danger if Lord Symington finds out."

"Albert suggested later, much later, that he dragged a branch behind him for a while covering the wagon tracks. The most unusual thing I have ever heard."

"Indians," Edith laughed.

"Indians?"

"I will explain it all to you later." She looked around as the sound of the front door creaked open. "First, we must get rid of Millie."

He rose from his chair and extended his hand to Edith. "You have been gone all morning. You must be exhausted."

"I found the strawberries, milady." Millie held up the bonnet filled with the red fruit.

"Take them to Mrs. Dawson," Edith ordered in a soft restrained voice. "And Millie, servants use the kitchen entrance, not the front door."

"Yes, milady." She stood for a moment and then turned toward the kitchen with bonnet in hand.

"Do not fret about Millie, Father. I will have Mrs. Dawson trump up something to get her dismissed. She has never trusted, nor liked Millie anyway. Mrs. Dawson said she was a very lazy girl."

The rest of the day went quickly for Edith. After they had their evening meal, she excused herself to seek the refuge of her room. It had been a long strenuous day for her and the full impact of Rachel being gone for good caused her enormous pain.

She walked over to the large window in her room and stared out at the red sky and brilliant yellow globe edging its way out of sight. "Are you looking at the same sunset as I, dear Rachel? I shall miss you so terribly."

She glanced around her warm and cozy room that she, and Rachel, had spent so many hours in. She looked at the wallpaper with its small, yellow rose pattern and smiled thinking about the time they tried to count the yellow roses on one wall. They fell asleep before they got to fifty.

The ceiling-to-floor window curtains were of blue and white striped cotton, trimmed in white lace. A couple of chairs placed around a small round table had bright yellow cushions on them. There were nightstands on either side of her bed, where each of them would place their candle, or cup of hot tea.

A white, feather quilt was on top of her bed, and the under-skirting was the blue and white striped cotton, just like the curtains, only larger stripes. Her four-poster bed had a canopy trimmed with yards of lace that hung gracefully overhead. Nothing in the room was very expensive, but done with love and devotion from her father. It was a chilly evening, so there was a warm fire glowing in the fireplace next to her bed.

There was a soft knock on her door, "Yes," she called out.

The door opened slowly and a portly, middle-aged woman wearing a white cap over a shock of grey hair entered the room. Edith could hear her petticoats rustle from under her gray, gingham dress and white apron as she placed a large lit candle on the stand next to her bed. "I thought you would be needing this." Her voice was gravelly, belying the kindness in her eyes and rotund face. Her large green eyes traveled around the darkening room. "Shall I light the other candles?"

"No, that is very thoughtful of you Mrs. Dawson," she turned and smiled warmly at the cook. "I will be retiring shortly."

"Your father has told me about that little chit, Millie." She quickly added, "Pardon, I meant no disrespect."

"There is no one around now, Mrs. Dawson. You can speak informally as much as you wish." She walked toward the older woman and gently patted her arm. "I don't care if other people think it is improper. You have been like a mother to me. I love you dearly."

"And I love you, too. Now, let me help you get undressed." She turned Edith around and began to undo the buttons to her dress. "I dismissed the ... Millie this evening. Your father is too good to her. Do you know he gave her a month's wages? 'Tis a fine thing to do," she grumbled sarcastically. "She barely worked around here at all. Always asking questions and sneaking around the house. Never trusted that girl."

Mrs. Dawson turned Edith back around and waited as Edith untied the ribbons from the front of her empire-styled dress. The long, blue muslin dress came off easily, and fell softly to the floor.

"I would not trust anyone that Lord Symington recommended." Edith pulled at the ribbon around her waist that held up her nude-colored pantaloons until they too fell to the floor.

"There," Mrs. Dawson helped Edith step over the clothing on the floor. "Now, milady, you get into your nightgown and get into bed."

"You called me milady in private," Edith smiled and hugged the large woman. "You have raised me from a newborn. I never wanted you to call me milady in public or private. But you insisted on calling me milady. So we made a pact that you only call me milady in public, remember?"

"Yes, I do remember," she gave Edith a quick hug and pulled away. "What a horrible day this must have been for you? I shall miss little Rachel, too." Quickly, she pulled several folded handkerchiefs from a pocket in her apron. "I thought you may need this, my dear." She took one for herself and dabbed at her eyes and nose.

"Yes," Edith's voice was barely above a whisper. She took the handkerchiefs from her and placed them on the table next to her bed. She reached for her nightgown, placed on her bed earlier, and slipped into it.

"I will take care of your things," Mrs. Dawson scooped up the dress and pantaloons from the floor putting them neatly in the armoire. She hurried over to Edith's bed and pulled back the covers for her. "I will have a really fine breakfast for you in the morning, my dear. Sleep well." She smiled and nodded toward Edith as she headed for the door.

"Thank you for everything, Mrs. Dawson. Have a good evening." Edith finished adjusting the nightgown of soft white cotton around her.

"Good night, dear Edith," she opened the door, gave a little curtsey, and shut the door very quietly.

Edith leaned over placing her hand around the glass chimney of the lamp and blew out the candle. Darkness now descended all around her. She slipped into bed and pulled the covers up around her neck. Then the tears started; the pain of it all overtook her. She took the handkerchiefs from the table. It was going to be a long, hard night full of tears, and she knew it.

Edith awoke to a sunless room. The day was dark and overcast with gray and white clouds saturating the sky. A gentle knock at her door caused her to stir. "Yes," she called out weakly.

"Good morning, my dear," Mrs. Dawson came into her room carrying a large tray of breakfast foods. She moved the candleholder and set the tray on the table next to Edith's bed. "I know 'tis a sad day, but you must eat. After you are done eating, I will come back and help you get dressed." She put her hands on her hips when Edith made no effort to move.

"You see," Edith, pointed toward the window, tears forming in her eyes. "She took the sun with her."

"Now, now, my dear," she picked up the tray and held it in front of Edith. "You have to eat something. Come on, sit up."

Reluctantly, Edith pulled herself up, propping a couple of pillows behind her. "I am not very hungry, Mrs. Dawson."

"I know, my dear. I know," she put the tray in front of Edith and reached over, took the napkin off the tray, and placed it on her chest. "But you must try to remember why Lady Rachel had to leave. 'Twas for her own good."

"I know." She nodded slowly. "I know, but it still does not take away the pain. I feel as if my heart is empty right now."

"Well, just fill it up with the special breads I baked for you," she patted Edith's hand, and left the room.

A little while later Mrs. Dawson came back upstairs to Edith's room. She had left the door slightly ajar, but closed it now as she glided into the room. "Well, 'tis a good thing you managed to get some of the food down." Mrs. Dawson picked up the tray eyeing the partially eaten food, and put it on the table near the window.

"The chambermaid will be up shortly to clean up, so I suggest you get up now, and I'll help you dress." She pulled back Edith's quilt and took her elbow assisting her out of bed.

As soon as she had finished her toiletries and gotten dressed, Edith walked downstairs to the library in search of her father, but he was not there. None of the servants knew where he had gone.

Suddenly, Edith felt a strong urge to be comforted in the arms of her love. She grabbed her shawl, gloves and bonnet, and gave orders for the stable boy to get her buggy readied and, without an escort, drove toward Ian's humble cottage in the valley.

A slight smile crossed her face at the thought of the large, gentle Scotsman who had captured her heart. He was not a Lord or an Earl, but he was a nobleman to her. Her Ian was very tall and broad in the shoulders. His blue-gray eyes looked at her with such love it astounded her.

She loved the way his reddish-blond hair always looked tousled and unkempt, and how he would constantly run his fingers through his unruly hair. He had a bit of noble blood in his background, but his family came upon hard times, and all he owned now was this little cottage near the edge of what used to be his family's vast property. He managed to make a decent living with his carpentry, especially with the beautiful pieces of furniture he created.

Edith was relieved that the roads were empty of travelers. She turned off the main road and headed down a small, winding path. Twenty minutes later, she reached his home. He was there to greet her as she pulled up in front of his door.

"Why are ye out alone?" He asked, surprised that Edith was unaccompanied by a servant or Rachel.

"I have much to tell you." She reached her arms down for him.

"What has happened?" He gently lifted her to the ground.

"If you would be so kind as to put a pot of tea on, I will tell you everything that has happened."

"But we would be alone in the cottage," he looked around to see if anyone else was about.

"Are you afraid of me?" She chided softly.

"Aye, for yer reputation I am," he lifted her chin up. "It is not proper for a Lady to be with a man alone if they are not married."

"Alright, you stand out here, and I will go and fix me some tea and drink it by myself." She brushed past him and went into the neat little cottage.

"Saints preserve us," he shook his head, looked around, and walked to the buggy. "I am going to put the horse and carriage in the barn, just in case someone happens by."

"A very good idea, Mr. Atterby," she said walking through the door. Surprised and pleased to see the tea already brewed, she took two cups and poured the tea. She walked around the table placing the cups and saucers on it, sat down, and waited for Ian, who hurried back into his cabin.

"This has to be very important for ye to come all this way alone. What has happened?"

"Everything happened so quickly. I did not have time to tell you before now." Tears formed in her eyes, and her hands dropped to her lap.

"What is it, dearest? What has upset ye so?" He dropped down on one knee next to her.

She pulled on the drawstrings of her finely sewn reticule to open it, took out a handkerchief and began dabbing at her eyes and nose. "Please let us have some tea, and I will tell you everything. I hope you will not be displeased with me when I tell you what has happened."

"Nothing ye could ever do would displease me." He got up and moved a chair closer to her. "Now, my dear, tell me what is troubling ye so." He sat down and waited for her to begin.

Between her story, and her tears, she finished telling him about Rachel's escape with the young Lieutenant. She waited for his response. She was afraid to look into his eyes; instead, she focused on her hands as they twisted the handkerchief on her lap.

He placed one hand under her chin and gently lifted her face. "What ye did was a wonderful thing, my dear. That I would think less of ye for that is naught but foolishness. The tea is cold let me warm it for ye." He stood up and turned toward the small, pot-bellied, iron stove.

Edith stood up and grabbed his arm turning him toward her. "Oh, Ian, I do love you so," she threw her arms around his neck.

"And I ye," he nuzzled her hair, breathing in her scent. "I am counting the days until ye are here with me forever."

"As am I, my love, as am I." She pulled back and stared into his eyes.

Slowly, their heads moved closer. Her heart was beating wildly. She could feel his breath so warm near her lips. Then, she felt him begin to pull away. A low, almost growl, escaped from her lips as she grabbed him and kissed him full on the mouth.

At first, she felt him ever so slightly try to pull away. Then he pulled her into his arms and kissed her back. However, this time his lips parted and his tongue moved gently into her mouth. Edith was stunned at first, and then returned his kiss with a passion she had never felt before. He pulled away kissing her face, her hands, and like a starving man sought her lips again.

He moaned softly and began gently kissing her neck, moving his lips down to her shoulders, when he abruptly drew away from her. "I cannot do this to ye," Ian said as he pulled away from her. "Oh, my dear, I want to have ye more than ye will ever know. But we only have a short time to wait. I do not want to hurt ye in any way."

Edith had never before experienced or felt anything like the passion she was feeling. She stood there looking up at him trying to catch her breath. It was as if a fire inside of her was trying to consume her. "Why did you stop?"

"I told ye, my love, I did not want to have yer reputation hurt in any way."

"Why let it bother you. It does not bother me," her knees seemed weak as she grabbed the back of the chair for support.

"Oh, woman, ye could tempt the Gods."

"I do not want to tempt them, just you."

He pulled her to him and kissed her again, his body pressing hard against her. Suddenly, he broke the kiss.

"What is the matter?" She asked confused again by the strong feelings she was having. "I don't want you to stop."

"I hear horses heading this way," he said, and went to the window. "By the Gods, there are a couple of riders coming this way."

"How many times have I come to see you, and there has never been one, not even one rider." She exclaimed with disappointment.

"We must get ye to the barn." He took her by the elbow and led her out the back door to the barn. "Stay here until I come for ye."

Edith heard the horsemen ride up and then an exchange of voices. It seemed like forever before Ian opened the barn door.

"They were looking for ye."

"Me? Whatever for?"

"It appears ye have a visitor at the manor, and neither ye, nor yer father be there."

"Why do they not just come back when we are there?" A distasteful fear crept into her thoughts.

"Unless, it is that horrible Lord Symington. He is the only one I know who would do this."

"Ye must go before they find ye here," he brought her to his chest. "It is only for a short time, and then we will be together forever." He brought his lips down and kissed her gently.

"Yes," she sighed deeply. "You are right. I will go." She reached up and held his face in her hands. "We will be together soon, forever my love."

He took her cupped hands in his and kissed them gently. Ian sighed audibly as he pulled her to him for one last kiss. He put his forehead to hers for a moment and then said, "Wait until I climb to the top of the hill and make sure that no one is around." He helped her up into the buggy and opened the barn doors. "When ye see me wave that means it is all clear and ye can go."

She nodded and pulled the carriage out of the barn to wait for his signal. Edith watched him walk to the top of the knoll. Her heart was bursting with love for him.

He turned around a couple of times checking the roads, then his arm went up, and he waved for her to leave. She waved back as she rode down the dirt road. He stood there until she could no longer see the knoll or him.

Chapter 3

Edith's heart sank at the sight of Lord Symington's carriage parked in front of the manor steps.

Albert was waiting for her by the front of the house. He helped her down from the buggy. "He be in there, Lady Edith."

He didn't have to say "who" Edith knew. She walked calmly into the house toward the open doors to the parlor. She stopped short of the doors, took a deep breath, and walked casually into the room. A sickening feeling swept over her as she looked at Lord Symington sitting alone on a chair by the blazing fireplace.

The chair had been turned so that his back was to the warming fire. "Did you have a nice ride this morning?" His little, pink tongue flicked at his blackened lips.

"Yes, thank you," she said coldly. She took off her shawl and placed it on a nearby chair.

"Why are you here?" She did not sit; instead, she walked behind a chair and stood looking down at him.

A nasty smirk began to form across his face, "Blunt and to the point. So, I shall be blunt and to the point as well," he said in a steel-cold voice. "I have come about my wedding."

Edith's heart stopped for a moment. He must have found Rachel. She grabbed the back of the chair to steady herself. "The wedding?" She asked, trying not to sound too shaken.

"No, not "the" wedding – I meant my wedding. Oh, did I say 'my' wedding? I meant *our* wedding, of course." The black hole he called his mouth widened into a huge grin.

Edith was at a complete loss for words. She just stood there staring at him, not really believing what she had heard.

"Are you not pleased?" He sneered ever so slightly.

Edith regained her composure, "Have you been kicked in the head by a horse recently? I do not intend to marry you now or ever. If you are not aware of this fact," her eyes narrowed contemptuously at him. "I am promised in marriage to someone else."

"Hmmm," he toyed with a black leather glove in his hand. "Yes, I have heard, but you are a sensible girl, and I really do like your spirit."

"Well, this spirited girl would like to show you to the front door." She turned and walked toward the parlor door.

"You will be a widow before you are ever married." He never took his eyes off her as he slapped his gloves hard against his hand.

"What?" She gasped and whirled around.

"You heard me, my dear," he smiled at her again. "You would also be an orphan. Your father is such a gentleman it would be a shame if he had an accident, too."

Edith stumbled to a chair near the door and fell, more than sat, back into it. Not prepared for such treachery her mind began to reel from shock and confusion.

"You took my bride from me, so it is only fair that you replace her," his beady-black eyes narrowed into tiny slits. "I told you that you were not as clever as I am." He leaned back in his chair and smiled. "So, my dear," the word dear was filled with contempt, "when shall we plan this delightful event. I believe a month is more than enough time for you to ready yourself as my bride."

"I cannot do this," her voice was barely above a whisper, but he heard it.

"It is up to you whether your beloved Ian Atterby, a man of no consequences I might add, and your father live long and healthy lives." He stood up and bowed slightly toward her. "And do not think of running off with this Mr. Atterby, I have taken precautions this time. And, do not worry about your father, he will understand."

"My father will never let me marry you," she spat out the words.

"Oh, yes he will. Just tell him it is a business arrangement. Your father is in town now trying to acquire credit. It seems that he has incurred more than a few debts."

"My father does not owe money to anyone."

"Oh, but he does, my dear. Your father was misled into some very unworthy business ventures," Lord Symington said smiling wickedly as he walked to the door. "I shall gladly pay off all of his debts just to make his daughter happy." He stopped at the doorway, "Now. I think I shall see myself to your front door."

"I will tell my father of your treachery, he will deal with you," she spoke loudly and calmly.

"Then he will die before the week is out." His face twisted in hatred. "Our banns will be posted tomorrow." He slammed the front door as he left the manor.

Edith sat there in shock. What could she do? What was she to tell Ian? What was she to tell her father?

"Dear little Edith," Mrs. Dawson and Albert stood at the parlor doorway. "Albert and I heard everything. What can we do to help you?"

"Oh, this cannot be," Edith sobbed into her hands. "What am I going to do?"

"There, there, my dear," Mrs. Dawson spoke softly. "Give Albert and me some time to come up with some ideas of our own to help you."

"I must get to Ian and tell him," Edith began to rise from her chair.

Albert rushed to her side, "Lady Edith, right now would not be a good time. I think that miserable man left somebody outside to watch the house."

Edith nodded and stared down at the floor. "Why are there people like that in this world?"

"You have your good men like Lord Brekmore, Mr. Atterby, and Albert here, maybe God throws in evil men like Lord Symington, just so we can appreciate the good ones."

"Excuse me, Lady Edith." Albert bowed and headed toward the door. "I think sneaking out the back door may be the way to find the black-heart. I will go and check to see where he be."

"I am so numb. I cannot feel anything."

"We will think of something." She patted Edith's hand. "We will."

It was dark before her father's carriage pulled up to the house. The sound of the stable boy running to fetch the carriage and her father's slow footsteps coming in the front door brought Edith to her feet. She could tell that her father already knew by the look on his face.

She ran into his arms, and he held her tightly.

"I am so sorry my child. So, sorry," he kissed her cheek and released her.

"It has nothing to do with you, father. It is all the doing of Lord Symington." She looked into her father's troubled face and gave him a small smile.

"He promised it would be a way for me to leave you a small fortune for your future. He tricked me into these business ventures that turned out to be hollow." He sat on the love seat with his head in his hands. "How could I have been so stupid?"

"You are not stupid," she sat next to him and took his hands. "You are a good, kind, loving man who would never cheat anyone. Why would you think someone would do that to you?" She held his hand and shook her head. "Father, I am fated to marry Lord Symington. However, he will be the one to regret this marriage."

"I cannot let you do this," his voice filled with rage. "The thought of that foul man touching my lovely daughter. I will kill him first."

"Father, I would rather die than have that hideous man touch me. I will think of something, please trust me on that." She pulled his hands to her face and kissed them. "Mrs. Dawson and Albert heard Lord Symington's madness. They want to help. And I am sure we can come up with something. Although, getting out of this marriage I cannot see."

"I cannot let you do this," he stood up and began to pace the floor. "We will plan your escape, just like you did for Rachel."

"No, he already has someone watching me, just in case." She left out the part where Lord Symington would have him killed if she ran off with her Ian. "He is planning the wedding in one month's time. I must have a good plan ready by then."

"My dear, dear, Edith," all he could do was shake his head and repeat her name repeatedly. He sat down next to her again. "How can I live with this horrible thing I have thrust upon you? I cannot."

"Father, stop," she hugged him and then stood up. "Let us never talk of you dying again. If you were not in my life, it would be unbearable. I will be alright, trust me." She hoped her last words sounded more convincing than she felt. "It is getting late and I am tired. We will talk more of this tomorrow." She leaned down and kissed the top of his head.

In the morning, Mrs. Dawson rushed into Edith's room and shook her awake. "Come on we have work to do."

"What are we going to do?" She asked groggily.

"Not we, you. You are going to your Mr. Ian and tell him what happened."

"How can I do that?" Edith became immediately alert, and Mrs. Dawson had her complete attention. "Lord Symington has someone watching the house at all times."

"Yes, for you," Mrs. Dawson smiled and threw a huge lump of clothing she was carrying onto the bed. "But they would not be following me, now would they?"

Edith looked down at the clothing on the bed. It was one of Mrs. Dawson's gray gingham dresses, and her large sunbonnet.

"A little padding and no one would be able to tell it is you."

"Do you think it will work?"

"Yes," she grabbed Edith's elbow and helped her out of bed. "Now get to your toiletries, so we can get started."

A short time later, Edith, wearing Mrs. Dawson's dress over her own clothing, headed down the hallway toward the stairs.

Albert peeked around the kitchen door and whispered. "The carriage is waiting by the back door."

"Thank you, Albert." Edith said softly and turned to Mrs. Dawson. "What would I do without you two?" She hugged the robust woman and kissed her on the cheek.

"Now, now," Mrs. Dawson seemed slightly embarrassed. "You must go quickly.

Edith walked out of the back door and climbed into the waiting buggy. She gave a small wave of her hand and adjusted the large bonnet over her head being careful to hide her face.

Mrs. Dawson watched as Edith pulled the large bonnet further over her face and headed down the road. "What would I do without *you*, my sweet child? I promised your kind and gentle mother, I would watch over you. I have watched over you like my own, I have, and I will until the day I die."

Mrs. Dawson ran to the window and carefully peeked out to see if the man watching the house would see through the disguise. He was hiding behind large bushes off in a distance exactly where Albert first spotted him. She watched as he moved out from his cover to see who was leaving the house. He held the reins of his horse in his hands. She held her breath until she saw him return to his hiding place and tethered the horse back to a tree.

Edith controlled the impulse to slap the horse into a faster pace. She had to look like she was not in a hurry, just like when Mrs. Dawson drove into town. The road to town and the road that veered off to Ian's were far enough away from the prying eyes of Lord Symington's henchman. She turned down the path to Ian's and let out a yelp giving the horses their cue to move faster, and raced toward his cottage.

Ian was at the front door, and a surprised look came over his face from the sight of Mrs. Dawson in her buggy racing toward him. "Something has happened to Edith," his voice filled with worry. He hurried toward the buggy as it pulled up in front of him. "Mrs. Dawson what is it?" Edith raised her head.

"What the ...?"

"Hurry and help me down," she said urgently. "Please hide the carriage in the barn. I will explain all of this. Just hurry."

Noting the urgency in her voice, he helped her down and quickly took the buggy to the barn as Edith raced into the cottage and shut the door.

Ian hurried back to his cottage. "What are ye doing here? What are ye doing in that outfit? By the Saints," he exclaimed. "What happened since yesterday?"

Edith finished taking off the bonnet and outer clothing of Mrs. Dawson. She ran to him throwing her arms around him sobbing uncontrollably. It took him a while to settle her down and to tell him exactly what had happened. She sat quiet for a moment, and when she started to speak again her voice trembled. "If I do not marry Lord Symington my father will end up in debtor's prison, or worse."

Ian sat there quietly for a while, his eyes lowered, and then his large hand curled into a fist slamming onto the top of the table. "We will leave, now."

"We cannot, my love," she shook her head. "He will kill my father."

"Then, we will all leave together." He looked up at her, his eyes brimming with tears.

"It is impossible," she reached over and took his face in her hands. "He has us watched now at all times."

"But we could disguise ye and yer father like that," he gestured at Mrs. Dawson's clothing lying crumpled on the floor next to them, "and then we could all ..."

Edith stopped him. "It is no use, my love. They have someone watching my father and me at all times. I was almost afraid to come here for fear they would have someone watching you, too."

"Are ye sure ye are safe coming here?"

"Yes, Albert checked it out, last night and this morning. He said one is following my father, and one watches me right now."

"Marrying him is the end of us." He jumped up and began to pace the floor.

"It would not be if you listen to what I have to say," she lowered her eyes for a moment.

"I do not understand ye at all," he stopped pacing and stared down at her.

"Please sit, Ian," she took a deep breath and waited until he sat down in a chair facing her.

"My heart is breaking, Edith. What can ye say to ease this pain?"

Another deep breath and Edith blurted her plan to him, "I want to have your child."

"What could ye say … huh?" He sat stunned.

"I want to have your child," she continued nervously. This was the boldest thing she had ever done. "Albert heard Lord Symington's men bragging about how he planned to bed Rachel as his wife just to get a boy. Once she was with child he would not touch her again, unless she pleased him of course. So, you see once I am with child he will not touch me either, because trust me, he will never be pleased with me."

"He would kill both of us if ye were with child when ye married him." He ran his fingers through his wavy hair. "What kind of madness is this? Edith, he must bed ye to think the child is his."

"Yes, but" she produced a small pouch from her pocket. "This is an herb that Mrs. Dawson uses to sleep better at night. Over the years, she has heard that Lord Symington always has a glass of wine before he goes to bed. I shall slip this in his drink, and he will sleep the night through."

"If he falls asleep, he will know that ye two did nothing." He shot up from his chair and began pacing again. "This is the worst day of our lives. How can this be happening?"

"Please hear me out," She grabbed one of his hands and pulled him back to sit next to her. "I love you more than life itself. If you truly love me, I only ask that you lay with me, so I can conceive our child."

"Edith what ye ask is wrong."

"Wrong?" Her voice filled with hurt. "Wrong? How can the love of two people be wrong? Do the vows of the church make bedding a man you are forced to marry right? Do you think God planned this? I think Lord Symington is Satan himself. I love you. I would gladly boast about my bedding you to the whole town. I care not what anyone thinks, save you."

Tears ran down his cheeks. "All that I have ever wanted has been ripped from me by this evil man. He took our family lands and title. But this

… this is the most painful thing of all. He has taken you from me; he has destroyed our dream."

"Our dream is not destroyed, just broken a little. Oh, Ian, I do not want him to win the hideous game he is playing with our lives. Please, let us have a child, a child who will always remind us of our love. He is an old, foul man who I pray is not long for this Earth. Once he is gone, we shall be together. I need you to do this for me. I must have your child." Her eyes began to fill with tears.

"I know what ye say is right." He placed his hands over his face and leaned forward in his chair. "And, by the Gods, I so desire ye."

"Please, do this for us," she knelt down beside him and gently took away the hands that shielded his face. "I cannot bear the thought of being with anyone else but you."

Startled by the strength and quickness of him when he grabbed her to his chest, Edith almost lost her breath. "Nor can I." His voice filled with pain. "I have loved ye for so long. I have failed ye."

"'Tis not you that have failed me, but my own acts that have brought this upon us. My love for you is so strong; it is almost more than I can bear.

What have I done to us? What have I done?" She laid her head against his chest.

"My dearest, ye tried to help a loved one. I believe that if ye knew that things would have turned out this way, ye still would have helped yer Rachel. That is why I love ye so dearly." Gently, he stroked her hair.

She pulled away from his embrace and looked into his deep blue-gray eyes. Her face was filled with anguish. "Oh, no! What have I done to you? How foolish of me. I am sorry I have put you in such an embarrassing situation. I have acted shamelessly and I deeply regret my thoughtlessness in putting you in such a disagreeable position. I have acted like a wanton harlot."

"Say not such things. It is not for me that I ponder about what is right and wrong; it is only for ye," he said caressing her face gently. "My dear, dear Edith, ye are a woman in love with a weak man, for as surely as I sit here, if you stay but a moment more I will bed ye."

"But you would think ill of me later. I could not bear the thought of you thinking of me as evil or as a woman of easy virtue."

He pulled her to him again. "There is nothing in this world that would make me think of ye as anything but a Lady. My Lady. My lovely, sweet Edith."

"Then, take what I offer, that which is rightfully yours … my heart, my soul, my body. I need you, my love. Now, more than ever. I beg of …" Her voice was silenced as his lips covered hers.

Chapter 4

It was late afternoon when Rachel and Phillip finally reached the ship. Phillip helped Rachel out of the carriage, while Horace signaled two young seamen to fetch their trunks. After Horace gave Rachel a polite nod and bow, and Phillip a quick pat on the back, he jumped up into the driver's seat of the carriage. Rachel watched as Horace started down the busy wharf and out of sight.

"He has to return the carriage and get to his ship. His ship leaves in a couple of days, so he has plenty of time. Plus, I might add, my father paid him handsomely." Phillip led Rachel toward the swaying, wooden ramp that came from the ship and rested on the worn, wooden dock.

The wood creaked beneath Rachel's feet as she walked up the ramp to the ship. It was the first time in her life that her world seemed so alive, so real and yet, so unreal. There were curious mixtures of aromas that filled the air; the scent from the sea breeze, the strong odor of fish, and strange scents she could not identify. The smells from the ship surprised her, too. There was a heavy odor of musk, lye, and mildew as she stepped down onto the deck of the ship.

However, it was the smell of freedom that rallied her senses. It was a long, anxious, yet, exciting day. She was now Lady Prescott, and her new life was just beginning. Rachel was almost giddy with excitement.

A short, burly man took them to their quarters below deck. It was a small room sparsely furnished. There was a bed attached to the wall, and a small, round window that looked out over the wharf. A basin, resting on a wooden stand, was embedded into the wall, as was a small table that jutted out slightly.

There was barely room for the train of her dress to fit into the tiny room. She turned as Phillip closed the door and latched it shut. He whirled around and grabbed her so fast it startled her. She looked up into his eyes and saw something she had never seen before. He pulled her close to him and pressed his lips against hers.

Her arms reached up and went round his neck pulling him even closer.

His breathing began to increase, and she felt his hands moving up from her waist toward her breasts. She tried to pull away, but his hold on her only increased. One hand cupped her breast, and the other hand started to work at the tiny buttons of her pelisse. Phillip began to walk her backward toward the bed as his lips pressed harder and harder against hers.

"Lieutenant?" There was a loud rap at the door.

"What is it?" Phillip almost growled.

"The captain would like to see you topside," there was a slight pause, and added, "Right away, sir."

Rachel could hear the shout of the captain giving orders to his crew, and the sound of wood grinding against wood.

Phillip placed his head on her shoulder, heaved a big sigh, and pulled away from her. "I will be right there." He yelled at the man on the other side of the door. His finger reached up and moved slowly along her jaw line. "We will be heading out to sea soon, my wife, to our new lives." His hand ran quickly over her body. "We will continue this when I get back."

Rachel stood still and said nothing as he walked out of their room and shut the door behind him. She backed up until the bed stopped her and sat with a rustling of her muslin dress.

Her hand ran across her bruised and swollen lips, as she tried to comprehend what was happening. He had never kissed her like that before and certainly never touched her. What was she expected to do? Why was he breathing so heavily?

She looked down at the bed and ran her hand over the rough blanket tucked neatly in on all sides. There was only one bed in the room. Where was the other bed? Were they supposed to sleep in the same bed? She got up quickly and walked around the tiny quarters. Where was she supposed to change and do her toilet? "Continue what?" She questioned softly. She sat back down on the bed in complete confusion.

There was a sharp rap on the door that interrupted her thoughts. "Ma'am?" A young man's voice filtered through the door. "I brought ya some things from the captain."

Rachel rose slowly from her bed, still bewildered by what had just transpired. She stiffened her back, adjusted her hair, and walked the few steps to the door with her head held high. She pulled the latch and opened the door. A young lad, who looked to be about twelve years of age, stood there holding a pitcher filled with water, and over his left arm dangled a couple of washcloths and towels.

"Thank the captain for us," she smiled warmly and stepped aside so that he could carry the items into the cabin.

His curly, shoulder-length, light brown hair brushed against his white shirt. The young boy set the pitcher and cloths neatly on the table in the corner of the little room. He gave a slight bow and quickly made an exit from the room shutting the door behind him.

She pulled off her gloves and the floor-length pelisse holding it up in front of her. The empire design was simple, yet, elegant and matched her dress beneath. She was grateful that she, and Edith, had made the pelisse out of wool with a cotton lining, or the carriage ride would have been a lot colder.

Her periwinkle blue, empire dress was high at the neck where white lace delicately graced her throat. The train on the dress was shorter than usual and trimmed in three rows of lace. Long sleeves of sheer muslin ended in a row of lace, just like the lace on the bottom of her dress.

She reached behind her neck and unfastened as many of the little buttons she could reach. She thought about taking her bonnet off, but thought it would be faster in doing her hair if she left it on. After all, she was just refreshing herself before he returned.

Struggling, she managed to pull the dress off without damaging it, or dislodging her bonnet, and let her dress fall to the floor. Carefully stepping out of it, she picked it up and draped it over a small chair in the room. She undressed down to her long shift, and her knitted cotton stockings tied on by blue, cotton ribbons.

Rachel took advantage of the water, splashing it on her face and letting it run down her neck, stopping it just before it disappeared down her shift. It felt cool and soothing; she almost wished that it was large enough for her entire body to be submerged.

She rubbed the wet cloth over her bare arms. Rachel reached down and pulled her shift up, so she could untie the ribbons around her stockings, when the door to the room opened.

Phillip stopped, and she heard his intake of air. He quickly turned shutting and locking the door behind him. "This is more than I had hoped." His voice was hoarse from excitement.

Rachel grabbed her dress from the chair and held it in front of her. "Phillip? What are you doing?"

"What all husbands do, my dear," he moved closer to her.

She backed up into the stand that held the water basin, causing some water to spill over its side. "Phillip? Why are you looking at me that way?"

"I am looking at you because you are so beautiful, and you are all mine now. Only mine. You are my wife."

"But I . . ." She never finished her sentence, as he moved swiftly and covered her mouth with his.

Phillip pulled the dress still clutched in her hands away from her body and threw it on the floor behind him. He took off her bonnet and undid her bound up hair. His hands roughly grabbed her breasts. She could feel his hot breath on her shoulder and neck, as he began to pull the shift over her head. Rachel's body stiffened.

"Relax, my dear." He whispered softly into her ear.

"I want to leave this on," Rachel grabbed at her shift and pulled it back down.

Phillip laughed, "I am your husband and there is nothing for you to be ashamed about. However, for this moment, I will honor your request." He lifted her up and carried her to the small bed they were to share. "Now, you will become my wife. I adore you, my beautiful Lady fair. My Rachel."

"Yes," she stroked his hair as he placed her gently onto the bed. "I love you, too." She looked into his face, reaching up to stroke it. The intensity in his eyes was something she had never seen before. His lips met hers again, this time she responded with all the love she felt for him.

It was over quickly. She was unsure of what had just happened. Was it supposed to hurt? He made strange noises and grunting sounds like a wounded animal. It frightened her. They lay quietly in each other's arms for a while, until Phillip began to stir again.

Rachel smiled after the second time; at least, there was no pain for her this time. She was not sure how long they slept, but when she awoke she found herself cradled in his arms. She squeezed him tightly. "Phillip, does this wife and husband duty cause you pain?"

"Pain?" He laughed and slapped the palm of his hand to his forehead. "Pain? No, my dear. I feel no pain. Pleasure, yes." He brought his hand down and touched her cheek.

Rachel had felt no pleasure, except the pleasure of being close to him. She said, "It's just all the noises you made I thought you were in pain."

"No, I make the noises because the pleasure is so great," he smiled and rolled on top of her. "In fact," a hand slipped beneath the covers and began tickling her side. "Time for some more noises."

There was a knock on their door. "The captain wishes you to join him at his table for the evening meal at half-past the hour."

"Thank you," Phillip shouted through the closed door. "We would be honored." Slowly, he pulled himself off Rachel, gave her a quick kiss, and jumped out of bed. "We should probably get some fresh air before we partake of our evening meal."

Rachel closed her eyes at his nakedness and waited until his toilet and washing was completed. "Please," she said softly. "I do need a moment for myself."

"Of course, my dear," he finished dressing and walked back to the bed. "Hurry up. We do not want to keep the captain waiting."

"Are you not going to leave the room?" Her eyes widened in shock.

"No." His eyes scanned the room. "Hmm, I think I'd have a better view from here." He sat down at the table and pushed the chair back. "I intend to watch every move you make. I have waited months for this."

"But" she said in complete shock, "surely, you do not expect me to do my toilet and wash with you watching me. I would rather not share that experience with you."

He hesitated for a moment and then laughed, "This time I will not watch, because I can see you are embarrassed. However, there are some things you will have to get used to in the future, Lady Prescott." He got up and went to the door. "I will wait outside until you call me so that I can button up your dress."

Rachel felt uneasy as she climbed out of bed. She pondered on how being married was nothing like what she had imagined. Was this what marriage was all about? It was supposed to be just little kisses, hugs, holding hands and being together. This was not what she had expected at all. A soft rap on the door brought her out of her reverie.

"Someone is coming," Phillip said softly. "I'm coming in."

Rachel was relieved that she had finished washing and quickly stepped into her dress on the floor. She pulled it up and held it in front of her when the door opened.

Phillip quickly stepped inside and shut the door. "That was close." He studied her for a moment and then laughed. He reached over and gently pulled the tightly held dress away from her and held it up for her to slip her arms through. He turned her around and began to button her dress up. "I have two brothers and two sisters, so nakedness is nothing new to me, nor should it be something to be ashamed of, especially when you are with your husband."

"I only have one brother," she shrugged. "He never was naked around me; although I heard some of the servants say that my father procured him girls when he was very young. What does that mean 'procured'?"

"It means I am done closing the buttons," he turned her around and looked at her hair. "Your hair needs to be straightened up."

"Dear me," Rachel sighed. "It is a good thing Edith and Mrs. Dawson showed me how to take care of it. I will meet you up on the … the …"

"Deck, my dear, it is called a deck. That is acceptable. I will meet you when you have finished." He kissed her forehead and left the room.

Rachel gave a sigh at the sight of the small mirror against the wall. It was going to have to do. Tiny ringlets fell down her forehead as she pulled her long hair into a bun at the back of her head. She put on her cap, looked into the mirror, and felt comfortable enough with the outcome.

She opened the cabin door to her room and walked down the narrow corridor. A set of wooden steps led up to the door that opened onto the deck. Carefully, she picked up the small train of her dress and made her way up the stairs.

Rachel looked for Phillip, but he was nowhere in sight. She spotted the captain standing on the other side of the ship.

The captain did not appear to be as old as she thought he would be. He looked to be in his late twenties or early thirties; she thought, studying him. He was at least a head taller than her husband. Although he was not a very handsome man, there was something attractive about him. She was not sure if it was his dark-brown eyes, and black hair or the way he carried himself, with his shoulders and back straight as a board.

When he walked about the deck, she watched as the sailors hurried about their work, and as he passed by them, the respect they had for him was evident in their faces.

She quickly stopped assessing him when the captain turned and met her gaze with his piercing brown eyes. Rachel blinked a couple of times in embarrassment, gave a weak smile, and turned her attention to a couple walking on the dock toward the ship.

A woman, wearing a big bonnet that concealed her face, was carrying a large valise. She walked with a slight limp as she hurried toward the steps. The ship pitched slightly as she stepped onto the uneven wooden planks of the ramp causing her to lose her balance. The large man behind her grumbled something, as he grabbed her arm and yanked it hard to keep her from falling.

He continued to hold her arm until they reached the end of the wooden ramp, and then gave the small woman a shove causing her to stumble again.

Rachel almost laughed. The man obviously did not know his own strength. She rushed over to assist the woman. Rachel was glad there would be another woman aboard the ship for her to chat up. When she reached the woman, she held out her hand to help steady her against the slight roll of the ship. Docked at port, it still moved about from the rough waters brought in by the current.

The woman brushed past her hand and stood with her head down until the man who had been behind her grabbed her arm. This time Rachel heard the woman give a little gasp when he pushed her roughly toward the passenger quarters.

"You stupid, clumsy baggage!" He snarled at the tiny figure in front of him. He turned and grabbed the door to pull it open when a strong gust of wind blew it shut. At the same time, the wind blew the large bonnet of the woman up, giving Rachel a chance to see her face for the first time.

Now, it was Rachel's turn to gasp. Both eyes of the woman appeared blackened. Her lips were bloodied and swollen, and large black bruises covered one side of her face. Their eyes met briefly, and the sadness in the woman's eyes made Rachel want to run to her and hold her.

Quickly, the woman reached up and pulled the bonnet down to cover her battered face. The big man glared at Rachel at first, and then the strange look that came over Phillip's face early in their room appeared on the strangers face.

"Milady," he made a slight gesture of respect by touching his hat and nodding in her direction.

Rachel gave a slight nod. The man's sneering smile reminded her of the one Symington had on his face the last time she saw him. The difference between the two was extreme, as this man was handsome, taller, and much younger. Even though he was one of the handsomest men she had ever seen, she was not attracted to him. There was something about him that she did not like. "I am sorry. I was just trying to help her up. She's injured."

"Yes," he said still smiling down at her. "Our carriage overturned and she was hurt. The doctor said she will be fine for travel."

"Simon," Captain English yelled for the young cabin boy. "Take them down to their quarters. I believe, under the circumstances you would prefer your meal in your quarters?"

The young woman gave an audible sigh of relief and nodded in agreement. However, her companion had other ideas. "No, we will have our meals with the rest of you. She will be fine, right, my dear."

She dropped her head and nodded in agreement.

"You see. She agrees." He turned her around and headed down the steps leading to their quarters. "When shall we be expected?"

"We shall dine at half past the hour. If you will all excuse me." Captain English gave a slight bow and headed away.

"You look positively fetching," Phillip said behind her.

"Phillip," Rachel hurried toward him. "Did you see that poor woman? She looked dreadful. I am sure she did not want to join us for dinner, but that horrible man made her." She ran with her arms open toward him.

He abruptly stopped her from hugging him, "I am in uniform. No hugs," he said softly.

Embarrassed and hurt, Rachel stepped back and looked at him. "It appeared not to bother you when we would meet in town."

"That is because now we are on a ship, and the Captain is watching us," he spoke a little sharper.

"In town, there was no one to see us. Remember?"

"Do you wish for me to walk on one side of the boat, and you on the other?" She said sarcastically.

"Let us not start a row, shall we," he bristled. "And, just to make sure you understand something very important; this is a *ship*, not a boat."

"Well, I shall endeavor to remember such a very important thing." She turned and walked away with tears forming in her eyes.

"Rachel!" Phillip called after her, "Rachel!" He moved swiftly toward her and grabbed her arm spinning her around to face him. "Do not ever, ever walk away from me when I call you. Do you understand? Do you understand that?"

"I will walk away whenever I choose," she yanked her arm from him. "You will treat me with respect. Do you understand *that*?" Tears streamed down her face.

"I am the man and you are the woman." He hovered over her. "You have to learn your place."

"Learn my place?" She said incredulously. Rachel dabbed her eyes dry with her handkerchief and pushed past him. "I know my place. It is you who do not know his place, at least not yet."

"Rachel, come back here at once," he yelled after her.

She did not turn or look back as she headed down to her cabin.

"It is better to leave them alone for a while," the captain said coming down the stairs. He stood and stared after Rachel. "Did you ever notice that women are like the sails of a ship? They unfurl with the gentle winds, but close up during a storm. Another thing I was surprised to hear about was not hugging in uniform. Soldiers hug their women all the time in uniform. Plus, this is a passenger ship, not a military vessel."

"I am still an officer in Her Majesty's Royal Army," he blurted out indignantly. "We must maintain a decorum at all times."

"That is your personal choice, not mine," the captain stepped aside as a seaman pulled a large crate past them. "Your father must be a very important man to grant you passage on this ship while your regiment is aboard a military ship."

"Yes, he is a renowned barrister and highly respected," he shrugged. "I am meeting up with this new regiment in Boston and will transfer to the military ship there to go to Nova Scotia."

"What of your wife?"

"She will continue with me until we reach Boston. Then, we will figure out how and when she will accompany me."

"Figure out?" The captain was stunned. "You are taking your wife to a strange country, and you have not figured out how she will accompany you to wherever you are going?"

"There are other wives accompanying their husbands," Phillip said confidently. "If other wives are going, she can go with them if need be. I am not worried about it. It will all work out. Besides, with no disrespect, sir, I do not see how this concerns you."

"You are right," he bowed slightly. "The meal is ready to partake of, so I suggest we head to my cabin."

Phillip followed him quietly down the dark stairs to his quarters. It was a spacious room with a large rectangular table in the center and five chairs around it. There were two wooden chairs along each side and one at the end for the captain. Three lanterns in the room cast a warm glow over the food on the table.

The captain gave the cabin boy orders to fetch the others. Within minutes, the cabin boy brought the other couple to the room. The man stopped and bowed slightly from the waist. "I forgot to introduce myself," he said. "I am Count Tychovsky. You may call me Peter."

"And your lovely wife," the captain motioned toward the frail woman standing next to him.

"Of course," he nodded in her direction. "This is my wife Countess Tychovsky. You may call her Elnora."

"With your permission, Countess?" Captain English asked courteously.

She looked up at her husband, and he gave a nod of approval. "Yes," her voice was barely above a whisper as she looked down at her hands twisting nervously. The lighting throughout the room made her blackened eyes and bruises show up even more grotesquely.

He pointed to two chairs alongside of the table for the Count and Countess to sit, and indicated for Phillip to sit on the opposite side. The captain pulled the chair out for Elnora, nodded respectfully, and sat down.

Phillip sat nearest the door watching anxiously for Rachel to appear. Shortly, she entered the room with her head held high and purposely avoiding eye contact with Phillip. Her eyes were red and swollen from crying.

Phillip jumped up and pulled a chair out for her. "I apologize for my wife's lateness." After receiving a disdainful look from the captain, he abruptly changed the subject. "I think the food looks wonderful, do you not agree, dear?" And quickly added, "Forgive my rudeness. I am Lieutenant Prescott. I would like to present my wife, Lady Prescott."

Rachel did not respond to his comments. Instead, she nodded politely toward Captain English and the other couple.

It was a long meal for Rachel as she sat and listened to the constant droning of the Count's voice. He bragged constantly about everything he had accomplished.

As far as Rachel was concerned, the only thing that he had accomplished was marrying a Count's daughter, a very rich Count's daughter.

The Count spoke of how careful they have to be because of the family jewels and gold that her father gave them. He continued to boast how he told her father, he wanted to live in the Americas and run a plantation. Therefore, her father gave them the start-up money to begin a grand plantation.

The only time in his entire dialog that he mentioned Elnora was in describing how they met and how badly she had changed. "She was once a beautiful young woman who loved to laugh. It was fun to be around her. Now, she is like an old woman and never smiles or laughs anymore." He shrugged casually.

Rachel could take it no longer, "One can only wonder why she does not laugh or smile anymore."

The Count did not miss her sarcasm; he shot a cold look directly at Rachel. "It certainly had nothing to do with me, if that is what you are implying." He said waspishly.

"The Lady has a point." The look did not escape the captain. His hand gripped a metal goblet tightly. "And you, sir, *do not* challenge anyone at my table, especially a Lady. If you cannot conduct yourself with more restraint you shall be confined to your quarters for the rest of your meals."

"I am quite sure my wife did not mean anything by her comment," Phillip quickly added to try to placate the situation.

"Captain," Rachel put down her goblet and stood up. The captain and Phillip were on their feet instantly. "If you would be so kind as to excuse me. I would like to retire. This has been a very long and tiring journey for me."

"Of course, Lady Prescott," the captain bowed toward her and gave her a warm smile. "As I am sure the rest of you must be equally tired." He motioned for the cabin boy to open the door. He moved behind Elnora and pulled her chair out.

"Yes," Peter said indignantly. "We are very tired as well." He grabbed Elnora's arm and pushed her ahead of him.

The captain's jaw tightened and his eyes filled with anger, but he said nothing. Phillip caught the look of anger on the captain's face as well and gently took Rachel's arm as he escorted her to their cabin. Once inside he spoke quietly to her, "Rachel, do not embarrass me again by interfering with another man's personal belongings."

"Did you say 'personal belongings'?" Rachel's eyes grew wide in shock. "Do you consider me your 'personal belongings'?"

"Well, my dear, if it was not for men, what would you women do? How would you ever exist without us? Men are tougher, smarter, stronger, and braver than women could ever be."

His sincerity irked her even more. "Why did you never speak like this before?"

"I did not think it was necessary," he began taking off his uniform. "Women should know their place, especially by the time they are your age."

She blinked in utter confusion at his attitude toward women. It was no better than her father or brother's. "This is absurd."

"Yes, finally you understand what I have been saying is correct," he sat down and pulled off his boots. "You can see how absurd this whole conversation is, in fact, it is rather funny when you think about it. Let us not quarrel any further." He moved toward her with his eyes filled with passion. "There are better things to do than to argue,"

"Why my dear, I have no desire to argue anymore either," she smiled sweetly. "I shall sleep in this bed, and you can sleep anywhere else that pleases you."

"And, just where do you think I am supposed to sleep?" He asked incredulously.

"I realize it will be very difficult for me to sleep in this comfortable bed all by myself, but seeing that you are smarter, tougher, stronger, and braver you will find a place somewhere."

"Maybe I have been a little unreasonable," he stood staring at her and then the bed.

"A lot unreasonable," she quipped.

"Would it make a difference if I said I was sorry?" he asked hopefully.

"It would be a very good start," she said trying to hide a smile in spite of everything.

"What if I throw in I adore you, and let's forget about this little tiff?" He rolled his eyes in mock pain and threw himself on his knees.

His antics caused Rachel to laugh. "You just want to share this bed with me. You will say anything."

"That is very true," he looked up with a boyish grin.

"What am I going to do with you?" She asked looking at the impish behavior of her beloved husband.

He moved closer to her on his knees. The impish look was gone, replaced with a serious frown. "I truly hope we shall not argue again." He wrapped his arms tightly around her waist pressing his head against her stomach.

She stroked his hair gently, "Come to bed, my love. Come to bed."

It had been only two weeks at sea as the ship glided effortlessly through the quiet ocean waters. It was a dark night. The only sounds were the water slapping against the ship as it sliced through the calm seas, and the intermittent groaning of the ship.

The moon hid behind the massive clouds overhead, as a couple of the night crew watched warily at the approaching storm off in the distance.

A small figure waited by the doors at the top of the stairs that led to the deck. She waited until the night watchmen passed the door and headed away from her. The Countess snuck onto the deck in her bare feet and nightgown carrying the heavy valise. She moved to another spot closer to the edge of the ship and waited.

The two night watchmen talking quietly were unaware of the small figure climbing over the side rails of the ship.

Elnora let out a gasp as she almost dropped the valise onto the deck of the ship. It would certainly have gotten the attention of the watchmen. She wanted to make sure they had not heard her; she waited, and then pulled the heavy bag over the side of the ship with her. She had seen the rope ladder hanging against the side of the ship and hoped it would still be there. It was.

The coarse rope was rough against her tender skin as she climbed farther down toward the swelling ocean below. She felt the first brush of water against her bare feet. She let go and fell quietly into the black waters of the ocean. Just before Elnora's heavy valise pulled her under the water and into its cold, dark embrace, a smile spread across her battered and swollen face.

Chapter 5

My Dearest Edith,

We were married and reached the ship safely, no sign of that hideous Lord Symington. By the time you receive this letter you will be a happily married woman, just like me. I must admit being married holds a few surprises. Yes, there were quite a few surprises. It is very interesting to find out what your husband really thinks. We have had some rather long and shall we say enlightening talks. However, I am sure this is natural between husbands and wives.

The ship's captain is a very competent and respected seaman, so I feel safe about our journey across this never-ending span of water.

Another couple, a Countess and a Count, have joined us on this sailing. However, we

do not see much of them, as they stay off by themselves, except for dining. I have only managed to converse with her a couple of times and find her to be so sweet of nature.

Well, I wrote down the highlights as they happened. It is so hard to say everything on one little piece of paper. The captain said he will give this letter to a ship headed back to England as soon as we reach port.

Give your father a hug from me, and Ian, Mrs. Dawson and Albert. Of course, the biggest hug of all goes to you. When you feel a cool breeze brush against your cheek, it is just me sending you a kiss. Write soon and tell me everything. I miss you so desperately. With love and highest regards, Your Rachel

Days flew by quickly for Edith, too quickly. Her marriage to Lord Symington was to take place in less than three days, and there was still much she had to do.

The only thing that kept her spirit up was being with Ian three times a week, and that he said he would wait for her.

She had worked out a plan after she was married to visit her father, and then dress like Mrs. Dawson again to see Ian. At first, Ian was reluctant to see Edith after she was married, not because he did not wish to see her, but because he feared what Lord Symington would do to her if he found out.

Meanwhile, Edith and Mrs. Dawson worked out the perfect scheme to prevent her from having to endure any of the foul advances of Lord Symington.

It happened on a cool, predawn morning a week before the wedding.

Mrs. Dawson shook her awake, "Lady Edith. Edith, my dear."

Startled, Edith's eyes flew open to a darkened room. "What is it?"

"We must hurry." Mrs. Dawson pulled back Edith's quilt. She already grabbed a dress from Edith's wardrobe and a warm pelisse throwing them quickly on the bed. "Hurry, my child."

"Yes, yes," Edith shook her head to wake herself up. "What of the henchman?"

"Albert said he is sound asleep. I think the warm cup of tea I sent him last night helped him sleep better. Or rather, the sleeping herbs I put in it." She pulled the dress over Edith's nightgown. "He was ever so grateful." She chuckled, and handed her a pair of slippers. "We still must hurry and be back before he wakes up."

"You trust this woman?" Edith asked, adjusting the last slipper. "There, I am ready."

"Yes, I trust her completely." She grabbed Edith's elbow and guided her to the door.

They waited until the snoring of her father assured them he was asleep and crept through the house for fear of waking any of the other servants. As soon as they got to the kitchen, they raced out the back door. Albert was waiting for them. They hurried behind the barn where they would be totally out of sight of anyone in the house and the henchmen, just in case he awoke.

"You be careful," Albert whispered to them. "Tis a dark morning to be doing this. The moon is not bright enough to see very well."

"We will be careful," Edith moved quickly toward the road where Albert had tied the horses and carriage to a sturdy tree.

Albert helped them climb inside and hurried toward the front to untie the reins. He rushed back and handed them to Edith. "Go quickly and safely." He waved after them as they moved away into the early-morning darkness.

"Mrs. Dawson?" Edith could not help but wonder why Mrs. Dawson was so sure about the person they were going to meet. "Why do you trust this gypsy lady?"

"Because," Mrs. Dawson reached over and patted Edith's hand, "she is my sister."

"Your sister!" Edith gasped.

"Yes, my real sister," Mrs. Dawson said.

"I never knew you were a gypsy," Edith looked over at the portly woman sitting next to her.

"Are you disappointed in me?" Mrs. Dawson glanced at her young mistress.

"Disappointed? Absolutely not," Edith smiled. "Surprised, yes. How, why, when?" Words tumbled out of Edith faster than Mrs. Dawson could reply.

"I will tell you," she scooted back into the carriage seat. "It was before you were born that I met your mother. God rest her soul. The kindest lady I have ever known." She paused in a silent respect for Edith's mother and continued. "I was a gypsy in a caravan. We were working our way through the countryside when we came upon a village south of London. It was a terrible scene, just terrible."

"Oh my, what happened?" Edith exclaimed.

"We had stopped to put on a show and sell our wares as we usually did in any of the villages we came upon. But these villagers were awful people who shouted unkind things at us. In addition, someone began throwing stones at us. Little stones at first and then larger ones were hurled at us."

"That is terrible," Edith gasped. "I am sorry, continue."

"We grabbed up our wares as quickly as we could and put them in our wagons. As fast as we could we headed out of town. My family's wagon was the last in line and one of the rocks that were thrown struck my father down."

"Oh, Mrs. Dawson, how awful."

"I jumped down off the wagon to protect him. He said he was fine and climbed up and grabbed the reins. I smacked the horses and ran to the back of the wagon to get in when I was struck on the head. I awoke to find this lovely, young woman putting a cool cloth over the wound. I was frightened at first, but when I looked into her kind eyes I knew I was in a safe place."

"What of your father?" Edith asked.

"My father and the others made it safely out of town; except for a few bruises from the stones, they were all fine."

"How did you get left behind?"

"My father thought I had climbed into the back of the wagon, and those inside of the wagon thought I was riding up front. They did not know I was missing until they stopped far from the village."

Mrs. Dawson nodded in memory. "From what I was told your mother heard the ruckus from her home and came out to see what was going on. She was shocked to see the village people throwing rocks at us. She saw me fall to the ground. The brave little lassie ran between the rocks and me."

Mrs. Dawson chuckled, "Your mother was so angry with the crowd. She began chiding them for what they had done. Your mother was very well loved and respected in that village."

"My mother was a great lady, was she not?"

"That she was, my dear, that she was," she continued. "In fact, that was the day your mother met your father. He was on his way to London in an open carriage, when he saw what was going on. He was furious, but he was too far away to stop them. When he finally approached the center of town, he saw this young girl reprimanding the actions of the town's people. I think that was when he fell in love with this brave, young girl standing up to an unruly mob."

"It is unfair that she was taken away so soon," Edith shook her head.

"Yes, my dear, yes it was," Mrs. Dawson nodded in agreement. "Even though you did not come along for several years after they were married. It was still too soon." She glanced over at Edith. "Let me tell you, your father and mother were envied by everyone around them."

"Truly?" Edith smiled.

Truly. There was always laughter, and their love for each other could be seen in everything they did. It was such a joy to be around them. There was never a time that your mother did not treat me with kindness. Never spoke a harsh word to me, or any of the other servants. I truly believe she was an angel and that the other angels missed her so much they came and got her."

"I miss her even though I never knew her," Edith said sadly. "But wait. When your family realized you were gone what did they do?"

"My sister, who is a lot older than me, snuck into town and found out I was taken in and being cared for by your mother. She was afraid to get near me so one of the gypsy men, dressed as a roving preacher, got a message to me telling me where and when to meet up with the clan." She reached over and patted Edith's hand. "Am I talking too much, my dear?"

"No, please go on."

"It was if I were being torn in two as to what I should do. You see I once had a daughter and a mate, but both were lost to a fever that swept through our camp. My daughter would have been a few years older than you if she had survived. Anyway, for some strange reason, I felt as if your blessed mother and I were destined to be together. Does that seem strange to you?"

"No," Edith pulled back slightly on the reins. "I understand that feeling completely. Please go on."

"The duty to my father and the clan was very strong, so I left your mother as instructed," she continued. "I met up with my clan and traveled with them for a while, but my thoughts always came back to your mother. It was my sister who noticed how sad I was and, after a clan gathering, I was given permission to leave. They were quite wonderful about it, and as I left they said I would always be welcomed back. I have kept in touch with them over the years and sent them money whenever I could."

"That you came back to us was a lucky day for all of us. Look," Edith pointed at a lone figure standing in the road. "Is that her?"

"Oh my, oh my! Yes, it is. Rosita," she shouted the name. The carriage had not come to a complete stop when Mrs. Dawson jumped from it and ran to embrace her sister. She kept saying her name over and over as she hugged her firmly.

Edith noticed the resemblance immediately, only Rosita was taller than Mrs. Dawson. However, she had the same portly build, same smile, and raucous laugh.

"Let me breathe," Rosita laughed. "Let me look at you. It has been years."

"I have missed you terribly," Mrs. Dawson cried and enfolded her sister in her arms again.

"I received your message and the money." She glanced up at Edith and pulled away from Mrs. Dawson. "Carlotta, is this the young woman in trouble."

"Yes," Mrs. Dawson brushed away the tears rolling down her cheek. "I knew if anyone could help us; it would be you."

"Oh, I can help a great deal," she turned toward her sister. "Come, Carlotta, I have much to show and tell you before the day breaks. I have built a small fire over there behind the tall trees."

"Did you come alone?" Edith asked.

"No," she motioned for a tall figure standing in the shadows to come forward. "This is my oldest son, Juan. He is very good at what he does, and I believe he will be of help to you Lady Edith."

Edith noticed how tall and muscular the man was, and that his hair was almost coal black. He had a large nose and a small mustache over his full lips. His eyes were as piercing and black as the night.

"I am very curious about all of this." Edith scrambled out of the carriage and hurried to join Rosita and Mrs. Dawson.

Juan disappeared into the blackness of the night as he led the horses to a small stream. After the horses were watered, he brought them back to the campfire and tied them to a low shrub.

"Juan, I have given her the herbs to keep this foul old man asleep, now you tell her what she must do." She quickly turned to Edith. "Just remember these herbs are very powerful compared to the ones I give Carlotta."

"These herbs are known to put someone in a deep sleep, too much would kill him. Do you wish to kill him?" Juan asked nonchalantly.

"I wish he was dead, but I do not want to kill him," Edith sighed. "I just want him to leave me alone in our wedded bed."

Juan threw back his head and laughed. "That is not the first time I have had that request." He caught the hurt look on Edith's face and the chastising one from his mother and aunt. He quickly added. "It is not enough that you put him to sleep."

He shrugged and continued. "When this old man falls asleep you must whisper in his ear that you have consummated your marriage vows. Make suggestions to him that he did not enjoy any of it. However, you must explain to him in detail what transpired, and when he awakes in the morning, he will actually believe it happened. Um, do you need me to explain what should happen?"

Mrs. Dawson let out a small gasp, "Indeed not, young man."

Edith pulled a small pouch out of her handbag and handed it to Rosita.

"What is this for?" she asked.

"I want to pay for the wonderful service you have given me," Edith extended a pouch filled with gold coins to her.

"I have already been paid. The rest I do for my sister. I need no payment," Rosita bristled slightly.

A long arm shot out and grabbed the pouch from Edith's hand. "We may need extra money to help her."

"Yes, Juan, you are right," Mrs. Dawson said. "Rosita, please do not be offended by this offer.

My Edith means only to show her appreciation for all that you have done for her."

"No offense taken," she smiled at Edith.

Edith smiled back. "Trust me, I will find ways to get money from this little toad. So, if you need more contact us the same way, and I will try to get you as much as I can."

Juan opened the pouch and let out a whistle. "This will do nicely."

"Quickly," Rosita pointed to the light breaking on the edge of the field. "You must get back before you are discovered. I will keep in contact with you until this is finished."

Juan helped them into the carriage and led it to the road. He slapped one of the horses on the rump sending the carriage racing down the road. Edith took the corners on the road at a fast clip, almost turning them over a couple of times. They arrived back at the house as the first rays of light began to fall over the darkened ground.

Albert woke up as the two women ran into the barn out of breath. He got up quickly and headed out the back barn door to fetch the carriage they left at the edge of the road.

The two women bent down low and hurried toward the rear of the house. Edith raced into her room with Mrs. Dawson right behind her. They quietly shut the door behind them. Mrs. Dawson crept to the window and pulled the curtain back just enough to see if the henchman had seen them. She smiled as she saw the man get up off the ground and stretch his arms.

"He did not see us," she sighed with relief.

Edith went to the door in her room and cracked it open ever so slightly to see if anyone in the household had seen them come in. There were no sounds of movement. "All looks good here, too," she said.

"I will go down and make us some breakfast," Mrs. Dawson headed toward the door.

"No, you must be very tired," Edith took a hold of her arm to stop her.

Mrs. Dawson embraced Edith quickly, "This has been an exhilarating experience. I am not tired at all. However, you must be exhausted."

"I am way beyond exhaustion. In fact, I am feeling just the opposite," she began laughing and whirling around her room.

"Get to bed," Mrs. Dawson chided. "You're looking too happy this close to your wedding day."

The day of the wedding was one that Edith would always remember and hate. Usually, weddings were performed at the home, but Lord Symington wanted everyone in the village to see them wed. Edith knew it was because he wanted to humiliate her.

She hoped and prayed that she was having a nightmare, and when the doors into the church opened it would be Ian waiting at the altar. But it was not Ian. There standing, like a puny monkey, at the altar was Lord Symington.

Her father took her arm, and began the long walk down the aisle.

Edith made sure that before she stepped foot in the doorway to the church that Lord Symington had paid all of her father's debts and had given him a substantial bride price.

She had hired a solicitor from London, who was also very powerful and rich, so that Lord Symington could not buy him off. The solicitor made sure her father's sizeable bride price was safe from any of Lord Symington's treachery. At least, her father would be able to live the rest of his life in comfort.

Edith planned to marry Lord Symington in an old dress of hers; in fact, she was going to borrow one of Mrs. Dawson's, until he heard about it. He would not have any bride of his in an old dress. He wanted his bride to be resplendent and handpicked the gown she was to wear. She had to wear the dress he picked; it became one of the conditions made in her bride price.

She wore a long, empire-style, white silk gown trimmed in layers of Brussels lace, mixed with layers of red roses. The cap sleeves were puffed and trimmed with tiny, red roses. The train made of white silk, trimmed in matching Brussels lace, flowed out behind her almost ten feet. Her long gloves were made of lace and tied on with white ribbons.

Edith thought it was such a shame to hate a dress as beautiful as he had chosen, but she detested the dress and everything it stood for. She picked her veil, which had long layers of white tulle in the back with no trim. However, to the shorter layers in front, she kept adding tulle until it totally obscured her face.

The Vicar was reading something from the bible, and blessing their union; all the while, she felt the urge to retch. Her mind wandered away from the long-winded ceremony, and she wondered what Ian was doing. The thoughts of him brought a small smile to her lips and the way she had beaten Lord Symington at his own nasty little game.

Edith heard the Vicar clear his throat loudly. She looked up, and he was staring directly at her. "Do you take this man to be ...?" He was speaking, but she didn't hear a word he was saying. She stared back at the Vicar as he waited for her to say, "I will."

The people seated in the pews began to whisper. She looked over at Lord Symington, who was glowering fiercely at her. Her mouth opened, but no words came out.

"She said it," screamed Lord Symington. "I heard her say it. Pronounce us now," his lips twisted in anger.

"I now pronounce you man and wife," the frightened Vicar said.

It was over. She was Lady Symington, married to the most despised man in the village. He tried to reach up to lift her veil, but he was too short. He ordered her to bend down so that he could lift her veil and kiss his new bride.

"Kiss me? Never. I have never heard of such a thing in a church." She hissed at her new husband.

He stomped his foot and yelled at her, "I demand that you ..." He turned seeing everyone staring at him. He covered his embarrassment by shouting out, "She is not feeling well." He grabbed Edith's arm roughly and led her down the aisle to the bright sun outside. "You will take off that ridiculous veil, or I shall have my men rip it off."

"Do you think I care?" She yanked her arm from his grasp and almost ran to the waiting carriage. "Do not touch me like that again you miserable little man."

"I see you will have to be taught some manners later," He climbed up into the carriage letting her fend for herself.

She gathered her long train in her arms with the help of the coachman and climbed in sitting across from her new husband. “If you or anyone in your household lays a hand on me; you will regret it the rest of your miserable life.” Edith spoke venomously through her teeth.

“I see you are going to be a challenge,” he sat back and smiled his black-toothed smile. “This is going to be more fun than I had thought. None of my other wives were so headstrong and feisty. I think I am really going to enjoy this marriage.”

“That makes one of us,” she snapped as the carriage pulled away and headed toward the large manor.

Lord Symington’s large hall was set up to serve thirty invited guests. Edith wondered if he had to pay these people to attend. As per the proper social decorum, Menu Cards were placed between every other person at the table.

Edith was not interested in eating, but she loved the wine. Although, lately everything seemed to upset her stomach, but she just attributed it to her awful, upcoming marriage to Lord Symington.

The footmen began serving the guests. This was Edith’s first formal dinner party, and she was amazed at how it worked. If a dish of food was placed too far for the guest to reach, he or she had to try to get the attention of the footman to bring that dish to them. She noticed before the start of the evening meal, each guest gave the footman money so that he or she would be sure those dishes of food that were out of their reach would be brought to them.

After everyone had finished with their meal, the men retired into the library leaving the women alone at the table. Edith found it strange that not one of the women tried to elicit a conversation with her. Not one of them would look her in the eye.

Edith stood up abruptly, startling the ladies seated at the table. "If you will excuse me, I am very tired. I will be retiring to my room. Good evening."

Soft little murmurs of good evening and the slight nod were all she received. Quickly, she left the room and headed for the grand staircase that led to the bedrooms. Yesterday, she had followed the maid upstairs to her room where her luggage and personal items had been deposited.

She climbed the stairs and entered the huge room filled with beautiful ornate furniture and luxurious silk comforters in gold and deep rich purples. A canopy of lace over the bed fell softly to the floor in a pool by each bedpost. It was a room grand enough for a queen she had thought.

Edith turned to stare at the two massive doors that led from her room to his; she shuddered at the thought of what was to come. Her heart was beating wildly. Everything seemed so easy and simple when they concocted their plans. Now, she prayed it would work according to plan. She ran to her door leading into the hall and cautiously peered out. No one was there.

Edith could hear the band starting to play and sighed with relief for the distraction. She locked her door and then hurried to the two doors that connected their rooms. Another sigh of relief, they were unlocked. She cracked one of the doors open just enough to peer inside to see if anyone was in there. The room was empty.

She looked back around her room and spotted her valise sitting on an oriental chair against the wall. The small key to it hung from a chain around her neck discreetly hidden down the bodice of her shift. She pulled it out and opened the valise. Inside, was a small bottle and in it was a clear liquid from Rosita. She returned to the connecting doors and peered inside one more time to make sure there was no one there.

The door creaked as she pulled it wide enough for her to slide through. Her long train did not make it easy for her to slip in and out of the doors. She found his goblet on the nightstand next to the bed. Edith began shaking so badly she was afraid she would spill the potion before it got into his goblet.

She froze at the sound of footsteps heading toward the room. Quickly, she counted four drops and raced back to the doors that connected their rooms. She had just managed to pull the last part of her train through when someone knocked at the door to her room. Her fingers were shaking so badly she barely got the plug in the bottle. "Who is it?" She called out trying to sound nonchalant.

"Lord Symington saw that you left and 'ad gone to your room. 'e instructed me to 'elp you prepare for bed."

Edith ran to her valise placing the little bottle in its hidden compartment and locked it, and hid the key under the chair's seat cushion. She unlocked the doors, walked to the chaise lounge, and sat down as if she were tired. "Come in," she called out in a feeble voice.

The door opened and a thin, middle-aged woman entered the room. She had on the usual servant gray dress, with a white pinafore and cap. "Are ye feelin' not too well, yer ladyship?"

She wanted to yell at her, 'would you feel well being married to that odious man?', but instead, just said, "I am tired from the long day's events."

The woman walked over to one of the three large armoires and took out a beautiful cream colored, silk and lace negligee, a matching dressing gown and slippers, and placed them carefully on the bed. "That is a most beautiful wedding gown, Milady."

"Yes, yes it is," Edith said looking down at her dress. And tomorrow it will go up in flames, she thought as she looked over at the peat burning hotly in her bedroom fireplace.

The servant did not exchange another word as she prepared Edith for her wedding night until she had finished. "Good evening, yer ladyship," the woman curtseyed and exited her room.

Edith looked at herself in the fancy full-length mirror in her room. She sighed at how beautiful the negligee was and how she had longed for Ian.

She stopped abruptly, grabbed the key from under the cushion, and opened the valise again. Searching frantically, she found the other bottle. Opening the cap, she dabbed a little of the liquid behind her ears and some between her breasts. Quickly, she placed the bottle back in the valise, locked it up and hid the key again. She wrinkled her nose at the strange, offensive aroma that was coming from the "perfume" that Rosita had given her.

Her heart skipped a beat when one of the connecting doors opened.

And there stood her worst nightmare, Lord Symington. "Ah, you look lovely, so lovely." He stepped back and motioned for her to come into his room. "I paid my dues, now you must pay yours." He rubbed his hands together as if they were cold and nodded toward the large bed behind him.

She deliberately walked past him slowly, hoping he would catch a whiff of her acrid perfume. Suddenly, she froze in place. Horror raced through her entire body. There were two goblets sitting on the nightstand and they both looked identical.

"You look frightened," he chuckled. "You should be." He wiped his mouth with the back of his hand and moved behind her. His hand reached over and stroked her firm buttocks.

She jerked away from him in abject terror. "Come, come," his sneering laugh had returned in full force. Suddenly, he stopped and wrinkled his nose. "What is that foul odor? Never mind, I have such plans tonight for my little virgin. Get on the bed, now!" His voice filled with lust for her.

She did not move; all she could do was stare at the two goblets.

"If you plan on being uncooperative, do not," his hand gestured toward the door in his room that led into the hallway. "I have two, shall we say helpers, standing outside, in case I have need of them. Do I make myself clear?"

It was all Edith could do to keep from crying. There were only two options for her now; he would fall asleep very quickly, or she would.

"Wait," he walked to the nightstand and picked up the two goblets filled with wine. "Let us make a toast to our wedded bliss."

She hurled a hateful gaze at him. It galled her that he had won after all.

She walked to the bed. Her glare became even more intense as he smiled and licked his lips as he walked toward her.

He extended a goblet to her, but when she went to reach for it, he yanked it back. "You are not going to cheat me out of taking you and seeing how much you hate it. I know what you are planning on doing."

Edith gasped as her hand went to her throat. How could he possibly know? Her heart sank; all was for naught.

"I saw how much wine you drank tonight. You will not pass out on me, my dear wife; you are going to be sober and sorry, very sorry." Lord Symington looked her up and down, and slowly drank both goblets of wine.

Edith could not believe it. She sat there for a moment stunned, but quickly realized she had to get his skinny body in bed or the henchmen posted outside the door would hear him fall to the floor. Edith climbed into bed as if expecting to perform her marital duties.

"Smart girl, you know when you are outdone," he pulled his long nightshirt up as he climbed into bed. "Now, I shall show you what I expect and demand." He turned toward the door to the hallway where his two henchmen stood. "Leave us," he shouted. "I have her under my control."

He straddled over her and roughly grabbed her hair. "Now, this is my favorite part." His hand shot out and slapped her across the face. He smiled at the shocked look on her face and struck her again. "I really do enjoy this," he raised his hand to strike again and stopped. His eyes glazed over, and he fell to his side on the bed.

"This is my favorite part," she grabbed his skinny, bent legs and yanked them straight. "Let us get you in the proper position, you disgusting pig." She moved his body so that his head rested on a pillow.

Edith remembered what Juan had said and began to talk slowly and purposely to him. Now, that she knew what Lord Symington wanted to do she kept repeating it. She talked to him about the cruel and unpleasantness of their union. In addition, she made sure he would think he did not enjoy it very much at all. She kept mentioning the bad smell around her, and that it repulsed him, and he had no desire to be with her when they were awake.

After an hour, and almost hoarse from trying to "place pictures in his head" as Juan called it, she went to her room and took out another tiny jar that was mixed in with her toiletries. She went back into Lord Symington's room, and with great effort, resisted the urge to spit on him. She walked to the side of the bed where he last saw her.

Carefully opening the jar, she spilled a small amount of pig's blood where she had been, then with absolute disgust, she lifted his nightshirt and poured some directly over his wrinkled little penis. She pulled his nightshirt back down over his private area and covered him up. Rosita had told her the blood would be a sign of her having been a virgin, but to use it sparingly.

Edith hurried back into her bedchambers and into a small room off her bedroom that housed a fancy wooden commode and basin that held a pitcher of water. She took off her nightgown pouring a little blood on the back of it and threw the gown on the floor. She rinsed out the small amount of pig blood left in the jar, put on a clean linen nightgown, and walked back into her bed-chambers.

After placing the empty jar back in her valise Edith peered in one last time at Lord Symington to make sure he was still asleep. She sighed deeply with relief; he was.

Quietly, Edith pulled the connecting doors closed and locked them. She leaned back against them. Her whole body was trembling so badly she had to wait for a moment before she could move. Still shaking, she walked toward her bed, pulled back the comforter, and crawled between the silky sheets. She was asleep before her head hit the pillow.

Chapter 6

My Dearest, darling Rachel,

I almost squealed with delight when I received your letter.

Yes, I agree that marriage can lead to many unknown and somewhat interesting things. Although, I have to admit that I have not had the time to engage in too much conversation with my husband. Nevertheless, I believe I know what he is thinking. Furthermore, he has proven to be a very sound sleeper. I always thought I knew what my husband was really like, and I was definitely not wrong in my opinion of him in any way.

I had a most beautiful wedding gown, but the day after the wedding hot coals were accidentally spilt on it. It quickly went up in flames.

But, I care not, for I have my Ian. Each moment with him makes me want him more. I have such love for him that I fear for us each time we are apart.

Well, my love, I must end this letter so that I can give it to our mutual friend. I will check in a few months for a letter from you. There is not a day that goes by that I do not think of you. All my love, thoughts and prayers go with you, your Edith.

Angry shouts coming from topside broke the usually quiet mornings on the ship. Rachel moved groggily at the sound of footsteps pounding down the wooden stairs. There was a sharp knock on their cabin door. Phillip got up sleepily and opened the door.

"I beg yer pardon, sir," the young cabin boy tried to peer around Phillip's tall frame. "Is Countess Tychovsky in yer cabin?"

Phillip blinked his sleepy eyes a couple of times. "What are you talking about? Why would the Countess be in our room?"

"We are just checking every place possible on the ship. It appears, she has disappeared," he said nervously.

Now Phillip was wide-awake, "What do you mean she has disappeared? How can anyone disappear on a ship?"

"That's what the captain is trying to figure out," he bowed slightly. "Sorry I bothered you, sir." He turned and ran up the wooden steps.

"Did you hear that?" Phillip turned to Rachel. "The Countess has disappeared. That does not make much sense. I am sure she is on the ship somewhere. I'll get dressed and see if I can help in the search."

"I have heard him hitting her more than once in their cabin."

Phillip let out a deep sigh, "Well, my dear. She probably did things to upset him." He looked over at Rachel and raised an eyebrow. "Women must not upset their husbands. I trust you will remember that as well."

"And husbands should not upset their wives." She stared back at him defiantly. "Edith and I have heard about women being struck by their husbands. We always said our husband better never strike us."

"Now, what could you possibly do if he did?" Phillip said in total exasperation.

"We would wait until he was asleep and then hit him in the head with a poker stick."

Phillip stepped back and gulped.

Rachel was unaware of his startled response to her comment and continued. "Anyway, I hope she has found a good hiding place. Let me know and I will bring her refreshments for the remainder of our journey." Rachel pushed the blanket off and dropped her feet over the bed. "I am going to help, too."

"I would prefer it if you just stayed in here." He finished dressing and put his hand on the door. "Lock this door after me."

"Phillip?" Rachel gripped the wooden side rails of their bed. "What is going on with this ship? It seems to be a little rougher than before."

"I'll be back," Phillip stared hard at Rachel as he left their room.

Rachel locked the door, but proceeded to dress herself. It was rather cold in her cabin, so she grabbed her warm pelisse and buttoned it up the front. She unlocked the cabin door and headed for the deck. Water sprayed down on her as she braced herself going up the wooden steps. Seamen were running everywhere, lifting and pulling on anything that could hide someone. She heard the sound of angry voices directly behind her up on the bridge. It was Count Tychovsky screaming at the captain.

"You are responsible for your passengers and their valuables," the Count screamed. "Someone has stolen all of my money and jewels. I need that money now."

"We are doing everything we can at the moment," the captain's voice was cold as steel, "to try to find your *wife*." His stare bore into the Count.

"She has stolen my money," he raged. "She did it on purpose. I'll teach her when I get my hands on her."

"The only one doing any teaching will be me," the captain snapped.

"When you find her," the Count's teeth bared. "I want you to put that valise with all of my money and jewels in a safe place where she can't get her hands on it."

"My concern is for your wife, not your money." The captain clenched his fists.

"Her father has plenty of money," the Count's eyes narrowed as he thought aloud. "I will just demand that he sends me more money. That will be the end of that." He sighed as if content with his financial outcome.

"It appears to me; you are far more concerned about money, as opposed to the well-being of your wife," the captain stepped back eyeing the Count menacingly.

"Why should I worry about her?" He shrugged. "She's hiding on this ship somewhere. It might be best if she stayed hidden." His anger was building.

"Why would your wife want to hide somewhere on my ship? Hide from what?" The captain continued sarcastically. "I do suppose if we cannot find your wife, whom you claim has your money, then it would appear you cannot pay for your passage on my ship. Therefore, you will have to work your way to the Americas."

"Work?" The Count spat out the word as if it were the vilest word in the world. "I will not 'work' as you say for my passage. My father-in-law will send you the money for my passage."

"I doubt that very much, especially after I inform him of her physical condition and your less than gentlemanly manner with her." The captain turned his attention from the Count, and looked down from the bridge at his crew who had congregated on the deck below.

Captain English's first officer came on the bridge. "Sir, the crew, and I have looked in every conceivable place she could have found to hide. Sir, I think …"

The captain waved his hand to stop him from continuing. He closed his eyes for a moment and shook his head, "I am afraid your wife is no longer aboard our ship." His voice was filled with sadness.

"What do you mean she's no longer aboard this ship? What did she do with my money? Where is my *money*?" The Count screamed into the captain's face.

Captain English was the same height as the Count. He stepped in front of the raging man. They were eye-to-eye. The captain's eyes flashed dangerously. "I do not care what happened to your foul money." He brought his hand up and began rubbing his chin. "But wait, there's that little problem again - you have no money to pay for your trip."

"That's a lie," the Count yelled. "She paid before we came on board."

"Actually," the captain's face registered a slight smile. "I do not remember that transaction. I always give a bill signed paid in full. Do you have such a thing?"

"Of course not," he shrieked. "I let her go down to the docks and pay for it, not me. I can't be bothered about such peasant trifles."

"Yeoman," he did not take his eyes off the Count. "Take the Count's belongings and throw them into the crew's quarters. He will be taking the rest of the trip there. First Officer," he called out, still staring into the Count's anger filled eyes. "Make sure you have some very *interesting* jobs for this ... interloper."

The Count took a couple of steps away from the menacing face of the captain. "There's nothing you can do. I completely refuse to work."

"First Officer, this crewman is refusing a direct order from his captain," the captain's eyes narrowed. "You and the rest of the crew will please escort this person to his new quarters."

"Well," the Count said smugly. "I see you have come to your senses. My father-in-law will hear about your offensive treatment to me. I will have him reduce you to a cabin boy."

"Get him out of my sight," the captain snarled.

"Aye, sir," the First Officer smiled and nodded. The First and Second officers grabbed the Count roughly by the arms.

"Get your foul hands off of me," he snapped. "This is a very expensive shirt to be having your filthy hands touching it."

"Is it now?" The First Officer asked wryly.

The First and Second Officers looked past the Count at the captain. He gave a knowing smile and nodded to his officers. They escorted the Count roughly down the steps from the bridge.

The Count turned toward the passenger quarters, but instead the two large officers turned him around in the opposite direction. "What are you doing? I told you two to keep your filthy hands off me. Are you too stupid to understand?"

The other seamen formed a circle around him. "Captain, call your filthy hounds off. Now!" He ordered. There was no response. He turned to see that the captain was no longer on the bridge. His eyes widened in disbelief and fear as the crewmen closed in on him.

The captain and Phillip left the bridge to escort Rachel back down to the passenger quarters.

Rachel jumped when she heard a blood-curdling scream. "Oh, no, did they kill him?"

"No," Captain English said sadly. "Nothing that good. They probably ripped off one of his finely tailored sleeves, and introduced him to his new quarters."

"Where are his new quarters?" She asked.

"The brig."

"What's a brig?"

"It is a ship prison, my dear." Phillip looked at the captain and shrugged. "This is her first experience on a ship."

"You need not make any excuses for your wife," he smiled down at Rachel. "Questions are always welcome."

"That is very kind of you, Captain," Rachel said. Her shoulders heaved slightly, and her voice filled with sadness as her thoughts were about the Countess. "She cannot be dead. Maybe she is somewhere still on the ship. She may come back."

The captain and Phillip exchanged knowing looks.

"My dear, she is not coming back." Phillip gently started to turn her toward the door to their cabin.

Rachel gasped. "Oh, no," she brought her hands to her mouth. "The last time I talked with her; she said something that I thought was most peculiar."

"What was that?" Captain English asked courteously.

"I just happened to run into her on the deck one night. I so longed to talk with another woman. She was of such a sweet nature. However, it was a curious thing. In the moonlight, her bruises appeared dimmer, and she looked quite beautiful. She looked so sad, as she always did, and I wanted to say something to make her feel better. I complimented her on how lovely she looked, and that all her beautiful dresses paled in her comparison. It was not said falsely, I meant every word."

"Yes, I can believe that." The captain smiled, tipped his hat, and turned to leave.

"There is more. After I said that a smile crossed her face, and she grabbed my hands in hers. She asked me if anything happened to her would I promise that the jewels of the Tychovsky's be sent back to her family where they belonged. She held onto my hands so tightly they hurt until I promised I would do so for her. Then she heard the Count calling for her. She leaned close to me and whispered something like, 'the jewels are hidden hollow and awash from the sun's light. Never. Never let the Count know. She asked me to promise. So, I promised again. Then she hurried down the stairs to her quarters."

"That is a curious thing indeed," the captain said.

"Oh, my," Rachel hesitated. "I made a promise to send back the jewels, but she must have taken them with her when she... "Rachel could not finish her sentence. When she spoke again it was softly. "How can I keep such a promise?"

"You should never have made such a promise in the first place, my dear." Phillip said in a chastising manner.

"Yeoman," Captain English called to one of his crew. "Make sure the Count does not re-enter his cabin for anything or for any reason." He turned to Rachel, and said gently, "You were the only friend she had, and I think that was important to her."

"I wish I could have done more," Rachel gave a small curtsey to the captain and went into her cabin.

A short time later, Phillip entered the room. "Rachel, do me a favor and do not make any more promises you cannot keep.

"I won't, Phillip." She said solemnly.

"Done," he picked her up and placed her on the bed. "I'd rather not talk at all right now."

During the long sea voyage, Rachel became seasick and had stayed sequestered in her cabin. However, today was the first day she felt like she wanted to live again. She dressed, put on her warm pelisse, and went on deck. It was a chilly day at sea, and the ocean was still a little too choppy for her. Nevertheless, she needed to get out of her stale cabin into the fresh air.

In a few days, they would be pulling into the Boston harbor, and she was looking forward to getting off the rolling ship and endless sea.

She was still a little weak from not being able to keep anything down for a few days and staggered slightly when the ship lurched.

The doors to the deck were open and Rachel saw the Count moving around down below. She vaguely remembered Phillip telling her that the Count decided being in the brig was not the best place for him to be. He was kept busy with the most disgusting jobs the crew could find. They also refused to have him share their quarters, so the captain arranged for the Count to stay in the storage room until they docked in Boston.

Count Tychovsky was just coming up the steps from below deck to get the bucket of lye that sat close to the doors. It was another job the Count hated. The cook always made his own soap for cleaning his galley, and he put the Count in charge of making it for the whole trip. Count Tychovsky looked up and caught sight of Rachel standing at the top of the steps. A nasty sneer crossed his face.

The ship lurched again, and Rachel fell against the hot bucket of lye causing it to splash down the steps onto the Count's face. His screams brought everyone on deck.

The captain and First Officer raced to see what had happened. Immediately, the captain hollered to the cook, and grabbed a bucket of swill water throwing it on the thrashing Count to try to wash off the caustic lye. The cook appeared with a substance that looked like milk and poured it over the face of the Count.

Rachel stood on deck in total shock. "It was an accident. I am so sorry. I am so sorry." She cried repeatedly.

Phillip had been on deck talking with the navigator when all the commotion started. He raced to Rachel's side and put his arm around her.

"Get her back to your cabin," the captain ordered Phillip.

Rachel did not see the Count again for the rest of the journey, and asked Phillip how he was doing. "According to the captain, the Count was told to stay in his quarters for the remainder of the trip. Oh, Captain English asked me to tell you that you should not worry about the Count, because it appears there are no serious injuries, except one of his eyes may have been damaged a little. The Count's face is red and raw looking, but he probably will only have a few scars."

Rachel gasped. "What have I done?"

"Nothing. I also forgot to mention the captain said it was not your fault," Phillip shrugged. "He told me that the lye had to remain on deck until it cooled, and it should never have been left unattended. However, the Count left the bucket of lye up on deck, in front of the steps, and on a choppy day at sea. His negligence caused this accident, not yours. It could have been anyone walking in front of the bucket."

"I wish you had told me sooner," Rachel's eyes brimmed with tears. "I have been feeling just awful about this whole thing." She sighed deeply, "I still do."

"Well, now you know," he shrugged. "Besides, why should you care for a stranger anyway?"

A few days later, the ship docked at Boston Harbor. Rachel was beyond happy: they had arrived. All she wanted to do was feel solid earth beneath her feet. Rachel climbed the wooden steps from her cabin and came face-to-face with Count Tychovsky.

His once handsome face was gone. The right side of his face was bright red, and he had a black patch over his right eye. Hatred poured from him, and she could have sworn he growled at her.

Captain English quickly placed himself between them. "I have enclosed a small amount of money for you, although you do not deserve it. Now, get off my ship," he ordered the Count. He had the Count's clothing and other items stuffed into a duffle bag, and had his first officer give it to him as he was leaving the ship.

"You will regret this," the Count said venomously.

"Threaten me again and I will show you who will have regrets," the captain glowered.

The Count grabbed his bag and hurried off the ship, disappearing amid the chaos on the dock.

Rachel gave a sigh of relief that they would finally be getting off the ship.

The captain walked over to her and bowed slightly. "Lady Prescott it has been a pleasure knowing you. Stay safe and be happy," he bowed again and walked away.

Rachel stood and watched him go. There was something sad about parting with him. He was wise, kind, and very informative on places and things she had never seen or heard of before. She loved listening to his stories at his dining table, and he made her laugh frequently. She felt a small ache inside knowing that she would probably never see him again. It was like losing a dear friend. Then her face lit up when Phillip walked toward her, and as always, her heart seemed to skip a beat.

They walked to the rail of the deck and looked down into the mayhem on the dock. "Where do we go from here?" Rachel asked.

"I have to go to Nova Scotia," he put his arm around her shoulder and pulled her close to him.

"When do we leave?"

"Unfortunately, I cannot take you with me."

Rachel pulled away. "Whatever do you mean?" Her voice quivered slightly.

"I have to go alone," he took her hands in his. "Do not worry, my dear. We will find an inn for you to stay at until I can send for you."

Rachel was so shocked she just stood there looking at him, not knowing what to say.

"It will be fine. It will not be long. I am an attaché to a very powerful general. So, you can rest assured you will be sent for almost immediately." He smiled down at her. "Look, my father sends me money every month. I will instruct him to send a little money directly to you."

"I do not understand?" She asked still stunned about being left alone in a strange city.

"I told you, he would send some money to you. You are my wife. Although, I must admit he was not totally pleased with my marrying you. However, my being his favorite son," he stopped, smiled, winked and continued. "He met personally with the regimental colonel to get his approval for our marriage. They really do frown upon military men being married. I hope that does not go against me."

He stopped as if pondering his last statement and then continued. "Nevertheless, it has all been taken care of. I told him that you were a fine young Lady, and that I could not bear the thought of being without you. He still wasn't too pleased, but I am sure everything is just fine with him now."

Rachel stood still, her mind reeling. She was being left alone in the wilds of America. She could hear Phillip talking, but she was not really listening.

"Father is now in the process of buying me a captain's rank. A captain is due to retire soon, and he has put in a bid for that commission. We will be making more money with that commission. Of course, father is going to have to send even more money as I have to pay for my new uniforms. In addition, I will be expected to have larger living quarters, and to entertain on a grand scale. I will have to buy a horse, and saddle, and probably have to hire a groom as well. It will cost quite a bit more. Hmm, I will need a manservant as well. These are things I will have to plan for."

"Phillip? Phillip!" She pushed on his chest sending him staggering back a bit. "What are you talking about? Does that matter now? Where am I to go, and what am I to do while you go to Nova Scotia?"

"We will check the city out for the cleanest and best inn we can find," he said regaining his composure. "There is no need to get testy about this." He straightened and fussed with his uniform jacket. "It is just a temporary thing."

"No need to get testy?" Rachel put her hands on her hips, and her foot began to tap against the deck. "You are going to Nova Scotia and leaving me here alone. Does that not worry you?"

"I said we would find you a decent place to stay, and you will have all the money you will need to get by on," he shrugged. "What more do you want from me?"

"Did you not think of this in your plan when we eloped?"

"I knew I would figure something out when we got here, and I did," he said defiantly.

"Excuse me," the captain stood next to them with a duffle bag slung over his shoulder, and his cape blowing out all around him. "Forgive me for intruding, but if you would permit me, I may have a solution."

"Thank you, sir, but we do not need your ..." Phillip's sentence was never finished.

"Any suggestions from you would be most welcome," she sent Phillip a warning glare.

"Of course," Phillip said, taken aback by Rachel's fierce determination.

"I have two delightful aunts who live in Boston. They have a very large house, and I am sure they would welcome Lady Prescott with open arms." He looked quickly at Phillip. "Boston can be a very dangerous place to live if you do not know where to go or what to do. My aunts live in a very safe area, and Lady Prescott would be well taken care of."

"Well, I do not …" Phillip began to speak, but again, Rachel cut him off.

"That sounds wonderful to me," she sighed in relief looking up at the captain. She turned to Phillip and asked with one eyebrow raised. "Do you not think so too, my husband?"

"It may solve a slight problem at hand," he nodded.

"Slight problem?" Rachel bit her lip for fear of saying anything unpleasant that would be hard to retract later. "Captain, would it be imposing on you to take us there?"

"That is always my first stop when I come into port. It would be my pleasure," he turned to Phillip. "You will rest easier once you have met them, and know that your wife will be safe and well cared for until you send for her."

"Alright, it is settled then. I will just have time to go with you to his aunts, and then I must leave immediately." Phillip said.

The determination on Rachel's face faded at hearing he would be leaving her so soon. Tears began to form in her eyes.

"Stop that! Don't embarrass me." Phillip said. "Officer's wives do not cry when their men leave them. It is what we do, and you must endure. No soldier wants to go off to battle remembering a red-eyed, simpering wife."

A deep sigh of exasperation escaped from the captain, "Then let's make haste and get her situated. My ship leaves in a couple of days, and I too, have many things I must get done."

"Excuse me," Phillip raised his index finger. "Do you stay with your aunts while you are in town?"

The captain stepped in front of Phillip; their eyes locked. "I have my own place." In an almost threatening manner, the captain asked, "Do you have any other questions?"

"I apologize if what I asked was out of line."

"It was, and apology accepted."

Rachel walked away to check her trunk being brought up from their cabin.

Phillip looked into the captain's face. "This was a side of her I have never seen. I have my work cut out for me," he laughed and winked. "But it won't take long to break her strong will."

The captain's jaw tightened, "Excuse me," he said and walked away.

Shortly, Rachel, Phillip and the Captain climbed into a carriage waiting on the dock. Captain English gave the driver his aunts' address, and they settled in for the ride.

"You seem young to be a captain of such a large ship," Rachel said.

"I started out as a cabin boy, and worked my way up." He smiled.

"You worked your way up from a cabin boy into a fine captain. Phillip was commenting on how well trained your men are, and how much they respect you. Didn't you, dear?" Rachel smiled at the tall man sitting across from her, and then back to her husband.

"Actually, I did," he said. "We went through two horrific storms, and you lost no one." Now he smiled at the captain. "And, thankfully, you didn't lose the ship either."

"Thank you," he nodded. "I take that as the sincerest form of flattery."

"Something has been bothering me for a while." Phillip looked with a display of arrogance at the captain. "Why is it that you do not have your hair powdered? All officers are required to have their hair powdered under penalty of imprisonment. I was reprimanded severely for not putting enough on one spot of my hair."

"I am not in the military," the captain said flatly. "And I find powdering my hair a tedious, frivolous waste of time. No offense to those who do, of course."

"No offense taken," Phillip said.

After a bumpy and long ride, the carriage came to an abrupt stop.

Captain English quickly opened the door and climbed down, holding his hand for Rachel to exit. She put her hand out to take hold of his extended hand and stopped. Behind the captain was a beautiful, large manor that was at least twice the size of her father's. She stepped down and waited for her husband to exit the carriage.

He, too, stood and starred at the home of the captain's aunts.

"I say," Phillip managed finally to speak. "This *is* a much better place for you to stay than an inn."

The door to the manor burst open and two elderly women came rushing out. "Nathan! Nathan!" They both yelled rushing to him with arms open.

Captain English turned and walked hurriedly to his running aunts. "Easy, my loves; I don't want you falling and getting hurt." He threw his arms around them, crushing them in one of his mighty hugs. After they had finished greeting their nephew, they peered around him at the couple standing back and watching them.

"Who are these charming young people?" Aunt Clara asked. Her portly frame was elegantly dressed. Her bright blue eyes lit up at the young couple.

"Oh, my, yes," Aunt Libbie was as thin as Clara was heavy. Her gray hair was neatly done up into a bun, but a few strands of hair had escaped and were blowing in the breeze as she walked around and greeted the couple. "Are they staying with us? I hope."

"I was going to ask if it would be all right for the young lady to stay with you as her husband has to return to his military duty today."

"Of course, it is," Aunt Libbie said happily. "You will be gone for a couple of years or more?"

"I don't think more than a couple of months," was Phillips startled reply.

"Oh, bother," Aunt Clara, said sadly, then, she perked up. "A couple of months are better than no months. Right, sister?"

"Absolutely," Aunt Libbie clapped her hands. "This is going to be so much fun. Let us all go to the house. I will send our help out to get your things."

They started walking toward the house when Phillip grabbed Rachel's hand and pulled her back to him. Everyone stopped and turned, until the captain ushered his two aunts into the house. "Let them have their private moment," he said as he kissed the tops of his aunt's heads. "Besides, I have something for each of you."

The aunts squealed in unison, "oh, wonderful." Captain English knew his aunts were wealthy enough to buy anything they wanted, but they always seemed excited about the small gifts he brought them.

"Is it from the Orient?" Their questions became fainter as they entered the house.

Rachel fought back the tears that made Phillip angry as he put his hands on her shoulders. "I will send for you as soon as I can. You must thank the captain for giving you a safe place to stay. I will be able to concentrate on military matters better now, knowing that you are here with his aunts."

He leaned down as if he were going to kiss her and then pulled away. "I would kiss and hug you good-bye, but I am in uniform. You must know my thoughts are of you and our nights on the ship. I must gather my strength to leave you. I shall miss you, my sweet. The captain graciously gave me the address here so that I may write a letter to you. Stay brave. That's the most important thing."

"I will, my love. I will." Her voice broke.

Phillip climbed into the carriage. The driver pulled the carriage out into the street and headed back toward the dock and the ship waiting to take him to Nova Scotia.

A lone figure sat back in his carriage. The black curtains drawn so that no one could see in, but he could peer through the break in the curtains and watch what was going on. Hatred filled his soul. He studied the house the captain had entered, and then ordered his driver to follow Phillip's carriage. "I will make sure you all pay for what you have done to me," Count Tychovsky whispered. "You will all pay dearly, especially you, Lady Prescott."

Chapter 7

My Dearest Edith,

We have finally arrived. Land has never looked so good. So many interesting and unexpected things happened on this trip.

It saddens me to say that the young countess I mentioned before did not make the entire journey. She was a very frail young woman, and I know she is at peace at last.

I have some interesting things to tell you about the ship. Did you know that ships have prisons on them? They are called brigs.

We encountered a couple of rather large and scary storms, but Captain English got us through them with no problems. Well, at least no problems that I was aware of.

So, Ian is a sound sleeper. My darling Phillip is not. We have preconceived opinions of our husbands, but how much do you really know about someone until you marry them? Although, my opinion of Phillip is still the same, he is wonderful.

Phillip had to leave to go to Nova Scotia. He will be gone a couple of months, but he has found me a wonderful place to stay. I am staying with two very charming and delightful women who live in one of the biggest manors I have ever seen. I believe it is even bigger than that awful Lord Symington's manor. Speaking of that foul man, has he found another poor girl to marry him? I send her my warmest regards, and greatest sympathy.

I am sorry if my letter rather rambles on a bit. I am trying to say everything at once.

Well, my dearest, write soon, as I am so anxious to hear from you. With all my heart and good wishes, your loving Rachel

The bright morning sun crept into her room climbing up the wall and resting on Edith's face. She moaned and slowly stirred. Suddenly, she sat up and looked wildly around the room. "Oh, dear God," she whispered. "This is not a nightmare."

There was a tap on her door. “Who is it?” she called out.

“’Tis me, Abbey,” was the timid reply of her personal servant.

“One moment,” Edith crawled out of bed, put on her robe and slid into her slippers. She walked slowly to the door and unlocked it.

A young, very thin girl entered her room carrying a tray with tea, poached eggs, and bread. “’is lordship does not wish for you to join ‘im for ‘is morning meal.” She lowered her light brown eyes and curtsied. “I am sorry, yer ladyship.”

Edith gave a little laugh and said more to herself than Abbey, “Sorry for what, that I don’t have to look at his old wrinkled face. I don’t think I could have eaten a bite in his presence.”

Abbey tried to hide a giggle and placed the tray on a table near the window. She pushed a light-brown strand of hair back under her cap, gave a small curtsey, and left the room shutting the door behind her.

After Edith had finished what little food she could eat, she heard the rumble of a carriage pull up to the front of the manor. Her window faced the front of the house, so she could see who came and who went. She got up and peered out the window, keeping to the side of it so she wouldn't be seen. Lord Symington looked up at her window for a moment, but she was sure he had not seen her looking down. One of his henchmen helped him into his carriage, and it drove down the long, winding road that led away from the manor.

She went to the long cord hanging on a wall by her bed and gave it a short yank. It rang a bell in the kitchen that sent Abbey running up the stairs. She knocked on Edith's door.

"Come in," she said jovially. "Do you know when his lordship is coming back?" She asked the nervous young girl.

"I 'eard 'im say something about meeting with some foreign bankers in town and that 'e will be back in time for an evening meal. That is all I 'eard, your ladyship."

"That is good enough for me. Thank you Abbey you can go now." She smiled at the thought of the little toad being gone all day long. "First things first," Edith said and went to her armoire and pulled out her wedding dress. "You were a very pretty dress, but I hate the thought of every seeing you again." She laughed as she stuffed it into the hot embers. She sat and watched it burst into flames until the last remnant was turned to ash. "And that is that," Edith said with a smile.

Edith opened the doors to her room and found two servants waiting for her to leave so they could make her bed and clean her room. Edith nodded and smiled as she walked past them. She saw the startled look on the two women standing there. Edith knew that acknowledging any of the servants was against social etiquette, but her father raised her to be respectful to everyone no matter their station in life.

She descended the staircase and marveled at the beauty of the marble, black-and-white square tiles that led down a hall to the kitchen area. She moved from room-to-room looking at all the finery he had amassed over the years.

Plush chairs and divans filled the drawing rooms, along with ornate tables and fixtures. Gilded picture frames lined the walls with their life-size portraits dominating them. The picture of a young, skinny male hung over the fireplace. It looked like Lord Symington when he was young. "My goodness," she exclaimed. "You looked old as a youth." She moved closer and stared into the eyes in the portrait. "You had evil eyes even back then." An involuntary shiver ran down her spine.

Each room she went through was ornate and extravagant in style and taste. She moved to the library and stopped in front of a life-sized portrait of a lovely young woman. There was a sadness emitting from the picture that reached out and tugged at her heart. A servant was in the room dusting the large table that sat behind a divan.

"Who is she?" Edith asked.

The servant stopped dusting and looked at the painting. "She was 'is last wife. Poor thing." The last words were barely audible to Edith.

"So young and fair," Edith studied the face in the painting and shook her head. "What exactly happened to her?"

"We don't know, yer ladyship," she turned and started dusting again, only with more enthusiasm than before.

Edith walked over to the servant who was nervously dusting the already dusted table. "It is strange that you have not heard, because rumor has it, she fell from one of the towers."

"Those be the rumors, yer ladyship. Those be the rumors."

Edith walked to the large library doors and closed them. "I will not repeat anything you tell me, you have my word on that. Please tell me what really happened." Her voice was soft and gentle to the frightened woman.

The servant looked warily around the room. Satisfied she could speak freely she began in a soft voice. "The young girl was very sweet, yer ladyship. 'er ladyship refused to bed 'im and 'is 'enchmen beat 'er very badly. She ran up the steps to get away from them. But 'is lordship, and that nasty 'enchman, Lobart, followed 'er up the stairs. Then we 'eard a terrible scream. That is all I know. Please do not let 'im know I told ye anything, yer ladyship. I get ta talking, and I cannot stop."

"He will never know from me," she smiled and patted the servant's arm as she left the room.

Terror welled up in Edith as she climbed the stairs to her room. Her husband was capable of doing anything, even murder. She had hoped they were merely idle gossip, but now the fear mounted in her.

Four months went by and Edith used the sleeping potion on her husband every night. She continued talking to him while he slept; telling him that he hated being around her; that she did not please him; and he would only have her in his bed until she was with child.

Everything was working out well for Edith, except that her father was not feeling well and bed-ridden. She visited her father two or three times a week, and would stay with him until he fell asleep. Then, while he rested, Mrs. Dawson would send the other servants on errands that would keep them gone for hours; Edith would dress as Mrs. Dawson and go to Ian.

Lord Symington used to have his men hide in a thicket a distance from the manor, now they blatantly stayed in front of the house watching who came in and out.

This day was no different as Edith gave Mrs. Dawson a quick hug and hurried out to the buggy waiting for her by the back door.

An hour later, the sound of a buggy was heard pulling up to the back door of the kitchen.

Mrs. Dawson gave a slight smile. "I am so glad she is back early. I had this awful feeling that something bad was going to happen today." She kept talking under her breath, "Those darn tea leaves this morning said there was danger. I am just a superstitious old, gypsy woman," she chided herself.

Mrs. Dawson opened the kitchen door, and froze. It was one of Lord Symington's men. He was just as startled to see her as she was him.

"What be ye doing in there?" He asked surly. "I saw ye leaving a bit a go."

Mrs. Dawson, flabbergasted, stared hard at the burly man for a moment. Gathering her wits about her, she quickly said, "Are ye daft? I am here, and I do not have to explain when and where I go to the likes of you. Now get your carriage off this land."

"Ye dun't scare me, ye old crow," he snarled back.

"You would be wise not to anger me," she narrowed her eyes and stared hard at the henchmen. "I am a powerful witch, and I will put a curse on you if you ever set foot on this land again."

The henchman laughed nervously. "I dun't believe in any of that stuff."

"Then you are far more stupid than you look," she reached behind her and pulled out the broom that was leaning against the kitchen wall. "Let's see what I can do to make you believe." She began wailing and waving the broom through the air.

"You be a daft ole woman," he said as he flipped the reins to the horses and rode as fast as he could away from her.

Albert came rushing from the barn. "What was that all about? I couldn't hear from the barn. What were you doing with that broom?"

"Oh, nothing, just getting rid of a few spider webs," she said, and then with extreme urgency she blurted out, "Albert, that henchman saw me here. He knows it was not me in the carriage. You have to get to my dear Edith and warn her. Take the shortest route you know, and hurry."

Albert was already racing to the barn. He grabbed one of the horses and threw a saddle on it. He hurried to the end of the barn, pushed away some straw, and opened a small trap door. He took out one of the pouches and put it in the saddlebag. He carefully opened the back door of the barn. Satisfied no one was watching him; he raced his horse to Ian's cottage. As he got closer to the cottage, he began yelling as loudly as he could. "They be coming! They be coming!"

Edith and Ian raced out of the cottage at the sound of Albert's voice.

Panic gripped Edith at the thought of their being discovered. She threw her arms around Ian. "He will kill you."

"I can take care of myself," Ian said and grabbed Edith's arm as they raced to the barn.

Albert saw them heading toward the barn and rode directly in it.

Ian was starting to ready her carriage when Albert yelled.

"No, no! There's no time to hitch her horse to the carriage." Albert climbed off his horse and grabbed the reins. "Take my horse it will be faster."

Ian helped Edith up onto the horse's back, and then changed his mind. "No, ye cannot go." His arms reached up to help her back down from the horse. "It is ye, I fear for. I cannot let ye go back to him now. It is too dangerous for ye."

"Don't worry about me," Edith leaned down and gave him a quick kiss. "You take care of yourself, my love."

"Take the horse over the McDermott hills," Albert said, grabbing the horse's reins. "I just came that way. The ground is dry and not too rough."

Ian led the horse to the edge of the road. "Edith, I fear for ye," his voice was cracking.

"I will be alright," she said soothingly.

"No time for talking," Albert said swatting the backside of her horse. "The trees should hide you and the horse."

Edith raced her horse in earnest toward the grassy lands and the McDermott hills. Ian waited until she was out of sight and stormed into his cabin with Albert right behind him.

"Now, Mister Ian," Albert grabbed his arm. "Pack up what you be needing and leave. Do not come back for a while."

"I am not going to run away from this little man," Ian stood defiantly in the middle of his cottage. "I can take care of myself."

"Listen to me young man," Albert put his hands on his hips. "You are not dealing with a man of honor. He will have his men sneak up and strike you down from behind. They will kill you. You must think of Edith and do this for her. It will be one less person for her to worry about."

Albert reached into his pocket and pulled out a small pouch. "Here, Lady Edith been taking money from that miserable old miser and saving it just in case it should be needed. I was told that if this should happen, you were to get this money. It be enough to get you away until it be safe to come back." He picked up Ian's hand and dropped the purse on it. "Now, get the stuff you be needing and get going. Do it for her, my lad. Do it for her peace of mind."

"For her I shall do this," Ian grabbed a large canvas bag and began stuffing it with just the things he would need.

Albert heard the sound of horses in the distance heading their way. "Quickly, man, they're almost here."

Four riders stopped in front of Ian's cottage. Four large men, brandishing pistols climbed down from their horses, two walked into the barn, and the other two-kicked open the door to Ian's cottage.

"How dare you?" Albert yelled at the two men standing in the doorway. "Are ya animals? You're supposed to knock on someone's door, not kick it in." He sat staring at the two tall men in the doorway.

"What are ya doing 'ere?" Lobart, the leader of the henchmen asked. His tall, burly frame almost filled the doorway.

Albert picked up the steaming hot cup of tea and waved it in front of the men. He moved a pail of water that contained one of the cups Edith and Ian had been using. "That's better I've been kicking that pail all morning," he lied as he placed the pail behind the kindling next to the fireplace, so they couldn't see the extra cup. "I'm drinking a cup of tea."

"I can see that," he snapped. "What are ya doing in this man's cottage?" Lobart nodded for the other man to check out the place. It was a small cottage with one bedroom. He came back and shook his head.

"Well," he shrugged. "Not that it is any of your business, but I am taking care of Ian's place until he returns."

"What?"

"Does Lord Symington hire only deaf people?" Albert sipped casually from the teacup. "I said I be looking in from time to time on his place so squatters don't feel like they can take over this cottage."

"Where be this Ian?" Lobart demanded.

"Gone," he put the cup on the table. "You gentlemen like a cup of hot tea?" Albert thought he had better ease up with his insulting comments for fear they may do him harm or worse. He got up and went to the cupboard as if he were getting them cups. "Sorry, if I have been less than hospitable, but you all scared the bageebees out of me, you know, kicking in the door like that."

The men from the barn came back, and one of them whispered something to Lobart. "It appears that there be only one 'orse in the barn."

"Of course, it's mine," Albert purposely spilt the hot tea on his hand, and jumped around yelling. The henchmen laughed at his mishap. Albert attempted to keep the henchmen off guard. "It would be a long walk now, wouldn't it?" He was still flapping his hand as if it still burned.

"So, ya 'ave no idea of the whereabouts of this Ian? Ya think to be so clever. Don'tcha? What of the woman dressed like Mrs. Dawson and riding out this morning with Mrs. Dawson being in the house and all?" Lobart asked.

"Now, laddie, how would I know about that, with me being here and all?" Albert sat back down.

Lobart turned to the other henchmen, "Do you remember this bloke being at the manor this morning? Is he lying?"

One of the henchmen spoke up, "I be there all morning, can't say I recall seeing him there. And, the 'orse in the stable over there 'as not been ridden in a while."

"Look, from one servant to another if I knew I would tell you, so that you would not get in any trouble with Lord Symington. Besides this Ian was not good enough for yer ladyship. Lord Symington is a much better match. A very rich match I might add," he winked at them as he lied.

"We'll check out yer story," Lobart said.

"I can imagine how angry his lordship would be if he thought you let this man, Ian, get away. But it is not your fault." Albert shrugged. "I think he has been gone a few months. Just about the time of the marriage of Lady Edith to Lord Symington. Couldn't bear the thought of her with him, I guess."

Lobart studied Albert for a moment. "I am not sure of yer story. But we will find out shortly. If Lady Symington's hiding 'round 'ere waiting for us to leave she will never get to the manor before Lord Symington." He smiled broadly. "Come on, we don't want to miss the fun." Lobart motioned for the others to back out of the room. "Let's get going. Lord Symington's been informed of the trickery. I want to be at Brekmore Manor when 'e arrives."

Albert got up and walked to the door. The four men got on their horses and raced down the dirt road toward Brekmore Manor.

Albert walked back to the kitchen table and shook his head. "My friend, Ian. You rode like the devil itself was chasing you, and the devil was, as far as I am concerned. Be safe my friend, be safe." He raised his tea cup in a salute and took a sip.

Lord Symington had his footmen drive the horses as fast as they could go. He arrived at the front door of Brekmore Manor and did not wait for the footman to open the carriage door. He flung it open and rushed toward the house. He burst through the front door startling Mrs. Dawson so badly she dropped the tea tray she was carrying.

"Where is she?" He demanded. "Where is she?"

"How dare you come breaking through the door like a common criminal?" Mrs. Dawson stood over the little man, her bosoms almost in his face. "You do not own this property or this land. Now get out of here."

"Don't you dare to cross me, old woman," he gasped in anger. His frail body weaved slightly.

"Me? Old?" She gave a short laugh. "Have you looked into the mirror lately, you old fool."

"I will have you . . . " Lord Symington was interrupted by Edith standing at the top of the stairs.

"How dare you come into this house uninvited." The anger and hatred in her voice were not hidden. "You burst into my sick father's house and cause such a ruckus as to upset him. Get out!" She ordered raising her arm and pointing her finger to the front doors.

Lord Symington moved toward the steps' banister, and he swayed unsteadily for a moment grabbing at the finials. His footman ran to his side. "Get me up these stairs."

"Get out of my house," Lord Brekmore said weakly. "Get out and never come back."

"Father," Edith rushed to grab a hold of him. "You mustn't get up. You are too weak."

"Your strumpet of a daughter was with another man just a few moments ago," he called up. His black lips twisted in hate.

"My daughter has not left my side since this morning," he struggled to reach the top of the stairs.

"I don't believe you," he yelled from the bottom of the steps. "One of my men saw her dressed as your servant here leaving the house."

"Do you think I care what they saw or what you believe?" He started to sway back and forth. "If I was not so weak I would throttle you until you had no breath left in you." His body started to go limp in Edith's arms.

"Mrs. Dawson!" Edith called down to her.

"I'm coming, Lady Edith. I'm coming!" Roughly, she pushed past the footman who was partially blocking the stairway. She stopped and turned looking straight into the eyes of Lord Symington. "Get out of this house!" She said with her teeth bared, and hurried up the stairs.

"You are all liars," Lord Symington tried to shout, but his voice was weak. "Get me out of here!" He ordered. Once outside the four riders who had encountered Albert earlier were waiting by his carriage.

"Did you catch her with him?" Lord Symington could only gasp.

"No," Lobart said. "Their servant Albert was there. Said this Ian left 'is cottage the day ya were married to 'er ladyship."

"What was their man servant doing there?" He pulled a woolen blanket around his thin legs, even though it was a warm day.

"'e is keeping the place for this Ian so that squatters don't take it over. They are 'ard to get rid of once they take over a place."

"Squatters are like lice and gypsies. They are impossible to get rid of." He closed his eyes and fell back against the carriage. "Maybe they are telling the truth," his voice was fading. "They are *too good* to lie, especially Lord Brekmore. The man has a reputation of honesty at all costs. What a fool. Take me back to my manor, I feel very tired. I will think of what to do with all of them later."

Just then, a carriage appeared with a woman dressed like Mrs. Dawson. It went directly into the open barn doors. The henchmen looked at each other and shrugged. Lord Symington stared at the carriage and its occupant and then back at his men. "You ever send me on a wild goose chase again you will be the ones who pay dearly for it. Now, get me away from this place."

Edith and Mrs. Dawson helped Lord Brekmore back into his bed. Edith had tears streaming down her face. "Oh, father," she pulled a quilt up over his body. "You should never have gotten up."

"I should never have let you marry that charlatan," he said grabbing her hand. "I am so sorry, my dear. You have no idea how sorry I am."

"Father," she reached up with her other hand and stroked his face. "It was not your decision. It was mine. I can tell you now that he threatened to have you, and Ian killed if I did not marry him. It was my choice."

"You have sacrificed yourself for us?" He moved his head from side-to-side on the pillow. "This is unbearable."

"No, father," she squeezed his hand gently. "I have wonderful news for you. I am with child."

"Is this true? He shook his head confused. "And, you are happy to bear this foul creature's child?"

"Father, that hideous husband of mine has never touched me, although he thinks he has," she lowered her head. "It is Ian's child I carry. You are not ashamed of my actions are you?"

"I am going to have a grandchild," he smiled. "And it is not going to be from the odious little man you are married to. My dear I am completely amazed, and quite happy. Ashamed of you? Never. However, no one must know of this but us."

"We have been very careful, Lord Brekmore." Mrs. Dawson said.

"I am very tired and would like to rest now," he grabbed Edith's hand as she pulled it away. "You have made me very happy. I know not how you managed to do this, but it pleases me more than you know."

The two women left his room. "I'll make you some tea, my dear."

"Make *us* some tea, my dear, dear Mrs. Dawson." She walked with her to the kitchen. Both women were startled to see a woman dressed in Mrs. Dawson's clothing standing in the kitchen. The bonnet pulled low over her face blocking its view.

"What . . . ?" Mrs. Dawson was so startled, she could not even finish her words when the woman lifted her head and looked at them.

"Albert!" Edith ran and gave him a hug. "Albert!" She began to laugh heartily. Soon the three of them were laughing and hugging each other. Mrs. Dawson helped him take off the dress and bonnet.

"I was hoping they didn't come to see who be in the carriage. I figured the barn was far enough away from the house; they wouldn't see anything but a woman dressed like you, my dear."

"But how?" Edith asked incredulously.

"You left in such a hurry you forgot to dress like my Carlotta. It was in Ian's bedroom, so I stuffed it under the blanket on Ian's bed. It was not made up, so they wouldn't think anything of the lumps and bumps of the quilts and blankets."

Edith lowered her reddened face. "Oh, my!" She cleared her throat to regain her composure. "I forgot all about the clothing. I was in such a hurry to get here. I had just made it up the stairs when he came bursting through the door. I turned around like I had been upstairs the whole time." She looked at Albert, her voice filled with worry. "What of Ian? What has happened to him? Is he safe?"

"I made him leave, and that be a hard thing for him to do. I said you could rest peacefully knowing that he be safe, Ma'am."

Edith sank onto one of the kitchen chairs. "Yes, yes. Knowing he is safe is the greatest gift you can give me." She stared at the kitchen table for a moment. "There is something I haven't told you two." She looked into their concerned faces. "I am not really married to that hideous man."

"What say you?" Albert asked.

"I did not say my vows. I did not say I would marry him," Edith shrugged. "I opened my mouth to say them, but I could not say the words."

"Oh my, Lord Symington knows that. You may be in great danger," Mrs. Dawson said, her voice filled with worry.

"He will never admit that we are not actually married." Edith gave a short laugh, "his pride would not let it be known. All he wants is an heir. He will go along with this charade until the child is born. I am safe for now."

"I am worried about what is going to happen to you when you go back to that foul little man." Mrs. Dawson brought a cup of tea and placed it in front of Edith.

"He has a violent temper," Edith shook her head. "Even though he was proven wrong, I fear for what he will do because we ordered him out of this house. He does not take lightly to anyone besting him. Least of all me." She finished her tea and stood up. "I will go now and see what horrible plans this madman has for me."

"I will go with you," Albert moved by her side.

"No, but thank you, dear Albert," she heaved her shoulders slightly. "I want you two to take out the pistols and have them with you at all times. I do not trust this man." Her face filled with worry as she looked at Mrs. Dawson and Albert. "He may send his henchmen back to teach you all a lesson. Please, I beg of you be very careful."

"We will do that, my dear," Albert patted her arm. "We will be very careful."

"Don't you be worrying about us, my dear Edith," she smiled reassuringly. "We are smarter than his lordship. But we will be extra careful as well."

Edith looked in on her sleeping father one more time. It was the first time since his illness that he looked rested, and she could have sworn there was a slight smile on his face. She said her good-byes to Mrs. Dawson and Albert and rode back to the manor. The sun was setting, and darkness was descending over the dirt road leading to the manor. Edith felt a chill race down her spine as the top of the manor came into view. She knew what he was capable of, and fear gripped her heart.

Chapter 8

My Dearest Rachel,

I was so happy to get your letter. Your words are like home to me. I was saddened to hear about the poor Countess. May she rest in peace, and be comforted to know that she had a friend until the end.

Prisons on ships? I never knew that ships had prisons on them. The captain referred to them as brigs. Very interesting.

I hope Phillip is not away from you too long. Married life could be quite challenging, but Ian makes everything wonderful and worthwhile. I love him more each time we are together. He is the most gentle, loving man I have ever known.

Father has not been well lately, but he is starting to come around, so do not fret about him.

You asked in your last letter if Lord Symington had found himself another wife. Yes, but I think he has met his match in her. She is not like his last couple of wives - she fights back. I can only hope she is making his life a living nightmare, as I am sure, he is hers.

My dearest, I have such wonderful news. I am with child. Ian and I are going to have a child. I have never been so happy and so proud as to bear him a child.

Well, my dearest, many things are happening with you as well, let me know how you are doing soon. All my love, prayers, and good wishes, your Edith

Captain English had excused himself to take care of matters in town leaving Rachel alone with his aunts, Clara and Libbie, who made Rachel feel completely at home. They fussed over her until it was almost embarrassing for her.

"Come, my dear," Libbie said. "You must choose which room you want to sleep in."

"Oh," Rachel exclaimed. "Any room will be fine with me."

"Nonsense," Clara clapped her hands together. "This is the fun part. You get to see all the rooms and pick the one you like the best."

The two aunts grabbed her arms, one on each side. They escorted her up wide steps ending at a half-wall, where the steps split; one set of steps went to the right; the other to the left. At the top of the stairs was a large opening splitting the hallway in half. An ornate, iron rail ran along the open end of the landing where two large baroque doors stood.

"Our rooms are right there." She pointed to the two massive doors. "The one on the left is mine, and the one on the right is Clara's. Now, my dear, we have a few guest rooms to show you. If you are not pleased with any of the rooms on the left side of the house; we will find you one on the right." Libbie hooked one of her arms under Rachel's arm.

"Yes," Clara squeezed her other arm. "We know you young people do not like to be around us old folks. So, we always try to let them have rooms away from us."

"I love 'old people', as you put it," Rachel smiled at the two doting aunts.

"Oh, we are going to get along just fine. Just fine," Libbie said with satisfaction.

They gave Rachel a quick tour through the rooms, but the room Rachel like best was the one done in gold's and reds. It was enormous. Beautiful golden, silk drapes hung gracefully from the ceiling to floor windows and French doors. A gold quilt stopped half-way down the bed, and a beautiful lace bed skirt continued to the floor. Deep red, gold and lace pillows accented the bed perfectly.

"Perfect choice," Clara motioned her into the room. "This door is for your clothes." She opened the door to a long, narrow room. One wall was filled with pegs to hang her dresses, and the other side was filled with cubbyholes to place her shoes, purses, shawls, and parasols. At the far end of the room was a built-in dresser with drawers for her to place her very personal items.

Rachel was stunned. The closet was almost half the size of her bedroom back home. They hurried her out of the closet into the main bedchambers.

"This door," Libbie moved to the second door in the room, "is your private lavatory, or loo as it is referred to sometimes. However, we call it a bathing room. It is not a common practice to bathe as often as we do, but we so enjoy it."

"Oh, yes," Clara said. "We bathe every week."

"Sometimes," Libbie spoke softly, almost as if she were saying something wicked, "we bathe twice a week, and in the summer, we may take three a week."

Clara opened the door to the lavatory, and again Rachel was stunned. In the middle of the large room was a ceramic tub with claw legs. Off to one side was a washbasin on a pedestal, and a wooden commode was hidden behind a half wall. Instead of a fireplace, there was a small, ornate iron stove in the corner of the room. Large French doors, draped in the same gold silk and lace sheers, opened to a small balcony that connected to the one in her room.

"Nathaniel, we call him Nathan most of the time, put the stove in over there to keep the rooms warm in the winter, and to heat up the water for our baths." Libbie headed back into the bedchamber, with Rachel and Clara following close behind.

"Nathan, that dear sweet boy," Clara reflected. "He had this house built for him and his wife."

"Where is his wife now?" Rachel asked.

"Oh, the poor darling," Libbie said sadly. "She died in childbirth, along with the child."

Clara moved toward a chair next to a round table, and sat down. "She had the sweetest disposition. Gwendolyn was not the fairest young woman, but her kindness made her beautiful to us. She labored so long and was in such pain. She was such a frail young woman."

"I am so sorry," Rachel said sincerely.

"Come along," Libbie motioned for Clara to get up. "Let us go and partake of some tea and dessert cakes."

Clara almost jumped out of her chair. "Now, that is a great idea."

The aunts took Rachel down to their large parlor, and rang for one of the servants who appeared almost immediately.

"Tiffy, tea and dessert cakes, please," Libbie said.

"Yes, Ma'am," the dark-skinned girl curtsied and left the room.

"Years ago, Nathan found Tiffy hiding in an alley," Clara nodded in the direction of the servant girl who had just left the room. Clara sat down in a soft blue chair with a high back and intricate woodcarvings all around the back and legs. She clapped her hands together and continued. "It was a freezing cold day, and the poor little thing was in rags."

"She was afraid of him at first," Libbie quickly interjected, "but he persuaded her to come here. "Tiffy's mother had helped her run away with slaves who were heading north. Somehow she got separated from the others and was left to fend for herself. Poor little thing was badly treated by her owners. We could tell because there were scars on her back from where she had been whipped."

"We found that out when we made her take a bath," Clara laughed. "Mercy, that was a lot of trouble at first. However, now, she takes baths like we do and enjoys them, too."

Libbie sat down on a cream-colored chair that was less ornate than Clara's. "Nathan managed to buy her mother and a brother from their owners and brought them here. Her mother, Bimms, is a great cook, and her brother, Seth, is a very hard worker, and very protective of us."

"Nathan had quite a problem when he went to buy Tiffy from her slave owner, because the slave owner wanted to make an example of her for running away to his other slaves. However, Nathan offered him a great deal of money, and finally; the owner signed her papers over to him."

"What of her father?" Rachel asked.

"I believe he died on the way over to the Americas," Libbie just shook her head.

"Where do they stay?" Rachel sat down on a blue and cream love seat across from the two women.

"Oh, with us, of course," Clara spoke up. "We have very nice servants' quarters. They each have their own room, with fireplaces, and anything else to make them comfortable. Nathan made sure of that."

Libbie sighed. "I do not know what we would do without them."

"Do you have other slaves here?" Rachel settled back on the soft velvet cushions.

"Oh my, we do not have any slaves in our household." Clara gasped. "When Nathan came back he had a very powerful solicitor draw up papers showing that they were free, and not owned by anyone. He made sure it was shown on official government records."

"He offered them work, with very good wages," Libbie said. "And they have been here ever since. However, they are free to go anytime they so choose."

"Nathan seems like quite a man," Rachel said reflectively.

"They do not come any finer." Clara's face broke into a grin at the sight of Tiffy and the food tray she was carrying.

"Tiffy, Lady Prescott will be staying with us for a while. Will you have the men see to her trunks? Oh, have them put in the gold room. And, if you would be so kind to have one of the other girls help you put her things away." Libbie began pouring the tea.

"Yes, Ma'am," Tiffy looked at Rachel and gave her a big warm smile.

After they had their tea and dessert cakes, Clara looked up at the large clock sitting on top of the fireplace mantel. "Oh my! Is it that time already?"

Libbie looked over and stood up quickly. "Oh my! We are going to be late if we don't hurry."

Clara dabbed her mouth one more time with her napkin and stood up. "You must come with us." She said to Rachel.

"Oh, Clara," Libbie said. "She must be exhausted after her long journey."

"Why? They didn't give her an oar to row here. Besides, it is not far from here, and it is only for an hour or so." Clara looked down at Rachel. "Please come with us. I so want everyone to meet you. Even for just a moment. Tiffy is excellent with the hair and will help you get dressed."

"It would be quite nice to have you come along." Libbie said meekly.

Rachel was exhausted, and wanted nothing more than to crawl underneath the thick, quilted bedspread and sleep, but felt she owed them something for their grand hospitality. "I would love to go, wherever it is we are going."

The two aunts clapped their hands excitedly and called out for Tiffy, and Bimms. Tiffy hurried from upstairs, and Bimms came from the kitchen into the sitting room. Libbie spoke quickly. "We need your help. We have a tea, which I am ashamed we forgot about at Mr. Druketts. He wants everyone to meet his niece from London."

Clara picked up her skirt and began climbing the stairs.

"And Bimms, this is Lady Prescott." Libbie pointed to Rachel. "She will be staying with us for a while." She paused, "we are hoping a long while."

"Yes, Ma'am." Bimms smiled and nodded in Rachel's direction, as she followed the two aunts up to their rooms.

Tiffy waited until Rachel started up the stairs and then followed. Rachel stepped aside as a couple of men carried her emptied trunk out of her room and down the back stairs. Tiffy walked to the closet door and opened it. "What dress pleases you, Ma'am? Some of your dresses are very fine looking."

Rachel gave a short laugh, "Well, not as fine as I have seen, but thank you." She walked into the closet and stared at the dresses hanging there. Rachel let out a little gasp. The gowns of the young countess were hanging in her closet. Their elegance was unmistakable.

"How did these get in here?" Rachel ran her hand over the fine garments. Trust me, Tiffy; these garments are finer than anything I have. I could not wear one of them, you see, she . . . these are the Countesses, and she perished at sea."

"Excuse me for saying this," Tiffy held out a beautiful muslin blue dress. "But she can't be wearing them now, and it would be a waste to throw them away. Besides, you don't want to be embarrassing the Aunties now, do you?"

"Oh, no, I do not want to embarrass them." She eyed the blue gown in Tiffy's hand. "I don't think the Countess would mind my wearing this one."

Tiffy handed her the one piece, blue muslin dress with small cap sleeves. Silvery thread, in an Egyptian pattern, trimmed the empire-style bust line, cap sleeves, and the hem of her dress.

After Tiffy found a matching pair of low blue silk slippers, she found a purse, and matching bonnet and gloves to go with the ensemble.

Rachel looked for something warm to put over her dress, and found the perfect shawl to complement the entire outfit. Tiffy helped to fasten the bonnet, and pulled a few ringlets out over Rachel's forehead.

"You look so lovely," Tiffy said, staring at her.

"With your help," Rachel reached over and squeezed her hand. "Tiffy, I want you to help yourself to anything you find to your liking."

"Lady Prescott," she laughed. "I be twice your size. But thank you, just the same."

Rachel reached out and touched her arm. "There are no sizes to the parasols, shawls and purses, so anything that catches your fancy is yours."

"Thank you, Ma'am," Tiffy nodded and smiled. "You be very kind and generous."

Rachel quickly changed the subject. "Do you know anything about the young lady from London we are going to meet?"

"Only what the other servants tell me," she said as she began to work on the tiny buttons on the back of Rachel's dress.

"What is that?"

"It seems the Rutherford girls have not been very nice to her." Tiffy closed the last button and adjusted the small train on Rachel's dress.

"Who are the Rutherford girls?" Rachel asked.

"Their father be a very wealthy diplomat, and they be his only daughters. From what I hear, he spoils them quite a bit. One of their servants told me they be very jealous of this new girl. She is supposed to be somewhat pretty. And, I was told they be doing mean things to her all the time."

"Very interesting," Rachel checked her reflection in the mirror. "My word, she did have exquisite clothes."

"I beg your pardon, Ma'am?"

"Nothing, Tiffy. I think I am ready now."

Tiffy ran and opened the door. Rachel left the room feeling more elegant than she had ever felt in her life.

Clara and Libbie were just coming out of their rooms. Their clothes were as elegant as Rachel's, only the colors of their clothing were in darker shades of reds, and blues. When they spotted Rachel, they both let out a shriek.

"Oh," Libbie exclaimed with glee. "You are so beautiful, and elegantly attired. Do you not think so, Clara?"

"Of course, I do," Clara ran and grabbed Rachel's arm. "Let us go and show her off."

As they descended the staircase, the front door opened and Captain English walked in. He stopped in his tracks and just stared at Rachel.

"Nathan," his two aunts called simultaneously. They left Rachel on the steps and flew into his arms.

He greeted them warmly, taking each of their hands and kissing the back of them. He turned to Rachel, who now stood next to them. "You look absolutely wonderful." He picked up her hand and kissed the back of it.

Libbie and Clara hurried over to Bimms who finished adjusting their bonnets.

"I did not expect this pleasant surprise. I thought you would be tired from your trip and be resting." Nathan nodded politely to Rachel.

"I did not have to row the last few miles, so I am quite fine," Rachel smiled innocently at Nathan.

"Row?" He asked confused.

Rachel laughed heartily. "I would not disappoint your aunts for anything. And, I would not have had the attire suitable for such a visit, except I found a closet full of beautiful clothes. I can only wonder who is responsible for having the Countesses clothes brought here," she smiled knowingly at him.

He smiled and nodded. "It would have been a waste to dispose of such finery." He abruptly changed the subject. "Alright, my lovelies, are we all ready?"

"You are going with us?" Rachel inquired, somewhat surprised.

"Of course, he is," Clara put a finger to her chin. "Did we forget to tell you that? I guess we did." She shrugged and smiled. "Shall we go?"

"My carriage awaits you," he made an exaggerated bow, and his aunts giggled. "Seth?" He called out.

A tall, muscular, young black male came in the front door. "Yes, sir?"

"Would you please escort these darlings to the carriage?"

"It would be my pleasure," he smiled broadly and bowed his head to the two aunts.

They giggled, and each grabbed an arm of Seth's and walked down the steps to the carriage.

"Lady Prescott?" Nathan offered his arm to Rachel.

She looked up into his tanned face, smiled and took his arm.

The carriage stopped in front of a large brick house. Servants dressed in white pants and white jackets came to their carriage and helped them down.

No one was inside as they entered the manor. A wide winding staircase sat in the middle of a large hallway. Two large rooms were adjacent to the hallway. Nathan and his two aunts entered one of the sitting rooms, and Rachel was about to follow when she saw a young girl sitting in the other room.

Rachel entered the room and noticed that there was no one else in the room but the young girl sitting in a window seat.

"You can sit next to me," said the young girl sliding over to make room for Rachel.

"Thank you," Rachel extended her gloved hand, and the young girl took it. "My name is Lady Rachel Prescott, and you are?"

"My name is Lady Katherine DeLorie, but everyone calls me Kat." Her eyes traveled all over Rachel's attire. "You look so elegant."

Rachel wanted to repeat the compliment back to her, but she couldn't.

The young girl's disheveled light, red hair had large ostrich feathers shooting out at all angles. Her dress was made of a satin, which Rachel knew was not the proper material for an afternoon social. The color of her dress was a deep, dark green, with light green satin leaves sewn all over the entire dress. And, the young girl had too much rouge on her face, and her lips had a bright reddish cast to them.

Two young, slender girls elegantly dressed and around the same age as Kat, walked over to Kat sitting on the settee. "Who is your new friend?" The one with the black hair, and gray eyes asked rather snootily.

"I am Lady Prescott," Rachel raised an eyebrow in distain at the brazen girls. "Whom do I have the privilege of addressing?"

"My word," the other girl said, as sandy brown curls bounced freely against her forehead. Her brown eyes traveled up and down Rachel. "You really *are* an English Lady, and so beautiful."

"There are a lot of beautiful women in this room," snapped the first one.

"Where? We are the only ones in here." The other girl said, looking around the room. "My name is Beatrice Rutherford, and this is my sister, Melificent Rutherford. They call me Bea and her Mel."

"Charmed, I am sure," Rachel noted the beautiful gowns they wore, and no cheek or lip rouge on either one of them.

"Do you like the dress we picked out for our friend," Mel stood looking down her nose at the timid Lady Katherine.

"I am afraid my trunk full of my clothes was washed overboard on my journey here. So, they," she nodded toward Mel and Bea, "found some things for me to wear."

"I see." Rachel stared at the ugly dress on the lovely young girl.

"Who picked out this attire for her? I am curious." Rachel was fuming inside at how ridiculous they made Lady Katherine look.

"I did," Mel threw back her shoulders and acted as if she was proud of the horrible dress Katherine was wearing.

Captain English and his two aunts came into the room. "There you are," Aunt Libbie said.

"We wondered what happened to you," Aunt Clara smiled broadly.

"There doesn't seem to be many people here," Captain English said looking around the room.

"That is Kat's fault," Mel flounced around the room in her dress, swirling it this way and that way to show off her stylish tea gown. "She put down the wrong time on your invitation by mistake. Everyone will start arriving in about an hour. She said she thought she put the wrong time on someone's invitation, but she couldn't remember whose." She kept moving about showing off her frock in front of Katherine, until Rachel got up. Mel tried, very unsuccessfully, not to stare at Rachel's beautiful and stylish dress.

"If you will excuse me. May I have a moment of your time, Captain English?" She didn't wait for his reply. Rachel grabbed his arm and took him into the great hall.

"What may I do for you?" He asked puzzled.

"I wonder if you can get your aunts to distract those two young ladies in there so you can take Lady Katherine and me back to your aunts' house."

"What for?" He asked confused.

"I believe the Countess's clothing will come to the rescue, again."

Nathanial looked confused at first and then smiled. "That would be a nice thing to do. Leave it to me and my aunts," he walked back into the parlor and began talking softly to his aunts. Rachel could already see the mischief in their eyes as they nodded and began to giggle.

Nathan returned to Rachel and said very softly. "My carriage is at your command."

Clara and Libbie got up from their chairs and walked over to Mel and Bea. "You two are such lovely creatures. Since we have time, I would love to see the rest of the house. I am sure Lady De-Lorie would not mind."

"It's just a house," Mel said perplexed. "Have my father show you around."

"Oh, but you are right here," Clara grabbed Mel's arm. "We can all explore together."

"Yes, what fun," Libbie grabbed Bea's arm and led them out of the parlor.

Once they were out of sight, Rachel grabbed the startled Katherine, "Do not ask. Quickly, I want you to come with me." She rushed her out of the house.

Captain English was outside waiting with the carriage. He helped them get in, and they took off for his aunts' house. He got them to the house in record time and called out for Tiffy and Bimms.

"Yes, sir?" Tiffy and Bimms met him at the door.

Bimms took one look at the young girl, "Lordy, was she at a costume affair. Why is she dressed like a tree?"

"That is what we are going to correct," Rachel rushed the still puzzled girl up the stairs to her room.

Captain English did not follow; instead, he waited at the bottom of the stairs.

"Let us see what dress we can find that is more fitting for a young Lady. How old are you Lady Katherine?" Rachel asked.

"Thirteen, Lady Prescott. Please call me Kat," she replied looking around at the magnificent bed chambers of Rachel's.

"Thirteen? I will find something appropriate." Rachel sat Kat down at her vanity table. "Bimms, could you please remove that horrible rouge off her face and lips?

"She be dressed like a bird died in her hair," Tiffy said shaking her head.

"I knows, but we be gonna fix all of that," Bimms said with confidence.

"Yes, yes we are," Rachel said walking into her closet.

A few moments later, Rachel put her hands on her hips and smiled broadly. "I believe we are finished."

They all stood back and looked at their creation. The red rouge from her cheeks and lips were gone. Her almost translucent skin looked healthy and glowed. Gone were the large green ostrich feathers, and wild hair. Kat's long, wavy, red hair was pulled back at the sides and fell loosely down her back. Loose curls dangled on her forehead and by her ears. A few small, silk flowers placed in her hair replaced the huge ostrich feathers.

The two layered, green dress Rachel had picked out for Kat accentuated her green eyes. A sheer, light green, muslin dress flowed over a green muslin gown underneath. The matching green slippers were a perfect fit. The bust, hem, and train all trimmed in lace, bore delicate flowers embroidered above the lace. Rachel was thankful Kat was about the same size as her and the Countess as she grabbed a lace shawl and parasol.

"Now, look at yourself in the mirror." Rachel turned her around to look in the full-length mirror.

Kat almost started to cry, "I look so elegant."

"You look more than that, my dear." Rachel smiled at the work they had all done. "Bimms, you and Tiffy did a wonderful job. Thank you."

"That was fun," Tiffy replied.

"We have to get you back to your party," Rachel beamed. "I can hardly wait to see the faces of your 'friends'."

Captain English was pleased at the transformation of Katherine. "She looks beautiful," he said, bowing slightly.

"I think she is beautiful, too, but we have to get back as fast as we can." Rachel grabbed captain's arm, and he grabbed Katherine's arm, as they hurried out the front door.

"There will be no one who will be able to compete with you two beauties," he said helping them into the carriage.

They arrived to a house full of people, who were already milling around in all the rooms downstairs. Nathan found his two aunts sitting on chairs in the parlor.

"I do not think they like us very much," Clara snickered. "We even had them show us where the lavatories were, and the gardens that are no longer blooming."

"They got tired of us and finally snuck away." Libbie leaned closer to Nathan. "They have been looking for Lady Katherine."

Rachel slipped around the corner and joined the captain and his aunts.

The booming voice of Mr. Druketts interrupted the idle conversations of his guests. "I want to thank you all for coming here today to welcome and meet my niece from London, Lady Katherine DeLorie. Although, at the moment I cannot seem to find her."

Rachel looked over at the smug faces of Bea and Mel, and smiled.

The room full of people laughed, especially Bea and Mel, who nudged each other and giggled continually.

"Ah," Mr. Druketts said, "there you are."

Lady Katherine walked slowly around the corner. Ooh's and ahh's of approval radiated from everyone in the room. Everyone, except Mel and Bea. They stood with their mouths open and shock written all over their faces.

After a while, Katherine found her way to Rachel and Captain English. "How can I thank you?" She asked sincerely.

"Your smile is enough," Rachel said. "I will send some other things over for you to wear."

Mel and Bea approached Kat as she was talking to Rachel. "What happened to the dress we got for you? We are insulted that you replaced it with this."

Rachel stepped forward and looked into the faces of the two girls. "I cannot imagine Lady Katherine treating you as such if you were to visit her in England. She is in a strange country and has feelings just like you do. All she would like is a friend, a real friend. I truly believe you are very nice young ladies, but I think you have had enough fun at Lady Katherine's expense."

Mel looked down at the floor. "We did not mean any harm. It is just that she is so pretty, and well; we are not."

"Oh," Kat spoke quickly. "But I think you both are beautiful."

"You do?" Mel looked up in surprise. "I mean you being a Ladyship and everything you are too good to be friends with us."

"Oh no, you are so wrong," Kat took her hands. "I would love to be your friend. It would mean a lot to me to have you both as a friend."

They forgot about Rachel as they walked away. "Really? Gee, that is nice." Bea said taking one of Kat's arm and Mel the other.

Rachel watched them laugh and giggle about something. She smiled with relief that the girls would now be friends. Suddenly, Rachel started to become dizzy. The room was starting to spin as she swayed back and forth.

Captain English grabbed her around the waist and steadied her. "Are you all right, Lady Prescott?" His voice filled with concern.

"I think I am a bit dizzy," she replied weakly. "The long journey and then the unexpected excitement were probably too much for me."

He pulled up a chair from one of the tables for her to sit on.

"Thank you, captain." She sat down with relief. The dizziness soon passed, and she felt like her old self again. She looked around at the people in the room, and noticed that they were looking at her. "Oh, my," she tugged on his sleeve. "Captain, did I make a scene?"

"It would please me if you called me Nathan."

"Only if you call me Rachel," she said.

He laughed and looked around the room at the curious faces. He leaned down and whispered in her ear, "I believe they are looking at you because they have not seen someone as lovely as you in a long time."

Rachel blushed and turned to say something to Captain English. Her lips almost brushed against his. For one moment, their eyes locked, until Nathan abruptly pulled away. "Excuse me." He hurried off and disappeared around the corner.

Rachel sat there confused. What had just happened? Her heart was beating wildly. She wanted to get out of there. She wanted Phillip's arms around her. His face began to form in her mind, and she sighed. She remembered the closeness they shared on the ship. She loved him and him alone. She missed him so terribly. The minutes seemed like hours as the aunts introduced her to the curious people. Rachel nodded and smiled politely all the while wishing she could just get to her room and bed.

"Dearest," Libbie gently touched her shoulder. "We have kept you here way too long. You must be beyond exhausted."

"Come dear," the carriage is waiting. "Nathan had to leave unexpectedly, but he sent Seth back with the carriage."

Rachel didn't remember the ride home, or getting ready for bed. She was so tired that nothing mattered to her except the comfort of her bed. Phillip's face appeared before her again, but as she started to fall asleep, it began to waver.

Chapter 9

My Dearest Edith,

I am thrilled that you are with child. I am so happy for you and Ian. You will undoubtedly have the most beautiful child in all of England. I look forward to holding your child someday.

I was very pleased to read that your father is doing much better. I love that man very much.

So, Lord Symington's wife is giving him a hard time. How delicious is that?

My news is not that exciting. I have been completely accepted by Captain English's two aunts and their staff. They are all wonderful. Did you know that Captain English bought some slaves and then set them free? He is a very fine man.

We went to a party the day I arrived. Oh dear Edith, I was exhausted, but the aunts wanted me to go so badly, so I went. A young English Lady was there dressed in an inappropriate dress and a very ugly one. During her crossing her trunk filled with her clothing had been washed overboard.

Captain English had the fine dresses of the Countess brought to his aunt's house for me. He said it would be a shame to throw away such lovely clothing. Anyway, the party was starting late so Captain English and I whisked her away. I had such fun helping her find the right dress. The two girls who had dressed her so badly were stunned at how beautiful she looked. But everything ended well; they all became friends.

I am still trying to get over being on the ship. There was always constant movement on board the ship, and now I am on land where there is no movement, and I am still a bit wobbly. Captain English said I had to get my "land legs" back. Phillip has been gone such a short time, but I miss him so. Now, I

am missing two people I love. Your loving Rachel

The manor was dark, except for a small glow emitting from the fireplace in the parlor window. Edith pulled the carriage up to the front door. The livery boy promptly held the reins to her horse until she got off; she took a deep breath to steady herself and entered the house.

She walked into the large hallway and headed upstairs to her room, when Lord Symington called out to her. Edith paused for a moment, took another deep breath, and walked into the parlor.

Lord Symington was sitting on a chair pulled up close to the large fireplace. He had a shawl over his shoulders and a blanket over his lap. In his hand was a pistol. Three of his men stood stoically by the fireplace; all eyes on her.

Edith froze. Her heart began racing wildly. She waited until he spoke.

"I am not quite sure what I want to do with you," he never turned his head to look at her. Instead, he toyed with the pistol in his hands. "I can shoot you in the leg, or arm. It would probably kill you, but you haven't given me an heir yet. I wouldn't want you dead yet, now would I?"

Edith raised her chin and stood defiantly. She would not beg for her life, nor would she cry. She refused to give him that satisfaction. She did not reply to his question.

"I said, 'would I'," he tried to shout but his voice was weak. "Answer me."

She said nothing.

"I have been pondering over what action I can take to make you understand that you have no rights, no rights at all. That you are mine to do with as I please." He stared into the glowing coals burning in the fireplace. He began to laugh. It was a hideous laugh. "I have it."

Her thoughts were filled with terror for what he might do, afraid that it might cause injury to her unborn child.

"Put that poker into the fire," he ordered Lobart. "Let it get red hot." He turned in his chair and looked directly at Edith. "Let's see how brave she is when I brand her face."

Edith almost swooned, but forced herself to remain steady. Her stomach was in turmoil, and her head was pounding. She had no idea how she would endure the pain that was to follow.

The smell of the poker heating up began to fill the room. Lobart pulled it out of the fireplace and showed it to Symington. A broad smile crossed his face. "That is perfect." He weakly pointed a finger toward Edith. "You two hold her, and you," he pointed to Lobart, "hold me up so that I am the one to teach her a lesson."

His frail body moved slowly toward Edith. She did not try to pull away from his men. She would not give him the satisfaction of seeing her struggle. Her stomach began to churn inside as he moved closer to her with the hot poker.

The end glowed red, and weaved about from his unsteady gait. "Hold this. It is too heavy right now." He handed Lobart the glowing hot poker. "When I get close enough hand it to me." He smiled wickedly. They moved toward Edith slowly.

He was close enough now that Edith could feel the heat coming off of the glowing, hot poker in Lobart's hand. Lord Symington's face broke into a grin as he held out his hand for the poker.

However, he was not prepared for what happened next. Edith vomited. It was not just a gagging reflex; instead, it was so forceful it flew across the short distance between her and Lord Symington. It covered him and Lobart at the same time.

Lord Symington screamed in disgust and disbelief. He stumbled backward and began retching himself. Soon, one of the men holding her began to retch. The other henchmen let go of her and ran to his boss's side.

Edith took the opportunity to race up the stairs and into her room. She ran to her valise and opened the fake bottom. There, resting on the bottom was a loaded pistol. She waited to hear if someone was after her. The only sounds were of Lord Symington screaming and throwing up. The house filled with servants trying to help their master and clean up the mess in the parlor.

Edith locked the door leading into her room from the hallway. She pulled a chair in front of it and wedged it under the glass doorknob. She fell down sobbing on the seat of the chair unable to move.

A few minutes later, she could hear the weak cries of her husband as his henchmen carried him up the stairs and into his chambers. Edith froze. Had she forgotten to lock the connecting doors to their rooms? Slowly, she turned her head and watched in horror as someone tried the door handle. The door shook as they pushed on it, but the doors remained closed.

Edith put her head back on the chair and cried silently. The footsteps of his henchmen stopped in front of her bedroom door. One of them jiggled the door handle. There was silence. Edith held her breath until she heard their footsteps fade down the hall.

She raised her head; the pistol still in her hand. Edith knew in her heart that would never happen to her again. She would kill her husband and at least one of his men before they got to her.

Slowly, Edith got up from the floor. She took two chairs in her room and secured them under the doorknobs to their connecting rooms. Making her way to the bed she crawled on top of the comforter. Safely tucking the pistol under one of the pillows, she wondered what she could do to keep him from harming her again.

Darkness was everywhere when she got up, except for the bright light from the moon shining into her room. She grabbed the pistol from under the pillow and moved one of the chairs blocking the connecting doors. She entered his room quietly, checking the table next to his bed and then smiled. His wine glass was empty. Edith had poured the sleeping potion into his wine decanter and was delighted to see that he had continued his nightly nip of wine before bedtime.

She walked to his bed, the pistol still clutched in her hand. It would be so easy; she thought. Then she shook her head as if to clear the thought from her mind.

Edith would make sure he would never harm her again. To her nightly suggestions that she repulsed him, she added that he was not to harm her in any way. Edith almost laughed as his face twisted as if he had tasted something bitter. She continued with the suggestions for quite a while until she felt herself becoming too sleepy to continue.

She went into her room, locked the connecting door, and put the chair back under the knob.

Quickly slipping out of her dress, she crawled into bed and fell sound asleep.

A knocking on her door in the early morning awakened her. It was Abbey calling to her. Abbey's words were faint and jumbled as Edith tried to get her bearings. She got up and pulled away the chair that barred entrance to her room. "Are you alone?" Edith asked hoarsely.

"Yes, yer ladyship," she responded.

Carefully, Edith opened the door a crack and peeked out. Abbey nodded to affirm it was just her. Edith opened the door just wide enough for Abbey to enter. As soon as Abbey entered the room Edith shut and locked the door.

"Yer ladyship," Abbey said softly. She looked over at the two chairs blocking the connecting doors. "That be a good idea," she said smiling. "'is lordship is very angry this morning. I think it was because of last night when ya emptied yer stomach on 'im." She stifled a small laugh. "The whole 'ouse is talking about it. Lord Symington told me to fetch ya to come down to 'is library."

"Abbey," Edith raised an eyebrow. "Tell his lordship that I am too ill to come down. Tell him that I am with child. His child."

Abbey gasped, backing away from Edith. "Ye wants *me* to tell 'im what?" Her face filled with shock. "Shouldn't ye be telling 'im that?"

"No," Edith smiled at the startled young girl. "It is not something I want to discuss with him ... ever. I have not been feeling well these last few mornings. Please bring me some chamomile tea and toasted bread. Now, run off and give that message to his lordship."

Abbey stood in place staring at Edith. "But,"

"No, buts," she patted her arm and led her to the door. "You will be fine. He will not harm you for giving him such news. And, hurry back with the tea and toast."

Several minutes later, Edith heard shouts coming from down the hall toward her room; it was the voice of Lord Symington. He pounded on her door, and ordered her to open it. She opened the door slowly, stepping back so that he could enter.

"How dare you have a servant girl tell me that you are with child?" He shouted in anger. "How far along are you with child?"

"How long have we been married?" She replied coldly.

His black eyes narrowed and studied her for a moment. "Leave us," he ordered his men. "But don't go too far." He waited until the door shut.

"Now, you filthy, little peasant," he snarled. "You will not leave this house until the child is born, except to see your father. And, I do not know why I am even letting you do that."

Edith made a great effort not to smile. Going to see her father was one of her nightly suggestions.

Lord Symington pointed his finger at her. "After the child is born, I could not care less where you go or what you do. However, rest assured you will have no hand in raising my child. I am thankful that you will never sleep in my bed again. You repulse me."

He glared hard at her for a moment. "I will give orders that you are not to be harmed in any way until after the child is born, and then…" A slow smile crossed his face. He bowed mockingly toward her. "You must eat and take care of yourself until my child is born."

Lord Symington started to leave her room, stopped, and looked her up and down in disgust. "It had better be a son, or you will pay dearly, and so will the child." He left the room, leaving her door open.

Edith fell back against the wall with relief that he believed it was his child. The only thing that worried her was if her child were a girl. She decided not to think about that until she talked to Mrs. Dawson.

Abbey stood at the door holding a tray with tea and toast. Edith smiled and motioned for her to come into the room. Edith was delighted that she would no longer have to go into his room and make the sickening suggestions of intimacy to him.

It had been a couple of months since Lord Symington learned of her pregnancy. He still refused to have her join him for any meals, and only nodded to her in passing. The only time he spoke to her was to inquire if she was having any problems. She always replied that everything was fine.

Edith cherished every day because it did not include Lord Symington in anything, and she saw her father every day, except for those days it rained and the dirt roads were impassable. Her father's health seemed to be improving and life at her husband's manor was somewhat bearable.

The sound of a carriage coming to the Manor early one morning caused Edith to look out her window. The footman opened the door, and a woman in a long black pelisse stepped out. She wore a large hat, with black, feathered plumes that ruffled in the wind. One of the stable boys coming to get the horses got too close to her, and the woman reached out and smacked him on the head. Edith was startled. Who was the woman? Why was she here?

Edith didn't have to wait long to get answers as Abbey came to her room. "'is lordship requests yer presence in the parlor."

"Thank you, Abbey," Edith said and walked down the long, winding staircase to the parlor.

She entered the room and saw the woman sitting on a chair in front of the fireplace. Lord Symington was handing her a glass of wine and smiling down at her. Edith studied the woman who had slapped the poor stable boy and knew already she was not going to like her.

The woman turned her face to Edith and gave a practiced smile. However, Edith could see the cold disdain in her black eyes. Black strands of curled hair fell out of her cap and moved gracefully around her beautiful, aging face.

"This is my cousin, Lady Daphne Collingsworth," he turned his back on Edith, picked up the poker and began playing with the logs in the fireplace. He put the poker back and sat down across from Daphne. He never offered Edith a chair. She stood there her back straight, and her chin lifted. She waited.

"How do you do, my dear?" The voice of Lady Daphne was soft and almost soothing. "When I learned of his marriage and your delicate condition, I offered my services. His Lordship," she smiled over at Lord Symington, "requested that I come immediately and help care for you."

"It appears, he has wasted your time," Edith responded coldly. "I have no need of your services."

"Now, now, my dear," she smiled. "I am here to help you. We can be friends, can't we? After all, we are relatives now."

"I have no need to be friends with any of his relatives or acquaintances," Edith said.

"She is staying, and she will be with you at all times," Lord Symington sipped a glass of wine, rolling the wine around in his blackened mouth before he spoke again. "If you prefer, I can have one of my men be with you all the time." He turned to Lady Daphne, "I told you how she was. Now you can see for yourself."

"She is with child," Lady Daphne purred. "That may explain her bad disposition."

"Marriage to him has given me a bad disposition," Edith retorted.

Lord Symington leaned forward in his chair; his fist tightened, and hatred poured from his eyes. "You will do as I say. I can still make your life miserable." He settled back into the chair and spoke matter-of-factly. "Lady Collingsworth will be staying in the room next to yours."

"Give her time, dear cousin," Daphne said gently. "She'll come to like me. Won't you, my dear?"

Edith did not reply. She walked out of the parlor and ordered her carriage to be brought around. Abbey hurried over to Edith with her cape, as Lady Daphne slowly walked to Edith.

"Capes are rather passé, are they not, my dear?" She purred. "I see you are ready to go for a ride. I have been riding for hours. I do not feel like doing so any further tonight. We shall go another day."

"I am not asking you to go with me, nor do I wish for your company," Edith purred back. "I am going to see my sick father."

"Oh, but my dear," her voice was not quite as sweet as before. "Your husband wishes me to accompany you everywhere. We cannot disobey his wishes. Such a rich and powerful man should not be trifled with. I should know as I am his only living heir. I meant relative."

Sarcasm dripped from Edith's lips. "Disobey his wishes, did you say?" Edith looked up at the gray sky above. "Well, I wouldn't want to disobey his wishes. It is a very cold day today, wouldn't you say?" Edith gave her the same phony smile back. "If you wish to join me that is up to you. However, you are not welcome in my father's house. You will have to sit in the carriage until I come out. And, I spend hours with my father." She made a grand gesture for Daphne to join them.

"I'll be here when you get back," she stepped closer to Edith and said in a quiet voice. "Do not presume to do this again. I am more dangerous than Lord Symington. You have no idea with whom you are dealing." She moved back from Edith and said loudly with a sweet smile and a warning look. "Have a pleasant stay with your father. I'll be waiting for you when you get back."

Edith's carriage pulled up to Brekmore Manor. The driver helped her climb down before he took the carriage to the barn. Inside of the barn was a small room with a divan and chair that Albert used to relax. A potbellied stove kept the room warm in the winter months. The driver knew the way, as he always stayed there when he brought Edith to Brekmore Manor.

Mrs. Dawson greeted Edith at the door. Edith briefly told her that a cousin of Lord Symington was brought in to watch her.

After Edith had finished her visit with her father, she went down to the kitchen to join Mrs. Dawson and Albert.

"Mrs. Dawson told me about this new problem," Albert shook his head slowly.

"Fill me in on the details," Mrs. Dawson set a cup of hot tea in front of Edith and sat down in a chair next to her.

When Edith finished Mrs. Dawson gave an audible sigh. "This is not good. I don't trust that miserable old man, or any of his kin."

"She let it slip that she is his only living heir," Edith sipped the hot tea. "When she talks, she almost sounds like she is purring. I keep waiting for her to cough up a hair ball."

"His only heir? Except for your child, that is. This is even worse than I thought," Mrs. Dawson got up and began to pace back and forth in the kitchen. "She may have other plans than to watch over you, especially since she is blood kin to that foul man."

"But she is not a male heir. How can she think to get his money?" Edith asked.

"She probably figured all of that out before she got here. You have to be very careful around this woman."

"I will be extra careful," Edith said sadly. "I have this little one to think about. That madman I am married to said if it was a girl, we would both pay the price."

"Not as long as I draw a breath will that man harm you," Albert said angrily.

"'Tis a hard thing to try to protect you from here," Mrs. Dawson said. "I can't leave your father to be with you."

"Oh, my, goodness," Edith said watching her pace the floor. "I would not think of it. He needs you here. I am well and fit. I can take care of myself."

"Not against the likes of them," Albert almost shouted. "They are an evil breed that pair. Evil breed."

"I will try to be very careful and watch for any signs of trouble," Edith put her cup down and stood up. "I must be getting back. It is getting late, and I don't like traveling in the dark of night."

"Keep the doors to your room locked at all times," Mrs. Dawson stopped pacing and rushed to hug Edith. "Please watch out for him and this new one."

"I will," she hugged her tightly.

Mrs. Dawson clung to Edith. "Don't eat or drink anything that woman gives you. You have that young girl Abbey there. Only take your meals from her."

"Yes," Edith gave one last squeeze and released her. "That is good advice. However, I wonder how much I can trust Abbey."

"I know Abbey. She is a good girl," Mrs. Dawson said.

"Oh," Edith pulled out a pouch tucked in a hidden pocket of her cape. "Here is all I could grab last night. I thought for a moment he was going to wake up."

"My goodness, child," Mrs. Dawson laughed. "You have quite a bit of money and jewels stashed away right now. If you needed to get away I think it might be enough."

Edith shook her head. "I will need enough money to get all of us away from him, not just me. Don't forget we have to disappear completely. It would please him to have me thrown in jail for leaving my husband. It is the law."

Mrs. Dawson changed the subject. "Before you ask," Mrs. Dawson touched her arm. "We have not heard a word from Mr. Atterby."

"I was hoping you had heard something," Edith lowered her head. "I just want him to be safe."

"He is a big man," Albert said. "He can take care of himself. Don't worry about him right now. Worry about yourself."

"That's why I love Albert," Mrs. Dawson said. "He is so smart and right."

Edith's ride back to the Manor was cold and uneventful. She was relieved that no one was in the parlor, or any sign of Lady Collingsworth. Edith raced up to her room and opened the door. The candles were already lit as they always were by the staff.

Something moved in the dark shadows by the window seat. Edith jumped at the sight of Lady Collingsworth sitting in a chair by her window. "What are you doing in my room?" Edith bared her teeth in anger. "Get out!"

"Did you have a nice visit?" Lady Collingsworth did not move. "I was worrying about you on the ride home, the roads being dark and all."

"I asked you to get out," Edith's voice deepened. "Now, get out."

Slowly, Lady Collingsworth got up. She stood looking at Edith, all the while her fan tapped against the palm of her hand. "I shall come and go wherever I want. I have permission from my cousin to do so."

"He may have given you permission to come and go wherever you want, but I have not," she stepped closer to Lady Collingsworth. "You said you were more dangerous than Lord Symington, and that I have no idea with whom I am dealing." Edith stepped even closer. "Trust me when I say, it is you who have no idea with whom you are dealing. I am not a frightened child, or a weak woman. I can only suppose those were your victims. Now, I will not say this again. Get out of my room, and do not ever, and I do mean ever, step foot in this room again."

"You have not heard the last on this," she purposely bumped into Edith as she brushed past her. "We shall see who the victim is, shan't we." She slammed the door behind her as she flounced out.

Edith could see that Lady Collingsworth had examined everything in her room. Her heart sank when she did not see her valise. If someone were to discover the hidden bottom - she shuddered at the thought. She looked everywhere in the room for her valise and was becoming frantic.

There was a soft rap at the door, and then it swung open and Abbey rushed in closing the door behind her. She listened with her ear against the door and gave a deep sigh. "Excuse me, yer ladyship for bursting in like this," her voice was barely above a whisper. "But I took this before the awful woman came into yer room." She held up Edith's valise. "I 'eard Lady Collingsworth tell 'is lordship that she was going to search yer room. So, I raced up 'ere and threw some of your private things in it and raced out the door. I jest got to the servants entrance when she opened yer door and walked in. I 'ope I was doing the right thing, yer ladyship."

Edith rushed to her and threw her arms around her. "Abbey," she cried speaking in whispers. "You are wonderful. Of course, you did the right thing." Edith took hold of Abbey's hands that were still holding her valise, "but you could have gotten into a great deal of trouble doing that. I shudder to think of it."

"I would 'ave thought of something," Abbey whispered back as she walked to the vanity table and put the valise on it. "She is one mean woman. She backhanded me because I accidentally spilt some tea on the carpet. Be careful of 'er milady."

"Abbey, if she is aware that you like me, it could mean trouble for you. That has me worried. Please stay away from her."

Abbey laughed, "She already said I was to stay away from 'er. That I was a clumsy idiot." She laughed again softly. "I spilt the tea on purpose. I saw 'er 'it the stable boy, and I 'eard what she said to you, about being dangerous and all. So, I made sure she would not want me around 'er. I do not like 'er very much."

Edith laughed, "That makes two of us. She is not a very nice person."

"You 'ave always been kind to me. The other servants think you are a very kind lady, too. When you walked by our quarters and saw that we 'ad no coal or peat to put in our 'earths, and no warm blankets, you raided 'is lordship's cupboards and 'ad each of us take a blanket and some of the peat for our rooms at night. No one 'as ever cared about us - ever."

"Well, he will never miss any of those blankets, and I shall buy some to replace them, just in case he decides to look through the cupboards, which I doubt very much. And, Abbey just so you know; you are an easy person to like," Edith hurried to her door, opened it and peered out. She motioned for Abbey. "Go now, the halls are empty. And, please, please be careful."

"Yes, ma'am," she curtsied, peered outside for a moment, raced out the door and disappeared down to the servants' quarters.

Edith locked the door behind her and rushed to her valise. She trembled as she opened it. She pulled the items out and opened the bottom part. Everything was still there. Edith sighed with relief.

Edith pushed a chair in front of the door to her room. She wanted no more surprise visits from Lady Collingsworth. Edith got into her dressing gown, blew out the candles, put the pistol under her pillow, and tried to sleep. But sleep wasn't coming easy; she tossed and turned, until finally, she gratefully succumbed to the peace of sleep.

In the room next to her sat Lady Collingsworth. Her fingers tapped on her vanity stand as she sat in deep thought. "I am the only one entitled to the great fortune of this odious man," she fumed. After a moment, a smile crossed her painted lips, "You don't look like you have long for this world and are in much pain, my dear, cousin. What are families for but to help." A sly smile crossed her face. "I will help put you out of your pain, sooner than later. In the meantime, I will get rid of that child-bearing woman and the unborn child, and then I will be your only living heir." She got up and crawled beneath the warm quilt. "I have plans for you, dear Edith," she purred. "Let us see which of us is the deadliest."

Chapter 10

My Dearest Rachel,

The captain's two aunts sound wonderfully charming, my dear, but you must not let them wear you down too much. I do so look forward to meeting them someday, so that I may thank them in person for taking such good care of you.

Captain English sounds like a very kind and thoughtful man. You and Phillip are lucky to have him as a friend. You are so young. I am glad you are meeting other people, and going out and enjoying yourself. You helped one of the girls get a new dress for a soiree? I wish I could have been there. It sounded like such fun.

My life is also full of surprises. I came home one cold evening from visiting father, and my husband, always thinking about me,

had a warm fire going. He made sure it was kept warm with the fireplace poker. I have to be careful, with the cold and all, so I am taking all the precautions I can to make sure that my child, and I are safe – so do not fret.

There are a few changes in my life, one of which is I have a new houseguest. I had no idea that my husband had a cousin, a Lady Collingsworth. She is much older, probably in her late thirty's or early forties. Her attire is quite becoming on her. She came to help take care of me while I am with child. Although, I really do not need any help, as I am quite capable of doing for myself. However, I am sure my husband was concerned about the baby. Write soon, my love always, Edith

It had been a couple of weeks since Rachel stepped foot on Boston's dock and met Captain English's two aunts. They were more than wonderful to her, and kept her going for the last two weeks on sightseeing trips, afternoon socials, and other soirees. She was grateful that the seasickness she had experienced every morning for the last couple of months finally disappeared.

One day, two friends of Captain English showed up at their house. The captain had sent a letter requesting his aunts to let the two brothers stay at their house for a few days, as their house had just burned down.

Charles and Damian, two very burly men, were quickly accepted into the house by the aunts. Charles had light brown hair and green eyes and was the bigger of the two men. Damian's had dark-brown eyes and dark-brown hair that hung to his massive shoulders. The two men refused the guest accommodations upstairs, instead opted to share a room off the servants' quarters. The men slept at different times, when one was sleeping, the other was up. Rachel thought their behavior a little strange, but shrugged it off as an American quirk.

Rachel and the aunts were sipping tea in the parlor after a morning of sightseeing when the door opened, and Captain English came in.

"Well, my lovelies," he took off his hat and made a grand gesture of bowing to the three of them. "I have a message that you wanted to see me. I hope everything is alright?" He barely looked at Rachel.

"Of course, we wanted to see you," Libbie said pouting slightly. "We have not laid eyes on you for over a week."

"Two weeks," Clara corrected her. "Why are you ignoring us?"

"Yes," Libbie said. "You usually come and see us at least a couple of times a week when you are in port."

"I am afraid I have had much to do. There have been a few mishaps with my ships. Plus, I am preparing for my departure," he smiled weakly.

"Oh, are you leaving soon?" Rachel asked.

"I am replacing a captain who became ill," he nodded politely to her, but did not look her in the eyes. "My ship leaves in a couple of days."

"How long will you be gone?" Rachel asked.

"It is a short run down to the Carolina's," he said glancing at her for a moment. "I will be gone the better part of a month." He turned his attention back to his aunts. "So, what have you darlings been up to?"

"We have taken Rachel all over the city," Libbie said cheerfully. "And either Charles or Damian is always anxious to go with us. It is nice to have them around."

Clara looked over at Rachel. "She is not getting sick in the mornings anymore so we leave right after breakfast, and sometimes we are gone the whole day."

"You were getting sick in the mornings?" His eyes met hers for the first time since his arrival.

"I think it was something left over from the sea voyage," she smiled. "I am not very seaworthy. I would never have been a good sailor."

"How long did you have this morning illness?" His voice filled with concern.

"Let me see," Rachel thought a moment, and then said. "It was probably half way through our trip on board your ship. But just last week the sickness stopped."

"Are you tired a lot?" He asked.

"Yes, she is tired all the time," Clara interjected. "Sometimes she will fall asleep right next to us in the carriage."

"You two lovely creatures must stop tiring out Lady Rachel. I came by to make sure that you are doing well, and to say I miss you, too. If you will excuse me, I really have quite a lot to do." He bowed again, put on his hat and left, stopping only to chat briefly with Charles.

"My, that was abrupt," Clara said blinking her eyes several times.

"He has never done that before," Libbie pondered, and said. "It is probably his sailing to the Carolina's with the frequent storms that come along during this season.

The next couple of days were more relaxing for Rachel, and she relished just being around the house.

They were sitting near the fireplace crocheting when there was a knock at the front door. Libbie looked up at Clara. "That is unusual. Did someone leave a calling card?"

Tiffy went to the front door. Moments later, she came into the parlor. "It is Doctor Whittleson. He has a card for you, Miss Clara."

Clara opened the card, read it, and passed it to Libbie. "Show him in, Tiffy." Clara motioned for her to go back and let the doctor in.

A short, pudgy man with large, gray eyes entered the room. He took his hat off and bowed slightly showing a shock of white hair tied neatly behind his neck. "You read the card?" He asked rather arrogantly.

"Yes," she pointed to Rachel. "This is the person you are to examine."

Rachel was so startled she dropped her crochet needle. "Whatever for?"

"Captain English has asked me to make a call and see to your well-being." He moved to Rachel and looked into her eyes.

"I am fine, now," she replied still aghast.

"Even so," he looked at the two aunts for help. "I have my orders."

"Tiffy, go with the doctor and Rachel to her room, and wait in there until he is done examining her," Clara spoke very firmly.

"I am just a little tired. That is all," Rachel protested.

"Come, come dear," Libbie stood up and reached her hand down to Rachel. "Humor us two old ladies, will you?"

Rachel got up and reluctantly went up to her room, followed by Tiffy and the doctor.

After his examination, he just nodded.

"What are you nodding about?" Rachel asked trying to hide her annoyance.

"You are with child," he said nonchalantly.

Rachel was speechless. She just stared at him with a mouth that opened and closed soundlessly.

He leaned over and patted her shoulder gently. "I would say you are at least four or five months along." He turned, put his hat on, picked up his bag, and walked out of her bedchambers. She could hear the gleeful squealing coming from the two aunts downstairs.

"Is there anything I can do for you, ma'am?" Tiffy curtsied, and waited.

Rachel couldn't speak. She was with child. That is what the doctor just said. She was carrying Phillip's baby. Her heart soared. Phillip. She needed him now more than ever.

The door burst open and the two aunts raced in. "This is marvelous, wonderful." Clara was almost jumping up and down.

"We have to go shopping for baby things," Libbie was clapping her hands and walking around Rachel's room. "You will need clothes, and baby clothes. This is going to be so much fun."

"I still cannot believe it," Rachel sat on the side of her bed stunned. "I should be so happy, but suddenly I am afraid."

"There is nothing to be afraid of dear Rachel," Libbie sat on one side of her and put an arm around her. "We will be here with you the whole time."

Clara sat on the other side of Rachel and took her hand. "You will be fine. We will not let anything happen to you, and neither will Nathan."

"I have to write and tell Phillip," Rachel started to get off the bed.

Libbie pulled her gently back, "Would that not be better done in person? He is away doing his military thing, and it may cause him more worry."

"You are right," Rachel sighed. The thought of carrying his child was making her happier than she could imagine. "It would only add to his worry right now. He should be coming here soon to get me."

"In the meantime, we have a lot of things we have to do," Clara got up and grabbed Rachel's hand. "I believe a well-cooked meal is in order here."

"Why does that not surprise me?" Libbie said.

They went downstairs, each aunt holding one of Rachel's arms. After an early dinner, Rachel excused herself and retired to her room. She lay down on top of the gold quilt and looked up at the lace canopy overhead. Her hand ran over her stomach. She had thought her stomach looked as if it were getting bigger. And, at times, she thought she felt something move within her, but with all the strange food on the ship and at Nathan's aunts, she thought nothing of it. Rachel pulled the gold quilt around her and promptly fell asleep.

For the next few weeks, Rachel's days were filled with shopping, planning, and extreme pampering from the aunts. The aunts purchased baby furniture, along with bedding, baby clothes, toys and anything else Clara and Libbie thought the baby would need. They refused to let Rachel pay for anything, for which she was very grateful.

During these weeks, she had received only one letter from Phillip and was ecstatic when it came. She ripped it open and was disappointed at the brevity of the letter.

Dear Rachel, I know you want to write, but it would be best if you waited until you heard from me again. I have been reassigned, and we are marching to Fort Henry. I fear your letters will have no way to reach me at present. It will be a while before I can send for you. Wait for me to write again, I will write as soon as we get settled at the Fort. Your husband, Phillip

Rachel cried at the fact it would be a while before they could be together, and then the baby kicked her and caused her to laugh. She ran to Clara and Libbie and had them feel the baby as it moved. Rachel had come to love them as her own, and wished they really were her aunts. Tiffy, Bimms, and Seth had become her friends, and she cherished them just as much. As for Charles and Damian, they had been gone for a couple of days leaving the house as abruptly as they had come.

Rachel sat in the parlor crocheting a baby blanket as the wind howled around the house, slamming the rain into the windows. She looked out the window at the tall figure of a man in a hat and cape coming up to the front door. She recognized the walk instantly; it was Captain English.

"It's Nathan," she hollered.

The three of them raced to the door and threw it open. Libbie grabbed him and yanked him into the foyer. He dropped his duffel bag as Clara and Libbie hugged him.

Seth came around the corner, calmly taking his hat and coat, giving Nathan a wide grin.

"Good to see you, Seth," he looked down at his two aunts, and at a very pregnant Rachel. "It is doubly good to see you two, and you as well, Rachel."

Clara and Libbie grabbed his arm and led him into the parlor. "Tell us about your trip. You have been gone so long."

"There isn't much to tell," he smiled coyly. "But I have something for you. Seth, I have been waylaid by these pirates, could you please bring my duffle bag to me."

Seth laughed, picked up the duffle bag, and brought it to him.

Nathan reached in and pulled out a couple of wrapped gifts for Libbie and Clara, and a larger one for Rachel.

"What is this?" Rachel asked flabbergasted.

"I'll bet if you pulled off the wrapping paper, you would find out," his eyes traveled all over her, as if he were seeing her for the first time.

Clara and Libbie sat in their chairs near Nathan. They were excited about their pearl and diamond broaches, pinning them on immediately.

Rachel opened the present to find a very soft, stuffed animal for the baby. Her eyes almost brimmed with tears as she held it close to her. "Thank you. It is most thoughtful of you."

"How are you feeling these days?" He asked, looking at her swollen belly.

"Very large, thank you for asking," Rachel laughed.

"May I ask when the child is due?"

"In a month or two," Libbie said excitedly.

"Is your husband on his way here?" Nathan asked.

"No," Clara spoke up before Rachel could answer. "He wrote a note saying it was going to be a while. Although, it made Rachel sad, it made us very happy."

"He wrote something about going to a fort near Lake Ontario," Rachel held out the little stuffed squirrel and laughed. "It really is darling."

Nathan's brows furrowed, and his jaw tightened. He looked down at his adoring aunts and changed the subject. "Well, I have come a long way, and I am very hungry. Is Bimms food still as good as ever?"

From the kitchen, Bimms voice boomed out, "You bet it is."

Nathan became a steady visitor over the next few weeks. He would stay until it was time for everyone to turn in for the night. Sometimes, he and Rachel would be the only ones up, and they would talk, play cards, and laugh into the wee hours of the morning. On those occasions, he stayed in a room next to Seth, in the servant's quarters.

The doctor came once a week, although he didn't think, it was necessary. After all women have been having babies for thousands of years, he would huff. The fact that he was paid handsomely made him a regular visitor every Monday.

On Tuesday, Libbie and Clara had to go to an afternoon soiree for one of their neighbors. Nathan had some business to attend to in town, and Seth was gone on an errand.

Rachel decided she wanted to stay in for the day. She sat comfortably by the fireplace to do her crocheting. She rested her feet on a small foot stool, when suddenly a gush of water poured out of her. Terrified she screamed for Tiffy. Rachel stood up too fast, causing her to be dizzy and fell to the floor.

Bimms and Tiffy ran into the parlor to find her on the floor. "Go get the captain!" Bimms ordered Tiffy. "He be in town at his office. Hurry, girl." She began fanning Rachel's face with her apron skirt. "You be all right. Tiffy's going to find the captain."

Tiffy grabbed her coat and opened the front door to find Nathan standing there. "I forgot. The meeting is for tomorrow." He stopped and looked at the panic-stricken look on Tiffy's face. "What's wrong? What happened?"

"Here, Captain. It be Lady Rachel." Bimms called out to him.

Nathan tore past Tiffy and raced to Rachel's side. "Are you all right?"

Just then a pain seized Rachel, and she grabbed her stomach and moaned.

He reached down and gently picked her up. He felt the wetness on her gown. "Get the doctor." He ordered Tiffy. "Bimms come with me." He carried Rachel up to her room. She put her arms around his neck and held him tightly. Rachel let out another moan, only louder this time, squeezing his neck even harder.

"Bimms get her a dry nightgown." He held Rachel until Bimms brought one of her linen nightgowns. "Can you stand up, Rachel?"

She nodded, grimacing again at the pain.

"Bimms, I will hold her up, but I'll look away. Can you manage?"

"Yes, sir," Bimms said confidently. Quickly, the wet dress and undergarments were taken off, and a dry shift put on. "It be okay now Captain." She rushed to pull back the covers.

"Get me some cloths and cool water, Bimms."

He picked Rachel up again and gently put her in bed, and turned to leave. Rachel grabbed his hand firmly. "No, do not go. Do not leave me.

Please," she began to shake as another wave of pain struck her.

"I won't leave you Rachel," he patted her hand to try to comfort her.

Bimms brought in the bowl with cool water and some cloths. "I will go down and get that old man doctor up here fast, if I have to kick him in the seat of his pants to do it."

Rachel's face contorted as her pain increased.

"It is okay to scream, Rachel." He dipped the cloth in the water and wiped her sweated brow.

Rachel screamed in earnest, as the pain intensified. Her fingers dug into his hands, but he never flinched. Soon, the sound of people running up the stairs could be heard. Seth burst through her door followed by Clara and Libbie. "I took the carriage to fetch Miss Clara and Miss Libbie and when we came in the house we heard her screaming." Seth said looking from Rachel to Nathanial.

"We did not know what was going on," Libbie grabbed her chest and leaned against the wall.

"Seth was going to tear somebody apart," Clara patted her chest trying to get it back to normal.

"If you need me for anything, I be downstairs," Seth knew what was happening, and quickly left the room.

Rachel's pains were coming faster now, and her screams filled the room. In between the pain, she pleaded with them to help her get the baby out. Nathan kept trying to calm her telling her that the baby would come when it was ready. That everything was fine.

The doctor came into the room, and saw Nathan sitting by her bed. "You can go now. I will take it from here."

"No," Rachel screamed. "No, I don't want him to leave me."

"I will be right outside the door," He wiped her forehead one more time, leaned down toward her face as if he were about to kiss her, and stopped. He pulled himself up straight, squeezed her hand and left.

Hours passed as Rachel lay screaming in labor. Then, there was silence. Nathan jumped up from the chair he had placed outside her door. His heart almost stopped. There was no sound at all, until he heard the baby cry. After a few moments the door opened, Clara came out crying.

"Dear God, no!" He said in anguish.

"No, no, she is alright," Clara hugged him to her. "Both are doing fine. I am just so happy. It is a boy, and both are fine." She looked tired and haggard as she released him. "I am going down to get something to eat. Can I get you something?"

He shook his head and sank back down in his chair. His hands covered his face as he wept silently. A few minutes later, the door opened and the doctor came out. "That was not so bad now, was it?"

"For us, no," Nathan said. "Although, hearing her in pain was not very enjoyable."

"That is a woman's plight. It is their duty. What else are they really good for but to bear our children and raise them? We men have our own pains to bear. I will come back tomorrow and check on her and the baby." He walked down the stairs and out the front door.

Bimms opened the door and motioned for Nathan to come in. He stood in the doorway for a long time looking at Rachel holding the baby.

Rachel looked up and spotted Nathan in the doorway. She broke into a huge grin.

"Nathan," she motioned for him to come to the bed. "Look at him. Is he not the most beautiful thing you have ever seen?" She held her swaddled son out for him to hold.

He took the child from her very carefully, with Libbie and Bimms watching him nervously. "He is very beautiful, just like his mother."

"Oh, my word," Rachel laughed weakly. "I must look like an upside-down bird's nest."

"No," Nathan said tenderly. "You are quite beautiful." He quickly changed the subject. "Have you thought of a name for him?"

"Actually, Phillip and I never discussed having children." She became pensive. "I really don't think he wanted any, well, not just now. I will think on a name when I am a little less tired."

Nathan handed the baby back to her. "I will be staying here for the next couple of days, in case I am needed."

Rachel looked at the wonderful man standing by her bed, "you will always be needed, dear Nathan."

He bowed his head, and quickly left her room.

"Now, my dear," Libbie said softly. "You have had a very hard day. Let us take the baby, and you get some rest. There are plenty of us here to help with the baby, and we will all take turns, so we can get some rest, too."

It didn't take Rachel long to regain her strength. Nathan came to her room every day and even took care of the baby.

"Nathan," Rachel put down the piece of toast she was having for breakfast and looked at Nathan walking the baby. "I have decided what I am going to call my son."

"It is about time," he laughed. "I have been calling him 'hey you' for a couple of days."

"I think I should name him after his father," she said.

"That is generally what is done," he looked up at her and smiled. "Phillip is a good name, for a good man."

"Yes, I agree," she crossed her arms and looked at her son cradled in his arms. "His full name will be Phillip Nathaniel Prescott."

"Nathaniel? Is Nathaniel your father's given name?"

"I know of no other Nathaniel, but you." She smiled broadly. "I could think of no better name than yours, save my husband's of course."

"I am honored," he looked down into the baby's face and repeated his name to him.

Every day made Rachel stronger. Although, no one in the household would let Rachel do a thing. Nathan hired a wet nurse to help in the feedings, so that Rachel could get some sleep, and everyone took their turn changing and watching the baby.

Three months went by before Rachel received a letter from Phillip.

"Oh, how wonderful," Libbie said. "Read what parts you can to us," she giggled with Clara.

Dear Rachel, I think it is time for you to come to Fort Henry. We have not corresponded in a long time, and we have so much to talk about. I have made arrangements for you to meet up with a wagon train that will bring you here. You will take a stagecoach to Albany and meet up with the wagons there. I have enclosed a map as to their locations. Please get here as quickly as you can, Phillip

"Fort Henry?" Nathan got up from his chair and began pacing. "Is he not right in the mind? That is an uninhabited, wild country. There are reports of renegade Indians, and marauders. There are no decent roads, no decent anything, just plain wilderness. It will take you days to reach him, and the October days are coming to a close."

"My dear," Libbie began to cry. "Can you not just stay with us? It sounds like a dreadful place."

"It is," Nathan snapped.

"We do not want to lose you," Clara tried to find a handkerchief to wipe her weeping eyes.

"He is my husband," Rachel said. "I must join him."

"You have a wee baby, and you are not that strong. You cannot be serious about going." Nathan ran his fingers through his hair.

"I must," Rachel was close to tears. "It is my duty."

"I tell you it is not a fit place for a woman, let alone a tiny baby. How will you take care of yourself and him? The weather is cold this time of the year and the snows are deep in that area." Nathan's fists clenched, as he spoke softly to himself. "What husband would send his wife out into that wilderness?"

"My dear," Libbie said, finally pulling herself together. "Might I suggest something?"

"Of course," the tears were now flowing freely down Rachel's face.

"Please do not be offended by what I suggest, but I thought, well, maybe it would be better for Phillip Nathaniel to stay with us. I mean just until the weather breaks." Libbie waited anxiously for Rachel's reply.

"How could I leave him?" She began wringing her hands. "But I do not want to risk his life."

Nathan quickly knelt by her chair, "If we cannot talk sense into you for going to that God-forsaken piece of wilderness, then do the right thing for your son. I am telling you, as sure as I kneel here before you, he would not last the journey." He jumped to his feet and began to pace the floor. "Does your husband not know the dangers he is sending you into?"

Rachel looked at her son, sleeping soundly in the cradle next to her chair. "I am sure it has become less wild over the years. Phillip would not send me into danger."

"Your husband is very young," Nathan said, trying to keep his anger down. "He has marched through territories accompanied by a regiment of soldiers. I am sure they would not be easy targets for the Indians or marauders. Listen to me, Rachel. It is a very dangerous, uncivilized world up there."

"You have told me so, and I have heard you," Rachel said stoically. "I must go. That is the duty of a wife of a military officer. Phillip told me that many, many times." She looked down lovingly at her son. "It would only be until the weather breaks, and then I will come for him."

"We will take very good care of him," Clara said. "I promise."

"If I did not think he was in the best hands in the entire world; I would not leave him." Her lips quivered as she tried to speak bravely. She pulled a handkerchief from her pocket and dabbed at her eyes. "I must be brave. I am his wife, and I am doing the right thing, am I not?"

"Do not put that question before me," Nathan said firmly. "You would not welcome my reply." He walked out of the room and down the hall into the library.

Rachel followed him. "Do not be angry with me, Nathan. I could not bear it. You are my best friend."

Nathan turned around and looked at her. The light from the hallway cast a halo-like glow behind her head. "I am not angry with *you*. However, I am frightened for you."

She walked to him and studied his face. Rachel came to find his face so comforting to look at and his voice a joy to hear. She reached out and touched his arm, "I will be all right. I can take care of myself."

He took her in his arms and held her tightly. She wrapped her arms around him and snuggled into his shirt.

"Oh, God, why do I not want you to let me go?" She turned her face up to his. Her lips parted in a deep sigh.

"Rachel," his voice was husky. He looked down into her beautiful, innocent face, gave her a quick hug, and pulled away. "I . . . I believe I hear Phillip Nathaniel crying." He took her arm, and they walked out of the room.

The day finally came when Rachel was to leave. She cried so hard at leaving her son, Clara, Libbie and the others that she could barely talk. Nathan ushered her into the carriage and rode with her into town, where she was to take a stagecoach to Albany.

Nathan helped Rachel down from the carriage, and walked her toward a stagecoach and a large carriage being fitted up for travel. Rachel's eyes widened at the sight of the stagecoach, but she did not falter as she walked to it.

It was nothing more than a large wooden box on top of a freight wagon. She watched as several people climbed into the conveyance.

Rachel sighed, and spoke to Nathan. "Well, I believe this is my coach. I cannot thank you enough for all you have done for me and my son. I shall dearly miss him, Aunt Clara and Aunt Libbie, as well as the others." She reached over and touched his arm. "I shall miss you sorely, my dear friend. My captain."

Something was happening to her insides. Her heart was breaking at the thought of never seeing him again, never talking or laughing with him into the wee hours of the morning. Tears began to form in her eyes. She had an urge to reach out and grab hold of him and never let him go. Instead, she turned to climb up into the stage-coach.

"I believe you are getting into the wrong conveyance. He took her arm and led her to a carriage just behind the stagecoach. It had soft padded cushion seats and large windows to look out at the scenery. There were leather curtains that attached tightly when closed to keep the rain and dust out of the carriage.

Charles and Damian appeared from a building and walked toward them.

"Charles! Damian! It is wonderful to see you again," Rachel said as she smiled and waved at them.

They smiled and waved back at her.

"I have taken the liberty of securing you a carriage for your ride to Albany. Unfortunately, I am not able to assist you from there. I have hired Charles and Damian to drive you there. I believe you will find this a much more comfortable mode of travel."

"I do not know what to say," she said as she wiped away a tear running down her cheek.

"Thank you will do." He tipped his hat, and solemnly looked at her. "They will follow behind the stagecoach and make the same stops along the way."

Rachel rose up on her tiptoes, and kissed him on the cheek. He grabbed her for a moment, holding her against him, and then slowly released her. He smiled at her. But when he turned his head, she could not see the pain etched across his face. Solemnly, he helped her into the carriage. "You can still change your mind and stay." His voice was breaking.

The sound of the stagecoach pulling away drowned out their last few words.

"If, I could but stay," she said crying. "If I could only tell you …" She stopped and brought a handkerchief to her eyes and runny nose.

Charles and Damian climbed into the driver's seat, and with a nod from Nathan followed the stagecoach at a discreet and less dusty distance.

Rachel peered back at Nathan as the carriage pulled away until she could no longer see him. The image of his face would be forever etched in her mind. "Good-bye, my Captain, good-bye."

Chapter 11

My Dearest Edith,

You were surprised that Ian would have a warm fire for you when you returned home. Of course, he would. He has always been thoughtful and kind. I hope that you and Lady Collingsworth enjoy each other's company. If she offers to help you, let her, what harm can she do?

Are you ready for what I am about to tell you? I have a son. I cannot believe that you, and I were with child at the same time. Is that not amazing? You must have had your child by now, was it a boy or girl?

Edith, did you know when you were with child? I did not. Captain English was worried about my having morning sickness for a couple of months, and sent a doctor. When

the doctor told me, I was with child, I was shocked to say the least.

Captain English and his aunts have been nothing but kind to me and my son. I hope that you and Lady Collingsworth are becoming good friends.

I got a letter from Phillip. He does not know he has a son yet. I can hardly wait to tell him, as I will be joining him soon. I can see him now prancing about the room with pride and joy.

Well, my love, I will write soon, please write, with all my love, Rachel

In the morning, there was a soft rap at Edith's door. Thinking it is Abbey; Edith crawled out of bed, moved the chair, and opened the door. She was startled to see Lady Collingsworth standing there holding a breakfast tray. "I am afraid we got off to a rather bad start. I thought you would enjoy some marmalade on your toast for breakfast. Here," she tried to pass Edith and enter the room, but Edith didn't budge. "I just want to put it on the table by the window over there."

"Thank you," Edith smiled insincerely and said sweetly, "but I can manage on my own. It was very troublesome for you, and I don't want to trouble you any further." She reached out and took the tray out of her hands.

Lady Daphne stood there for a while, gave a half smile, turned and walked away. Edith watched until she disappeared around the corner of the hall. She closed her door and took the tray to the small table by the window.

"I wonder what part of the breakfast she poisoned." Edith placed her hand to her chin and stared down at the tea, bread, and marmalade. "Probably all of it." She picked up the marmalade and smelled it. It had a strange smell of almonds. She put it back on the tray. After a moment, she picked up the tray, took it to her private commode, and dumped the contents.

The water in the commode began to turn a strange color. Edith dropped the tray and stepped back in horror. She was jesting about Daphne trying to poison her; she just didn't want to eat anything the woman brought her.

Stunned, she went back to her room and grabbed the edge of the table. How was she going to fight this woman? What other ways was she going to try to kill her? What was in her food that would make the water change color? Fear began to grab at Edith's heart. What would that have done to my child?

There was another rap on her door, Edith jumped. "Who is it?" She asked trying to sound strong.

"'Tis me, yer ladyship, Abbey."

Edith ran to the door and was relieved to see Abbey standing there with another tray. "Come in, quickly."

Abbey came in, and Edith slammed the door shut behind her. "Yer ladyship, what's 'appened? Yer as white as a corpse."

"I think Lady Collingsworth just tried to poison me," Edith sat down at her vanity and looked up at Abbey with concern. "She brought me my breakfast this morning saying she wanted to start over. That we got off to a bad start. I didn't want anything from her, so I took everything she brought me and dumped it in my commode." Her eyes widened as she looked at Abbey. "Something made the water change color."

"Hmmm," Abbey put her tray on the vanity next to Edith. "One of the girls told me that Lady Collingsworth always orders two trays for 'er morning meal. She must be doing something to one of the trays, because only one tray of food is ever eaten, and the food from the other tray is found in 'er wastebasket. Oh, she is a sneaky one for sure."

"That would be a very true statement," Edith shook her head and looked at the food on Abbey's tray. "This looks exactly like the items she brought me. I am so hungry. Thank you, dear Abbey."

"That is the cook's marmalade, and it is very good. Don'tcha go trusting that evil woman. This food is good for you to eat, and safe." Abbey went into Edith's commode and picked up the broken items and the tray. She curtsied and left the room mumbling about the evil doings in the house.

Edith finished her breakfast and dressed in her morning gown. Lord Symington had all of her handmade clothes thrown out and replaced with dresses from France. He could not stand the sight of her "peasant clothes" as he called them. She hated wearing these clothes, but the surprise visit of his cousin almost made wearing the extravagant gowns bearable.

She chose an elegant, high-necked dress trimmed in lace, with long sleeves. The empire dress had simple Egyptian-themed embroidery in black and gold, running across the bust and hem of the dress. The train flowed magnificently behind her, trimmed in the same Egyptian theme. She donned her pearl necklace and earrings, and put on her morning cap trimmed in lace, which matched the lilac color in her muslin dress. She slipped into thin, silk shoes of black and gold.

Before she left her room, she walked to the full-length mirror near the armoire and smiled at her reflection. She grabbed a black shawl and fan, and opened her bedroom door to see Lady Collingsworth standing there.

"I was just getting ready to call upon you," she stopped and stared at Edith's attire. It was evident by the envious sweep of her eyes that she admired Edith's morning gown.

"What a lovely morning dress, my dear," her voice was soothing, but her eyes betrayed the envy seething inside of her. Her own empire gown was of a deep blue with several rows of beige lace trim on the bust and hem. Her blue cap trimmed in the same lace as was on her dress. However, it was not even close to the exquisite gown worn by Edith.

Regaining her composure, she peered around Edith and saw the empty tray on her vanity. A smile slid across her face. "Did you enjoy your breakfast this morning?" She asked coyly. "How are you feeling?"

"Actually," Edith smiled broadly. "I feel absolutely wonderful, and the breakfast was quite good. Thank you."

"You are quite welcome," her voice faltered for a moment and then resumed its phony purr. "Are you visiting your father on this cold day?" She asked demurely.

"No," Edith turned and began walking toward the kitchen. "It rained last night and the roads would be hard to traverse. So, I think not today."

"Wherever are you going?" Daphne asked, following her toward the kitchen area.

"I thought I would go into the kitchen and see what I can get into," Edith said lightly.

"Into the kitchen?" Daphne almost shrieked from shock. "What on earth for? That is strictly for servants."

"Well, I am told I have no rights. Servants have no rights. It is the same thing, is it not?" She hurried ahead so that Daphne could not see the smile across her face.

"We do not go into the kitchen, my dear." She ran and caught up to Edith and grabbed her arm. "He has women who oversee the kitchen. Ladies do not go into the kitchen where they prepare the food."

"If you haven't figured out that I am not a Lady by now, you never will." She pulled Daphne's fingers from her arm. "I am quite comfortable in the kitchen."

"You are doing this on purpose," she glared at Edith. "You know I will not go into that place for any reason."

"That is totally up to you. As for me, I like being in the kitchen. Now, if you will excuse me." Edith pushed open the swinging door to the kitchen and disappeared behind it.

"Well, I never!" Lady Collingsworth whirled around and flounced back to the parlor. "We'll see what my cousin thinks about that when he returns."

Edith walked to the long table where the staff ate their meals, pulled a chair out, and sat down. "What are you cooking today that smells so good?" She asked the heavyset cook, who smiled and began to tell her what meals were being prepared. Edith loved to watch them and learn the different ways to cook things. She also took the time to learn about their families and how they lived.

She had kept her visits to the kitchen from Lord Symington, because she knew he would forbid her from ever going into the kitchen again. It was totally unacceptable in high society to associate with the servants, but Edith did not feel like a high-society person.

Abbey walked over to Edith and sat down next to her. "Yer ladyship, whilst that woman is 'ere it is not a good thing to be in 'ere." She quickly added, "We enjoy your visits, truly we do. But that woman, Lady Collingsworth, will make it very difficult for you."

Edith looked over at the cook who just nodded. "You're right. I don't want it getting back to Lord Symington. He would totally forbid my coming in here. Or even worse, he may take it out on all of you." Edith stood up. "If he should ask what I was doing in here simply say I always check to make sure the kitchen is clean and that everyone is working. I am not asking you to lie, because I do check out how clean this kitchen is kept. I am impressed constantly." She sighed and left the kitchen.

She crept quietly past the parlor where she saw Daphne pacing back and forth in front of the fireplace. She hurried up the stairs and into her room. She went to a large trunk, took out her embroidering and sat down on the window seat.

It wasn't long before she heard the rattle of the carriage pulling up in front of the door. She looked out from her window seat and saw Lobart helping Symington down from the carriage. If she didn't loathe him so much, she might have pitied the pathetic creature trying to navigate the steps to the house. Lobart had to grab his arm a couple of times to steady him.

Edith put down her embroidery and silently went to the door to her room. She opened it just enough to hear Lady Daphne calling out to Lord

Symington to come into the parlor. Edith left the door to her room ajar and went back to the window, picked up her embroidery and sat down on the soft window seat cushion.

Shortly, out of the corner of her eye, Edith could see a hand pushing her door open. She did not look up. Lord Symington stood there shaking in anger. "How dare you act like a common servant? If you want to act like a servant, I will move your room to the servants' quarters."

"Whatever are you ranting about?" Edith poked her needle through the material and made another stitch.

"Lady Collingsworth has informed me that you sit in the kitchen with the servants. She was completely repulsed at such an act, as am I."

Edith looked up for the first time and saw Lady Daphne standing behind Lord Symington with a smug look on her face. "Milord," Edith said sweetly. "I did not tarry there. I merely checked to make sure that the kitchen is kept clean, and they are not sitting around like lazy doffs." She put the embroidery down next to her. "Am I wrong in making sure that your home is well kept and the staff is working?"

Lord Symington, taken aback, said gruffly to Lady Daphne. "How can she be down in the kitchen when she is up here? And, her position *is* to make sure the staff is working. Next time make sure you know what you speak of." He reached his hand out for Lobart, who guided him to his room.

Now it was Edith's turn to have a smug look on her face. Lady Daphne caught the look, whirled around, put her chin in the air and walked back downstairs to the parlor.

Abbey knocked on Edith's door a little later. "Lord Symington wants you to partake of the meal with 'im and 'is barrister. The barrister's wife will be there, along with that evil woman Lady Collingsworth. He grabbed me arm and said you 'ad better be in one of yer best dresses or else. I think 'e really means it."

"Well then, let's not disappointed him. I haven't gotten a large belly, as of yet. So, they all should still fit me." She walked to the armoire and took out the most elegant dress she owned. It was a pale rose color dress that was embroidered elegantly along the bust, hem and train with tiny, rose-colored gemstones.

Abbey helped pull her hair up into a chignon, while pulling curls out to frame her face. She placed a diamond and rose-colored pin in Edith's hair, and a rose-colored fan and shoes finished her attire.

"'Tis truly a most beautiful gown, yer ladyship." Abbey gently turned Edith to look at herself in the mirror.

"If only," Edith wished with all her heart that Ian would be the one greeting her at the bottom of the stairs.

"If only what, yer ladyship?"

"Nothing, Abbey. I fear I must go down and talk with them. Such a beautiful dress for such an ugly affair."

Time went slowly for Edith as she listened to the bragging of her husband, his cousin, and the barrister. It was only after the barrister and his wife left, and Edith said her condition made her quite tired, that he gave permission for her to retire. Lady Collingsworth asked her permission as well to retire. Lord Symington waved them both off with a flick of his wrist. He put his feet up and ordered Lobart to get him his favorite cigar, along with another glass of sherry.

Edith was grateful for the sanctuary of her room. She was quite tired and just wanted to get away from them and get some rest.

Suddenly, the house filled with screams.

Completely startled by the screaming, Edith grabbed her chest. She opened her door to see Lady Collingsworth racing down the hall screaming at the top of her lungs.

A minute later, she watched in amazement as Lobart raced up the stairs, his gun drawn and ran straight into Lady Collingsworth's room.

Shortly, Lord Symington and Lady Daphne came up the stairs. Two henchmen were on each side of Symington, with Lady Daphne, wide-eyed with fear, following behind them. They stopped outside of Lord Symington's room and waited until Lobart finally came out of Lady Collingsworth's room.

"Well," Lord Symington huffed crossly. "Did you find it?"

"No, yer lordship," he looked back at Lady Daphne and then back at Lord Symington. "I checked everywhere. There is nothing in her room."

"There is," Lady Daphne screamed. "I saw it with my own eyes. It was lying on top of my quilt. I will not go back into that room."

"You are becoming more of a pain in the ass than my wife," he said staring up at her face. "Put her in another guest room."

"She did it!" Lady Daphne pointed her finger at Edith.

"I did what?" Edith was still confused.

"How could she do it?" He snapped. "She was with us the entire time. I am too tired for all this. Lobart," he ordered. "Put Lady Collingsworth in another room." He looked over at Edith, "I wouldn't put it past her to do it. She might have figured out a way. Keep your door locked from now on."

The hall cleared as Lord Symington went into his room and slammed the door shut. Lobart helped Lady Daphne get some of her personal things from her room, promising they would get the rest of her belongings the next day.

As she passed Edith's room, she stopped and looked at Edith. "I know you had something to do with this. I am going to figure this out, and then you had better beware." Lobart led Lady

Daphne down the long hall and around a corner to her new lodgings.

Edith stood at her door in amazement. She had no idea what had happened, but whatever it was; it made her smile. She went to close her door, when a hand stopped her. Edith peered around to see Abbey standing there. "Oh, my dear," Edith grabbed her throat. "What a start I had with that dreadful woman's screams. I have no idea what that was all about?"

Abbey shut the door quietly, and talked in such a low tone Edith could just barely hear her. "There was a snake in her bed."

"A snake?" Edith started to say it aloud, when Abbey put her finger to her lips to silence her. Edith's voice was barely above a whisper. "Abbey, are you sure? A snake in her bed? Are there more of them? Maybe one got into my room." Edith looked nervously around her room.

"No," she smiled. "I put the snake in her bedroom."

Edith backed up and sat down on the vanity chair.

"Aww," Abbey said softly. "It didn't bite 'er or nuttin' like that, cause it was dead."

"How did you get it out of there? That horrible man, Lobart, couldn't find it."

"I was hiding in her armoire. I just waited until she screamed and ran out of the room. I picked it up and threw it out the window, and ran to the servant's door and waited. That Lady Collingsworth sure can move fast."

It took everything in Edith's power to keep from laughing. She got up and hugged Abbey. Her face turned serious when she looked down into the big brown eyes of Abbey. "Listen to me Abbey, be careful. Promise you won't do anything else that may get you harmed. Promise me. No more jokes. No more pranks. Stay away from her. Please."

"Yes, yer ladyship, I promise," Abbey dropped her head.

"Although, I really did enjoy all of that," she gave Abbey a gentle shove toward the door. "I rang you for some chamomile tea. If you wouldn't mind, I could still use some."

"Yes, ma'am," Abbey smiled, curtsied and hurried out the door toward the kitchen. The dim lamps in the hall cast shadows everywhere. Abbey moved cautiously toward the servant stairs. Suddenly, someone grabbed her from the shadows and threw her against the wall. "I know it was you, you filthy little urchin." Lady Collingsworth bared her teeth at the frightened young girl.

"I don't know what yer talking about milady," Abbey cried out.

"You are a nothing, a nothing," Lady Daphne's hands reached around Abbey's throat and began squeezing.

Abbey screamed and tried to stop her, but Lady Daphne was too strong for her. She couldn't scream anymore as she gasped for breath.

Edith was just shutting her door behind Abbey when she heard her scream out. She raced down the hall toward the scream, and saw Lady Daphne with her hands around Abbey's neck. "Stop it!" Edith threw herself at Lady Daphne pulling her hands from around Abbey's neck, as Abbey slid to the floor.

Lady Daphne freed one of her hands and swung at Edith. It struck her in the face. Edith doubled up her fist and struck her in the stomach. It caused Lady Daphne to stagger backward toward the steep, winding staircase. Her arms began to flail as she was losing her balance and about to fall down the stairs.

Edith grabbed her arm to keep her from falling and brought her around to the top of the stairs to safety. In a movement so quick that Edith didn't have time to react; Lady Daphne shoved Edith down the stairs.

Edith screamed just before her head hit a wooden rail knocking her out. Her body fell down the long staircase and finally came to rest with a thud at the bottom of the stairs.

Groggily, Edith began to stir. She felt the soft sheets underneath her and people talking around her bed.

"She's awake!" Mrs. Dawson rushed to her side. "My dear, Edith."

"How dare you speak so informally to her," Lady Daphne said arrogantly.

"Get her out of here," Edith tried to sit up, but couldn't. "I will kill her. I swear by all that is dear to me. I will kill her."

Mrs. Dawson's walked to the bedroom door and opened it. "You heard her ladyship, get out.

Because if she doesn't have the strength to kill you, you can bet I do." Her imposing stature and glare was enough to make Lady Daphne leave quickly. Mrs. Dawson slammed the door after her and rushed to Edith's side. "Little Abbey told us everything that has happened." Mrs. Dawson hurried to the table and brought a cup of broth for Edith to drink. She put the cup of broth down, and adjusted the pillow under Edith's head. "Here let me help you lift your head." Carefully, she reached behind Edith and lifted her up enough to drink.

"How long have I been like this?" Edith said after a couple of sips.

"Not long, a couple of days, that's all, my dear."

"How did you get here?"

"I don't want you to worry about anything right now." Mrs. Dawson gently released her hold on Edith and began fidgeting with Edith's blanket.

Edith reached over and gently took her hand. "Tell me everything."

"Abbey told us how Lady Daphne was trying to strangle her, and you came to her rescue. She said you stopped Lady Collingsworth from falling down the stairs. And, then she pushed you down."

"At least his lordship will know the truth," Edith shook her head. "How is Abbey?"

"Abbey is blamed for shoving you down the staircase."

"What?" Edith's head still ached. "How can that be?"

"Because that beast of a woman, Lady Daphne, said it was Abbey that shoved you down the stairs."

"But she didn't. It was Lady Daphne. Where is Abbey? I have to find her and protect her."

"Abbey said that Lady Collingsworth stood at the top of the stairs and laughed while you fell down them. Then, she hurried down the stairs and had her hands on your throat when the house staff came running to see what all the screaming was about. That evil creature would have killed you had the staff not come running. Abbey was at the top of the stairs, and she heard Lady Daphne tell everyone that Abbey was the one that pushed you down the stairs."

"Poor Abbey," Edith shook her head slowly.

"She managed to get to the stables, get a horse and ride to Brekmore Manor." Mrs. Dawson patted Edith's hand. "She is a clever lass, that one. I gave her some money and told her to disappear until you could straighten everything out."

"I have to get out of here," Edith tried to sit up again, but fell back against her pillow. "Why am I so weak?"

Mrs. Dawson got up, walked to the door, opened it and looked out. She closed the door and locked it. She came back and spoke in a low voice to Edith. "I have some bad news to tell you, my dear." The pain on her face was clear to see.

Edith began to cry. She knew what Mrs. Dawson was going to say, but she didn't want to hear it. "No, no," was all that she could say.

"Listen to me," Mrs. Dawson shook Edith. "Listen to me." She pulled a chair up next to Edith's bed.

Edith rolled her eyes, and her head rocked back and forth on her pillow. "No!" She started to scream, but Mrs. Dawson quickly put her hand over her mouth.

Tears streamed down both of their faces. Mrs. Dawson leaned in close to Edith. "My darling, listen to me." Her voice had urgency about it. "You must be still and listen." She dropped her head for a moment and then looked up into Edith's eyes. "Edith, if Lord Symington finds out you lost the child, he will kill you. Albert heard him talking in the parlor with that Lady Collingsworth."

Edith still did not want to listen. Her heart was broken, and she had no spirit left to fight. "I want to die. I don't want to live anymore." She moaned softly.

"Oh, I see," Mrs. Dawson bristled. "So, you want that creature that killed your child to win. Is that what you want? It certainly is what she wants."

"I don't care anymore," she cried. "They have won. I don't have the strength to fight them anymore. I don't care if they win. I want my child. I want Ian's child."

"I know how much pain you are in," she said comfortingly. "I have been in your place before. But listen to me, Edith, listen to me. We have heard from Ian."

Edith stopped crying and looked at Mrs. Dawson. "You are just saying that to make me feel like I want to live."

"Yes, I am saying that to make you want to live, but I am also telling you the truth."

"Is it possible?" Edith wiped her nose with the top sheet of her bed. "Please! Please, don't let this be a lie."

Mrs. Dawson smiled gently at Edith, "It is not a lie. In all the years you have known me have I ever lied to you."

"No," she answered feebly. "Where is he? I have to see him. I have to hold him. Please, where is he?"

"He is away right now, but you will see him soon enough. First, you must get yourself together. We can fight these two and win. Do you trust me? Do you trust Albert?"

"Of course, I do," she replied. "But the pain I feel is so great."

"You would not be my Edith if you did not feel," Mrs. Dawson got up and went to the door, unlocked it, and looked out again. No one was around. She shut the door and hurried back to Edith's side.

"The only ones who know you lost the baby are Albert and me."

"How is that possible? I saw that woman Daphne in here when I awoke."

"We have kept her out all this time. But I think she heard you had come around. She took me by surprise when she pushed past me as I opened the door. She kept trying to come in by herself. She has no idea that Albert and I knew what happened. She would tell me that I looked tired, and she would watch over you for a while. Albert and I have been taking care of you for the last two days, and have not left you alone for a moment. It has to be driving her crazy, especially now that you are awake."

"Who is watching over my father?'

"My sister and clan, of course," she leaned in close. "Now, here is our plan."

When Mrs. Dawson had finished outlining the plan, Edith nodded. "It is a very good plan. But pretending to be pregnant is going to be difficult to do. Honestly, Mrs. Dawson, do you really think we can do this and fool everyone?"

"You bet we can. Albert and I will be here for a couple more days. We will help get everything set up. Not only that," she looked around her and said more loudly than usual, "I am a mid-wife, and you must be looked in on from time-to-time." She leaned closer toward Edith and said much softer, "And that is exactly what I told Lord Symington. He agreed to it. But you should have seen him when we told him we were staying in your room until you were well enough to be on your own."

"He refused, until that Collingsworth woman ordered Albert and me out of his house. He got so angry with her for ordering someone out of *his* house that he said we could stay for a week, after that we had to leave."

"What of my Ian? Oh, can I see him soon."

"You will see him sooner than you think," she smiled and winked. "But first you must get strong."

"How can I pretend to be happy? I have lost our child."

"You can act like you always do here. Have you ever been happy here?" Mrs. Dawson asked.

"No," she said sadly. "I never have."

"And leave that Collingsworth woman to us. She will pay for what she has done. Now, one last thing. You must pretend that you do not remember anything that happened before the fall. That will keep that woman away from you long enough for us to take care of her proper. Agreed?"

"Agreed," Edith fought back the tears. "I wish she was dead."

"Oh, no, my dear," Mrs. Dawson smiled slyly. "That would be way too easy for her. Just rest assured she will be dealt with, and soon."

The door opened, and Lord Symington entered without waiting for permission. "I see that you are awake. I hear that the child is still safe. Lucky for you I would say. This creature can stay for a couple of days more. She will come back and check on you regularly so that my child is born alive." He walked away with help from his henchmen.

Lady Collingsworth stepped aside to give him room. She looked at Edith, "How are you feeling? Do you remember how you fell down the stairs?"

"I don't remember anything that happened just before I fell down the stairs. But my fall did not take away my memory of not liking you. Now, get out of my room. I don't want any comfort from you."

Lady Daphne turned in a huff and left her room, slamming the door behind her.

"Where is Albert?" Edith asked.

"He is taking care of a few details. But he will be here later. We have brought our pillows and blankets and will be sleeping on either side of your bed. No one is going to get past us to you. We locked the doors and put chairs under the doorknobs, and we don't eat any of his food. My sister sends one of the fairer-haired girls from our clan over with food every day for us." She fluffed Edith's pillow and kissed her on the forehead. "So, don'tcha go worrying about anything. Get some rest, my dear."

"I love you very much, Mrs. Dawson," Edith grabbed her hand and kissed it.

"And I you, my dear." She pulled the blanket up around Edith and stroked her hair. "Close your eyes and rest."

Edith closed her eyes, but it didn't stop the tears from racing down her cheeks. Her baby was gone. Her baby was gone. She turned onto her side and cried softly until sleep finally came to her.

Chapter 12

Dearest Rachel,

You had a son! My darling, little Rachel had a son. I am beyond ecstatic for you. All of my prayers and love go out to you both. I can hardly wait to see him one day. I am grateful that Captain English, and his aunts are there for you – I so wish it was I. He must be beautiful, just like his mother. I can just see Phillip strutting around bragging about his son.

As with me, my life is quite dull compared to yours, I am sure. You spoke of obtaining a couple of gowns. I, too, have acquired a couple of very fine gowns, not that I use them that much.

I got quite a start when Lady Collingsworth went into her bedchambers and saw a snake. Someone said they never saw anyone move so quickly. Of course, she was not hurt, just frightened. She tried to prepare a breakfast for me, and I have decided she is not a very good cook.

I took a slight fall a while ago, but do not worry Mrs. Dawson and Albert were there to help. I do not know what I would do without them. My father is feeling much better, and sends his love. We all send out love and wish you were here. Write me as soon as you can.

Your ever loving, Edith

Nathan had the carriage stocked with warm blankets, a basket with food and drink, and in a leather box inside of the basket was a pistol. Rachel, taken aback at first by the sight of the item, knew that Nathan had put it there for her protection. She withdrew the pistol, pulled the ribbons on her purse to open it, and carefully put the pistol inside. "I do hope I never have need of you," she said to the gun as she pulled the ribbons closing her purse.

Charles and Damian sat outside of the carriage, but were not as exposed as the stagecoach drivers. They also had two doors to enter, and two large windows on the sides, plus a roof that extended out over a half-wall that protected them from the weather. Nathan made sure Charles and Damian had warm blankets, as well as food for travel, and enough money for all of them to eat well at the frequent stops made by the stagecoach.

The roads were wide as they left the city, but the farther they traveled away from the city the narrower they became, until only one lane was open to travel.

Her journey was not going as quickly as she had hoped. The roads, deeply rutted from a recent storm, left giant puddles of water at some places, causing the stagecoach to become stuck numerous times. The male passengers had to help the stagecoach drivers push the coach out of the mud. Occasionally, the stagecoach would lose a wheel, and again; the male passengers in the stagecoach would climb out and help them put it back on.

The first stop they came to was a small inn. Two young boys raced out the door, unhooked the four horses on the stagecoach, and hooked up four fresh horses. When the young boys were finished with the stagecoach, they replaced the two horses on Rachel's carriage with two fresh ones as well.

Waiting in line for the outhouse, Rachel wished she had never left Boston. When she was done, Charles escorted her to the inn where Damian was waiting. The food was very strange tasting to Rachel; it was not good, but it was edible.

Afterwards, she asked Charles what she had eaten. "Squirrel, Ma'am," he said helping her up into the carriage.

Rachel resisted the urge to vomit, and thought back wistfully to the soft, stuffed squirrel for her son that Nathan had gotten him.

Later that day a torrential rain hit them causing the stagecoach to travel slower. A couple of times the stagecoach got mired in the mud, and they had to wait until it was pushed clear.

Fortunately, Charles and Damian could see where the stagecoach got stuck in the mud and were able to avert the same disaster. When the stagecoach finally pulled up to a large inn, it was getting dark, and the roads were becoming impossible to see.

Rachel managed to get a room for her, and one for the two drivers.

The only lavatories were outside, but she was grateful there was a chamber pot under her bed. A washbasin sat on a dresser in her room, and a pitcher of water next to it. Rags left near the basin for her to dry with were old, dirty and frayed looking. The room smelled musty, and looked like it hadn't been cleaned in weeks.

She pulled back the natty blanket, and saw that the sheets were not clean either. Rachel decided she would sleep on top of her blanket, and would use her pelisse to cover herself. There was a small iron stove in her room. She felt they must have just lit the stove, because the room was still damp and cold. For the next three nights on the road, Rachel found it necessary to continue her routine of sleeping on a blanket and covering herself with her pelisse.

At the last stop, one of the stagecoach drivers told Charles and Damian the place where all the wagon trains gathered for their journeys. It was in the flatlands, he said pointing toward the road they had to take.

Her carriage made its way down a winding dirt road until it came to a clearing. Campfires were sprinkled around the numerous wagons. People were too busy loading, cooking, and chatting with one another to take notice of Rachel's carriage.

Charles took off and began asking questions. After a while, he motioned for Damian to bring Rachel over to him.

"This gentleman said the wagon train that was going to Fort Henry left yesterday."

"Oh, no," Rachel gasped. "That can't be."

"Yep, sorry, Ma'am," he shrugged. "They left a day early. Had something to do with the rivers swelling up cause of all the rain. More rain is expected, and they wanted to get across it."

"Ma'am, we can take you back with us," Damian said.

"Thank you, no. I have come this far; I can make it the rest of the way. Is there any other way for me to get to Fort Henry?"

He nodded. "Yep, there's a family here that came in this morning, missed the wagon train going that way, too. Maybe they could take you along. Follow me."

They followed him to a wagon off to itself. A middle-aged man and his wife were heating their breakfast over a campfire.

Charles and the wagon train leader walked ahead of Damian and Rachel. She could see Charles's hands' moving as he talked with the couple. He nodded, pulled out a pouch and handed it to the man.

Rachel arrived in time to see the man stuff the pouch in his large vest pocket. "This is Mrs. Prescott. Her husband be a Lieutenant stationed at Fort Henry. She be going with you." He turned to Rachel. "I paid them in advance, so there should be no problem." Charles looked directly at the man. "I be an excellent tracker, and so be my brother here," he pointed to Damian. "I be expecting her to arrive at Fort Henry unharmed in any way."

"There is no need to make threats," the woman snapped. "We will make sure she gets there. You've paid us well, and we be honest folk."

"Thank you, I am sure you are," Rachel said sweetly. "I have a trunk in the carria . . . " She was cut off by the man.

"We can barely get our stuff in there," he shook his hands. "We ain't got any room for her stuff."

"How many days will it take us to get there?" Rachel asked.

"I 'spect about a couple of weeks or more," the man said. "I ain't pushin' my horses and having them quit on me."

"I will need to bring my valise," she said.

"Now, I jest told ya we dun't have hardly no room fer our stuff," he snapped.

"Give me back the pouch," Charles held his hand out. "You make room for her and the valise, or the deal is off."

He thought for a moment, "All right then. I'll make her a space."

"It will not take me long. When do we leave?" She asked.

"We be leaving as soon as ya get back here." He walked toward the back of the wagon and began moving things around.

Rachel hurried back to the carriage. She had them get her trunk out and took only what would fit in her valise. "It will have to do. I am sure I can get other things once I get to the fort."

Charles carried her valise over to the wagon, and waited until he saw it put in.

"We be going back now, Ma'am," he said, and then loud enough for the man and wife to hear. "You had better arrive safe and sound."

She reached up and gave Charles and Damian a hug. "Thank you so much. Give my love to everyone and let them know I am fine."

"Come on," the man snapped. "We be getting a late start as it is." He grabbed her arm and helped her up to the front seat of the wagon. She stepped over his wife and sat on the outside of the wooden bench.

He made a clicking sound and snapped the reins. They moved away from the other wagons and set out alone down a dirt road. "My name is Corinthia Kramer, just call me Cory. And, Elmer here be my husband."

It was a long, slow journey down the road. They stopped by a small creek for their afternoon meal. Elmer unhitched the horses and took them to the river for a drink. "Need to feed 'em and let 'em rest for a bit." He called out to no one in particular.

"We will have some jerky and bread for our meal." Cory grabbed a large burlap bag out of the back of the wagon. She untied the strings and pulled out some of the bread, and jerky wrapped in cloth. "Grab that pot," she said to Rachel. "We'll go down and get us some water." After they had gotten the water from the stream, they sat down to eat.

Rachel found the meal to be dry and tasteless, but she said nothing. After they were done eating she helped wrap the food back up and put the pot and cups back into the wagon. She was startled when Elmer yelled over to her.

"Did ya get your business done, so we dun't have to stop fer ya to go?"

"Just be careful of the leaves you grab to take care of your business," Cory said. "Some of them can give you a mighty bad itch and burning. Like them over there." She pointed to the poison ivy wrapped around a tree.

Rachel walked behind some bushes. She was horrified and mortified at having to relieve herself in the open, and with strangers knowing what she was doing.

She was barely finished when Elmer called out for her. "Come on," he yelled. "We can travel a little more before the sun goes down."

The wagon moved so slowly Rachel thought they would get to Fort Henry by the time Phillip Nathaniel was a grown man.

They stopped for the night in a clearing near a river. Rachel went about getting wood and sticks for the fire. Elmer brought in the larger logs, and once the fire got going; he threw them on.

Rachel filled the cooking pot with water from the river and watched as Cory made them a meal of beans and flour. It tasted awful, but she was so tired and hungry she ate it anyway. Cory brought out a burlap sack for Rachel to use as a pillow, and a couple of moth-eaten blankets. "Stay by the fire. It'll keep you warmer."

The strange sounds coming from all around Rachel didn't seem to bother the deeply sleeping couple. Terrified, Rachel grabbed her purse with the gun in it and kept it close to her all night.

In the morning, she awoke to find she was getting wet. The sky had opened up and was drizzling down on her. She made her way to the bushes, did her business, and hurried back to the campfire. Elmer and Cory already had their morning meal.

"Bout time ya got up," he snapped, and started hitching up the horses.

Rachel drank a bitter tasting brew called coffee and another piece of stale bread. She learned quickly how to climb up the wagon by herself. She had just crawled past Cory and sat down when the rains came down in earnest.

Cory wasn't much for talking, all she got out of her was that Elmer was a blacksmith by trade, and he was offered a job by his cousin who lived in a town near Fort Henry. Their two children died of cholera, and they had no family in Albany anymore.

It rained on-and-off for days as they traveled down the muddied roads. The team of horses trod even slower in the rain.

Rachel and everything she owned were soaked completely through. She started feeling chilled and feverish, but never told the Kramer's. They traveled a good part of the day when Elmer spotted a cabin just off the road. He pulled the horses down the little hill toward it and stopped in front of the cabin door.

"Hello," he yelled. "We be neighbors just passing through. Anybody in there?" Elmer yelled a few more times and got no response. He jumped down and cautiously approached the cabin door. It creaked as he opened it. He peered in then disappeared inside for a moment. He came back outside. "Nobody's home. We need to get ourselves dried off."

He spotted a small barn behind the house. "I'm gonna put the horses in the barn, and I'll be right back. Get some vitals started," he barked.

Rachel climbed down from the wagon, and opened the door to the cabin. It was dry. It was just one small room with a bed against one wall, a fireplace, a table, and a couple of chairs. The shelves against one wall had a few broken dishes and cups on them.

Rachel began to feel dizzy and swayed a little, but straightened herself out. She didn't want Cory to see her. She helped get the fire started, and began unpacking the food as Cory ran out to the well to get some water. The fire warmed the little room up quickly. They ate their meal in silence. When they were done, Rachel stood up to help rinse the plates when the room seemed to spin around her. She grabbed the table to steady herself.

Cory rushed to her side," Are ya all right?" She touched Rachel's forehead. "Elmer, she be burning up." Cory helped her lay down on the bed, and pulled a dusty blanket over her. Rachel closed her eyes and fell asleep.

The morning sun came out filtering its light through the broken wooden shutters on the windows. Rachel moaned and looked around. It was quiet in the cabin. "Cory." She called out weakly. "Elmer." There was no response.

Rachel crawled out of bed, and went to the window. She moved a broken dish that kept the wooden shutters closed and looked outside. The wagon was gone. She opened the door, hoping they were just around the corner, but they were nowhere around.

She managed to get back into the cabin and saw her valise in the corner. On the table were a couple of breads wrapped in cloth, and a fresh bucket of water by the fireplace. Rachel's mind was reeling. What was she going to do? They left her. She had no idea where she was, or where to go. Rachel staggered to the bed, and fell into it as blackness took her again.

She seemed to go in and out of consciousness, and feared the fever was making her see and feel things. A hand gently lifted her head and poured a bitter tasting drink down her throat. She would sip it slowly and then fade into blackness again.

Rachel began to stir. She felt the coarse blanket over her, and tried to remember where she was. "Help me," she cried out so weakly it was barely audible.

"Ah ha," a male voice said. "Someone be finally awake."

She turned her head and stared at the man sitting at the table. His skin was the color of ebony, and his hair and short beard were a mixed gray and white. "Hello, little Miss." His voice was friendly. "Ya've been pretty sick."

"Who are you?" Rachel asked feebly.

"They calls me Mountain Jack," he cocked his head and looked at her. "What do they calls ya?"

"My name is Rachel Prescott," she ran her dry tongue over her lips.

Mountain Jack got up and brought her some water, "Can ya sits up a little?" He asked holding a ladle full of water. When she tried and failed, he reached under her and lifted her just enough for her to take in some water.

"How long have I been lying here?" She asked.

He thought for a moment. "Let me see. It's been about three moons, and three sunrises. Now, can ya tell me how ya got here?"

When she finished telling him about her husband, trying to get to Fort Henry, and the Kramer's, he sat there a while taking it all in.

"We'll talk 'bout something a little later when ya be a bit stronger, little Miss."

A couple of days later, Rachel's health started to return. She had come to like Mountain Jack, who just happened to be a great cook, and storyteller, and took excellent care of her.

"Remember when I said we would talk 'bout something later, well; this be later. Sit at the table a moment little Miss."

Rachel put down the rag she used to wash the dishes and sat down. "Do ya know why they calls me Mountain Jack?"

She shook her head.

"Because I lived in the mountains way up there in Canerda. I could take ya to Fort Henry, but I only gots one horse. But I mays be able to trade it in fer a couple of mules."

Rachel jumped up and ran to her valise. She began pulling things out to get to the hidden compartment. She laughed as she pulled out a pouch filled with coins. "If you can get me to Fort Henry, I believe this will pay for two mules, and maybe a carriage. All of which you can keep."

"It be too long a journey, and too dangerous ta go up through New York. Marauders. Bad to go up through there now."

Rachel slumped in her chair.

"Now, dun't be so sad," he smiled a broad smile showing the few remaining teeth in his head. "We can takes the mules, and a carriage to the waterway. It will get us there a lot faster, and it be a lot closer." He jumped up and grabbed the money. "There be a trading post not fer from here. I'll be back with supplies and everything we be needing."

Evening was approaching and Rachel feared that he might have been robbed, or worse. But soon she heard the sound of a carriage and horses. She ran to the door and threw it open. It was Mountain Jack with a wagon full of supplies, two mules, and two horses.

He jumped off the wagon and greeted her with a little dance. His feet were flying and kicking up everywhere. "I be stuck here fer four seasons trying to gets enough money to gets back ta my mountains. Not enough trapping ta keep a fella alive here. And, there be way to many marauders and unfriendly Injuns fer me. But I be happy cuz now I gotta a way back to my Canerda."

"Then we are both very happy at this moment." She looked at his face. Something was bothering him. "What is it?" She asked.

"Those Kramer's you tolds me about. Seems they were attacked by some marauders nears the Adirondacks and kilt a couple of moons ago. If ya had been with 'em ya would have been kilt too."

"I am truly sorry to hear that. They were not bad people."

"Somebody shoulda warned them not to go that way by themselves. Even a full wagon train be at risk up there from them marauders and cutthroats," he stood up. "We leave tomorrow morning. I'll getcha to Fort Henry. I will. And it be a whole lots quicker than taken a wagon train."

Early the next morning, they left the little cabin and headed toward Lake Ontario. The roads had dried, and except for an occasional deep rut, they traveled at a fast clip. By late afternoon of the next day, they reached the shores of Lake Ontario. "If we travel down this road by this here lake, it'll take us to a city where we can get passage on a ship bound for Fort Henry."

It was dark, by the time they got into the city. Mountain Jack drove straight to the harbor. Several ships were moored there, and it didn't take him long to secure them passage up Lake Ontario to Fort Henry. But they would have to stay on the ship one night, as it was scheduled to leave first thing in the morning.

Rachel was almost beside herself with joy. She was finally going to see her Phillip. Her horrible journey was coming to an end; she made it.

One of the crew showed them to their separate quarters. Rachel closed the door and collapsed on the small bed in her room. All she could think about was seeing Nathan. She stopped and shook her head as if to clear her mind. She just wanted to see *Phillip*, not Nathan. She had closed her eyes and was resting when there was a knock on her cabin door. She opened it to find Mountain Jack standing there. He brushed past her, and closed the door behind him.

He pulled the little curtain to the window in her cabin closed. Then, he pulled the pouch out of his vest pocket and emptied the contents on her table. "Here, little Miss Rachel," he whispered. "I sold the carriage and the horse, but I brought all my supplies and two mules on board. This be all that's left."

"I owe you, more than two mules and a few supplies," she said starting to put the coins back into the pouch.

He grabbed her hands to stop her. "Listen, my darling girl. Ya be given me my life back. I be tricked by my miserable brother into coming down to New York. He took all my monies. Then I fell and broke my arm, and that laid me up a bit. I had no way to get back to my beloved mountains. Ya'll be given me that and more."

"I will keep some of these, but I insist you keep a few coins. You may need them until you get up to your mountain."

He took the coins from Rachel and put them in his pocket. "These will last me a couples of months, if not more." He patted the coins resting in his pocket.

Rachel threw her arms around him and hugged him. "You are a blessed man."

"No, just an honest one. Well, it be not proper fer me ta be in a married lady's room." He peeked out the door, saw no one, smiled one more time, and left.

She put the rest of the coins back into the pouch, and hid them in the secret compartment. She was beyond delirious with joy. The trip was over, and she was going to be with Phillip. Everything would be wonderful, and he would be overcome with happiness when she told him of their son.

Rachel locked her door, and crawled into bed. She pulled Phillip's face from her memory, but it began to fade. It was as if another face kept trying to replace Phillip's image.

Chapter 13

My Dearest Edith,

I was delighted to hear that your father is doing better. Snakes in her bedchamber? I certainly would have been moving very fast, too. I laughed at that part, and her not being a very good cook – me neither.

Finally, I received word that I can join Phillip. Captain English and the others feared the journey would not be good for my son, whose name is Phillip Nathaniel. So, with a broken heart, I am leaving him behind until the weather breaks, and we can come and get him. It will only be for a short while.

Captain English got me a carriage instead of my riding in a stagecoach. He had blankets and food for me, and even snuck some

money into my valise. He is so kind. I shall miss his friendship.

I missed the wagon train that I was supposed to meet up with, but another couple heading that way took me along. Half way there I got sick, but a wonderful new friend took care of me called Mountain Jack.

Now I am on a ship that will take me to my Phillip. I am so excited to see him, and I cannot wait to tell him about our beautiful son. Please write, I so long to hear from you.

Your loving Rachel

Edith had not been out of her room for a few weeks. She had no interest in going anywhere or doing anything. All she could do was hold her barren stomach and cry most of the day.

The days seemed to fly by quickly for Edith. Mrs. Dawson and Albert left a month ago. She remembered sitting there and watching them go down the road until their carriage was out of sight. She cried the whole day, missing them greatly.

The sun from the tall, French door-type window beat down on her. She began to feel too warm and got out of bed and went to the large window. She reached up and pulled the levers to open both sides of it. A cool breeze quickly surrounded her. She sat on the cushioned window bench tucking her legs underneath her.

Edith remembered Mrs. Dawson telling her not to worry about anything. That she would make sure her Edith would never be harmed again. And, she was not to worry about Lady Daphne Collingsworth, because she was going to be dealt with, and soon.

She was startled out of her reverie by Lady Collingsworth. "Are you feeling better?" Lady Collingsworth asked. The tone of her voice was not of someone who really cared. "The door was open, so I assumed it was alright to enter."

"Please close the door on your way out," Edith never turned her head to look at her. "I thought I had shut it. That was my mistake."

"I brought you something to drink and some toast and jam." She placed the tray on the small table near Edith.

Edith turned her head and looked at the woman she had come to loathe. "Fine," she got up slowly and walked to the table, all the while looking at Lady Daphne. She looked down at the tea serving and picked up the teapot pouring some of its contents into the cup. "Do you wish to sweeten your tea?" she asked the startled Lady Daphne.

Stammering for words, Daphne finally managed to smile sweetly and said, "I already had my tea this morning. This is for you."

Edith moved toward her carrying the filled teacup. She extended it to Lady Daphne, who was backing away giving no indication that she would take the cup from Edith's hand. "Well, take a sip." Edith's eyes narrowed. "See if it has been properly prepared."

"I can see you do not appreciate what I try to do for you," she said in an exaggerated tone of insult. "I will take my leave."

"I told you once before," Edith's voice turned threatening, "never, never set foot in my bedchambers again." She threw the contents of the teacup at Lady Daphne. The tea spilled down the front of her white muslin dress.

"You filthy, insolent, ill-bred peasant," Lady Collingsworth bared her teeth. "You will pay for this. You will pay dearly."

"Get out!" Edith screamed. "Get out before I pick up that knife," she pointed to the tray, "and plunge it into your black heart."

"How dare you threaten me?" She hollered back.

Edith turned and picked up the rather dull knife used for spreading jam; When she turned back to face Lady Daphne, she was gone. Trembling, she put the knife back on the tray. She wanted to scream at her that she killed her baby. She wanted to beat the breath out of her, but she had promised to let Mrs. Dawson and Albert deal with her.

One of Mrs. Dawson's new servant girls stood in the open doorway after Lady Collingsworth fled Edith's room. Edith smiled at the slim, pretty, young girl. Her light-brown hair fell in soft ringlets around her face, and her green eyes smiled warmly at Edith.

"Excuse me, yer ladyship," she curtsied. "I 'ave brought you food from the Brekmore Manor." She carried a large basket into the room and placed it next to Edith. "Mrs. Dawson said you are to eat all of it, or she is going to come over 'ere and feed it to you."

Edith laughed for the first time in weeks. "I believe she would, too." She picked up the cloth covering the basket and found breads, marmalades, teas and berries. Chicken and potatoes filled another tightly-wrapped dish. "This does look very good. Tell Mrs. Dawson not to worry, I will eat."

"Oh, she said you should be sure to eat the berries. It is good for the baby," she spoke the last sentence very loudly. The young girl pulled out a teapot bound tightly with material. Then she began to speak very softly. "This is tea water. She doesn't want ye to trust anyone over here. I must be getting back. Do you want me to close your door as I leave, yer ladyship?"

"Yes, please. Wait!" Edith looked at the young girl in front of her. "I'm sorry. I didn't hear your name."

"My name is Maggie," she smiled.

"Aren't you a little too young to be riding over here by yourself?"

"I 'ave a couple of very big brothers who ride with me. And, they 'ave their 'friends' with them. If you know what I mean."

It took Edith a moment to realize that her brothers "friends" were guns. "I feel much better. Thank you. And, be safe. Give my love to Mrs. Dawson and Albert."

"Yes, yer ladyship." She curtsied and closed the door as she left.

Edith got up slowly and walked to the closed door. She pulled out her key, locked it, and began speaking to the door. "I forgot to lock you after the servants came in to clean today. That is a very dangerous thing for me to forget." She returned to the table, removed the tray Lady Collingsworth had brought and put it on the floor. She pulled out the teapot filled with hot water, breads that were still warm, fresh marmalades, and ate until she was full. When she was finished, she crawled into bed and promptly fell asleep.

Edith awoke to a sharp tap on her chamber door. The room was dark. No candles were lit, and the dim light of the moon did not help illuminate much in the room. There was another loud tap on her door. "Who is it?" She called.

"I have come to light your candles, yer ladyship."

Edith recognized the voice as the woman who always lit the candles in her room. She fumbled getting the quilt off and made her way to the door. It took her a little longer to unlock the door because she had no light to see the keyhole. When she opened the door, the light from the candles in the hall cast long streams of light into her room. The woman waited until Edith gestured for her to enter. She carried a long stick with a flame at one end. She quickly lit the two lamps and the candles in Edith's room. "I will 'ave the steward come and make ye a warm fire, yer ladyship."

"Yes, thank you." Edith locked the door after she left. Stretching her arms, and yawning, she made her way to her private commode. When she returned, she took out the chicken, potatoes, bread, and cold tea, devouring them.

A short time later, there was another knock on her door. "Yes, who is it?" she asked.

"It is me, the steward, yer ladyship."

Edith got up and unlocked the door to let the steward in. He quickly went to her fireplace, and after a few moments, he had built a roaring fire. "That should keep you warm tonight, yer ladyship. I 'ave brought you peat to throw on when it starts to die down." He pointed to the open windows in Edith's room. "It is mighty chilly out tonight; do you want me to close the windows before I leave?"

Edith just didn't want to be bothered by anybody else tonight. "No, I'll see to them."

He nodded and bowed as he left her room shutting the door behind him.

Edith stood at the open windows looking into the darkness with only the pale glow from the moon casting shadows on the grounds below. She was just getting ready to shut the windows when she heard terrifying screams coming from down the hall.

She opened the door a crack and saw Lady Collingsworth racing to Lord Symington's chambers, and began beating on his door. Lobart opened the door. He took a step back amazed by the disheveled look of Lady Daphne. She pushed past him and ran to Lord Symington screaming that a man was outside of her window.

Edith crept closer to the open door to hear what was going on.

"Are you mad?" Lord Symington tried to yell, but was too weak. "You are on the second floor. There is no balcony off your room, or any room in this house for that matter. How can a man be outside your window?"

"I tell you he is there," she looked from him to Lobart. "I tell you there is a man outside of my window. He is wearing a black cape. I could see it swirling around him. He has no face. He has no face," she yelled to the disbelieving henchmen. "I swear it. He has a hood over his head, but there was no face. It was just the hood, an empty, black hood."

Her screaming brought a couple of the other henchmen to Lord Symington's room. "Go and see what has this woman screaming like a banshee. And, don't bother to come back to tell me anything. I don't care. Don't let this happen again. I was asleep, and resting. Lobart, give me another glass of wine, and then get out."

Edith ducked back so they didn't see her as they left his room. Curiosity got the better of her, and she followed discreetly behind them. Lady Collingsworth rattled on about the man flying by her window as they walked down the hall and rounded the corner.

Edith waited until they all went into Lady Collingsworth's room. She didn't want to get too close for fear someone would come out and find her there. She heard the henchmen open and close the windows, along with furniture being moved about the room.

"I am sorry, milady," one of the henchmen said. "There is no ledge for anyone to be standing on outside your window."

"I checked the room," the second henchmen said. "Nobody's in 'ere."

"I am telling you he was right there," she ran and pointed emphatically to one of the very tall windows in her room. "Check again!" She ordered. "I saw him. He was there flying about."

Edith heard the scraping sounds of the windows being opened and closed again.

"Like I said before, milady," Lobart's voice was very firm. "There is nobody flying outside the window. And, there is no way anybody could stand outside of this window, cause they would 'ave to 'ave very tiny, tiny little feet."

The other two henchmen began to laugh.

"Get out," she screamed. "Get out!"

Edith turned and fled down the hall, raced into her room and locked her door. She grabbed a chair and put it under the doorknob, looked over to make sure the two chairs were still under the doorknobs to Lord Symington's room, and heaved a big sigh of relief.

She saw movement by the windows. It startled her until she saw it was only the curtains blowing from the wind. She hurried over and closed the two windows.

Edith glanced down at the basket of food Mrs. Dawson had prepared sitting right in front of the big windows that had been open.

She hadn't eaten the berries and felt it would be a good thing to eat before retiring. Something caught her eye as she reached in to take the blueberries out. Sticking out from underneath the berry basket was a folded piece of paper.

She held the paper by the lamp. It was a note from Mrs. Dawson telling her that she had nothing to fear if a man should appear at Lady Collingsworth's window.

She didn't want the note to be found by anybody, so she quickly took it to the fireplace. She threw it on top of the flames and shook her head laughing about the whole incident.

"Tis the most beautiful sound in the world," a male voice spoke from the black shadows in the room. The shadowed figure moved closer to Edith. "Tis only dimmed by yer beauty and my love for ye."

Edith could do nothing but stare as he moved toward her. Her mind was numb. It was his voice. It was her Ian's voice. She wanted to scream out his name, to run to him, but her body and lips wouldn't move. She was afraid it was a dream, like so many dreams of him. She was afraid he would disappear if she called out his name. Her eyes followed him as he came toward her.

Edith's eyes filled with tears. "You are but another dream. I have dreamed of you so often. Am I still dreaming? I am afraid you will go away again like in my dreams. Are you real?"

He reached out and pulled her to him. His lips found hers and gently kissed her. "I am real."

Edith began frantically kissing his face, his hands, repeating his name over-and-over. She began grabbing his shoulders and his arms trying to make sure he was real. Finally realizing that he really was there with her, she threw her arms around his neck. "My love, my love." She drew back looking at him, and quickly pulled him to her again, holding onto him with all her strength.

Gently, Ian took her arms from around his neck and kissed her hands. The fireplace flickered and spattered behind her, framing her in a golden glow. He leaned down and kissed her, this time it was a kiss filled with desire and passion. She responded greedily.

Later, they lay wrapped in each other's arms, totally spent and exhausted. Edith ran her hand over his bare chest. Her head nestled against his shoulder, and her hair splayed all over their pillow.

"Oh, my love," Edith tried to hug his massive chest. "If this is a dream, I never want to wake up."

"I have never been this happy in my dreams," he leaned down and kissed her forehead. "Mrs. Dawson has told me everything. I felt it was my duty to be the one who paid Lady Collingsworth a visit."

"Where did you go? What did you do? How did you come back without being seen?"

"First question, where did I go? I went to Scotland to an old homestead that my family had bought many years ago. In fact, that was where I was going to live. And, then I met ye and knew I could never leave ye. Lord Symington took our lands here, but he never knew about our home in Scotland. When my parents left here they moved into the small manor in Scotland until they passed away."

He reached over and stroked her hair softly. "Second question, what did I do? Longed for ye every moment of every day. And wondering how I would ever get to see ye again. I stayed in Scotland just long enough to sell the property. Selling it, along with the money ye gave me, has allowed me to hire a few new friends. They are on the roof waiting for me as we speak. What was the third question?"

"How did you get back here without being seen?" She smiled and nuzzled against his chest.

"Oh, yes. Ye see, lassie; I had to see ye again. I could bear it no longer. I had to find out if ye were alright." His arm tightened around her waist, as she lay with one leg draped over his leg. "I went to a town where no one would know me, and bought some old clothes, a cane, and a big, ugly old hat. It has a great big burn hole in the middle of the brim. So my friends and I managed to arrive at Brekmore manor unnoticed. Did you know Mrs. Dawson has a very large family?"

Edith laughed and nudged him. "Go on."

"They told me what they were planning and were going to send Juan, ye know, her nephew to scare that evil woman. But I wanted to do this for us. And, it would give me a chance to see ye again. When ye first came into the room, I could not speak. All I could do was stare at ye. Ye were there, so very near to me. I too, was afraid I was dreaming. My heart was beating so hard when I saw ye, I was sure they could hear it down in the parlor."

"I have you back in my life," she pressed closer to him as a tear rolled down her cheek. "I will always grieve for our lost child, but God may bless us with another."

Ian's large hand wiped the tear from Edith's cheek. "My life is nothing without ye. Be with child or we cannot have another; we will have each other. I would pray that we be granted another, but if it is so decreed, then let it be just us."

"I have known such joy this night," she moved her head against his chest. "Tomorrow the nightmare will begin again."

"Don't be thinking about tomorrow my love. We still have a little time this night, and soon the rest of our lives."

"Say it again, please," she whispered.

"Which part?" He kidded. "It was all good."

Edith chuckled, "Then all of it."

He repeated. "We still have a few more minutes, and soon the rest of our lives." His voice softened on the last part of his sentence.

"That's the part 'the rest of our lives.' " She pulled her head off his shoulder and kissed his lips softly and then with an intensity that he eagerly returned.

A short while later she watched as he got dressed. "So soon?"

"My men will have been frozen on the roof by now. I have to think of them as well. Besides, we have to get back to Mrs. Dawson's before this household awakes."

"Yes, I know," she rose up on one elbow. "I will miss you beyond words."

"And I ye," he finished dressing and walked back to the bed kissing her one last time. "I have to climb that darn rope and get out of here before I am seen."

"Will you be coming back soon?" She asked, as she crawled out of bed, grabbed her robe, and put it on as she ran to him.

"I cannot promise when, but be sure to check the berries from time-to-time." He opened the window and yanked on the rope to signal his men he was ready to be pulled up. "I will be back for ye, my love." He grabbed the rope, slipped his foot in the noose, and disappeared from the window.

Edith ran to the window and leaned out to watch him climb safely onto the roof. He peered over the edge and waved. She threw him a kiss. He reached out as if he was grabbing the kiss, and then Ian and the rope disappeared from her sight.

She sat and stared out of the window. Edith wasn't sure how long she sat there until she saw the sun's misty rays beginning to mingle with the dark horizon.

The chilly night finally reached her core, as she shivered and closed the windows to her room. She threw a large piece of peat onto the fading embers. The dying embers embraced the peat, and soon she could feel the warmth from the fireplace returning.

Now, Edith was beginning to feel sleepy. She walked back to her bed, almost in a daze. Afraid that it had been just a dream, she stood looking at the bed for a moment before she crawled beneath the covers. Her heart soared; his scent was still strong in her bed. She knew it was not a dream and grabbed the pillow where his head had rested. She pulled it to her and hugged it as she fell asleep.

The sound of knocking on her chambers, only stirred her awake a little. "What do you want?" She asked sleepily.

"We are 'ere to clean your room, yer ladyship."

"Not today," she replied pulling her pillow over her head. "Not today."

Later that day there was another, but louder rap on her door. "I don't want the room cleaned today." Edith said firmly.

"I have no intentions of cleaning your room," Mrs. Dawson's voice chided her.

"Oh, one moment," Edith jumped out of bed, grabbed her robe and quickly ran to the door. She pushed the chair out of the way and unlocked the door.

Mrs. Dawson and Maggie, carrying large baskets, were about to enter her room when Lord Symington opened his door to the hallway.

"What do you have in those baskets?" He asked briskly.

"After her fall, we must be very careful what she eats," Mrs. Dawson bristled back. "And we have a few things that we have to check to make sure everything is still as it should be." She threw back her large chest and looked down at the little man in front of her. "Do you not want a son? Should I stop coming here to make sure she is doing everything right?"

His only answer was a flick of his hand, as if to say, "Don't bother me with these trifles" and walked unsteadily down the hall.

Mrs. Dawson glared after him as he walked away. His henchmen appeared and began helping him down the stairs. She heard Lord Symington berate his henchmen for not responding faster when he rang for them.

She went into Edith's room, closed the door, and put out her hand for Edith to give her the key to lock it. Once it was locked Mrs. Dawson and Maggie opened their baskets. One basket was filled with food; the other had rope and material in it. "You need to eat. That's one basket," Mrs. Dawson spoke low. "The second basket is for making you look six month, almost seven months, with child."

Edith just nodded. Before the fall, her once flat stomach was beginning to show there was a life growing in her. Now, when she looked down her stomach was flat again.

"Here put this corset on." Mrs. Dawson handed Edith a corset that just fit under the bust. "This has to look natural, so I suggest you do not wear any clothing that is of light material. Maggie, see what you can find in her armoire that will do."

Mrs. Dawson stepped back and looked at their concoction. The corset was just a pouch with thin straps that went over her shoulders. It had ribbons stitched across the top and bottom, so they could tie it around Edith's body. And, the pouch had a slit at the top so that they could add padding as the weeks went by.

Maggie held up a long gown of green velvet with an overdress of sheer muslin in a paler green. The empire-style dress had a shorter train, but yards of material hung in pleats on the front of the dress, making it perfect for an expanding tummy.

"Maggie, my child," Mrs. Dawson said gleefully, "that is perfect."

After they were through getting her dressed and pregnant looking, Mrs. Dawson stepped back to admire her creation. "Perfect, my dear, perfect." She clapped her hands with joy. "Rosita, and the other women and I worked for a couple of days on how making you look with child would work best. I think this will do nicely. Luckily for us, no one has seen you in weeks, so they would have no idea how big you are."

Maggie pulled out the breakfast food and placed it on the small table. "Yer ladyship, you must eat."

Edith looked in the mirror at her reflection. Sadness filled her eyes as she ran her hand over her protruding stomach.

"Now, now," Mrs. Dawson said, grabbing Edith's hands and gently leading her to a chair by the table. "Eat. We are going to take you for a short ride. A woman needs fresh air to have a healthy child."

"I am afraid that woman may get into my room," Edith said with concern.

"Maggie is going to stay here." She looked at Maggie, who nodded in agreement. "That woman will not be coming into your room. I will see to that." A strange smile crossed Mrs. Dawson's face. "Just give Maggie the key. She will be sure no one comes into your room."

Edith put on long-gray gloves and threw a warm, gray shawl over her shoulders and quickly grabbed a green parasol. After seeing Ian, she felt alive again. She was actually glad to get out of her room, and going outside for a ride greatly appealed to her.

Mrs. Dawson took Edith's arm before they left the room. "Now, my dear, I want you to promise not to notice anything out of the … well, shall we say normal sightings. You must not acknowledge anything that we should encounter on our ride. Promise me."

"Of course," Edith's brow furrowed. "But I have no idea what you are talking about."

Mrs. Dawson patted her arm, "You will, my dear. You will." She held Edith's arm as they walked down the long staircase. She called out for one of Lord Symington's open carriages. Edith thought that was strange, as Mrs. Dawson came in a carriage of her own.

Instantly, Lady Collingsworth appeared from the parlor. "Where do you think you are going?" She questioned looking at Edith and Mrs. Dawson.

"I feel her Ladyship has been cooped up in her room too long so we are going for a carriage ride." She smiled sweetly with as much sincerity as she could muster toward Lady Collingsworth. "You are welcome to join us. I am afraid her Ladyship needs some fresh air. It will help the child she carries even more."

Feebly, Lord Symington came from the parlor. Two men, on both sides of him, held him firmly.

"You will ride with them. It is for my son's sake," he snapped at Lady Collingsworth.

"Of course," she curtsied and called for her shawl. "It is rather a cold day for a ride. Are you sure this is good for his child?"

"Nonsense," Mrs. Dawson replied. "If he wants a strong and healthy son it will take lots of fresh air. My, that is a lovely purse you are carrying. It is a very unusual color of red. Don't you think so, Edith?"

Edith just looked at the purse and nodded in agreement. The bright-red color looked rather normal to her. However, she knew Mrs. Dawson was up to something.

Lord Symington looked at the purse and then back at Lady Collingsworth. "I brought you here to watch over her Ladyship, and you have done nothing. Nothing! Nothing but lounge around in my parlor, drinking up all of my port, and create havoc in my household." He gestured for his men to return him to his parlor.

A servant brought a shawl for Lady Collingsworth, and they made their way to the waiting carriage.

"Wait," Lady Daphne exclaimed. "This carriage has no covering. It is too cold for a carriage ride like this today."

"We are riding in this carriage," Mrs. Dawson said. "Unless you prefer we tell his Lordship you decided not to go with us."

Albert jumped down and helped Edith and Mrs. Dawson into the carriage.

Lady Collingsworth put out her hand for Albert to assist her. He brushed past her and climbed to his seat, while she stood in shock. She turned quickly to one of Lord Symington's servants and ordered him to assist her. The gardener, not being familiar with helping a woman in and out of the carriage, did not make her efforts to get into the carriage very graceful.

He reached down to pick up her train and put it in the Landau carriage, when Lady Collingsworth spotted his dirty hands. "Don't touch anything," she screamed, as she pulled and yanked her long train into the carriage.

They rode away from Lord Symington's manor down the main road toward town. After they had traveled a while, Albert turned the carriage down a narrow, less traveled, road. The carriage stopped abruptly.

"Why are you stopping?" Lady Daphne screamed at Albert.

"There's a puddle in the road ahead, milady," he answered back politely.

"Then, just go around it. You idiot." She said, agitatedly.

"Yes, milady." She couldn't see the smile on his face.

They came close to the trees, when suddenly a couple of Indians jumped out from the bushes, brandishing bows and arrows.

Lady Collingsworth screamed.

Mrs. Dawson grabbed Edith's hand and firmly squeezed it. "What are you screaming for and scaring the wits out of us?" She yelled to Lady Daphne.

Still screaming, Lady Collingsworth pointed to the Indians still standing in front of the bushes. Both, Mrs. Dawson and Edith turned and looked in the direction of the two Indians standing there.

"What Indians?" Mrs. Dawson asked. "What nonsense is this? There are no Indians in England."

Lady Daphne turned and shouted at Mrs. Dawson. "Turn around and look again. Look there!" She pointed in the direction of the Indians who were now gone.

"Albert?" Mrs. Dawson asked calmly. "Did you see any Indians?"

"What does an Indian look like?"

"Take me back to the manor this instant," Lady Daphne ordered.

"When we are done with our ride." Mrs. Dawson calmly ordered Albert to continue down the road.

They came to a path in the road where berries grew in abundance. "Albert, stop here. We'll pick some berries." She turned to Edith, "Are you up to it?"

"Absolutely," Edith replied happily. "I am very hungry for some berries. I can hardly wait." She knew something was about to happen, and she really couldn't wait.

Again, Albert helped Edith and Mrs. Dawson down, but ignored Lady Daphne.

"You go ahead and pick berries like the peasants you are. I will wait here." She turned her nose up at them and settled back into her seat.

Mrs. Dawson told Edith to pick the berries by the thick trees. Edith strolled toward the trees and down a slight embankment, disappearing from Lady Collingsworth's sight.

Ian stepped out from behind one of the trees and Edith ran into his arms. They kissed and held each other until the screams from Lady Collingsworth filled the air.

"I must go, my sweet, but I will see you soon." He gave her one long kiss and hurried back into the trees.

Edith hurried toward the carriage and saw Albert and Mrs. Dawson already there.

"What is it now, milady?" Albert asked feigning annoyance.

"One of those Indians stole my purse. He ripped it right from my hands and ran off into those trees. Go after him. Get it back!"

Albert shrugged, pulled his cape around him, and sauntered toward the thick bushes and the trees beyond.

Edith and Mrs. Dawson waited by the carriage when Albert returned, empty-handed. "I didn't find any Indians or a purse, milady." He shrugged and then helped the two women back into the carriage. He picked up the basket and gave it to Mrs. Dawson with a wink.

They drove back to Lord Symington's manor, and when they got to the front entrance, Lady Daphne climbed down and ran into the house. She hurried into the parlor. Lord Symington was asleep in his favorite chair by the fireplace.

"Your lordship," she called loudly.

He awoke with a start, and stared at the woman who was ranting and raving about Indians in the forest.

"There are no Indians in England," his voice was weak, but filled with disgust.

"They stole my purse," she replied hysterically. "You saw me take it from the servant. It was red. Even you could see that. Where is it? Where is my purse if the Indians didn't take it?"

"Lobart," he said weakly. "See if you can find her purse. This is making me very tired."

"Even you," she spat at Lobart, "can find a bright-red purse in the carriage. However, you won't because it was stolen."

Lobart went out to the carriage, and shortly came back into the room holding her bright-red purse in his hand.

"That is the same purse I saw you with earlier. Is it not?" Lord Symington asked getting more annoyed by the minute.

She grabbed the purse from Lobart and pulled the strings to open it. All of her items were inside. "This can't be. The Indian grabbed it and ran into the forest." Then she stopped and looked at Mrs. Dawson. Her eyes narrowed. "You," she hissed. She looked back at Lord Symington and smiled weakly. "You are right, your lordship. This is my purse. I was very tired this morning and must have fallen asleep and dreamt it. If you will excuse me." She didn't wait for him to reply, as she flounced out of the room and up the stairs.

"There's something very wrong with that woman," Lord Symington said, and turned to Lobart. "Get my barrister over here. Now!"

Albert and Mrs. Dawson helped Edith up the stairs and to her room. Maggie opened the door and motioned for them to hurry in. “I thought it was you coming back, so I went to the door. Then I ‘eard his lordships door open. I peeked out and it was Lady Daphne. She went into Lord Symington’s room. She wasn’t there but a moment, and then she came out, ran down the corridor and disappeared round the corner.”

“Thank you, Maggie,” Mrs. Dawson said. “We had better leave. We have much to do.”

Later that evening, Lady Collingsworth heard male voices coming from the parlor. She peered down the staircase; no one was in the foyer. She crept down and listened by the parlor door left ajar. She recognized the voice of Lord Symington and his barrister.

“I want her taken out of my will,” he said feebly. “I do not want that mad woman around my son. She is to get nothing. Do you hear me? Nothing. My will states my wife will receive nothing, and I want it written the same for that imbecile cousin of mine. Draw up the papers, immediately, and have them ready to sign first thing in the morning. I want them here almost before the sun rises. Is that understood? I am tired. Leave me. Pay the man." He ordered Lobart, who promptly gave the stuttering man a purse of gold coins.

Lady Collingsworth hurried down the hall to a door leading into the library and hid behind it until the barrister left. She went back up to her room, shut her door, and sat in front of the fireplace. Her eyes fixed on the glowing embers that smoldered and sputtered. "I have been poisoning you way too slowly, you vile, old man. I will have your money. I and I alone will have all of it … all of it."

Chapter 14

My Dearest Rachel,

I know how heart breaking it is to leave your young son behind, but I agree with them whole-heartedly. Once you are settled and he is a couple of months older, it will be easier on you both. Again, Captain English comes to your rescue. He truly sounds like a wonderful old man. And, a man called Mountain Jack? You must tell me more about him. He sounds like a wonderful man, too.

I am seeing a lot of Mrs. Dawson and Albert during this period in my life. I do not think I could do without them. I dearly love them both.

Lady Collingsworth still tries to bring me my morning meal. I keep telling her to stop, and as I told you before she is not a very good cook.

Ian is as wonderful, kind and loving as I could ever wish for. I cannot stop looking at his face. Every day for months, I would wake up and feel that he was just in my dreams. But then when his arms go around me, and I see his face; I know everything is right with the world.

A couple of days ago, Albert, Mrs. Dawson, Lady Collingsworth and I took a long drive in the country to pick some berries. It was a very interesting ride for Lady Collingsworth, you know, being new to our countryside.

Well, my dearest, I miss you desperately. I long to hear your voice, and see your sweet face. My heart, my thoughts, and love go to you, your loving Edith

The ship finally pulled into port. It was an uneventful journey to the military city nestled between the St. Lawrence River and Lake Ontario. As the boat moored, Rachel's heart began to beat faster. It would not be long before she would finally be with Phillip. "Everything will be back to normal," Rachel sighed.

The ship docked, and Rachel and Mountain Jack said their good byes. He waited on deck to get his mules and supplies, as she hurried down on the dock to try to find Phillip. She spotted a soldier in a bright-red uniform and stopped him.

"Excuse me," she asked trying to hold back her excitement. "Do you know a Lieutenant Prescott?"

"I'm sorry, Ma'am, that is not a familiar name to me," he replied respectfully. "You might try going to the fort. I'm sure someone will be able to help you there." He pointed in the direction of the fort, nodded politely, and walked away.

Rachel pushed through the throngs of people and the hustle of the busy dock. She walked for a while through the streets toward the fort looming ahead of her. A whimpering sound came from one of the side streets; it almost sounded like a child. She forgot about getting to the fort and headed down the alleyway toward the child's cries.

She stopped, aghast at what she saw. Two men were pushing around a small boy who could not have been more than six years old, and threatening him with knives.

"Excuse me," she said loudly, causing the two men to whirl around and look at her. "What are you doing to that little boy?"

"This ain't none of yer affair," one of them said nastily.

"Well, then I shall make it mine. Leave that child alone." She demanded.

"This ain't no child," the other man snapped at her. "This be an injun."

"That is a child, and you men should be ashamed of yourself frightening him like that." She glared back at the men.

"Why dun't you jest turn 'round and get back where ye came from?" He brandished the knife toward her. "Or when we be done with him, we can start on you."

Rachel held her ground, as her anger began to surface. She reached into her purse.

"Oh, looky that, she's gonna cry in her hankercheef," one of them laughed sarcastically.

Rachel pulled out the small pistol and aimed it at them, "I will not be the one crying. Now step away from the boy."

"Ohh, I am so afraid," he mimicked being frightened. "What you gonna do with that little thing?"

She lowered the gun and aimed it right between his legs, "I have two bullets, and I am not a very good shot, but from this distance, I believe this 'little thing' can do some damage."

"Hey, watch where you be pointing that thing," one of them yelled.

"Like I said I am not a very good shot, but at this distance, I can hit both of you in the same place." Rachel kept her eyes on the two men. Something moved behind them. She heard a soft chirping sound, and an arm came down and grabbed the little boy's outstretched arm. The arm pulled the boy up and out of sight from the two men.

One of the men took his knife and slashed behind him, thinking the child was still there. Stunned he began looking around when suddenly an arrow pierced his throat. His eyes wide with shock, he staggered a moment and then fell flat on his face. The second man started to run past Rachel when he fell with an arrow protruding from his back.

Rachel looked up and saw a couple of adult male Indians who were looking down at her. She had nowhere to run and there was nowhere for her to hide. She lifted her chin; she would die bravely. She waited for them to raise their bows and shoot her down. Instead, they disappeared over the rooftops.

Suddenly, a woman began screaming at the top of her lungs. Rachel quickly put the pistol back in her purse and tried to hurry out of the alleyway, when soldiers came running toward her. They saw the two dead men and gave orders to search the area for the Indians.

"Ma'am," one of the soldiers came up to her. "What happened back here? What did you see?"

The woman who screamed spoke first saying she just turned the corner, and there they were.

Rachel sighed with relief. "I was trying to find my way to the fort, and thought maybe this was a short cut in getting there. And, then, like she said, there they were. I was too stunned to scream."

"What business do you have at the fort?" He asked politely.

"I have come a great distance to be with my husband, Lieutenant Prescott," she said.

"I see," he nodded in her direction. "Sergeant, take this lady up to the fort. You will be safer with him, as we have renegade Indians in the city."

"What are renegade Indians doing in the city?" She asked sincerely curious.

"They usually come in to steal things, like food, clothing, and the like. Sometimes," he looked down at the bodies of the men, spotting a knife clutched in each of their hands. "Sometimes," he shook his head. "They send in the children, because they are smaller and less visible, to steal things for them. But these particular Indians," he looked at the feathers on the arrow protruding from the neck of one of the men, "very rarely do they kill anyone, unless they are protecting themselves or their family."

He looked down at the two men in disgust. "Get those arrows out of them. We don't want the people getting up in arms and rioting over this."

"Ma'am," the sergeant touched her elbow. "If you will come with me." They got to the main street, and he helped her into a buggy.

She reached the fort, and the sergeant gave her name to a higher-ranking officer, who asked that she follow him. There were hundreds of soldiers in the fort. Some of them were on guard duty; while others were in formation marching. Still others were milling or walking about.

The sergeant took Rachel to the building that housed the commander's office. He turned her over to another officer who asked her to sit outside the commander's office and wait. Unsure about Phillip's regiment information, she could only give an approximation of when he had arrived at the fort.

The hallway was cold, and the wooden bench uncomfortable, as she waited to hear from the commander. Soon, two officers came to the Commander's door, knocked, and told to enter. A short while later, the two officers came out and walked over to Rachel.

They introduced themselves as officers of Phillip's regiment.

"I am afraid Lieutenant Prescott was sent out on a reconnaissance patrol and should be back tomorrow, or it could be a couple of days more." They bowed courteously, and left her sitting there on the bench by herself.

Rachel was confused, alone, and now there was no place for her to stay. She got up and slowly walked back to the fort promenade. The sergeant who had brought her to the fort came over to her. "Ma'am, is everything all right?"

"My husband is away on some kind of patrol, and I have nowhere to stay until he comes back." She shrugged. "I don't know what to do."

"Here," he offered his arm. "I know of a very respectable inn for you to stay the night. Let me get the buggy, and I will take you there." They walked to the fort gates. "Wait here for just a moment." The sergeant disappeared through the gates. What seemed like hours to Rachel, but was only minutes, he returned with a buggy. He helped her get in and started back toward the town.

"How long have you been in the army, sergeant?" She asked trying to make small talk.

"Going on seven years, Ma'am." He kept his eyes on the road, making sure he did not run into any of the many people walking around them. "I just want you to know, I would have offered for you to stay with my wife and me, but we got six kids, and they are mighty noisy."

"That was very kind of you to think of me and to help me now."

"It was no problem, ma'am," he smiled down at her.

"How long have you and your wife been married?" She asked looking at the buildings and people.

"Well, her husband was killed a while back at Fort Erie, and she had to marry somebody within three days, or she had to leave the fort. She had three kids, and Fort Erie is out there in the wilderness. There are wild animals and Indians all around the fort. They woulda kept the kids if she wanted to leave on her own. But she picked me. She said I had kind eyes. Her husband had been kinda rough with her." He looked over at Rachel and shook his head. "A real man dun't have to hit a woman. Anyway, we've been married ever since. Had three young ones of our own."

"That is astonishing," Rachel's eyes widened hearing about Fort Erie. Her full attention diverted back to the sergeant. Had she kept looking at the people walking through the streets, she would have seen the tall man, with the black patch over his eye, stopping in his tracks as he recognized her. Nor, was she aware that he had turned and followed the carriage.

"There is the place, Ma'am." He pointed to a white building. "I have heard they have clean rooms, and serve three meals a day. I have to go back to the fort, so I can give them your information Then they can let your husband know where you are."

The sergeant pulled the carriage up to a wooden building with a large front porch. He helped her down and carried her valise into the main lobby. She got a room, at a reasonable rate with the sergeant's help. He bid her good-bye and left the building.

The innkeeper took Rachel to a sparsely furnished room, with one bed. A dresser was on one side of the room, and a small wooden table with two chairs sat under the window. He showed her where the lavatory was down the hall, and the chamber pot under her bed. He handed the key to her room and left.

She locked the door behind him, put her valise on the table, and looked around. At least this room looked clean, she thought. She walked to the bed and pulled back the quilt, and sighed with relief upon seeing clean sheets. She fell across the bed, and promptly fell asleep.

Down in the street, a man with a patch over one eye; his whole being filled with hatred, studied the boarding house. Count Tychovsky could not believe his luck. He knew how to find her husband, by the regiment he was in, and was greatly disappointed she was not with him. He wanted her punishment to be special. He had to think of what he was going to do first.

The next morning, after she had her breakfast down in the main dining area, she returned to her room to freshen up. There was a loud knock at her door. She opened it to find a couple of soldiers standing there.

"Ma'am we were sent by the Lieutenant to get you," he said politely. "Your husband's regiment has returned, and he is very anxious to see you."

Rachel grabbed her shawl, looked in the broken mirror over the dresser to adjust her bonnet, and locked her door as she left. She happily followed the two young soldiers downstairs. Rachel almost skipped to the front desk, gave the innkeeper the key to her room, and hurried out to the waiting carriage.

The two young soldiers took her to Phillip's quarters within the fort and left her standing outside of his room. Rachel took a deep breath, straightened her bonnet, and knocked on his door. There was no response. She knocked again. The door opened, and Phillip stood there looking at her. Rachel threw her arms out to him, but he did not respond in like.

He stepped back so that she could pass through, "It was good of you to come." His voice sounded hollow and cold.

"Phillip? What is wrong? Why are you acting this way?" Rachel asked confused at his greeting.

"I am sorry," he shrugged. "But that is the way it is."

"What is?" She asked completely puzzled.

He walked over to a table in his room, and picked up a long piece of paper. "Here you have to sign this," was all he said.

Rachel took the paper from him and began to tremble as she read it. She stumbled back against the door. "What has happened? Why are you doing this?" Her trembling hand moved to her forehead. "This cannot be happening." She dropped the piece of paper and just stared at him in complete shock. "You are divorcing me?"

"I told my father I was resigning from my post, from this infernal army," his fists clenched. "I want nothing that will remind me of this hideous place, and that includes you. And, I asked him to send me these divorce papers."

"You don't mean it, Phillip. You cannot mean it," tears streamed down her face.

"Oh, yes I do," he snapped. "My older brother was killed in a hunting accident, which now makes me the heir to the family fortune. My father wants me to marry someone with high breeding and a title. Of which, I agree. I need a wife who will fit into high society with grace and ease."

"But Phillip, each of us has gone through so much, alone and together. What about children? We have a . . ." Her words were cut off by Phillip.

"Children? With you? At least, I was spared enduring that mistake with you. My father said if I still have any lustful thoughts of you, I can visit you at my pleasure, after I am married to a woman of means and stature."

Rachel's body began to shake as she cried into her handkerchief.

"Stop sniffling. What do you know about anything? I have seen such horrors that will take a lifetime to wipe from my memory. I cannot bear another moment in this uniform, this place, or the sight of you."

"What have I done? What have I done to have you behave this way to me?" She sobbed.

"What have you done? What a wonderful question." He snapped and glared at her. "I took this position so that you and I could marry. I wanted to impress you. You see my father had secured me a position in London where I would not have to do any field duty. However, I thought I could not live without you, so I had him get me a commission … a commission to Hades is what this is. All because of you."

"All because of me," she repeated weakly.

"My post was not supposed to be in this infernal wilderness. I was supposed to be stationed as an attaché to a general, but he died. So, instead of sending me home, which they should have, they sent me to this Godforsaken place."

He turned on Rachel. His face distorted. "You have no idea what I have gone through. The pain, the anguish, and the suffering I have endured are beyond even my comprehension. I have seen things no man should ever have to see. Men shot, maimed, and killed. For what? It is all senseless. Marching for days, eating foul food, and watching men defecate in front of you. And, taking orders from low bred officers, who have brains the size of a bean."

"All because of me," she said through eyes blurred by tears.

"I want to go home." He said slowly and emphatically.

"I see," she reached down and picked up the paper from the floor. "Why didn't you just send this to me? Why did you make me come all this way? If you would have told me what you just did in a letter, I would have signed it."

"Because I felt you would understand it better if you knew how much I suffered. I wanted you to feel a little of what I have had to endure."

He turned away from her and got something from his dresser. "I must have you sign both. One is your copy to keep. I cannot stand the thought of ever thinking about this place, or the army, and you would be a constant reminder." He threw a pouch on the table. "Take this. I am being more than generous to pay for your passage back to England."

"I thought you loved me," her voice quivered.

"Love? What is love? I was supposed to be an attaché, no fighting, no filth, no marching, and because of you, my life has come to this." His fist clenched as he looked down on her. "I had much time to think of you. You are not the woman I want to be married to. You are obstinate and head strong. You are so ill-bred that you don't even know your place as a woman."

"Phillip, please, you don't understand. I have to tell you ..." Anguish welled up in her voice.

He raised his hand to silence her. "There is nothing, do you understand, nothing you have to say that would interest me. If you have to marry that old man, well that is not my problem; that is a woman's fate. My father and I agree this marriage is over. And, so that you completely understand, the thought of you disgusts me as does this post. I have passage on the first ship leaving this insidious place tomorrow morning. Do not be on it."

Rachel stood there holding the paper and trembling as she reached for the feathered pen. She dipped it into the inkwell, paused, and then signed both divorce papers. She opened her purse and took out a handkerchief, dabbed her eyes and wiped her nose. Rachel took the handkerchief and blotted the ink on one of the divorce papers, folded it up and put it in her purse.

She opened the door, hesitated for a moment, took the pouch of money, put it in her purse and pulled the ribbons to close it. It was for Phillip Nathaniel. She would need money to raise Phillip Nathaniel. She straightened her back, held her head high and walked out the door, never looking back.

The sergeant was at the gate, and spotted Rachel. He took one look at her face and knew something was wrong. He decided it was best not to pry and offered a carriage ride to the inn. All she could do was nod.

They rode in silence all the way there. He pulled up in front of the inn, jumped down, and helped her get out of the carriage. "War does strange things to men, Ma'am. Things will get better. You'll see. In the meantime, if you ever need a shoulder to cry on, mine are pretty broad. And, my wife is a great listener."

"You are very kind, sergeant," she managed a feeble smile. "Thank you. I will remember your kind words." He helped her up the stairs. She knew he could feel her trembling, but she didn't care. All she wanted to do was get into her room, and lock herself in. "Good-bye, sergeant." She didn't turn around, but waved her hand as she hurried into the building. The innkeeper was at the front desk and gave her the key to her room.

Rachel's hands were trembling so badly she couldn't get the key to work in her door, but after a few attempts it finally opened. Once she got inside, she struggled to lock it. She heard the click of the lock, and knew she was alone, and no one could bother her. She walked to the bed and fell on it sobbing quietly into the pillow. Her body and mind racked with pain, heartbreak, shame, guilt, and confusion.

She cried the rest of the day and long into the night. Exhausted from the emotional trauma of the day, she fell into a restless, but welcome sleep.

The morning sun inched its way to her face. She pulled a pillow over her head and moaned. Slowly, she got up and looked at her surroundings. The distorted and broken mirror on the wall only made her red and puffy eyes look worse. There was a knock at the door; her heart began to beat wildly, hoping it was Phillip. Maybe, just maybe he came to his senses. "Yes?" she asked hopefully.

"It's me, Josey, the innkeeper's wife. Everyone is down for their breakfast. My husband said he thought you might want to take yours in your room this morning," she said calling through the door. "He noticed you hadn't eaten yesterday."

"Yes, thank you. Please wait a moment." She got a coin out of her purse, and tried to straighten her dress and cap that she had fallen asleep in. The key was still in the lock. She turned it, and the woman came in carrying a tray.

"This will give you some strength," she said and put the tray on the table. "Is there anything I can do for you, Ma'am?" She asked sincerely.

"No, but thank your husband for being so thoughtful to me," she handed Josey a gold coin. She started to refuse it. "Please, it would make me feel better."

"Thank you, Ma'am," she looked at the gold coin, and then slipped it into her apron pocket. "If you want to take your other meals up here today, we can do that for you."

"I would like that very much," she walked to the table and was about to sit down.

"Ma'am, I would feel better if you locked the door after me." Josey waited outside the door until she heard the lock click in place.

Josey or her husband brought all of her meals to her for the entire day. Every time there was a knock on her door Rachel knew it was the innkeeper or Josey, but each time she hoped it was Phillip coming to apologize and tear up the divorce papers. She had never known anyone who was divorced. She had heard about it, but never thought it would happen to someone she knew, let alone her.

For two days, Rachel stayed in her room, only slipping out to use the lavatory. The innkeeper and Josey were very kind to her, bringing her meals and anything else she might require. In the middle of the second-day Josey called out to her that she had a sergeant there to visit her. Rachel unlocked the door, and invited the sergeant in, along with Josey.

He took off his hat, and looked down at the floor. "Ma'am, I came to tell you something I thought you would want to know." He looked up at Rachel. "Your husband is gone. The commander said he resigned from the army, but nobody can find a trace of him. All of his gear and military things are still in his quarters."

"That is understandable. He said he wanted nothing around him that reminded him, in any way, of his stay in the army." Rachel shook her head. "He was taking the first ship home; at least, that's what he told me."

"But one of our soldiers was seeing his wife off on the same ship as your husband, said he never saw him get on the ship," the sergeant shrugged. "I was hoping he was here with you."

"The last time I saw him was," she sighed heavily, "well, you know the last time I saw him."

"I am sorry, but we have to check everything out. I hope you are doing well." He put his hat back on.

"I hope all is well with you and your family, too." She waved good-bye to him as he left the room.

Josey closed the door after he left, and came close to Rachel. "There has been a man hanging around the building. He seems to be watching who comes and goes. He has been there for a couple of days. Except at night, I don't see him. Do you think it could be your husband? Maybe?"

"What does this man look like?" Rachel's voice filled with hope.

"He is a very large man," she thought for a while. "He does not wear a uniform."

"My husband is not too large, but he is not short either, and he would not be wearing a uniform. Is there anything else you can remember about him?" Rachel was getting excited that maybe, just maybe; he did love her enough to forgive her.

"Oh, yes," she said. "He wears a patch over one eye."

Rachel let out a gasp and grabbed her throat. "It cannot be." Fear began to form in her eyes.

"What is it?" Josey did not miss the terrified look in her eyes.

"That man means to harm me," Rachel blurted out. The thought of Count Tychovsky watching her terrified her. "He blames me for the loss of his eye and has promised to get revenge."

"I will tell my husband to chase him away," she said confidently.

"No!" Rachel grabbed her hands firmly. "He is a very, very dangerous man. I would not put it past him to kill you or anyone else that gets in his way. Please, promise me you will not have your husband get involved."

"Oh, my. I don't want anything happening to my husband. He is a good man, and they are hard to find." She thought for a while. "This one-eyed devil doesn't know we know about him, so we can try to see when he leaves. Then we can sneak you out and away from here."

"That would be wonderful, but only if you promise to stay safe."

"That is a promise," she said. "I have to go down and warn my husband about this man, so he doesn't do anything to get himself hurt."

Rachel locked the door after Josey left, and went to the window. She stood off to the side and carefully pulled back part of the curtain to peek out. She froze. It was him. He was looking directly up at her window. She pulled back and edged herself away.

She had to get away tonight. It was too dangerous for everyone if she stayed. Rachel packed everything up and went to the window. Carefully, she peeked out to see him still staring up at her window. "You don't know I know you are there. That may be my only chance to get away."

He leaned against the post, staring up at the light glowing from her window. A wide grin spread across the Count's face. "It took me a while, but I finally know which room you are in. Tonight. Tonight will be your last night." He watched until the lights in her room went out and walked away. “I will be back later to finish our business.”

Chapter 15

My Dearest Edith,

I am so glad that Mrs. Dawson and Albert are there for you. So, you are showing Lady Collingsworth a lot of interesting places. A ride in the country? How wonderful. I can imagine how much she enjoyed the fresh air, and all of the delightful surprises found in our beautiful English countryside.

And, you were right; this trip would have been too hard for Phillip Nathanial. I know he is being well taken care of, so I do not have to worry about him.

About Mountain Jack, well, he looks just like his name, rugged, tough, and very old. But he is an honest, honorable man whom I was lucky enough to meet. He managed to help get things straightened out and got me to Fort Henry safe and sound. It is quite an impressive Fort.

I have met so many kind and helpful people here. Phillip was out on some military maneuvers when I got there, but he was very anxious to see me. When we finally met it was an emotional experience beyond anything I could have ever imagined.

Well, I have much to do and miss you terribly. Give my love to all. Your loving Rachel

Barrister Smyth rode along the desolate road. The morning mist was heavy, and the air was damp and cold. "If that insidious little man didn't pay me so well I would never have agreed to come out this early in the morning. " He spoke out loud to himself. "He acts as if he is the bloody King of England."

The barrister had no qualms about taking anyone's money or property in Lord Symington's business dealings. He chuckled out loud. "Only a few more months and I will have taken enough of the little tyrant's money to never have to work again." It gave him cause to smile broadly at his cleverness. "I have out-cheated the master cheater."

The barrister stopped his horse for a moment. He thought he heard someone calling out for help. He listened and heard nothing, so he continued. Then, he heard it again, only closer this time. There seemed to be movement in the thick mist ahead. He took his pistol from his inside coat pocket and held it firmly in his hand. The barrister strained his beady eyes to see who was walking toward him in the mist so early in the morning.

"Oh," Lady Collingsworth sighed deeply. "Thank goodness you have arrived, sir."

He could see the figure and face of Lady Collingsworth. He relaxed and put the pistol down next to him on the seat. "Milady? What are you doing so far from the Manor?" He asked incredulously.

"I was out taking my usual morning ride, when my horse got spooked and threw me. In this fog, I had no idea which way to go." She limped toward his carriage.

"My dear woman," He got down and walked around to the passenger side of the carriage to help her climb up. "This is a terrible place to be out by yourself. I will take you back to the Manor." He hurried back around to the other side of the carriage and was about to get in when he looked up. Lady Collingsworth had his gun aimed right at his head. "What..." He never got to finish his question. The pistol went off cracking the morning silence.

She grabbed his leather briefcase, climbed out of the buggy, and hurried around to where he lay dead on the ground. She took all of his money and anything else that looked like it would be worth money. Lady Daphne raced to where her horse was tethered and headed back to the manor. She approached the manor carefully, making sure that no one was around. Once the horse was inside the stable, she quickly took the saddle and bridle off and put the horse back in its stall.

Her only escape, when she worked in France as a tutor to three unruly, nasty children, was to saddle a horse and ride the countryside alone. Hiding the briefcase under an oversized cape, she hurried into the manor through the servants' entrance, up the back stairs and into her room.

Shutting the door quietly behind her, she waited by the door to see if anyone had seen her come in and had followed her. There was only silence.

The fireplace glowed from the hot embers of the peat moss. But Lady Collingsworth wanted flames; flames to destroy the new Will. Earlier, when no one was around, she grabbed a couple of big pieces of wood from the parlor and brought them to her room. She picked one up and threw it on the hot embers. She would worry about getting rid of the briefcase later, now she had to get rid of the Will. Not bothering to read any of the papers in the briefcase, she threw the entire contents onto the hot embers. The papers caught on fire instantly.

She sat in front of the fireplace rocking back and forth with glee. She would get all of his fortune for sure. It was only a matter of time now. She knew the poison given to Lord Symington was going to kill him. It was such a painful way to die. She smiled.

Edith awoke to shouts coming from the hallway. There was a loud banging sound, but not at her door, it was at Lord Symington's door. Edith crept to the connecting doors and listened. She could hear the voice of Lobart talking with him.

"Yer Lordship," Lobart said excitedly. "The barrister 'as been murdered."

"What? What do you say?" He asked, still trying to wake up.

"The barrister 'as been murdered. Shot in the 'ead. Dead."

"Yes, that is usually what happens when someone is shot in the head," he said tiredly. "Now what is this about my barrister being murdered?"

"One of the men found 'is carriage on the road, and the barrister was lying on the ground, next to it, with a bullet in the middle of 'is forehead. There was no money or jewelry found on 'im. We think it was the gypsies."

"Oh, course it was the gypsies." Lord Symington began to cough and hack some more. "They are like lice; you cannot get rid of them. I do not want you to stop until you have cleared the land of their like. I want you and the men to go out and find them. Kill every last man, woman, and child."

"We will find their camp and get rid of all of them," Lobart nodded and left the room.

Edith gasped and backed away from the doors. She had to get out and warn them.

Had Edith stayed to listen to the rest of Lord Symington's conversation, she would have heard terrifying news.

"Speaking of someone being dead, you have not forgotten to take care of my wife have you?" Lord Symington's voice was getting weaker. "After my son arrives, she dies." He started to laugh and then began to cough and hack. "If it is a girl child, I want them both dead – like before."

"Yes, yer lordship," Lobart said calmly. "I will personally see to it again."

Edith knew that Maggie wasn't due to bring her food for a couple of hours. She ran to her armoire and grabbed a warm pelisse, bonnet, and gloves and raced out of her bedroom door. She ran into Lady Collingsworth at the top of the stairs.

Lady Collingsworth gestured for Edith to go first. Edith stepped away from the steps. "I think not," she said staring hard at Lady Daphne.

"Have it your way," Lady Daphne almost bounced down the steps ahead of Edith, who followed far enough behind to be a safe distance from any fast movements from her.

"I am going for a ride this morning," Edith waited for a response from her.

Lady Daphne turned and looked at Edith. "I really don't care what you do." She walked into the parlor. Edith thought she heard her humming a song.

That was all Edith needed. She was free and clear to warn Mrs. Dawson. She opened the front door to find one of Lord Symington's henchmen standing on the steps. He whirled around. "Where do ye think ye be going, yer ladyship?"

"I do not have to answer to you," she tried to pass him, but he stepped in front of her.

"Get back into the manor. Please." His voice was almost pleading.

"I will fight you if you try to stop me," she did not move when he stepped closer to her. "And if I lose this child. What will his Lordship do to you?"

"If I let ye go, I will lose my life for sure, yer ladyship." He stepped up to the top landing and gently took her arm.

"I am feeling ill, and I need Mrs. Dawson. I fear it may mean I will lose his lordships' child. She has special herbs to help me." She lied, feigning weakness as he guided her back into the manor.

"I cannot let ye out of the Manor, ye have to go back inside."

"What seems to be the problem?" A large burly-looking male stepped up behind the young henchmen. He wore a large hat that covered the top part of his face and a woolen scarf that covered the bottom half.

"Earl," he grabbed his heart. "You always scare me like that. You be as quiet as a ghost. The problem is 'er ladyship wants to go to Brekmore manor, and we were given strict instructions that she was not to leave the manor anymore until after the child is born."

"She seems like she is in a weakened state," he brushed past the youth, towering over him in size. "I will escort her back to her room."

"No," Edith pleaded. "It is a matter of life and death."

"I do not wish to carry you up those stairs, but I will if I have to, so please," he gestured for her to go back into the Manor. "Your ladyship." He picked up the front part of his hat and lifted his head from the scarf that was covering the bottom half of his face, and winked at her.

It took Edith a moment to recognize Juan. She almost cried out with joy at seeing him. "You are both beasts," she said, pretending to be angry.

Juan turned to the young man behind him, "I will make sure she goes directly to her room."

"Thanks, Earl, I really appreciate you 'elping me like this," he said.

Edith stomped up the stairs with Juan right behind her. At the top of the stairs, she pretended to lose her balance. Juan quickly reached over and steadied her.

"Juan," she whispered. "They are going to the gypsy camp and kill everyone."

"Watch where ye are walking, your ladyship," he said loudly. "I will stand here and watch until you are in your bedchambers."

Edith hurried down the hall as fast as she could, unlocked her door, rushed in, and slammed the door behind her.

A couple of hours later, there was a knock on her door.

“Who is it?” She called anxiously.

“It’s me, Maggie.”

Edith rushed to the door and unlocked it.

Maggie came in carrying the basket of food, as she always did. She had started to wear large bonnets that hid her face, and large flowing capes. She walked to the small table by the window and waited until Edith shut and locked the door.

Edith went to Maggie and asked in a low voice, “Did anyone get a message from Juan?”

Maggie smiled, nodded, and whispered. “He warned them, just in time.”

“Is the world so full of these evil people?” Edith slumped down in the chair next to her table. She motioned for Maggie to sit on the cushion in the window seat.

“I do not think there are that many,” she sat for a moment. “I think there be far nicer people in the world, but not in this ‘ouse.” The two women began to laugh.

They visited for a while before Maggie got up to leave, “I must get back. But Mrs. Dawson will be coming tomorrow to check in on you.”

"Stay safe, dear Maggie." Edith got up and unlocked the door.

"Oh, I will, yer ladyship."

Just as they opened the door they heard the door to Lord Symington's room open. Edith quickly closed her door, but left just enough room for them to see who was coming out of his room. It was Lady Collingsworth. Edith slowly shut her door. Lady Daphne's steps stopped in front of Edith's room for a while.

Edith and Maggie looked at each other in wonder. They waited until they heard the soft padding of her shoes walking down the hall. When the sound of her footsteps faded altogether, Edith opened the door slowly. She looked out the door and saw that the hall was clear. "Go the other way," Edith pointed to the backstairs the servants always used. "It will take you to the kitchen and from there they will tell you how to get to the front door. Hurry."

She locked the door after Maggie started down the back stairs. Edith ran to the window and waited anxiously until she saw Maggie emerge, and her brothers help her into the carriage. She slumped back in her chair and wondered what could possibly happen next.

The next couple of weeks were uneventful for Edith. Lord Symington's health was getting worse day-by-day, and she cared not.

Lord Symington never left his room anymore. He allowed no one in his room except his henchmen. They stayed with him at all times and took turns watching him in his chambers.

Lady Collingsworth was forbidden to set foot in his room. She tried a couple of times to get one of his men to leave so she could talk to Lord Symington alone. The henchmen refused to let her in alone or otherwise.

Maggie, in her large bonnet and cape paid her daily visits, and Mrs. Dawson started coming over three times a week instead of her usual twice a week. Edith, now restricted to the house, had decided to stay in her room, but now it was beginning to distress her. Although, she knew the real reason for her distress was because she had not seen Ian in a week.

Early in the morning Edith heard Lord Symington send Lobart to fetch a doctor from town.

Edith decided it was time to get a little fresh air, or at least a change of scenery. She pulled out one of her gowns and dressed herself. It was hard maneuvering around the rather large padding across her stomach. She struggled for a while but finally managed to get the one and only dress on that would fit around her. She had a terrible time trying to get her stockings and shoes on, and finally forgot about the stockings and just slipped on her shoes. She tucked her hair up into a large lacy cap, and grabbed a shawl.

Edith thought she might just walk about the grounds. She went to the window and looked out. There was a slight covering of snow, and she thought better of it. "Okay, I'll go down to the kitchen. I haven't been there in quite a while." She spoke aloud to herself. "Mrs. Dawson and Maggie are due here any moment, although from the looks of the road, it may take them longer today."

She unlocked her door, and relocked it as she left her room. There was no one in the hallway which pleased her greatly. Instead of going down the main staircase, she used the servants' staircase.

When she walked into the kitchen she startled the cook. "Yer ladyship, should ye be up and about? Can I get ye anything?"

"I am feeling fine," she said. "I just needed to go for a little walk."

"Would ye be wanting a cup of tea?"

"Yes, I believe I would," she was about to sit down when she heard a loud smashing noise coming from the parlor.

The cook, one of the servant girls, and Edith rushed into the parlor. They opened the door and cautiously looked in. Lady Collingsworth was standing in front of the fireplace. Edith moved in closer to her and saw the shattered pieces of glass around the hearth.

Lady Daphne was swaying back and forth staring into the fire. She turned and spotted Edith and the servants. "Get out!" She screamed. "Get out of my parlor!"

"As far as I know," Edith replied coldly. "This is Lord Symington's parlor." Edith still could not bring herself to call him her husband.

"That foul man?" She sneered. "That miserable old man shouldn't own such a place." Her words were slurred. She moved toward a chair by the fireplace and grabbed the back of it to steady herself.

Edith turned to the frightened cook and servant girl, "Go get Earl. Hurry, now!"

They took off running from the parlor. Earl was one of Lord Symington's new henchmen that they liked, although his size and appearance frightened them a little. He was a frequent visitor in their kitchen, even though he barely said but a few words to them.

"This is all going to be mine," Lady Daphne staggered and fell against a table, knocking an unlit lamp that shattered as it hit the floor. She moved toward Edith, a smile on her face. "I haven't been able to see him or you for a long time. However, seeing you now," she smiled broadly, "is like a gift." As she advanced toward Edith, she reached inside a pocket of her dress. Her eyes began to sparkle.

Edith was stunned at the sudden change to the expression on Lady Daphne's face. The hatred replaced with an expression of happiness.

When Lady Daphne stumbled again, out of instinct Edith rushed to steady her.

Suddenly, Lady Collingsworth's face twisted and contorted into rage as she shoved a knife into Edith's stomach.

Edith screamed in shock. She had nothing to defend herself with. She screamed again, as Lady Daphne raised the knife and brought it down to strike at her heart. Edith moved aside quickly, but the knife cut into her arm.

Daphne raised the knife again for the fatal blow, when suddenly she was lifted up from behind and thrown violently across the room. Like a toy rag doll, she flew across the room, knocking over a chair and table; her flight ended when her head hit the wood frame around the window. Knocked unconscious by the blow, she lay there in a heap on the floor.

"Oh, no," The servant girl screamed. "She stabbed the baby"

Mrs. Dawson came bursting into the room. "Juan, get her upstairs,. Immediately."

"That's Earl," the cook said, correcting Mrs. Dawson.

"Whatever your name is," she looked at Juan and then at Edith. "Get her up to her bedchamber, now."

Juan picked Edith up in his strong arms and carried her up the stairs effortlessly.

Mrs. Dawson reached for the key chain from around Edith's neck, and gently took it off. Maggie followed silently in the large bonnet that covered her face, and in her long, voluminous cape. Mrs. Dawson unlocked the door and ordered the cook and servant girl to fetch her some boiling water and cloths to treat the wounds.

They raced down the servants' steps to get the items Mrs. Dawson demanded.

Once Edith was safe in her room, Juan bowed and made his exit. "I have a matter that has to be taken care of in the parlor. If you will excuse me." He shut the door behind him.

Mrs. Dawson hurried to Edith. "Quickly, let me see the wound." She shook her head as she pulled the material away from the cut. "Thank goodness, it is not a deep cut. Here let me help you get your dress off."

Suddenly, Maggie doubled up and began to moan.

Edith and Mrs. Dawson rushed to her side. "What is it dear Maggie," Edith asked with deep concern.

"We must wait until they bring us the water and bandages. Oh, what is taking them so long?"

Again, Maggie groaned and doubled over.

A few minutes later, the servants entered with the hot water and clean cloths.

"That will be all," she ushered the two women out of the room and locked the door.

Mrs. Dawson undid the large bonnet, and pulled off the cape. Edith stepped back and then nodded. It wasn't Maggie, but a gypsy woman who was about to give birth.

"Is it time?" Edith asked. Her heart began to soar. This was the beginning of the end of her life as Lord Symington's wife. "Mrs. Dawson, I have to ask you, how can we be sure she's going to bear a son?"

Mrs. Dawson smiled. "This is not her first-born child. She said she carries the girl children differently than the boy children. Now, if she happens to have a girl, we have a backup plan, so don'tcha go worry about anything. There may be one slight little problem though."

"Mercy, what is it?" Edith clutched her heart.

"She is a month early. This is not good for her or the baby." Mrs. Dawson took a rag and wet it. She finished dressing Edith's wound, just as the woman gave out a scream, followed by several more screams seconds apart.

A henchman began pounding on the door, "'is Lordship be asking what the screaming is all about. 'e be not feeling well, and it be disturbing 'im."

"Tell him his wife is about to deliver his baby," Mrs. Dawson yelled back.

A few moments later, the henchmen yelled through the connecting doors. "'is Lordship said she can scream all she wants." He stopped and then continued. "Lord Symington wanted me to tell you that 'e be enjoying 'earing 'er scream in pain. And, it 'ad better be a son."

It was a couple of hours later, when the sound of a child's cry filled the room. Mrs. Dawson cleaned the child and placed it in the tired woman's arms. With Edith's help they pulled the bloodied blanket from under the woman and wadded it up throwing it out of their way. They gently pushed a clean blanket underneath her.

"'is Lordship wants to know if it is alive. And, if so, is it a boy?" came a call from the next room.

"You can tell his Lordship, it is a boy." Mrs. Dawson smiled and winked at Edith.

"How is she going to be able to stay with her son," Edith asked concerned that the mother and son would be parted.

"She is your new wet-nurse," Mrs. Dawson arched her back and sat down on one of the chairs blocking the connecting doors.

The sound of someone knocking on Lord Symington's door alerted the two women. They listened through the connecting doors.

It was one of his henchmen, "Lobart will be 'ere soon with the doctor you requested."

Lord Symington began ranting and raving at the frightened henchmen. "Bring ... my son. Get my son ... out of her hands."

Edith and Mrs. Dawson heard everything. They gently helped the young mother up, placing the clean blanket that had been under her over the chair seat. Edith grabbed one of her larger bonnets and tucked the mother's loose and wild hair underneath it. Mrs. Dawson grabbed the cape and threw it around her shoulders, closing it in the front.

"Open the door," the henchmen shouted. "'is Lordship wants to see 'is son. If you do not open the door I will kick it in."

"Just a moment," Mrs. Dawson yelled. "I will open the door as soon as she has been cleaned up."

Edith slipped out of her ripped dress, and crawled into bed. Mrs. Dawson handed her the swaddled baby, took a deep breath and walked to the door, and unlocked it.

The henchmen brushed past her, took the baby out of Edith's arms without saying a word and left the room.

Mrs. Dawson closed the door and locked it again. Edith jumped out of bed, and they ran to the connecting doors to listen.

They sighed with relief when they heard Lord Symington. "Look at his black hair and eyes-s-s. He looks-s-s just like me. Put him in his bed. I – no one - - anyone near him. He's-s-s mine alone. Find a wet-nurs-s - e. Only other person allowed … to touch him." His words were becoming slurred, and his voice much weaker.

Edith and Mrs. Dawson strained to hear him. "Where is-s-s Lobart ... doctor. He mus-s-s-t ... make me well again." His voice became weaker, barely above a whisper. "I want to be ... with my s-s-son."

Juan stood over the limp form of Lady Collingsworth lying on the floor. She began to stir, moaning softly.

One of the henchmen came in and stood looking over her. "I 'eard what 'appened. What are we going to do with 'er?"

"I know what I want to do with her," Juan snarled.

"We 'ave to wait for Lobart," the henchman shrugged. "Only 'e can tell us what to do with 'er."

"What happened?" Lady Daphne raised her hand to her forehead and asked hopefully. "Is she dead? Is the child dead?"

Juan grabbed her raised arm and yanked her to her feet, shoving her in a chair by the fireplace. "Sit there until I tell you to move."

The screams of the woman in labor reverberated down into the parlor.

"No," Lady Daphne said. "That cannot be her. I drove my knife into her belly. She cannot be having this child. She cannot. This is my manor now." Her voice was on the verge of hysteria.

As the minutes flew by Juan listened to the Lady Collingsworth rant and rave about all the murderous and evil deeds she did in her life, justifying them to herself. "I am a woman, in a man's world. I had to do these things to survive."

She rambled to herself, not even aware of the man standing by the fireplace: The man who was going to seal her fate. "And my beautiful mother hated me for causing her such pain. My father died and left us nothing. Everything went to my uncle. We had to survive, didn't we? We are women in a man's world."

One of the servants brought Juan a cup of tea. "The child is born. It is a boy. And, mother and child are doing fine."

"Nooo!" Lady Collingsworth screamed. She tried to get out of her chair and was roughly pushed back by Juan. "No," she sobbed. "No, it cannot be."

A carriage pulled up to the manor. Lobart brought the doctor whom Lord Symington had ordered.

He stopped at the parlor and spied the chairs overturned and the complete disarray of the room. "What 'appened 'ere?"

Juan and the other henchmen filled him in on what happened. "What do you want us to do with her?" Juan asked.

"Get rid of 'er, and I am not interested in 'ow you do it. Just do it." Lobart gave a half-smile and changed the subject matter abruptly. "So, it is a son, is it? I didn't think the old bugger 'ad it in 'im. Well, I 'ad best get this doctor up to see 'im before all 'ell breaks out." He left the parlor and motioned to the doctor to follow him.

Juan moved toward Lady Collingsworth, who didn't appear to have heard anything. Her eyes were wildly looking around the room. He grabbed her arm and yanked her up from the chair. "Let's go for a nice ride," he said baring his teeth.

"Get your hands off of me, you filthy beast." She ordered trying to pry his strong fingers from around her arm.

He turned to the other henchmen. "I will take care of this one." When he turned back she lashed out at him with her knife cutting part of his leather coat. Juan struck her on the chin with his fist, and she fell to the floor in a heap. He picked up her limp body throwing her over his shoulder like a sack of grain and headed out the door.

"I am glad I'm not 'er," said the henchman watching the dangling body of Lady Collingsworth go out the front door.

Juan made a quick stop at Brekmore manor before he continued his journey.

Lady Collingsworth awoke in a dark room. Her head and chin hurt her. She reached up to feel her face when something on her wrist made a rattling sound. She moved her legs to sit up, and again heard the rattle sound. She looked at her wrists and then her ankles and began to tug on the chains. "What are these things? Get these things off of me." She hollered. "Where am I? What place is this? Get me out of here, now." She screamed again.

Sounds of people screaming and moaning were all around her. A faint light filtered in through a tiny window high up in the door to her cell. "I am Lady Collingsworth. I am of noble blood. Get me out of here." She screamed repeatedly.

One of the caretakers at the asylum sauntered to her cell and peered in through the tiny window. "Shut up. Yer waking the other patients."

"Get me out of this filthy place, this instant, you foul peasant," her lips curled back in hatred as she screamed.

The caretaker shut the little door to the window and walked down the hall to the staff's quarters. "They said this one would claim she was a duchess or something like that. Crazy as a loon, that one. They said to watch out for 'er because she 'as killed a couple of people, may be more."

"Yeah," the other caretaker said. "A real fine duchess she be. She looks more like a gypsy to me in the clothes she be wearing. We get all kinds in 'ere. A Lady, she be claiming. They said she thinks Indians are going to attack us." Both attendants broke out in laughter.

"That 'lady' is going to be with us for a long, long time." They could still hear her screaming all the way down the hall. "We are going to 'ave to stop 'er from doing that. But not tonight, cause we 'ave more important things to do. She will learn soon enough. Never can take those chains off though, cause she be too dangerous for that."

"It be yer move," the caretaker pointed to the checkerboard on the table.

"Wait till I shut the door, so 'er screamin' won't bother us."

They both looked at each other and broke into laughter again. "We'll put 'er with all the others in the morning. It oughta give us some fine entertainment."

Chapter 16

My Dearest Rachel,

I am glad that you and Phillip have finally found each other again. I can well understand the pain of not being with the one you love. I would have liked to have met your friend Mountain Jack in person. He sounds like a wonderful man, especially since he took such good care of you.

We have had a bit of excitement here. It appears that Lord Symington's barrister was murdered. No one knows who did it. On a more cheerful note, Lord Symington is very ill, and they do not expect him to survive the month. Therefore, my darling, you and Phillip can come home any time you wish.

Ian had to go away on a business trip, and I am so lost without him. However, he shall return to me soon, and I can hardly wait.

One of Mrs. Dawson's nephews helped Lady Collingsworth find a new place to stay. Mrs. Dawson felt that Lady Collingsworth needed a more befitting home for her position. I do not believe she will be coming back. I am told she found a place where she will stay and be looked after for as long as she lives. She so deserves that.

Well, my love, it is getting late, and I must get this letter to our mutual friend. With all my love and sincerest regards, love Edith

Rachel waited until Count Tychovsky returned to starting his vigil of watching her room. She smiled. "You go ahead and watch the front of the building." She put her bonnet and shawl on, and grabbed her valise and purse. She cautiously opened the door, and hoped everyone would be in the dining room having their meals. She sighed with relief: The hallway was empty. Rachel hurried down the backstairs.

The backdoor creaked as she opened it slowly peering out to see if anyone was lurking around. It looked empty. Carefully, she stepped outside into the alley, seeing no one she took off running toward the docks.

A man stepped out of the shadows. He watched her run down the alleyway toward the docks. He raced around the building to Count Tychovsky. "I think the lady we have been watching just left from the backdoor."

"Come on. Let's go," the Count said.

The other man reached out and grabbed the Count's arm. "She better have all the money you say she has on her."

Count Tychovsky yanked his arm away. "She does." He smiled to himself, because it wouldn't matter if she had the crown jewels of England in her purse, he planned on killing the man after he caught up to Lady Prescott.

They ran across the street and down the alley in the direction Rachel had gone.

Rachel ran between the buildings, hoping she was heading in the direction of the docks. The alley opened up to a forest on one side and buildings on the other.

Fear gripped her as she thought she heard the sound of someone running after her. She looked back and saw the form of two men running after her, and one was definitely Count Tychovsky. She tried to run faster, but the heavy valise and purse were slowing her down. She began screaming for help. The buildings looked empty, but that didn't stop her screams for help.

"Stop her," the Count ordered to the other man.

She turned as she was running and saw them closing in on her.

"I said to stop her. Shoot her in the leg, anywhere, but don't kill her." She heard the Count yell to the other man. She looked back and saw that the other man had stopped and had raised his pistol. She kept running, hoping it was too far for the bullet to travel.

Suddenly, there was a scream behind her. She stopped, out of breath, and looked back. The gun had dropped from the man's hand as he clutched his chest. A stunned look was on his face as he looked down at the arrow protruding from it. Count Tychovsky turned and ran back down the alley, with arrows whizzing around him.

Rachel felt someone behind her. She turned and came face-to-face with an Indian. He had a tomahawk in one hand and a knife in another. A couple more Indians came from the wooded area, and quickly grabbed up all of their arrows, including the one sticking out of the chest of the dead man.

The Indian just nodded toward her, pointed down a small alleyway, and then quickly disappeared back into the forest with the rest.

Rachel didn't hesitate. She ran down the alleyway that eventually opened up to the docks. She managed to find a ship that was going to a port off Lake Ontario in New York. She would try to retrace her steps to Boston. If she could get to Albany, there would be stagecoaches to get her back to Boston.

The ship's cabin was very tiny. The small window in her cabin was round and opened inward. There was a walkway right outside her window. She could see the crew and other passengers as they walked past her window. Some looked in, while others paid no attention to the window. Rachel locked the door and closed the small curtain that hung by the side of the window. She was feeling better. She escaped the Count. Now, she was on her way back to Boston. She wanted so desperately to see Phillip Nathaniel, Aunt Libbie and Aunt Clara, and Nathan again.

They sailed for a while in somewhat calm seas, until the ship began to pitch violently. Rachel opened her curtain to see waves rising and falling in great heights. Freezing wind and snow belted the tiny ship as it battled against the elements. It was hours before the seas were calm enough for the ship to pull into a port and dock.

She opened her door and stopped a crewman walking by. "Have we arrived?" she asked.

"No, Ma'am," he said. "We pulled in here to wait out the storm. There is another front moving in. It is too treacherous for us to continue now. But if you like, there is a tavern just a bit down the way. They will have food and drink for you. I would go if I were you, because we may be here a long time, and we don't have food on this ship for passengers." He tipped his cap and left.

Rachel grabbed her purse and valise and headed down the wind-blown gangplank. The winds were strong against her back as she made her way along the slippery, stone street.

She spotted a sign buffeted by the strong winds that said Tavern on it. She didn't care what kind of establishment it was, just so she could get out of the freezing rain and wind. She struggled to open the tavern door, and was startled when the wind ripped it out of her hand, sending the door slamming against the wall.

A young barmaid ran and pulled the door closed against the strong wind. "Nasty night to be out and about. Come this way." She took her to a table near a large, roaring fireplace. "You look wet and cold. I'll get you some warm ale."

Rachel had a tasty meal, but she had learned not to ask what it was.

The barmaid stood at the window looking out at the black sky, and blustering winds. "You'll not be traveling on that ship for a day or more. That is a big storm brewing over there. I usually don't offer any rooms cause this place is just a tavern, not an inn. But I have an extra room that you can rent out above the tavern if you be needing one." She brushed a red curl away that escaped from her cap and fell on her forehead. Her green eyes smiled warmly at Rachel.

"Yes," Rachel said. She looked at the pretty barmaid and smiled back at her. She did not feel like spending the night on a ship and tossed about in a storm. "But I have one request. If someone should ask about me, or ask if a woman is staying here, I do not want them to know. I will pay you well." There was a hint of fear in her voice and eyes that the barmaid did not miss.

"Running from a bad husband," she said. "I had one of those. No one's gonna know you are here, but me. My name is Mary. The other girl never showed up today. I be the only one who knows where you are and no lousy husband is going to find you. Let me just clear this stuff of your table first. After she had cleared and wiped the table, she turned to Rachel. "Come on; let's get you a nice warm bed to sleep in."

Mary took her to a room that was not facing the street. "This side of the tavern is better for you. Nobody can see your light from the street below. I'll be back to get you a nice warm fire in the stove."

Mary returned and got the fire started. She left the door open so that she could hear if any customers should happen to come in. They talked for a while until the sound of the door banging open from the wind sent Mary downstairs.

Rachel closed her door and moved her chair closer to the stove. It was more than an hour before she heard Mary coming down the hall. She got up and opened the door. Mary went into a room that overlooked the street. After a few minutes, Mary raced toward Rachel's room.

"I think he was here," she said in a low voice.

"Oh, no." Rachel exclaimed.

"Your husband have a patch over his eye?" She asked.

"That is the man I do not want to find me," Rachel gasped.

Mary shuddered. "He was a really nasty customer, that one."

"What happened?"

"He came in and asked if I had a woman staying at my inn. I told him this was a tavern, not an inn, and nobody was welcome to stay here, except my husband and me. I didn't want him thinking I was here by myself. My husband will be back sometime tomorrow, but I don't know when. He went up to the neighboring town to get some supplies."

"Your husband is the one who beat you?" Rachel asked.

"Lordy, no," she slapped her thigh. "That mean son-of-horse thief is dead. He used to slap and punch me around all the time. He was always sorry later. Blamed all his meanery on something I did. One night he went to bed after he beat me pretty good. I picked up my iron skillet and smacked him over the head while he lay there sleeping. Man never did wake up. This husband I have now is a kind, older man, never says a cross word to me."

"That is good for him," Rachel laughed. "And the man downstairs is not my husband. I met him and his wife onboard a ship. She looked like he beat her regularly. I accidentally caused his face to be burned and for him to lose one eye. The Count wants his revenge."

"A Count you say? Don't have much use for any kind of them royalty folks. He went and ordered some food and drink, and asked me if I knew about a place to stay." She began to laugh, "I sent him down the road on the opposite side of the docks. It's really storming out there. I 'spect he will be good and wet, by the time he gets there. And, just in case he was watching, I went into my room, lit some lamps, started a fire, and walked in front of the window to let him see it was just me."

"Do you think he is gone?" Rachel asked nervously.

"I told him I was closing up the place as soon as he left," she shrugged. "I don't think he'll be hanging around outside for long. Let me see if he's there." Mary left and went into another room across from Edith's that faced the street. The room was completely dark. She peeked out the window carefully so he wouldn't see her, and then raced back to Rachel's room. "I don't see him, and I don't think he'd be stupid enough to stand outside in this storm on a chance you may be here."

"But just in case he decides to check out the back of the building." Rachel leaned over and blew out the candle sitting on the small table by her bed.

Mary quickly closed the heavy drapes in front of her window. The stove in Rachel's room gave very little light, and the drapes would hide that.

"You get some sleep now," Mary stood up and stretched. "I'll have a good breakfast for you in the morning."

Rachel climbed into bed in her clothes, took the pistol out of her purse, pulled the quilts up around her, and fell into a restless sleep.

Morning came with the smell of coffee and bacon cooking downstairs. Mary opened her door and brought in a cup of hot coffee, some bacon, eggs, and toast. "I don't think he will be coming back here for breakfast, but we can't be sure."

Rachel had taken off her bonnet and dress during the night, and was just sleeping in her shift. She was starving and ate every last crumb on her plate, and even drank the bitter tasting coffee. Mary was an excellent cook, not like Edith's Mrs. Collingsworth.

She pondered about the people she had met in her life, from Edith to Mary. There were so many wonderful and kind people out there. However, unfortunately, there were many evil ones, too. Rachel was dressed and headed down the hallway toward the steps when she heard the Count's voice. She ran back to her room, grabbed her things, and waited.

It was a long time before Mary came upstairs. "Rachel?" She called out softly.

Rachel opened the door. Mary did not come in; instead, she just leaned against the doorframe, keeping a watchful eye on the hallway. "He was back again this morning. Said he was still looking for his 'wife', that he checked the ships docked here, and found out which one she was on. The ship she was on left the harbor and his wife never returned to it. He asked me if a woman traveling alone, stopped in my tavern for breakfast this morning. Said he has checked all the places that serve breakfast and no one had seen her."

"What did you tell him?" Rachel asked.

"I told him no single woman had been in here in the last couple of days. I asked him to describe you, and if I should see you, I would let him know. I asked him where I could get in touch with him if I saw you. He told me he was checking out the town to see if someone gave her a place to stay for the night. He said he would be back and check with me, and the other taverns later to see if she had come around. He got up, paid for his food and ale and left. I waited until he was out of sight before I came up here to tell you."

"Thank you, Mary." She reached out and gave her arm a gentle squeeze. "I must get a carriage and head for Albany. Is Albany far from here?"

"It be a pretty far distance, maybe one or two days from here if you are going by carriage, and a good couple weeks, or more if you be walking."

"I heard there are marauders and Indians out there."

"Not so much if you stay along the coastline of the lake."

"I cannot wait. I have to get out of town before the Count finds me, and he will. Is there anywhere I can buy a horse and carriage?"

"No buggies. But if you want to buy just a horse, I have one in the barn behind the tavern. My husband takes turns using them to go on his buying trips. We have a saddle, but it is not for an English Lady to ride. There is no way to ride it sidesaddle."

Rachel smiled. "I can ride the horse astride."

The transaction was completed. "Now, I will show you just how to bridle and saddle a horse. I will explain what and when to feed it, so the horse gets you to Albany."

Just as she promised, she showed Rachel how to put the bit in the horse's mouth, and where to put the reins. She pulled out the dusty blanket for the horse's back, and showed her how to pull the straps from the saddle under the horse and to adjust them securely. Rachel was terrified she would forget something, and repeated everything Mary said several times.

Mary told Rachel to wait for a moment; she had to get some things from the tavern. She came back carrying a couple of things in her arms. "Here's some bread for you. You might get hungry." She reached into her apron pocket, and pulled out a large pistol. "Here, I have a couple more in the tavern. You may be needing this." She pulled an old saddlebag from a hook, and wiped off the dust. She flipped the leather flap back, and shoved the pistol inside of a pocket. "You might want to get rid of your valise, and put what you can in the saddlebags. Be a mite easier."

Rachel took the few things in her valise and stuffed as much as she could into the saddlebags.

Mary brought over a step stool for her to stand on. "I don't know how a little thing like you is going to keep getting on and off this horse without a block or something to stand on." She scratched her head and shrugged as she hoisted Rachel on the horse with her shoulder. "I wish you the best of luck. It woulda been nice if you could have stayed longer. I really enjoyed talking with you." She led the horse to the closed barn doors.

"You are a wonderful person, and I shall always remember you and your kindness," Rachel said reaching down to grasp her hand one last time.

"Aww, it wasn't nothing. Now you wait and let me check and see if the horrible Count is around." Mary opened the barn door and walked around outside for a moment. "It looks okay. Go out of here to the left, and stay by the road along the lake. Now you be careful."

Rachel waved good-bye, as she turned left and headed away from the town. Riding horses was nothing new for Rachel, but riding in this position was going to prove to be interesting she thought.

She was relieved to see the last block of city buildings. With any luck, he would still be looking for her in the town. Once she got beyond the hill in the road ahead, he would not be able to see her.

The rains were coming in again, and the roads were deep with mud. She tried to keep the horse off the middle of the road and onto the side of the road that seemed less muddy.

Suddenly, ahead of her, she saw the Count running from between a couple of buildings set back off the road. He was trying to reach the road to cut her off.

She kicked the horse in its side, and it began to move faster. The Count was closing in on her. I'll never make it; she thought. She lowered her head and yelled for the horse to go faster. As if it understood, the horse immediately began to gain speed.

The Count was almost on her. He let out a scream as he leaped toward her and the horse, only to miss by inches and fall into a thick pile of mud. He pulled out his pistol and fired at her. The bullet missed.

Rachel withdrew the pistol Mary had given her and fired back at him. She saw him dive off the road. "Now, you know I am armed as well." Her horse raced over the hill and out of sight.

When she was sure that the Count was not behind her, she slowed down. Rachel kept the horse off the road as much as possible, choosing to ride on the berm. The hard rain caused the roads to be slippery, and the mud deep. She was completely drenched and shivering from the cold winds that accompanied the rain.

A couple of men on horseback passed her on the road; each one turning to look at her strangely. She reached into the saddlebag and pulled out her pistol. The men slowed for a moment and then, spotting the pistol, kept going. Rachel was relieved that they did not come back for her and that their horses would help to cover her tracks.

Her travel was slow, but she kept going. Rachel's bonnet provided the barest of protection by keeping the pelting rain out of her eyes. She pulled the horse up and stopped. There was a fork in the road. Which one was she supposed to take?

She was exhausted and wet. She tried to think. The horse had been plodding along in the deep mud, and Rachel knew it needed to rest. She patted the horse's side, not knowing which road to take she shrugged and picked her course.

About a mile down the road, she saw a dirt road and a cabin sitting back in the woods. She reached the cabin, and got off the horse. It was a barren cabin, no chairs, no beds nothing except a musty old blanket and a fireplace.

Rachel took the horse to a small shed in the back. At least, it was warmer and the freezing wind and rain had stopped.

She took off the bit and bridle, and loosened the cinch to the saddle pulling it off the horse and draping it over the half-wall of its stall. She found some old hay and brought it over to the horse. Next to the shed was a bucket filled with rain water. Quickly, she filled the horse's trough and took the remaining water, along with the saddlebags, into the cabin.

The first thing she did was to try to get a fire started in the fireplace. There were some pieces of wood beside the fireplace. She looked around for the flint to start the fire, and found it on a dusty shelf. However, she needed kindling to get the fire going. She looked around but could not find any, until she remembered her divorce decree. She grabbed her purse and yanked it out. She tore it into small pieces, wadded it up, and put it under the wood. It took her a while, but finally, she had a warm fire going. She took off her wet clothes and hung them on pegs near the fireplace.

She opened the saddlebags, and was thankful they were made of leather, because the bread was as dry as when Mary had put it in there. After she had finished eating, she pulled the dusty blanket over her, curled up by the fireplace, and promptly fell asleep.

Rachel woke up to the sun trying to shine through the broken shutters and window. Her body ached all over as she got up off the floor. She checked her clothes and was relieved that they had almost dried through the night.

After she ate a little bread, and drank some water, she hurried into the barn. The horse was still there, and looked rested. She remembered all the things that Mary had quickly shown her about putting the bit, bridle, and saddle on the horse.

She led the horse to the front porch. It was the perfect height for her to get on. Rachel threw the saddlebags over the saddle, stepped into the stirrup, pulled the front of her dress up a little, and slung her leg over the horse.

The sun helped to take some of the chill out of the morning air. Nevertheless, it was still going to be a long cold ride. She traveled for hours, stopping frequently for the horse to eat, rest, and drink. By nightfall, she reached the outskirts of Albany. The sight almost made her cry. She urged the horse down into the town. Rachel found a livery stable for her horse, and an inn nearby. The innkeeper told her the stagecoach would be leaving first thing in the morning. Rachel purchased her ticket, ate a meal, went to her room, and fell asleep.

The next morning she was up early. Rachel looked at the saddlebags and knew they would not do for the next leg of her journey. She asked the innkeeper where she could purchase a valise. He said there wasn't anything open that early in the morning, but he had one someone left behind and would exchange it for her saddlebags. The valise was old and worn, but it would suffice just fine for her. Rachel quickly transferred everything from the saddlebags to her valise. She hurried downstairs and gave the innkeeper the saddlebags, and went out to the stagecoach.

Count Tychovsky spotted a cabin off the road and rode toward it. He approached the cabin cautiously; he knew she had a pistol. He took his horse around to the back of the cabin, first looking in the barn. Finding the barn empty, he moved to the cabin, with pistol in hand, he kicked the door open. Disappointment consumed him.

The Count moved toward the fireplace, and felt around the still warm embers and found a partially burnt portion of a divorce proclamation. He saw a bucket with a little water in it and a blanket that was left by the fireplace. He knew she had been here.

He kicked the bucket across the room and screamed, as if in pain. "If I had just taken the other road, I would have found her." Soon a smile crossed his face, "I know where you are heading. There is no place on earth where you will be safe. I am coming for you, Lady Prescott. I am right behind you."

Chapter 17

Dearest Edith,

I was not surprised that Lord Symington is very ill, nor can I say I was sorry to hear it. He has to be over a hundred years old, well, maybe not, but he looks it. Life has a way of changing directions, and sometimes, not the way we want them to go. However, I am glad that Lady Collingsworth has finally found a place where she will be taken care of for the rest of her life.

Edith, I have met so many wonderful people over here. They have been kind and helpful, at least all the ones I have met so far.

This is a very big country. I have seen quite a bit of it. Oh, and Edith, I have even seen a couple of wonderful, real, Canadian Indians. They were beyond amazing. I think when I return I am going to take up archery.

I have stayed in some interesting inns. I was on Lake Ontario when a horrible storm struck. However, the ship's captain pulled into the first safe port, and they had us all spend the night on shore.

Here is hoping you, Ian and your child are doing well. You forgot to mention if you have a son or daughter. I am anxious to hear all about your beautiful child. Give my love to Ian, your father, Mrs. Dawson and Albert.

An innkeeper said he would take care of this letter for me. I am heading to Boston now and am looking forward to seeing Phillip Nathaniel and everyone else.

Well, my dearest, it is getting late, and I am hoping you will get this letter soon. With all my love, Rachel

The doctor pulled Lobart into the hallway to speak with him. Edith and Mrs. Dawson snuck to the door and listened. "I am afraid Lord Symington is a very sick man. I don't think there is much I can do for him. Try to keep from upsetting him. He is very weak. Not only is his body weak, but so is his heart. I will bring my leeches in and see whether that will help him in any way. Although, I do not think they will help with his speech."

"What do ya mean?" Lobart asked.

"I believe he can understand everything we are saying and doing, but he can no longer speak, at least coherently." He turned and looked back at the frail man. "He appears to be in a great deal of pain."

Shortly, the doctor came back and began applying leeches all over Lord Symington's body. The more leeches he put on him the more agitated Symington became. He could not speak coherently, but he finally managed to let the doctor know he wanted the leeches off him. Then he gestured for Lobart to get rid of the doctor.

Lobart really didn't understand a word he said, but he could tell by the waving of Lord Symington's thin arms that he wanted the doctor gone.

"I did not bring anything for pain," the doctor said putting the leeches back in a jar. "I was not prepared for him being in such agonizing pain. I have only seen this much pain once before, but that man had been poisoned."

“Poisoned?” Lobart had a look of surprise on his face. “Ah, Lady Collingsworth,” he murmured. “So, thoughtful of ‘er. Always leaving a fresh bottle of wine for ‘is Lordship, because ‘e so enjoyed a glass in the evening.” He chuckled to himself.

“What did you say?” The doctor asked.

“Nuttin,” he said chuckling some more.

“Oh, well,” the doctor said. “I would appreciate a ride into town. I have some business to attend to tomorrow.”

“I will ‘ave one of my men take you there,” Lobart helped the doctor carry his medical bag down to the carriage.

Lord Symington lay in his bedchamber alone. Edith motioned for Mrs. Dawson to help her move the chairs that were in front of their connecting doors. She entered his room and shut the door that led to the hallway. She raced over to the crib and gently picked up the baby who was sleeping peacefully. She walked over to Lord Symington’s bed and stared down at the loathsome man lying there.

His face twisted in hate as his black eyes bore into hers. She held the baby down for him to get a good look. "Do you see your son?" She rocked the child in her arms. "Do you think he looks like you?" Edith leaned down and stared into the black pits he called his eyes. "This is *not* your son." She leaned down even closer. "Did you hear me, you foul excuse for a human being? This is not your son. You have never, and I repeat that, never touched me. Not even once." She smiled at the bewildered look appearing on his face.

He looked at her and then the baby. Edith sat on the edge of the bed. He tried to raise his arm up to strike her, but was too weak.

"What is even more delicious than that is the fact that this child's mother and father," she paused, "are gypsies."

Lord Symington began making gurgling sounds from his mouth. His eyes were wide and hatred spewed from them.

"A gypsy child is going to inherit all of your money and all of your estates. A gypsy child."

Weakly, he began thrashing around on the bed, his head rolling from side-to-side.

"And I do not want to forget to tell you that I have been sleeping in my bed, right next door there," she pointed to the connecting doors to their rooms, "with my beloved Ian Atterby."

The rage in Lord Symington caused the veins in his neck to stick out from under his wrinkled, thin skin. He grabbed her by the arm, but he was too weak to squeeze it. His hand fell down and flopped against the bed.

Edith heard Mrs. Dawson talking with Lobart at the end of the hall. She looked down and smiled at his twisted and purpled face. "Sleep well, Lord Symington. If you need anything just call me. I will be next door sleeping in my lover's arms." She put the child down in his crib, and raced back into her room.

She quickly locked the doors and put the chairs under the doorknobs, when Mrs. Dawson came back into the room.

"I can tell by the look on your face, you had a good time in there," she kidded quietly.

"Oh, yes," she laughed. "Oh, yes."

Lobart and one of the other henchmen came into Lord Symington's room. Lord Symington was rolling, coughing and began babbling incoherently. He kept frantically looking at the child sleeping in the crib.

"Oh," Lobart picked up the child. "He wants to make sure his son is still here." Lobart brought the child to his bed, and Lord Symington let out a small scream and began shaking his head violently.

"I know what 'e wants," the henchmen said. "Mrs. Dawson brought a wet-nurse for the baby. He probably wants 'er to feed the little tyke."

"Take the baby to 'er," Lobart ordered. "But make sure that baby gets put right back in 'ere. You can see 'ow upset it makes 'im, not to see 'is son and all."

"Gotta be 'ard for the old bloke to know that 'e won't be around to see 'im grow up."

"We are being well paid to watch over that boy," Lobart grinned. "And we will live quite well while we be doing that. Now, off with ya. Take that boy to get 'is food."

Lord Symington heard everything they said. He tried feebly to get out of bed. Lobart saw him and quickly rushed to push him back on the bed. "Now, dun'tcha worry. Your son will be back after the feeding."

Lobart leaned down and spoke quietly to Lord Symington. "I 'ave not forgotten my promises to get rid of Lady Symington. That Mrs. Dawson be staying for a couple of nights to look after 'er, but as soon as she is gone, I will take care of Lady Symington for good."

For two days, Lord Symington lay in bed, his body racked with excruciating pain. Every attempt to appease him with his child brought violent reactions. His face would turn dark red. Veins popped out on his forehead, face, and neck, and he thrashed about wildly. He could no longer speak, but he understood every word that was said.

Lobart left the room and went down to the kitchen to have his mid-day meal.

Lord Symington's eyes moved toward the sound from the baby fussing in his crib. He moved ever so slightly toward the end of the bed. Each movement brought him even more pain. He didn't care. He struggled until he was at the edge of the bed and let gravity take its course. He fell to the floor without a sound. Inch by painful inch, he crawled toward the gypsy's baby. It would die with him. A smile crossed his face. He had bested her. He was the winner.

Lobart came back from having his meal and found Lord Symington dead on the floor. He was inches away from the baby's crib; his clawed hand still out-stretched. "Look at that," Lobart said sadly. "It almost brings a tear to my eye. The poor man tried to drag 'imself to see 'is son for one last time."

He called out to the other henchmen, who came running. "Lord Symington is dead."

Edith and Mrs. Dawson heard him call out that Lord Symington was dead. They both smiled and hugged each other. "You are safe now, my darling. I am going back to Brekmore manor and look in on your father." Mrs. Dawson turned and looked at Collette, the mother of the baby. "You did well my dear, very well."

"Yes, very well indeed," Edith smiled.

Mrs. Dawson patted Edith's arm as she grabbed her cloak and gloves. "I am going to have them hitch up my carriage, but I will be back tomorrow." She left the room and hurried down the servants' staircase to the stables.

"Come on, Collette," Edith motioned for her to follow her. "I think I hear the baby starting to fuss a little. He may be hungry."

Lobart and the other henchmen were gone when she entered her deceased husband's room. They had put Lord Symington's body back in bed, and his quilt pulled up to his waist. His hands were out and crossed over his chest. It almost looked as if he were just sleeping. "Take the baby, and I will carry the crib back to my room." Edith grabbed the crib and hurried out of his room.

Edith placed the crib by the fireplace, while Collette changed his rags, and then started to breast feed him.

"You must be starving," she said to Collette, who just nodded her head. "I will go down to the kitchen and fix us something to eat."

Edith made her way down to the kitchen. The cook was still there and helped prepare a meal for them. It was a while before Edith got back to her room. Collette had finished feeding the baby and was just putting him in his crib. He was sound asleep.

They ate their meal in total silence. All Edith could do was think about Ian. Where was he? She was a free woman, and she was free to marry him. She put down a piece of bread and sat back in her chair. The food on her plate held no interest for her. She was too excited to eat. She had to tell Ian. She had to find him.

Edith looked out her window. Winter came and so came the shorter daylight. She grabbed a warm cape, with a nice large hood to keep her warm, and headed to the stables. Her silk slippers did not keep her feet warm on the icy-cold ground. She hurried faster. The door to the stables was ajar; she pushed it open and walked in. There was no one around. She called out, but no one answered her. Suddenly, the door behind her slammed shut. She whirled around to find Lobart standing there.

"I figured you would want to go and visit your Mrs. Dawson," he moved toward her, as she backed up. "So, I just waited. Sent the other two men ahead to meet us at Lanigan's cliffs. Now, we can do this the easy way or not."

"Why should I make this easy for you?" She snapped, as she looked around for something that she could use to protect her.

"I am not talking about making it easy for me. I am talking about making it easier on you."

"So, you think I am just going to climb into this carriage and have you drive away and then let you kill me without a struggle?"

"Oh, I am 'oping you are going to struggle," he licked his lips. "Now, get into the carriage."

"Why not just kill me here, then?" She asked, still trying to figure out how to get out of this.

"Why? She asks, 'why'?" He almost snarled at her. "Because you are a Lady, and I am a peasant. I would dangle from a tree for it. One of them servants may 'ave seen me come in 'ere before you. I am not taking any chances. That is why I sent my men ahead, so that no one will bother to connect me with you. Now, get into the carriage. You're going to 'ave a very bad accident."

"Why are you doing this? Of what possible good would my death do you now?"

"I cannot 'ave you around his Lordship's son. You would 'ave control of everything."

"No, that is where you are wrong," she hoped this would be her way out. "He left me nothing. Nothing. I have no money, no manor, no servants, and no baby."

"No," he said playing with a splintered piece of wood on a post. "Barrister Smyth's paperwork is missing. That includes the Will excluding you from everything. As it stands now, your son will inherit everything, when 'e becomes of age. In the meantime, you are legally 'is guardian and will 'ave access to all of 'is lordship's money. I am afraid that is a job for only one of us, and that one is me." He stopped fidgeting with the wood post. "Now, get into the carriage." He growled menacingly.

Edith picked up her dress and climbed into the carriage. She had to think. This couldn't be happening, not now.

It seemed like such a short ride to the cliffs, and Edith knew there was no chance for her to survive this. The carriage stopped, and he climbed down and opened the door. He reached in to grab her; instead, she pulled the door shut and climbed out the other side of the carriage.

She was startled to see the other henchmen sitting on their horses in front of her. Their hoods pulled down over their faces, and their capes whipped wildly around them. They sat stoically, not one of them moved. The bright moon was behind them casting eerie shadows under their hoods.

Edith picked up a large stick on the ground. She straightened her back and held the stick out toward Lobart, who was walking around the carriage.

He threw back his head and laughed. "Now, do you really think that is going to protect you?"

"Maybe not," she said, stick poised and readied in her hand. "But at least I will give you something to remember me by, and with any luck, I will break your head. And, that should be easy, because that is your weakest point."

All the henchmen laughed. "Shut up." He snapped. "I am about to teach this lady a thing or two."

The henchmen slid off their horses and walked toward Edith. "That's right, come closer, men," he smiled down at Edith. "You all are about to learn something." He turned to his henchmen when a fist shot out knocking him backward.

"What the 'ell are you doing?" He grabbed his chin, and moved toward the henchman who had struck him.

Suddenly, all four of the men took off their capes. "Ian!" Edith screamed in elation. She dropped her stick as one of the men went to her side and pulled her out of harm's way. Edith's knees were weak from sheer relief at the sight of Ian, Maggie's brothers and Juan.

Lobart went for the pistol in his belt. Ian knocked it out of his hand, and struck him again. This time he knocked him to the ground.

"You would not be so brave if they were not 'ere," Lobart gestured toward the others.

"I believe it has been my fist, and my fist alone that is doing the work here. Although, I might add that my friends would really like to share in the fun. However, I am such a selfish person. I want all the fun myself."

Lobart turned and raced toward the carriage; he managed to grab a pistol hidden underneath the driver's seat. He aimed it at Edith first, his eyes aglow. Ian rushed to protect her, when a shot rang out.

Edith screamed and tried to push past Juan to get to Ian, but Juan held her back.

All the men had drawn their weapons, but not one of them had fired. They all had their pistols aimed at Lobart, who was staring at them in a strange way. His eyes were wide with shock as his pistol slipped out of his hand and landed on the ground by his feet.

There was movement from the trees, and they all turned their pistols in that direction. "Don't shoot," Albert yelled as he walked to the group still standing there in stunned silence.

Juan saw Ian moving toward Edith. He smiled and stepped aside. Edith shrieked at the sight of Ian and threw herself in his arms.

"Did I ever tell you I won prizes at the city fairs for shooting?" He looked at everyone still staring at him. "Hmm, guess not." He walked over to Lobart, who was still standing, and with one finger touched him. Lobart fell backward; his eyes still open. "Nasty piece of work, that one." He reached down and picked up Lobart's pistol from the ground, and handed it to Juan.

Everyone came alive and began laughing and hugging Albert. "I think this is a good time to go back to Lady Symington's manor and have us a good glass of port.

"Albert, I love you dearly, but please do not ever call me that hideous name again," she laughed and grabbed his arm and then stopped. "Oh, no, I do not want to go back to that house. His dead body is still in there."

"Well," Albert grabbed her hand and turned her back to the carriage. "I think Mrs. Dawson and her clan have fixed that by now. I am sure they have found a proper place for him, my dear."

"I will ride with you, my love," Ian helped her get into the carriage.

Maggie's brothers picked up Lobart's body and threw it over the horse Ian had ridden. Albert whistled, and a horse came out of the woods. He tied it to the back of the carriage and got up in the driver's position.

"Let's go home," Albert cracked a whip in the air, and the horses took off for the manor. "Good thing I followed all of you. I knew we were gonna have some fun."

"It is over, Ian," Edith rested her head on his shoulder, as he cradled her in his arms.

"Yes," he kissed her forehead. "Now, we can start this out right. I am not taking any chances. We are going to the Vicar's early in the morning and post our banns."

"That sounds wonderful to me. I was so happy to see your face back there. But what happened to Symington's other men?"

"We were all on our way to the manor when Juan saw them riding away from it. We stayed hidden while Juan rode over and asked what was happening. They told him Lobart was bringing you to the cliffs to get rid of you, and he wanted them there to make sure nobody interfered. We interfered."

"How can we forget the horrible things that have happened?"

"I will spend the rest of my life trying," he tilted her head upward and kissed her.

The carriage pulled up to the manor, and Mrs. Dawson was the first one out of the door, followed close behind by Rosita. "Thank be the stars, you are alright."

"Of course, she be alright," Albert said, as he got down off the carriage. "She had all of us there."

"Wait," Edith pulled back from going into the house. "Is he gone from here?"

"Come inside and we will tell you," Rosita said.

Laughter and music filtered out to the small-group standing there. "Come on in." Mrs. Dawson hugged Ian and Edith. "I have a couple more surprises before the night is finished."

Ian and Edith walked into the manor with their arms around each other. All the furniture in the large parlor was now against the walls, and all the area rugs rolled up out of the way. Gypsy fiddlers were playing music, and the middle of the room was crowded with everyone dancing and laughing.

Mrs. Dawson led Edith around to the fireplace. Edith let out a yelp of joy when she saw her father sitting by the fireplace. She ran to him and threw her arms around him.

"This is one of the happiest days of my life," he kissed her cheek and stroked her face gently.

"Mrs. Dawson, you have made this a most perfect night," Edith said, her face glowing with happiness.

"It is not done, yet," she waved her hand and the music and revelers stopped.

A gypsy male came forward. Rosita introduced him to Edith and Ian. "He is the leader of our gypsy clan, and will wed you two tonight. In the eyes of the gypsies, you will be man and wife."

"Does that not suit you?" Mrs. Dawson peered around Albert to look at Edith and Ian.

"It is fine with me," Edith said.

Ian tightened his arm around Edith, "I see no problem with that either."

"Lord Symington's body is not really in the house is it?" Edith asked Mrs. Dawson.

"It is not in this house," Mrs. Dawson said smiling. "But he is definitely in a house." Mrs. Dawson looked at Edith, and back at her sister. "Should we tell her?"

"My dear Edith," Rosita began to laugh. "The Wilkenson's are going to find a surprise when they go out to do their business in their outhouse. We made it look like he was trying to crawl out of one of the openings. He was so puny; we almost lost him a couple of times."

Edith was relieved that Lord Symington was nowhere in the manor. She relaxed and smiled. "Then I want the gypsy marriage ceremony to begin."

The gypsy leader performed the hand fasting. When it was done he let out a yell. "They are now man and wife."

Music and laughter filled the house long into the night. Edith and Ian danced and laughed to the wild and sometimes soulful music of the gypsies.

Finally, weary from the day's events Edith and Ian bid their goodnights, and told everyone they were welcome to stay through the night.

Mrs. Dawson and Albert helped to take her father upstairs. They found him a warm and cozy room and got him ready for bed.

Edith wanted a room as far away from Lord Symington's room as possible. The servants found them a large room in another wing of the house. They started a fire for the newlywed couple, put clean bedding on the bed, and quickly left them alone.

Edith reached up and pulled him to her. "Now we can start forever."

Chapter 18

My Dearest Darling Rachel,

You and Phillip have been traveling across the countryside of America? How exciting! I would love to come to the Americas, well, except for the long voyage. You saw Indians? How exciting. You must tell me all about them.

Oh, my dear, Rachel, I have so many things to tell you. First, being married to Ian is the most blessed thing I can imagine.

Second, Lord Symington died. They say he was found in the Wilkinson's outhouse. I guess it gave Mrs. Wilkinson quite a fright. The local officials feel that he was not thinking right, went for a walk, had to use their outhouse and fell in because he was so thin and frail. Quite befitting, would not you say?

If Phillip should ever go on a long military maneuver, or transfer to a post where you cannot join him, Ian and I will send you the monies needed to come home.

My dear, I have so much I wish could be told, but it would fill pages. Did I mention that father has come to live with us? We have a little bit bigger house, of course.

Did I ever mention that I love gypsy music? Dear me, I am rambling. Possibly, because I have never, never felt such contentment. As for writing about my beloved child, well, it would take volumes of paper. Write soon my love, write soon, as always your Edith.

The stagecoach was waiting outside the inn. Rachel climbed in to find there were three rows of benches and enough room for nine people. They all entered from a door in the front and had to crawl over the bench seats with no backs to get to the last row. There were two little windows covered with leather placed high near the top.

Rachel found a seat up front on the first bench away from the door grateful she did not have to crawl over any benches to get a seat.

After all the passengers were ensconced in the stagecoach and seated, she heard the crack of a whip, and the coachmen yell at the team of horses. The coach lurched forward causing Rachel to put her hands out to stop from hitting the wooden wall in front of her. Wind and dust seeped through the cracks in the wood frame, as they took off down the dirt road.

Rachel could not sleep or rest, because the coach had no springs to buffer against the jolts caused by the ruts in the roads, and occasionally they had to wait for large herds of cattle, or sheep to pass before they could continue. It was a long, cold and tiring ride, even though they stopped periodically to change horses, and for the passengers to use the outhouses and get refreshments.

After three days, they reached Boston. Rachel stood looking at the bustling city, and wanted to cry from sheer joy at finally reaching Boston. She hired a carriage to take her to the office building that Nathaniel's family owned. It started to rain, as she went inside and asked if Captain English were around, and was told that he had gone out to sea.

Hearing that Nathan would not be at the house saddened Rachel. She knew a sea voyage could take months before he returned.

Once outside she found another carriage to take her to his aunts' home. She could hardly wait to hold her son in her arms. The carriage pulled up to the house and Rachel hurried down the walk to the front door. She was almost lightheaded at being back among those she loved. She knocked on the door and waited. Rachel listened to see if anyone was coming to the door. She knocked again, only louder. There was still no response. She tried the door handle, and the door opened.

"Aunt Libbie? Aunt Clara? Anyone?" She called out loudly, as she walked into the darkened house. She closed the door behind her and walked into the parlor. The house smelled strongly of smoke as she headed toward the kitchen.

A lamp was sitting on the kitchen table. Rachel went to the stove and picked up a thin stick used to light the lamps and candles around the house. She opened the stove and caught the end of the stick on fire and lit the lamp on the table.

She was startled to see scorch marks on one side of the kitchen wall. Boards covered the gaping holes to keep the elements out. "That is very strange. The stove is across the room from those burn marks."

The heat from the oven drew her to it. "The stove is lit so they must be here," she said happily. "They all must have gone out somewhere, but they will be back."

The rain increased in its intensity, beating on the boards that covered the damaged wall. Exhausted from her trip, she went up to her bedroom. Relief settled over her as she entered the room; the fire had not touched it.

Unaware of her actions, she automatically turned the key to her bedroom and locked the door. She put the lamp down on the table, and put the valise on top of the bed. She began emptying it, and shaking her head at how little was really in there. She took out the large pistol Mary had given her and placed it on the table next to the lamp.

Rachel pulled out the small pistol wrapped in cloth that Nathan had given her. She went over to the stuffed chair in front of the French doors and sat down. Carefully, she began to unwrap the little pistol.

She sat there and stared at nothing in particular. She was too tired to think, but she didn't want to sleep. Rachel's eyes began to close. She tried to stay awake, but sleep soon overpowered her. The small pistol fell out of her hand and slid down next to her between the cushion and the chair.

Her dreams were filled with all the events that had happened; it was a deep, restless sleep. She dreamed someone was pounding at her door and rattling the doorknob to her room. And, then it stopped abruptly. Groggily, she looked around the room. The pounding noise must have been the wind beating against the windows; she thought.

Rachel smiled. She was back in Boston, in her room. She looked out the French doors. The wind was still strong, but the rain had stopped. She stretched her arms, and wondered how long she had slept.

Then, Rachel remembered that she had locked the door when she came in, and laughed at the silliness of it. She got up slowly and walked to the bedroom door. She unlocked it and opened it to look out and see if they had come home. But the house was still dark.

Something caught her eye as she went to close the door. It looked like mud and water had accumulated by her bedroom door, she shut the door behind her, and looked down at her shoes, there was no mud on them. She turned walking back to her chair still looking down at the dry hem of her dress.

Suddenly, she sensed something was wrong. She felt as if someone's eyes were boring into her. Her entire body tensed. Her eyes traveled from the bottom of her dress, and moved across the rug and up to the French doors to her room.

There was the dark figure of a man standing outside of her room. He kicked the French doors open, almost ripping them off their hinges. Rachel screamed and tried to run, but he grabbed her and threw her roughly into her bed.

"I have been waiting for you," Count Tychovsky said, eyeing her up and down like a cat with its prey. "I knew you would come here. I was very disappointed that nobody else was here." He brandished a pistol in his hand. "I was going to get rid of them all. But they are all gone. Disappeared. No one knows where they went. So, I thought just getting rid of you would have to do."

"I have money, a great deal of money," she lied. "I can make your life very comfortable."

He moved quickly to her bed and stood over her. "Look at my face!" He grabbed her arm and yanked her to him. "Do you think a woman would want to live with this? This is what you did to me."

"It was an accident. I would never have hurt you intentionally," Rachel was staring into the face of a mad man; a mad man full of hatred.

"Intentionally or not, you did this to me." He thrust her back on the bed. "I have thought about this for weeks. You have no idea how happy I am now that I finally have you." He walked over to the table with the lamp and picked up the large pistol. "Well, well, what do we have here? You won't be needing this." He threw the pistol out the broken French doors.

"What good would your killing me do? It won't change anything." She moved closer to the edge of the bed. She had to get away from him.

"What good would it do? It would make me feel very good. I have no intentions of killing you right away. You are going to suffer, like I suffer every time I look in the mirror. Wait!" He said. "I want to hear you beg. If you beg maybe I'll kill you quickly. But then again, maybe I won't."

Rachel stood up and defiantly said, "I will not beg."

He whirled around and backhanded her, sending her to the floor. He reached down and grabbed her by her hair pulling her to her feet. He slapped her again, sending her toward the fireplace.

"Too proud to beg are you?" His face twisted in a perverse smile. "Your infantile husband was not. He was really very good at it. Said he wasn't the one who had disfigured me. It was you. Offered you up to me on a silver platter, he did. Said he hated you and hoped I would find you."

"My husband is a better man than you could ever be. And that is not saying much," she snapped.

His eyes narrowed and then he smiled. "Husband? He told me he had divorced you and even produced papers to prove it. He said those papers were the only thing he cared about."

"You are a pathetic man," she said shaking her head.

He threw back his head and laughed, "I'm pathetic? You should have seen the look in his eyes when I ripped those papers up and threw them in the river. Oh, he was a terrified little man. I was tired of him, so I just shot him between the eyes. I didn't even have to push him in the river. He fell backward. What a splash he made."

Rachel gasped, her eyes filled with horror.

"The ones I wanted to kill were you and that captain. Your husband was just, shall we say, practice. Divorcing you, huh? That is quite funny if you think about it. I should have saved the papers, just so I could look at them and laugh every day."

Slowly, Rachel began backing away from the madman in front of her.

"I kept the captain pretty busy for a while, setting fires to his ships and anything else I could think of to cause him trouble. They caught me setting fires to merchandise on the docks, but I managed to escape and made my way to the Carolinas. But the captain caught up with me and had me thrown in prison. Do you know what it's like in a prison? I am a Count! I am not a filthy prisoner. I am royalty!" He hollered at her, jabbing the gun in his hand at Rachel.

She backed up to the fireplace, and into the poker stand. Her hand came around the end of an iron poker. She grabbed hold of it and quietly pulled it away from its holder.

He continued to rant and rave about being of royal blood, robbed of his title and rights. His eyes narrowed as he looked at her. "I pretended to be dead, and escaped. Headed back to this grand house," he spat out the words grand house. "You had already gone. I wanted to get rid of you first, and then get rid of the captain. But I couldn't help myself. I started a nice big fire at the back of the house. Unfortunately, it started to rain heavily that day."

He looked around the room, and shook his head. "It must have put my pretty fire out. Of course, I didn't know that at the time, because I had gone down to the docks to find out where your husband's regiment had gone. Said I was your husband's brother. It didn't take long before they told me he was in Nova Scotia, and from there I found out he was transferred to Fort Henry. It appears his new commanding officer didn't like him very much. Sent him to Fort Henry, he did."

All the while he raged she kept looking for a way out. Then, she spotted a glint of her pistol in the chair by the window. Rachel inched her way slowly in front of it to block his view, terrified that he would see it first. She held the end of the poker behind her, waiting for her chance to strike.

His eyes narrowed, and a grin began to form on his lips, as he waved the pistol in front of her. "I figured you would come along soon enough. I joined a band of men who raided and robbed ships, wagon trains, travelers, and whoever they wanted. Sometimes they killed just for the fun of it. I only joined them because I kept hoping I would find you tucked away neatly on a ship or wagon train. Funny thing is, I really enjoyed being with them, so when I am done with you, I plan on rejoining them."

There was a loud banging sound downstairs. He turned his head. Swiftly, Rachel swung the poker at his hand holding the gun. He dropped it, letting out a yelp of pain. She swung the poker around and hit him on the side of his head. Rachel lunged for the chair and grabbed the pistol and turned facing him.

His face contorted in a rage as he started to go after her, but stopped when he saw the pistol in her hand. "Do you think that little thing is going to stop me?" He growled at her.

"I believe we are close enough for this to do some real damage." Her eyes narrowed.

"You're not going to shoot me," he started lowering himself to reach for his pistol on the floor.

"I am telling you once, just once, don't move, or I will shoot." Her voice cracked, but she held the gun firmly in her hand.

"I'm not taking orders from anyone, especially a stupid woman." He bent down and reached for his pistol.

A shot cracked through the air. The Count looked up at her, his face registering shock and disbelief. He fell forward onto the floor.

Rachel backed away from him until she hit the bedroom door. She turned around and yanked it open running from the room hoping someone was downstairs.

But the banging sound was only the sound of a shutter hitting against the window. She ran to the front door, pulled it open and ran outside screaming for help.

The mud on the road was deep, as she tried to run. Suddenly, she heard the Count calling from behind her. She turned and to her horror, she saw the dark, shadowy figure of the Count staggering toward her. He was holding his bleeding chest with one hand and brandishing a pistol in the other.

Rachel grabbed up the muddy and now heavy hem of her dress to make running easier. Her slippers were lost somewhere in the mud behind her. A shot rang out, and she felt a bullet whiz past her.

She saw a carriage coming at a fast clip toward her. She called out for help, but the Count was gaining on her. Rachel kept running as fast as she could, slipping, and sliding on the muddy ground. Another shot rang out. She felt something graze her arm, but she kept running. She heard someone from the carriage yell "get down." Almost on cue, she slipped and fell down on the ground and immediately several gunshots exploded around her.

The carriage stopped, and Nathan flew off the carriage to Rachel. Charles and Damian passed him to get to the Count's body sprawled out face down in the mud.

"Rachel! Rachel!" Nathan said repeatedly, as he gathered her up in his arms. "Have you been injured?"

Rachel grabbed him, pulling herself into him as far as she could. She was trembling. Quickly, he took off his coat and wrapped it around her, picking her up and taking her back to the carriage. Once inside he piled blankets on her, and pulled his large jacket around her. "You are safe now. I won't let anything happen to you."

Charles and Damian, and two other men, picked up the dead body of Count Tychovsky and threw it behind the carriage. They got in and drove the short distance to the manor. "We'll take care of him," Damian said matter-of-fact gesturing toward the lifeless body of the Count.

Charles jumped off the carriage and grabbed some rope from under the Count's body. "I know he be one dead man, but I am not taking any chances on getting hit on the head from behind." He tied the hands and feet of the Count securely, and climbed back on the carriage.

"Are ya daft?" Damian asked. "Why are you tying up a dead man?"

"Is this some strange American custom?" A male in a deep Russian accent inquired.

"No, but he pretended to be dead at the prison and killed a guard. I not be taking any chances."

"But he has big hole in his head," the second Russian male stared at Charles in disbelief.

"How dead do you think he's gotta be?" Damian said shaking his head.

"Still, I dun't trust this one," Charles climbed back on the carriage.

The two men from Russia just shrugged.

Nathan got out of the carriage first and held his arms out for Rachel. Still trembling she reached down, and he swiftly picked her up in his arms and took her inside of the house. He took her upstairs to her room, and saw the blood on the floor by her bed. He quickly took her to another room and sat her in a large, overstuffed chair.

He ran and got a basin of water and rags to wash her muddied face and hands. After a futile attempt, he decided a complete hot bath would work far better. He grabbed a quilt from the bed. "Here, take off your clothing and wrap this around you. I will go down and get some coal for the stove and fireplace." Before he left he leaned down and gently touched the bruise on her face. "You are safe now."

After he had gone, she pulled off her dress and undergarments and kicked them away from her. Still shivering, she pulled the quilt around her naked body.

Nathan returned shortly with two buckets. One filled with coal, the other water. He lit the small stove in the bathing room first so that the water could be heating up, and then the fireplace in the bedroom. It wasn't long before the room was warm, and she stopped shivering. He moved a chair next to hers and put his arms around her, pulling her close to him.

"I thought you had gone to sea. How did you find me?" She asked resting her head against his chest.

"I had a visitor from the prison come to the house. He told me that Count Tychovsky had escaped, and killed a guard. I knew he would be looking for you and me."

"Oh, my word," she exclaimed.

"I raced back to the house with Damian and Charles, two of the toughest and most trustworthy men I know, to make sure everyone there was alright. When we got there Seth, Bimms, and Tiffy had just put out a fire that had been started from outside. They never would have been able to save the house if it hadn't rained as hard as it did. I moved them to a safe place, and put guards around them day and night."

"Charles and Damian were staying with us a while back and then left abruptly. Why were they there and why did they leave so quickly?"

"Someone recognized the Count as trying to burn down one of my ships. I hired Charles and Damian to make sure that all of you were safe. Once we captured the Count, and he was thrown in prison, I had no need for them to be at the house."

"I see," Rachel said. "They were there to watch over us."

"Yes," Nathan said and went into the bathing room.

She could hear him pouring water into the ceramic tub. He came back picked her up, quilt and all, and carried her to the partially filled bathing tub.

He already placed a cloth and a bar of soap in the water. Nathan pulled a chair up and placed its back to her. He sat down and continued facing away from Rachel.

"I knew that madman was going to go after you, so I took the fastest ship I owned and sailed for Fort Henry. When I got there I was told they had found Phillip's body floating at the river's edge. He was shot. No one knew where you went. I figured ... well, I was hoping you would head for Boston, and here."

"How did you know I was here at the house?" She poured the water over her head to rinse her hair.

"I returned to Boston; only a couple of hours after you arrived. Our ship met some very foul weather on the way. Anyway, I stopped at my office building, and was told a beautiful young woman had stopped in to see if I was there. I knew it had to be you. We grabbed a carriage, and almost ran over the few people walking in the rain to get here as fast as we could."

"I am done she said," she looked at the muddied quilt. "But I think that muddied quilt would reverse my bathing."

"Yes, of course, it would." Keeping his eyes off her, he left the room. Shortly he opened the door and, still averting his eyes; he placed a nightshift and robe onto a chair in the room. "Excuse me," he said and left the bathing room.

Rachel got out of the tub and dried off. She tried to dry her long hair to no avail. She wrapped a soft cloth around her hair, and got into the items left by Nathan. She opened the door to the bedroom, but Nathan was not there. Rachel found a brush on a dresser and began working on her wet hair.

Several minutes later, Nathan came back carrying a tray and looking refreshed himself. "I thought you might like some hot tea. And, I thought I should clean myself up as well." He walked over and put the tray down on the table.

"How is Phillip Nathaniel doing? When can we go to him?"

"I know you are anxious to see your son. He is a fine boy I might add. However, he would be asleep by now, so first thing tomorrow we shall go to him."

"Yes, oh yes. That would be wonderful." She walked to him and put her arms around him. He gently held her in his arms. "Nathan. My dearest, Nathan." She said as her arms tightened around him.

She lifted her face to him, her lips parted to say something, but before she could speak he brought his parted lips down and kissed her.

Rachel was stunned and pleased at the same time. Phillip had never kissed her with an open mouth. She felt her body start to tingle with excitement as Nathan's tongue gently began to explore hers. Rachel returned his kiss with an intensity that almost scared her.

Finally, Nathan pulled away. "I fear I am taking advantage of you in a weak moment." He started to release her.

"I do not feel that this is a weak moment," she grabbed his face and pulled him to her kissing him and enjoying it.

"Rachel," his voice became huskier. "I will not be able to stop if we continue like this."

"Good," she said kissing him again.

He picked her up and laid her gently on the bed. Their eyes met. Rachel saw the love in his eyes and hoped he could see the love in hers.

Later, much later, they lay spent in each other's arms. Rachel could barely speak, as tears rolled down her cheeks.

"What is it Rachel?" His voice filled with concern. "I am sorry," he dropped his forehead to hers. "I should never have let this go so far. You are feeling remorse for our actions."

"No," she said. "I feel wicked, because I want more." She touched his face and began kissing him again. She laughed. "I have never known pleasure like that before."

When they were spent for the second time, Rachel pulled herself up on her elbow. "Nathan," she said softly, stroking back the curl that fell on his forehead. "Do you know what real love is?"

"I believe I do. There are all kinds of love, my sweet. Sometimes you love someone because of their sweet and gentle nature." He gently tapped her nose. "Sometimes you think you love them because of your desire for them. However, the greatest love is to love someone for who they are. First, they should be your friend. A soul mate, if you will. Of course," he added flippantly. "It helps to desire them, too!"

"That is what I feel as well," she ran her fingers across his chest. "You were my friend first, and then I began to love you with an intensity that scared me."

She heard a small gasp coming from him.

"That is why I had to go to my husband, because I knew we could never be, and it was breaking my heart. I thought if I saw Phillip my feelings for him would return. I kept telling myself that it was Phillip I loved, and I would try to see his face. But it would fade, and yours would steal into my thoughts." She pulled away from Nathan. Tears began running down her face. "I cannot do this to you."

"Do what?" He asked somewhat confused.

She got up slowly, and put on her robe. She turned to him and began to cry, her hands covering her face.

"Dear God, Rachel," he jumped out of bed and went to her. "What is it?"

Rachel put up her hand to stop him from coming closer. Her lips trembled as she tried to speak. "I am a divorced woman. A woman of shame. I burned my divorce papers in the cabin to help start a fire. Count Tychovsky said he destroyed the copy of Phillip's, but Phillip's father is the one that sent the papers."

Nathan stood there for a moment and then threw back his head and laughed. In one step, he enveloped her in his arms. "Do you think that matters to me?" He said incredulously. He gently caressed her back. "Do you know what your being divorced means to me? It means... if you will have me, we can marry."

"You do not care about this shameful thing I would bring upon you?" She lifted her head and stared into his eyes.

"Well, you mentioned that Count Tychovsky destroyed Phillip's copies, and if you destroyed yours as well, that means you are not a divorcee, but a widow. But my love, there is nothing shameful about a divorce. And, for you to worry that it would cast shame on me, with no concern for yourself, is why I love you so."

"Would you say that last part, about loving me, again?"

"I love you, Rachel; with such a depth, I see no end." He gently rubbed his chin on the top of her head. "I will never forget the beautiful young woman who came aboard my ship and the strength and kindness in her. She cared not for herself, but for others. My love for you deepened with each day, only to bring me such great pain knowing that you could never be mine." He pulled away from her, and kissed her.

Rachel's arms went around his neck, and when the kiss ended she looked up at him, "Nathan, I am feeling wicked again."

They spent the rest of the night loving, laughing, and sometimes sleeping.

Chapter 19

Early the next morning Rachel and Nathan took a carriage to a house in the county. The doors to the house flew open and Libbie and Clara raced down the walkway, while Tiffy stood at the door holding a small child in her arms.

The two aunts greeted Rachel and Nathan warmly as they hurried them back to the house.

Rachel saw Phillip Nathaniel and held out her arms to him. He hid his head on Tiffy's shoulder. Nathan took the boy from Tiffy's arms, and kissed his cheek and hugged him. "It will only take a few moments, and he will warm up to you. Come," he held his free hand out for Rachel, and they walked into the parlor. Nathan was right. Within minutes, Phillip Nathaniel was all over Rachel laughing and playing.

"While you are playing with him, I have something that is yours," Nathan left the room and came back carrying a small silken sack. "This is yours."

"Lady Rachel, it is his meal time. May I take him to feed him?" Tiffy asked politely.

Rachel hesitated for a moment. "Of course, Tiffy. I just cannot seem to get enough of him." She sighed, as she watched Tiffy carry him out of the room. "He is so beautiful, is he not?"

"He looks just like you," Aunt Libbie said. "He is one beautiful little boy."

"Wait for us," Aunt Clara got up and quickly followed Tiffy.

"He is the most precious child ever, well, since Nathan. Excuse me." Libbie called out as she left the room, "Aunt Libbie's coming sweetheart. Aunt Libbie's coming."

"They all love him very much, as I do," Nathan said.

Rachel leaned over and kissed him softly on the lips. "I love you, Captain Nathaniel English." Then, she looked down at the sack on her lap and opened it. Startled by all the gold coins inside, she asked confused. "Whatever is this for?"

"Remember when the Countess gave you a riddle?" He asked.

"Oh, yes," she shook her head. "But I cannot remember exactly what the riddle was now."

Nathan smiled. "I remembered. She said 'the jewels are hollow and awash from the sun'."

"Yes, that was it," Rachel exclaimed.

"I found the jewels she was referring to hidden in the hollow wash basin in their cabin. I lifted the basin, and there was a large sack stuffed underneath it. The jewels were all inside. I contacted a friend of mine who managed to get a letter to her family explaining the events of her death. It appears the Countess' family moved from Russia and took up residence in the south of France. He told me that two brothers of the Countess' had arrived in Boston and were looking for the Count. Somehow they learned of the bad treatment of their beloved, little sister."

"Those two gentlemen with the strange accents?" she asked.

He nodded. "I turned over the jewels to them, and they gave me a reward. The reward is really yours, because if you had not mentioned the riddle the jewels would never have been found."

"But" she looked inside the pouch again. "There is a great deal of money in here." She closed the pouch and handed it to Nathan. "You take it. It is really yours."

"No," he gently ran his hand along her jaw. "It is yours." He pulled back and grabbed her shoulders. Now, I have another surprise if you were so inclined to hear me out."

"Another surprise?" Rachel started to laugh, "I love your surprises."

"What would you say if we all, and I mean all of us, take a trip to England?"

Rachel's eyes began to tear up. "Nathan, do you really mean it?"

"Of course, he does," Aunt Clara came back and sat down.

"We have been packing for days," Aunt Libbie followed behind and sat on the chair next to Clara. "Bimms, Tiffy, and Seth have never been to England. I think they will like it."

"Our company has purchased a ship that has improvements made on it that will get us there a lot quicker." He folded his arms and sat back in his chair.

"When do we leave?" Rachel asked excitedly.

"As soon as we are married," he said.

"Ohh," both aunts screamed together happily.

Nathan leaned forward, his face filled with concern. "Unless you preferred not to marry. I mean, we will all still go to England."

"I will not go... unless my name is Mrs. Rachel English," she feigned a pout.

"By the stars, I love you," he kissed her quickly on the lips. "But my love," he smiled sheepishly. "It will be Lady Rachel English."

"Oh, yes, my dear," Clara clapped her hands in excitement. "You are looking at Lord Nathaniel English."

"He will always be 'my captain' to me." Rachel said lovingly.

Nathan and Rachel were married that week, and the very next morning everyone was boarded and bound for England.

Although, Rachel was prone to being seasick, it only happened in the morning, and the rest of the time she was busy enjoying every moment.

A few weeks later, their ship docked at the London harbor.

When they disembarked from the ship, Nathan ordered two carriages that took them to a vast estate in the country. Servants rushed from the manor to assist in carrying the luggage into the house.

Nathan helped Rachel out of the carriage and made a sweeping gesture at the grandness of it. "This is the family estate. It is a couple of hours away from your Edith, but you may visit her anytime you wish. Would that please you?"

"Beyond words," she replied, throwing her arms around him. "To have you and Phillip Nathaniel with me is the greatest joy I have ever known." She pulled him to her, "I must tell you something, my love."

"What? You want a bigger house than this?" He said kiddingly.

"No, I would live in a one-room cabin as long as it was with you," she laughed. "I am with child. We are going to have a child."

Nathan stared at her, his mouth agape. "We are going to have a child? How did I not see this?" He grabbed her up and whirled her around. "My dearest love, you have made me very happy, and I care not if it is a boy child or a girl child. It will be our child."

It did not take them long to settle into the beautiful manor. They couldn't walk around the lush gardens because of the constant rain, but soon the spring rains stopped, and the lush green foliage began to emerge.

On a brisk spring day, Rachel received a letter. She read it carefully, and her face filled with sadness.

"What is it my love?" Nathan asked.

"I was curious as to what my father and brother were doing, so I contacted a barrister. I received this letter telling me that my brother had married Lady McLean, but my father was in debtor's prison."

"I see," he said calmly.

"My father never showed me love, but he is my father. Knowing how much I love you, if something happened to you ... I do not want to think about that." She shook her head, as if trying to shake that thought out. "What I mean is he loved my mother so much that when she left him, he cared for nothing else."

"Let me see what I can do," Nathan said.

Rachel went to a large wooden box and pulled out the reward money from the return of the jewels. She walked over to Nathan holding it in her hand. "Will it be enough to relieve his debts?"

"I will go into London this day, and see what I can do." He kissed her forehead and walked toward the door.

"No, wait," she called after him. "You forgot this, money. Please. Please take this and use it, all of it if need be."

Reluctantly, he took the sack of money and went into London. He was gone for four days, when Rachel saw his carriage coming toward the manor. She ran out to greet Nathan, and spotted her father sitting solemnly next to him. Nathan jumped down from the carriage and embraced Rachel. "Lord Ramsford, if you please." He made a gesture for him to exit the carriage and join them.

Slowly, her father got out of the carriage. His eyes were downcast. He could not look Rachel in the eyes.

"Father," she said. "It is good to see you."

"I do not deserve this kindness from you," he said quietly, with his head still bowed.

"No," she said firmly. "No, you do not. However, you are my father, and maybe, just maybe we can heal our wounds and start over."

He looked at her for the first time, tears forming in his eyes. "You can forgive me?"

"I will certainly try," she said walking over and taking his arm. "It is chilly out here. Come inside and meet your grandson and your new family." She held out her other arm for Nathan to take, and they walked into the house together.

Clara and Libbie made a fuss over her father. And, then Rachel heard something she had never heard in her life before; her father's laughter. He was on the floor with Clara and Libbie playing with Phillip Nathaniel.

Edith sat in her parlor by the fireplace; her belly swollen with child. There was a sharp rapping on the door. Abby went to the door and opened it. A young black woman was standing there.

"This is a letter for Mrs. Atterby," Tiffy said. "I will wait for a response."

"One moment," Abby took the letter to Edith.

"Oh, it is a letter from my darling Rachel," she exclaimed, and quickly opened it and began to read it aloud.

My Dearest Edith,

Lord Symington is dead? I cannot say that I am sorry to hear such news. He was an evil man. But that they found his body in the Wilkinson's outhouse left me laughing quite heartily.

Lord Brekmore has come to live with you? How wonderful for you. Gypsy music? I have never heard gypsy music, but if you like it, I am sure I will too. So much has happened and I have much to tell you.

I have sent you something from the Americas, and I hope you are pleased with it. It is at your front door as you read. Your loving Rachel

Edith got up from her chair and went to the front door. She saw the young, black woman standing by two carriages. A man she had never seen before got out of the carriage and extended his hand for someone to get out.

"Rachel!" Edith screamed. "My darling Rachel."

Rachel ran up the stairs and into Edith's open arms. They hugged each other as best they could with their swollen bellies.

"Be careful my dear," Ian said, rushing to her side. "You must be careful in your condition."

"And you as well, Rachel," Nathan said, walking up the steps of the manor behind her.

When Rachel and Edith finally pulled away, tears streaming down their faces, they looked down and saw that each was with child. They grabbed each other again and began squealing and laughing.

"We stopped at Brekmore Manor, and were told this is where you live now. I am so confused." Rachel said.

Nathan reached around her and held out his hand to Ian. "I am Rachel's husband, Nathanial English." They shook hands and nodded to one another.

Edith blinked a couple of times looking at Nathan, "Rachel. You think you are confused? Oh, my."

"I have other family members outside, may they come in?" Nathan asked.

"Of course, of course," Edith replied jubilantly. "Mrs. Dawson! Albert! Come quickly."

Nathan gestured for everyone to come into the manor. They all stood looking at each other for a moment, when Mrs. Dawson and Albert came running into the room.

"How delightful, we have company." Mrs. Dawson said happily, and looked questionably at Edith. "Who are they?" Then she spotted Rachel and let out a shriek, hugging and kissing her.

"Family!" Edith said, "They are all family." Suddenly, she spotted Phillip Nathaniel. "Oh, my word. Oh, Rachel, he is so beautiful. Phillip Nathanial ... Nathanial? Captain Nathanial English? Oh, my, we do have to talk."

Phillip Nathanial shyly put his head on Seth's shoulder. Edith laughed, "You will get to love your Aunt Edith. Oh, yes, you will."

"I will have the kitchen staff make a special meal for tonight," Mrs. Dawson said.

"I would love to learn how to cook a traditional English meal," Bimms looked eagerly at Mrs. Dawson.

"I can make that happen," Mrs. Dawson grabbed Bimms and Tiffy's arms. "Come on. Follow me."

Albert motioned for Seth to follow him, "Let's follow the ladies." He leaned over and said quietly. "Come on, young man, you are about to be spoiled and fussed over."

"This is a lovely home," Clara said. "Don't you agree, Libbie?"

"Why, of course," Libbie said following everyone into the parlor.

Edith grabbed Rachel's arm and pulled her back. "You have a lot to explain. That is not Phillip." She said looking confused.

"And you have a lot to explain, like why you are living in Lord Symington's manor?" Rachel said.

The both started to laugh and hugged each other. "Do you happen to have the letters I wrote to you?" Edith asked.

"I have every one of them with me. Do you have mine?"

"Yes, my dearest I kept them all. We have much to talk about later." She took her arm and together they walked toward the parlor.

"We can start with the first letters and explain in further detail." Rachel said smiling.

Edith patted Rachel's hand and said, "Oh, my dearest, if we could only have read what was hidden between the lines.

The End

Dear reader,

We hope you enjoyed reading *Hidden Between The Lines.* Please take a moment to leave a review, even if it's a short one. Your opinion is important to us.

Discover more books by Sally Laughlin at https://www.nextchapter.pub/authors/sally-laughlin

Want to know when one of our books is free or discounted? Join the newsletter at http://eepurl.com/bqqB3H

Best regards,
Sally Laughlin and the Next Chapter Team

You might also like:

Fly Toward Death by Sally Laughlin

To read the first chapter for free, please head to: https://www.nextchapter.pub/books/fly-toward-death

About the Author

What makes a person want to write, to tell a story, whether it be fact or fiction? For every writer, there is a different reason why they write, but we all have one thing in common - we are storytellers.

My journey into writing was a very difficult one. Education in the inner city of Cleveland, Ohio in the 1950s was at iffy at best. Some kids got good teachers, but unfortunately, I was not one of them. When our family moved to a more upscale suburb of Cleveland, well, it didn't improve much. English teachers would hold up my papers and use them as an example of what not to do. Instead of trying to guide and help me, they chose to ridicule me. The stories churning about in my mind slowly began to fade away.

Soon reality, and everything it held, silenced my stories. I married and had two daughters. Many years later, there was a divorce. A few years after that, I married and acquired three more daughters. During this second marriage, I became a police officer, and a year later I became a detective. My job was to investigate child and elder abuse, along with training police officers in how to deal with domestic violence. I spoke before the Ohio State Senate to bring about the reform of the domestic violence laws in Ohio. The ugliness associated with my investigations brought back my love of reading. It took me away from all the troubles the victims were going through – if even for an hour.

And then it happened. The stories that I had silence in my head were starting to resurface. The more I read, the more restless they became: I had to write.

After the kids were grown, and I was an empty nester, I decided to go to the university and get my degree. And to my surprise, and relief, my papers were no longer held up for ridicule. It gave me the confidence to start my journey into writing.

Suddenly, writing became my world. I became obsessed with it. I would awake early in the morning before I went to work to write. After work I would sit and write until the wee hours of the night, and loving every frustrating moment. There never, at least for me, seemed to be a loss for ideas. My first four books, a science fantasy series, were so much fun for me to write. I fell in love with that genre after reading J.R.R.Tolkens, *The Hobbit.* Reading is so selective to everyone, some like their fantasy novels to be dark – never liked dark. The job I had to do was dark-enough. So, I made the choice that my books would be filled with adventure, humor and great characters.

When I was sixteen years old, my grandfather came to live with us. I was bored one day and asked him if I could go through his old trunk that was stored in our attic. He smiled, and said absolutely. What I found triggered the next book I wrote: an old diary written by one of my relatives from around the early 1800s. She was escaping to the Americas to avoid being married to a foul old man. She had eloped with a British officer and was subsequently disowned by her family. I was half way through the diary when my mother, unknowingly, threw away the "old, torn, dirty-looking book" resting on my nightstand. The last thing I remember reading in her diary was "never ending water." This, along with my History degree, gave me the impetus to finish "her journey."

Currently, I am happily living in northern Ohio with my sane sister, nutty dog and brat cat.

Hidden Between The Lines
ISBN: 978-4-86752-223-3 (Large Print)

Published by
Next Chapter
1-60-20 Minami-Otsuka
170-0005 Toshima-Ku, Tokyo
+818035793528
27th July 2021

Lightning Source UK Ltd.
Milton Keynes UK
UKHW040626170821
388717UK00012B/71